After Hours at Dooryard Books

Cat Sebastian

AFTER HOURS AT DOORYARD BOOKS. Copyright © 2025 by Cat Sebastian. All rights reserved.
ISBN: 979-8-9935934-0-1

For booksellers and librarians
and everybody else who's gotten the perfect book
into my hands

Author's Note

This book deals with grief and some other serious topics. A full list of content notes can be found on page 348.

Part 1
DEBRIS AND DEBRIS

Patrick

1

At the jangling of the door chimes, Patrick glances up, eager to find out what kind of lunatic goes shopping for secondhand books when the sidewalks are ankle deep in trash. Sanitation workers have been striking for over a week and the city smells like a sewer. Patrick hasn't had a customer in days. It's been amazing.

But it isn't a customer. It's Mrs. Kaplan, the store owner, who isn't the kind of person to be deterred by blockades of rotting garbage or anything else. She's wearing what he recognizes as her Good Dress, a navy blue number with brass buttons and a drop waist. It must have been brand new during the Hoover administration, and only gets brought out for funerals, air travel, and doctors' appointments.

She isn't alone.

"I brought you someone!" Mrs. Kaplan calls out, the

chimes ringing again as the door swings shut.

Patrick replaces the lid on his paste pot and studies Mrs. Kaplan's new project. This one's even more dubious looking than usual, and that's saying something: he's thirty-five, maybe even forty, milk-pale, brown hair past his collar, dark eyes that dart around the shop like he thinks cops might jump out from between the overstuffed bookshelves. None of his clothing fits right, likely because Mrs. Kaplan went to the thrift store without knowing his size, so Patrick can't tell whether he's thin or just plain skinny. He has the wary, vigilant look of a man with a warrant out for his arrest.

"This is Nathaniel Smith," Mrs. Kaplan says, all smiles, like she's proud to have produced this specimen.

It's always the same story: it's her hairdresser's brother, or her rabbi's wayward nephew, or a guitarist she found busking in the Union Square subway station. They're dodging the draft or kicking a habit. Maybe they wake up in cold sweats twice a night, thinking they're still in a faraway jungle, or maybe they've just gotten out of Riker's.

Patrick knows himself and his shitty disposition well enough to admit that he'd judge every last one of these strays if he hadn't been one of them himself. A decade ago, he'd been a surly teenager with nothing to recommend him but a black eye and a chip on his shoulder. Mrs. Kaplan not only hired him, but let him sleep in her spare room. It's a miracle the woman's managed to reach the age of seventy-five without getting herself killed, but Patrick's afraid there's time for that yet.

"Smith," Patrick repeats. "Sure, why not." Half of them are something like Smith or Jones. Hell, Patrick might have been a Smith or a Jones too if things had gone a little differently. "I'm glad you're here," he adds, and it's true enough, because the inside of a safe, warm bookstore is better than anywhere else this guy is likely to find himself, and Patrick is, generally speaking, against people freezing to death.

Mrs. Kaplan beams at Patrick, dentures gleaming, like he's the smartest boy in the whole class. He tries to look like he isn't actively preening.

"Nathaniel," she says, "Patrick runs the shop for me." And then, to Patrick, "I'm sure Nathaniel can tidy up or learn to do inventory." She manages to say this without making it sound like she's accusing Patrick of having failed to tidy up or take inventory, even though they both know he very much failed on both scores: the store is dusty, even by the lax standards of secondhand bookstores, and some boxes upstairs have been sitting around, persistently uninventoried, since before Prohibition. The last time he opened one, the first thing he saw was a 1927 issue of the *Daily Worker*. He sealed that box right back up.

"What are you working on?" Mrs. Kaplan asks, peering at Patrick's desk.

"Fixing the binding on that first edition of *Twice Told Tales*."

"The one you picked up for a quarter?"

"Twenty cents." He found it at an estate sale in Pelham, on a shelf with outdated almanacs and church fundraiser cookbooks. He'll be smug about it for a good long while.

"Can I?"

"Go right ahead."

She picks it up, careful not to disturb the half-finished binding, and makes the kind of approving noise she usually saves for new babies and nice loaves of bread.

"Nathaniel needs somewhere to stay," she says,

putting the book down. "Is that apartment on the third floor still empty? Sylvia's getting her gallbladder out, so I'm off to Florida to look after her."

Usually the strays stay in Mrs. Kaplan's floral-wallpapered spare room in Forest Hills, eating schnitzel and brisket until they get back on their feet. But obviously she isn't leaving junkies—Patrick's learned it's best to assume they're all junkies until proven otherwise, no hard feelings, there but for the grace of god, et cetera—unsupervised in her home while she's out of state.

"Sure it's empty," Patrick says, instead of asking how long this man has been staying with her and why Patrick's only hearing about it now, or pointing out that she'd know better than anybody if there was a new tenant, because not only does she own the bookshop, she owns the rest of the building too. "We'll have to sweep it out, put some clean sheets on the bed, but otherwise it's in decent shape."

"I can clean," Nathaniel says, the first words he's spoken since entering the shop. "I don't mind cleaning," he repeats, the slightest emphasis on *I*, with a bitchy little glance at the dirty windows. Or maybe the glance isn't bitchy so much as appalled.

"Well, pal, it's your lucky day," Patrick says, gesturing expansively at the vast array of cleaning opportunities the shop provides.

"Where do you keep your broom?"

Patrick has no idea where the broom is. None of his business, frankly. "Settle down, Cinderella. The dust has been here longer than you. It isn't hurting anybody. Just—have a drink or something. There's a box of cookies around here somewhere, and there's a kettle in the back room. The tea is…" He's pretty sure he saw that box of teabags yesterday. Maybe the day before.

Mrs. Kaplan and Nathaniel exchange a glance, then Nathaniel heads toward the rear of the shop.

"He even looks like a bookseller," Mrs. Kaplan says.

"What's that supposed to mean? I look like a bookseller. I am, in fact, a bookseller."

She pats his arm. "You look like a Coney Island strongman. All you need is the handlebar mustache."

If she means the bodybuilders who used to pose in leopard-skin leotards, Patrick has no idea whether it's supposed to be an insult or a compliment.

"Get me something to read on my flight, will you?" Mrs. Kaplan asks.

The Kaplans opened Dooryard Books in 1920. Anyone might have thought nearly half a century in the business would have left her with some strong opinions about what she likes, but instead she plucks books off the shelves virtually at random and reads them cover to cover. Patrick has seen her do that with a cookbook. A road atlas. A collection of jokes for kids.

When she asks for recommendations, Patrick tries to assemble the three most disparate books possible, the literary equivalent of going to the A&P and buying a rack of lamb, frosted flakes, and a bottle of drain cleaner. Today he brings her a novel about a village in Kenya, a doorstopper on the Spanish Civil War, and a mystery in which a cat solves crimes.

"Thank you," Mrs. Kaplan says, taking the books and dropping them all into her enormous purse without even glancing at the titles. "I know the shop is in good hands."

"Anything I need to know about your new friend? Should I lock up the booze? Worry about loud noises? Hide any sharp objects?"

She hesitates. Mrs. Kaplan is not a woman who

hesitates much in her life. Patrick knows the darkest secrets and medical histories of her entire extended family. If she's hesitating now, he doesn't like it.

"He may be a little paranoid," she says. "Skittish."

"Drugs?" Patrick asks. "Or the war?" Nathaniel's old enough to have fucked his brain up in two wars. Plenty old enough to have fucked his brain up in a bunch of ways.

"He's getting better," she says, which isn't an answer. He's about to ask where she found this man, what his story is, but she checks her watch and says, "I'd better go. I left the cab waiting."

Patrick walks her to the door. As the cab pulls away, a gust of icy wind whips down the length of the street, lifting tiny whirlwinds of coffee grounds, eddies of cigarette butts and onion peels, and resettling them in drifts of debris along the sidewalk.

At four, Iris and Hector from apartment 3R come clattering into the shop in a tumult of bookbags and soda bottles, in the middle of an argument they abruptly cut off with hissed whispers. Mrs. Valdez is a hospital nurse who works odd hours, and Mr. Valdez does something backstage at a midtown theater, so there's often nobody home after school. Ever since they moved in two years ago, Patrick's been letting the kids do their homework at the table in the back of the shop as long as they keep quiet and stay out of his hair. Hector and Iris are good kids—or as good as a pair of fifteen-year-olds are going to get, which probably isn't anything to get excited about.

Today, Patrick orders a couple pizzas—Hector alone can put away an entire pie—tipping the delivery boy extra for having to wade through trash to reach the door. He explains to Hector and Iris that Mr. Smith is the new shop assistant and will be staying across the hall from them in apartment 3F. Iris casts an assessing eye over Nathaniel, and Hector waves distractedly before returning his attention to an old transistor radio he's been taking apart and putting back together over the past few weeks.

Not wanting to leave a strange man alone with the kids, Patrick finds a reason to stay in the back of the shop.

Dooryard Books is the kind of secondhand bookstore that might pass for an antiquarian bookshop, if you're in the market for nineteenth-century American poetry and fiction. There's always one or two good editions of *Leaves of Grass* in the glass case upstairs. But, like a lot of secondhand bookstores, it's turned into a chaotic warehouse of books Patrick can't even remember acquiring.

The way the shop is set up, most of the first floor is covered in bookshelves. Along the walls, shelves stretch from the battered wooden floorboards to the tin ceilings. More shelves, not quite so tall, form alleys and pathways that Patrick swears made sense when he put them there back when the store moved here from its old Fourth Avenue location, but since then seem to have tangled themselves up, like a piece of string left too long in your pocket.

The walls, in those rare places where they aren't hidden by shelves, are painted a nondescript shade that must once have been a dusty green, years ago when this shop was something else—a pharmacy or a grocery store, judging by the contents of some of the junk that was lying around when they moved in. Upstairs are more bookshelves, a locked glass case displaying some rare books, a safe containing the very rare books, and Patrick's apartment jammed into a back corner, looking out over the scraggly courtyard.

On the first floor, at the front of the shop, are the cash register and Patrick's desk and typewriter. Toward the back, the maze of shelves gives way to an empty space that's just big enough for a table and four chairs crammed close together.

Beyond that is the back room, a dusty hellhole full of boxes upon boxes of uncategorizable stuff and one electric kettle balanced on top of one of the more stable piles. Patrick threw some boxes in there when they moved in, but those boxes have multiplied, divided like amoebas, invited their friends over for drinks, and in general taken over the place. He keeps that door shut so he doesn't have to think about it.

Patrick gets distracted comparing two editions of *The House of Mirth*, and when he turns around both pizzas are nearly gone—they left him two measly slices—and the twins are doing what looks like algebra.

"Where are we?" Nathaniel asks, looking at the poster-sized subway map that hangs on the door to the back room.

"New York," Iris says, without looking up from her paper, and with the bored patience of a child who's humored her share of Mrs. Kaplan's strays.

"New York City," Hector clarifies. "Manhattan. You're on Jones Street in the Village."

"Not Great Jones Street," Iris says. "People get confused."

"You do not want to go to Great Jones Street," Hector agrees. "Well, unless you want to buy—"

"Hector!" Iris hisses, low enough that Nathaniel probably can't hear. "He looks like he has the supply chain figured out."

Patrick winces. When he was fifteen, he was a lot of things, but a reliable judge of what drugs a person might be on was not one of them. The spectacle of people enjoying varying degrees of success with an assortment of substances is hardly rare in the city these days. Iris and Hector know what to think when they see a pale, underfed man in secondhand clothes.

But Patrick thinks the twins misunderstood Nathaniel's question. He goes over to the subway map and points to a space between the Christoper Street and West Fourth Street stations. "We're right here."

Nathaniel smooths both palms over the paper. He leans in close, squinting at the words, and Patrick tries to decide whether they need to take a trip to the eye doctor and pay for it out of petty cash. When five minutes pass and Nathaniel still hasn't moved, Patrick figures bad eyes might not be the problem here. Iris and Hector exchange a knowing look.

When Nathaniel turns around, he peers at the twins' homework. "What did those poor numbers ever do to you?" he asks. "Or, rather, what are you trying to make them do now?"

"We're simplifying equations," Iris says.

"Hardly. Who told you to do it that way?"

"The teacher?"

Nathaniel takes Hector's notebook and scowls at it. "Your teacher needs to be brought before a tribunal."

Patrick snorts and Hector laughs outright, but Iris folds her arms over her chest. "It's how he taught us."

"If you enjoy doing things the slow and silly way, I won't stop you," he says, then pulls up a chair and proceeds to erase half of Hector's homework. Iris looks outraged, but Hector just looks glad someone else is doing his math for him. After a moment, Iris leans in and starts asking questions.

"Oh, Mr. Fitzgerald," Hector says, ignoring his sister and Nathaniel. He leans out of his chair and pulls something from between two books about bird identification. "Did you lose this?"

"Can we stop with the 'mister'?"

"No, sorry. I'm more afraid of my mother than I am of you."

"Fair." Patrick sighs and takes the envelope that Hector's holding out. It's the electric bill. He's been looking for it for days. "Thanks," he says. "I was going to have to call Con Ed to get a new one.

"How do you lose the electric bill?" Hector asks. "You always have a stack of bills on your desk. How did that one escape?"

For Patrick to know the answer to that question, he'd need an entirely different personality. He takes care of the bill and when he returns to the back of the store, the twins have moved on to biology homework.

"You mind if I read that?" Patrick gestures at the copy of the *Times* sticking out of Iris's satchel. He hadn't bothered going to the newsstand that morning. Iris is the kind of person you can count on to carry around reading material, a snack, and first aid supplies. She hands it to him without comment.

He unfolds it like he's braced for a punch, or maybe like he's driving past a graveyard. Above the fold is a picture of children in Saigon amid the rubble of their smoldering home, using buckets to put out the fire. He skims the articles about the sanitation workers' strike and makes himself read every word about Vietnam.

He doesn't feel guilty about not being there, not

exactly. For one, America doesn't have any business in this war, and secondly, the army doesn't want queers, and so they can't have him. The bartender at a place on West Street got out of the draft with a letter from a psychiatrist and an affidavit written by the Mattachine Society. Patrick could have tried something like that, if he'd been called up. Or maybe he'd have burned his draft card like the kids in Washington Square Park. But he never did get called up, and now he's twenty-seven, so he's home free. Dumb luck.

"Good news," Iris says, tapping the bottom corner of the front page. The state legislature is about to vote on expanding abortion rights.

"Good news," Patrick agrees.

Iris takes the paper from his hand, flips a few pages, and folds it back to reveal a full page ad against the war. "More good news," she says.

It's an ad against the war, but mostly for Eugene McCarthy, who's challenging President Johnson for the Democratic nomination in this fall's election. The ad reminds him, very unnecessarily, that sixteen thousand Americans have died in Vietnam. Another hundred thousand are wounded. No mention of how many Vietnamese civilians are dead or wounded, but Patrick supposes that isn't the kind of data that wins hearts and minds.

"Subways are filthy and the stations are foul," the ad reads. "Our cities are dying of neglect." It sets Patrick on edge, because yes, the subways are filthy and yes, the city never has enough money, but that doesn't have a damn thing to do with asking American kids to commit war crimes a few thousand miles from home. This is *his* horrible city, graffiti and rats and all.

It's sweet that Iris can see this ad and think it's good news. Patrick was an optimist, too, when he was fifteen.

Nathaniel's watching them. Patrick passes him the paper, then watches out of the corner of his eye as Nathaniel reads the front page, his lips pressed together, then flips to the second page. Patrick can't tell if he disapproves of the news, or of Patrick and Iris, or if that's just what his face looks like when he's reading. He hasn't said much, but there's something in his voice that makes Patrick think about golf and the stock market. Nathaniel doesn't sound like someone Patrick would expect to be on his and Iris's side—and the fact that there are sides is increasingly obvious. Still, Patrick has yet to meet a conservative with hair as shaggy as Nathaniel's. But who knows, maybe Nathaniel missed a few haircuts while he was busy going off the deep end, or doing whatever it was that landed him at Mrs. Kaplan's house.

As the afternoon slides into evening, Patrick watches Nathaniel closely, mostly to make sure he isn't slipping off to get high, but also to figure out what kind of sad story he is. There are only so many ways a person can hit rock bottom, and Nathaniel—distinctly twitchy, wearing clothes that don't belong to him, living on a stranger's charity, using a fake last name—has all the signs of someone who just scraped himself off the cellar floor. Usually it's drugs, booze, jail time, or mental trouble. But there have been a couple women who left bad situations. At least once a year there's a kid who's run away or gotten kicked out, and Patrick spends the next month grimly furious.

Hector and Iris go home, Patrick closes the shop, and he and Nathaniel head up to the third floor with a broom that Nathaniel managed to turn up and a set of sheets Mrs. Kaplan brought, correctly guessing that Patrick's own spare linens are wadded up in the bottom of his closet, waiting for a trip to the laundromat.

The apartment is furnished, for a given value of furnished: a couch, a bed, a table and chairs. There are two bedrooms, even if the second one is tiny, empty, and only has the sort of half window that looks out onto a ventilation shaft.

Once Patrick switches on all the lights, he checks the bathroom for soap and toilet paper, and the kitchen cabinets for the same old pots and pans and mismatched dishes he found the last time he got this place ready for a tenant. He and Nathaniel make the bed. Nathaniel sighs and readjusts every single corner of the fitted sheet.

"This is cop behavior," Patrick says as Nathaniel checks that the top sheet is symmetrical on both sides.

"Take a look at your desk and then tell me which of us is the pig," Nathaniel says. Patrick, caught by surprise and always a sucker for a pun, laughs. For a moment, under the too-dim overhead bulb, Nathaniel looks delighted with himself. He isn't smiling, exactly, but his face is lit up. And Patrick, who spent the afternoon treating Nathaniel the way he treats all Mrs. Kaplan's strays—like he's signing a check for the minimum payment on a cosmic debt he racked up years ago, a truly shitty way to treat a person but there you have it—is brought up short. The unforgiving light turns the dark circles under Nathaniel's eyes nearly purple, and Patrick has to add a few years to his earlier estimate of Nathaniel's age. But there's no mistaking the look of unholy glee on his face—at roasting Patrick, and maybe also at making Patrick laugh. It makes Patrick feel like he's seen too much, like he's peeked through a keyhole. Like he's gotten a glimpse of something he wouldn't mind seeing more of.

Nathaniel's about twenty years too old to be a runaway. At some point runaways graduate into drifters. They drift in, they drift out. Patrick gives them a hand and he wishes them well when they leave. No point in getting attached.

Speaking of which. "There's an A&P around the corner," Patrick says, one foot in the hallway, thirty seconds from being on his sofa. "They'll still be open, if you need anything." Mrs. Kaplan will have given Nathaniel at least five twenty-dollar bills, smooth and clean and fresh from the bank, plenty for a man to buy his own groceries. It isn't wages, it's a gift, she always tells them: Mr. Kaplan's life insurance payout put to good use. If they want to stick around the bookshop and work, Patrick pays them for their time and teaches them a little about buying and selling books. Usually, though, they just need a few weeks with food and rent taken care of to get back on their feet, and then they come up with a plan of their own.

Nathaniel looks a little stricken—and, fair, nobody wants to buy groceries at eight p.m. in the coldest part of the winter, even when the streets aren't paved with garbage. But that prospect would make most people look annoyed, not like a mouse freezing at the sound of an owl's hoot.

"Or we can figure out groceries in the morning," Patrick says. "Don't worry about breakfast. I have coffee and milk in my apartment. I might even have cereal. I'll get you tomorrow at nine?"

Nathaniel looks more grateful than anybody should about some corn flakes, and that just pisses Patrick off, which means it's time to go. He says a terse good night and is halfway down the stairs before he hears the apartment door shut.

2

"You're allowed to take breaks," Patrick says when Nathaniel finishes sweeping the floor and cleaning the grimy shop bathroom. It isn't even noon. Patrick's exhausted just watching him. "Go have a cigarette or something."

Nathaniel glares at him. Patrick isn't sure whether the glare is for suggesting a break or for letting the shop acquire what Patrick likes to think of as a respectable patina. It doesn't matter. This is his shop. Or, Mrs. Kaplan's, but she lets him have free rein. The old Fourth Avenue store housed three stories of disorganized books and over four decades of dust. By comparison, this place is practically an operating theater in its cleanliness, a minimalist paradise in its aesthetics. Dooryard Books is the Mies van der Rohe of used bookstores. Hell, some of the shelves are even alphabetized.

He tells Nathaniel this. Nathaniel stares at him for ten

full seconds, his face a study in disapproval, then goes back to cleaning the windows. "Mies van der Rohe," he says a moment later. "Spare me."

Patrick prefers bitchy Nathaniel over quiet and terrified Nathaniel, partly because terrified is, objectively, not a great state, but mostly because it's just a sad fact of Patrick's life that he's drawn like a magnet to the most irritable bastards on the planet. Give him a man with a pretty face and a list of complaints and Patrick is putty in their hands.

It's too quiet, so Patrick puts on the radio. WBAI is playing "Alice's Restaurant." Patrick keeps an eye on Nathaniel, looking for signs he disapproves of protest music, but Nathaniel just wipes down the radiator, the cash register, the telephone. "Okay, quit it," Patrick says when Nathaniel gets too close to his typewriter. "Leave that alone." Nathaniel cleans the rest of Patrick's desk, leaving a neat perimeter of dust and smudged ink around his typewriter.

There aren't any customers, which may have something to do with how there's even more trash on the streets now than there was yesterday. Patrick's managed to make his groceries last for a week, but he's down to a few tablespoons of milk and a brown banana, so he'll have to go out in this mess.

He finds Nathaniel in the back of the shop, dusting the bookshelves. "Want to go to the A&P?"

Nathaniel freezes, feather duster in the air. Patrick would love to know where he found a feather duster.

"I can watch the shop," Nathaniel says.

"Don't you need groceries?"

Nathaniel looks like he wants to say that he doesn't need food, that he'll figure something else out, like photosynthesis, or maybe starvation.

"Mrs. Kaplan gave you money?" Patrick asks. Nathaniel nods. "And you still have it?" he adds, because maybe Nathaniel sneaked off in the middle of the night to get a fix, who knows.

"Yes," Nathaniel says, mightily offended.

"Okay, then you should spend some of it on food. It looks like it's about to snow, so we should hurry."

"What if you have a customer?"

"We can lock the door and flip the sign to Closed for half an hour." That's what Patrick does whenever he leaves the shop during business hours, unless Mrs. Kaplan wants to come in for a bit.

Nathaniel shoots a wary look toward the front of the shop, toward the street, and it's the same reaction as last night when Patrick suggested that he buy groceries. Maybe he can't take cold weather. Maybe he likes rotting garbage even less than most people. Or maybe he has a screw loose in his head, like some people do about getting stuck in elevators or washing their hands. Patrick's experience with people who find themselves homeless and alone is that it'll loosen a few screws all right. It took Patrick a while to tighten his own back up.

"Or," Patrick says, "I can pick you up a few things."

"Yes," Nathaniel says. "Please."

They make a list. It's the saddest grocery list Patrick's ever seen, and he has ten years of sad grocery lists under his belt. Milk, cereal, bread, coffee, peanut butter, a few cans of soup and tuna fish.

"Do you want to cook anything?" Patrick asks. "There are some pots and pans in your apartment."

"No," Nathaniel says, appalled, like Patrick suggested cannibalism. That's pretty much Patrick's own attitude toward cooking, so he can't really judge.

Patrick buys some eggs anyway, and also some butter to cook them in. Then he remembers that fruit exists, so when he comes home it's with two overfull paper sacks. Nathaniel's waiting at the door like he wasn't sure Patrick was going to make it back alive, which is fair, because the trip took twice as long as it should have. Before he even got to the grocery store, he found a coatless girl at the entrance to the Sheridan Square subway station, a look of grim determination on her face and the piss poor judgment to solicit clients in broad daylight in front of what's pretty widely known as a gay gym. He can't afford to buy coats for every kid on the planet, but he can make sure girls barely older than Iris get a hot coffee and cab fare, so that's what he did. It's about ten percent of what Mrs. Kaplan would have done.

Nathaniel takes his share of the groceries and scrupulously gives Patrick ten dollars. Patrick rolls his eyes and gives him back eight dollars, because just how much does this guy think a jar of peanut butter and some tuna fish cost.

While Nathaniel is bringing his groceries upstairs, Patrick checks the cash register. Nothing is missing. He isn't particularly surprised. Whatever Nathaniel's problems are, the contents of the cash register aren't going to solve them.

Mr. Valdez has the night off, so the twins go straight home after school. When seven thirty rolls around with no customers and the sky is dumping snow onto the streets, Patrick closes the shop.

"If you let me use your kitchen, I'll scramble some eggs for dinner," Patrick says. Sometimes, inspired by the novelty of it, he'll cook a couple eggs in a little pan over the hot plate in his apartment, but there's no way that pan will fit enough eggs for two people.

Nathaniel accepts so readily that Patrick is sure at least one of them should be embarrassed about it.

"These eggs aren't very good," Patrick observes when they sit down to eat. They're badly overcooked, but with some raw egg still visible. He doesn't know how he managed that.

"An abomination," Nathaniel agrees, and Patrick nearly chokes on his admittedly abominable eggs. Well, whatever Nathaniel is afraid of, at least he doesn't seem to be afraid of Patrick. Patrick knows he isn't exactly approachable. Hector—six feet tall and built like a truck—skittered away from Patrick for a full two months after the Valdezes moved in. Patrick isn't sure what exactly he's doing to be scary—maybe it's his size, maybe it's the beard—but whatever it is, Nathaniel's apparently immune.

"I promise never to cook for you again," Patrick says.

"In exchange, I can promise never to cook for you either. A fair trade."

Now Patrick is sure of it: Nathaniel's voice doesn't fit. If Patrick shut his eyes, he'd expect that voice to come from someone in a suit and tie. He doesn't, as a rule, spend a lot of time with people in suits and ties.

Patrick is trying to decide whether he's going to ask some questions he won't like the answers to or whether he's going to go watch *Star Trek* in the peace of his own apartment, when the buzzer rings—not the one in this apartment, but the shop doorbell all the way downstairs. The only reason he can even hear it this far up is that it sounds like someone's leaning against it. For fuck's sake, nobody needs a book that badly.

"I need to get that," Patrick sighs, checking his watch.

The shop would normally still be open. It could be a late delivery. He runs down the stairs, aware of Nathaniel's footsteps behind him. On the second floor landing, there's a locked door that leads to Patrick's apartment and the upper story of the shop, but it's easiest to take these stairs right down to the street, then use his key to let himself back in through the shop's front door.

When he reaches the sidewalk, he's hit with a blast of freezing air and powdery snow. A customer is waiting at the shop door, a woman with long black hair cut in a fringe across her forehead, a suitcase at her feet and a— he's very much afraid that's a *baby* in her arms. She turns to face him.

"What the *fuck* is all this garbage for?"

"Susan?" He's known her longer than he's known practically anybody but she's so out of context that he doubts his own eyes. "I'll explain the garbage if you explain the *baby*," Patrick retorts. He pulls the key chain from his pocket and unlocks the door, then impatiently waves everyone into the shop. Why Nathaniel is still there is anybody's guess.

"You knew I was pregnant," Susan says in the near dark of the closed shop. "What did you think was going to happen?"

Patrick's been doing his best not to think about it at all. He still can't make sense of Susan—the same Susan whose locker had been next to his, the Susan who rolled his first joint and helped him definitively determine that he isn't into women—as a *mother*. Twenty-seven is a perfectly normal age to have a baby, but it still seems implausible, even with the proof staring him in the face. *Susan and Michael have a baby* is a nonsense series of words, like the phrases they make you repeat when you're learning a foreign language. The monkey has a hat. My aunt has the pen. Susan and Michael have a baby.

"A baby," Nathaniel says, sounding about as stricken as Patrick feels.

"I'm so glad we've all agreed that Eleanor is indeed a baby." Susan shifts the infant higher on her shoulder, and Patrick sees that she has her guitar case on her back.

"Susan, Nathaniel is the new clerk. He's staying here."

"How old is she?" Nathaniel asks Susan.

"One week."

"You flew across the country with a brand new baby?" Patrick asks. Shouldn't they both still be in the hospital? Or at least in bed?

"I didn't feel up to driving," she snaps, and that shuts him up fast. "Why are we standing around in the dark?"

Patrick runs his hand along the wall until he finds the light switch. When he turns back around, the sight of Susan brings him up short. She's so pale she's nearly gray. The only color in her face is her bloodshot eyes. A dusting of snow is in her hair, still unmelted, and it's that, for some reason, that sends a shiver down his spine.

The last time they talked—only a month ago, Susan blithely racking up a phone bill that made Patrick crazy to even think about—she was in San Francisco with no intention of going anywhere else. The band was in its final death throes, Michael was in Vietnam, and a baby was imminent but not discussed. She wasn't happy, but he didn't get the sense that she was sitting in her apartment crying her eyes red, either.

"Susan," Patrick starts, but he's interrupted by the baby mewling.

"May I hold her?" Nathaniel asks, which Patrick might have found odd if everything else about this encounter wasn't far weirder.

As Susan gives Nathaniel the baby, something shifts in her expression. Patrick knows this look all too well. It's the "I'm dropping out of college and starting a band" look. It's the "We're getting married and you're coming whether you like it or not" look. This look is the equivalent of an air raid siren. Patrick steels himself.

"Okay," she mutters, digging in her pocket for something. She's wearing the kind of dress that's more a nightgown than anything else, with only a cardigan over it. It's completely unsuitable for a snowy day in New York, and probably isn't even warm enough for California. At least the baby is bundled up, wrapped in a woolly blanket, only her tiny pink face visible. "I'm not going to say it," Susan says, and Patrick only has a second to notice that she sounds choked up before she shoves a crumpled piece of paper into his chest.

It takes him a few seconds to smooth it out, and then another few to identify it as a telegram. The words assemble themselves out of order. "Regret to inform" and "Department of Defense" and "Private First Class Michael Fitzgerald" all hang there in his consciousness before he's able to understand that he's holding the sort of telegram they send in movies to tell you someone's dead. His brain stalls out for a minute before he grasps that the dead person is Michael. He reads it again, just in case he's wrong. He feels, inanely, like he really ought to double check.

This time his gaze catches on the date: the telegram is dated today. Susan must have gotten it that morning, packed her suitcase, grabbed the baby and her guitar, and hailed a cab to the airport.

"Susan," he says, without a single clue what to say

next.

"I think I might be about to make some bad decisions," Susan says, her voice wobbling. "And nobody I know in San Francisco knows how to look after a baby."

Patrick opens his mouth to say that he doesn't have the first fucking clue how to take care of a baby either, that he's never so much as held one, that he's only aware in the broadest terms how babies even *work*. But he knows about running away, and he knows about last resorts.

He gives the telegram one final look before folding it back into a lopsided rectangle and sticking it in his pocket, stowing it away with whatever he might be feeling.

"Come here," he says, and he sounds steady, almost like someone you can count on. She's in his arms instantly, like she was waiting for the go ahead. A memory slips in sideways, the last time he hugged her, the scratchy lace of her wedding gown strange and stiff under his palms, Michael's arms around them both. He threatened to kneecap Michael if he hurt Susan, and threatened to kneecap Susan if she hurt Michael, and thought he was so amusing.

A few yards away, watching them, Nathaniel holds the baby against his shoulder. The baby is so small she's nearly swallowed up by the bulk of Nathaniel's too-big thrift store sweater.

There are three people counting on Patrick. They need a crib for the baby. Probably AA meetings or something along those lines for Nathaniel. God only knows what for Susan. Probably a dozen other things Patrick hasn't thought of yet. It's a relief, really, to have all that to think about.

"I'm glad you came," he tells Susan, and he's almost positive it's the truth.

After the kind of night that's so cold the radiators never stop clanging away, Patrick gives up on sleep. He wants to put on clean clothes but can't figure out how to do that without putting the baby down. He isn't sure where you put babies when you don't have a crib. The floor is dirty. The bed feels unsafe. He'll have to ask Mrs. Valdez.

Every time Patrick looks at Eleanor, he thinks: who the hell are you? Which isn't what anybody's supposed to think when they're holding a baby. But right now the fact that he's standing at his hot plate, sterilizing a bottle according to the instructions on the can of formula, feels about as likely a thing for him to be doing as piloting a spaceship.

He's pretty sure he's in shock, the kind of shock they treat with brandy or sugary tea in old movies, or maybe a brisk slap to the face, but there's nobody to slap him or give him anything to drink. He wants to call Mrs. Kaplan, but this isn't her problem and he'd only make her worry.

Before crawling into Patrick's bed, Susan swallowed a frightening number of pills, washed them down with a swig of Ballantine's she found on Patrick's bookshelf, and nearly gave Patrick a heart attack in the process. He spent the night alternately checking that she was still breathing and staring at the baby, seeing traces of Michael all over her face. *Eleanor.* Christ. That's Michael's doing. What would they have named her if she'd been a boy?

For lack of any better ideas, Patrick carries Eleanor down to the shop as soon as she finishes her bottle.

The Hawthorne he was repairing is still on his desk. He'd been looking forward to finishing it today, then going to the gym and maybe letting himself get picked up by that fireman who keeps monopolizing the bench press.

Now all that seems impossibly remote, a glimpse into the life of some other man.

It's six o'clock in the morning. Over a week's worth of accumulated garbage has been joined by heaps of snow, so the last thing Patrick expects is for anyone to knock on the door. He switched his desk lamp on when he came downstairs, and it's pitch black outside, so all he can see in the shop door is his own reflection. Still, he slides loose the deadbolt and opens the door, reasoning that burglars don't usually knock.

It's Nathaniel, holding two cups of coffee in mismatched mugs. "I thought you might be up."

Patrick takes one of the cups, angling it away from the baby. She hollers when he tries to take a sip, like she's personally going to see to it that he suffers. Patrick sighs. "May as well open the shop."

Somewhere in one of his pockets is the key to the cash register, but he has no idea how he's going to reach it without putting down either the baby or the coffee. The question of how to get the key out of his pocket feels like the kind of riddle they print in kids' magazines.

"I can hold her," Nathaniel says.

"It's okay." Patrick puts down the coffee and juggles Eleanor onto the opposite shoulder so he can reach into his right pocket. Eleanor screeches into his ear. The key isn't in that pocket, only the telegram. Patrick wants to kick something.

Wordlessly, Nathaniel takes the baby from Patrick's arms. Eleanor immediately stops crying.

"How did you do that?" Patrick demands.

"Babies don't like to be still," Nathaniel says, and sure enough, he's swaying a little while patting Eleanor's back. She's stopped crying, but now she's banging her little head against Nathaniel's shoulder. "She's hungry." There's no mistaking the reproach in his voice.

"She just finished a bottle. She's what, seven pounds? She can't need a quart of formula in an hour." Somewhere in this shop there must be a book about babies. It's not the sort of book Patrick usually stocks, but neither are cookbooks and somehow there's a whole shelf of them anyway.

"For heaven's sake, make her another one," Nathaniel says.

Patrick runs upstairs, makes a bottle, then grabs a can of coffee grounds and the entire coffee maker and carries it all downstairs, a quart of milk wedged against his chest.

Nathaniel is sitting at Patrick's desk, Eleanor nestled in the crook of his arm. She's staring at him with wide blue eyes, not screaming in the least. Nathaniel, meanwhile, is staring back at her in such plain distaste that Patrick might find it funny in any other circumstance. He doesn't buy it, though: last night, Nathaniel asked to hold her.

Nathaniel stands up and moves to pass Patrick the baby.

Eleanor immediately starts screaming. When Patrick sways, the way Nathaniel had done, she screams louder. She's screaming so insistently she doesn't even seem to notice that there's a bottle literally in her mouth.

"You're holding her like she's an undetonated grenade. Who *wouldn't* cry? Let me," Nathaniel says, extracting the baby from Patrick's arms. Patrick watches as Eleanor drains the bottle and goes limp.

"I think she hates me," Patrick says.

"Some babies hate everything," Nathaniel says. "Some people are born knowing the world is a terrible place."

This is heartening. Maybe he and Eleanor have

33

something in common.

"Your friend should have the empty apartment," Nathaniel says after carefully placing the sleeping baby in Patrick's lap. "I can find someplace else to stay."

There's no way Patrick's turning this man onto the streets after less than forty-eight hours. The whole point is to get him on his feet. But Patrick can't say that, because forcing charity on people is a great way to get them to head for the hills.

"That apartment is too much space for one person," Nathaniel goes on. "And your apartment isn't nearly big enough for three people." He'd seen Patrick's apartment—all five hundred square feet of it—yesterday morning when Patrick fed him cornflakes.

Mrs. Kaplan meant for Nathaniel to have apartment 3F. But if Patrick called her right now and explained the situation, she'd tell him to give Susan the apartment and ask Nathaniel to stay in Patrick's minuscule spare room—after scolding him for wasting money on a long distance call, that is. *I don't have stock in the phone company, Patrick.*

She might also remind him that some people, before they can let themselves be helped, need to do something to balance the scales. Patrick still changes the oil in Mrs. Kaplan's 1957 Ford Fairlane station wagon and goes out to Queens to put on snow tires whenever she needs them.

"All right," Patrick says. "Thank you. I do have a spare room. It's tiny and kind of awful, but you're welcome to it."

At least he has sheets for the narrow bed, purchased last year when Michael was in town without Susan, and was too cheap to pay for a hotel. They'd spent the entire visit sniping at one another about Michael's deranged refusal to wait out the war safely enrolled in graduate school, finishing his degree. He kept saying things like *this is my country* and *it's my duty* but also *if I keep deferring they'll just send some kid.* Patrick had never wanted to strangle someone so badly. And what's insane is that Patrick still wants to strangle him.

The door chimes ring, and Patrick looks up to see a figure swathed in a huge gray coat. The smell of garbage wafts in along with the cold.

"That's a relief," she says, and Patrick doesn't know if she means the heat or the fresh air.

"Professor," Patrick says. Vivian stops by the shop nearly every Wednesday and Friday morning on the way to teach a poetry seminar at NYU, but she hadn't come in earlier this week. If he's honest with himself, he's relieved to see her. Most customers are a pain in the ass but he starts worrying when he doesn't see the regulars. Even though he knows they're all avoiding the streets because of the strike, it still makes him uneasy.

"What on earth." Vivian stares at Eleanor. "I didn't know you were married, Patrick."

Patrick snorts. Sure, if a man is walking around with a baby, there's a good chance that baby belongs to him, and that he has a wife nearby.

But Vivian has salt and pepper hair short enough that she must get it cut at a barbershop. She wears men's shoes and used to come in with a woman who wore a fedora and smelled like cigar smoke. Patrick thought they were on the same page about the likelihood of either of them getting a baby the old-fashioned way.

"Haven't gotten knocked up yet," he says dryly. "Can't figure out why."

"Well," Vivian says. "She looks just like you."

Patrick's stomach drops. "She's—not," he says. "She's,

ah—" He swallows. "Her mother's visiting and her father isn't around." God, Michael would be so offended, but going off to die in a war is the pinnacle of *not around*. "She was my brother's. Is," Patrick corrects. "Vietnam." That's the fewest syllables it could possibly take to get the point across.

A few yards away, he hears Nathaniel make a sound. Patrick doesn't know if in the confusion of last night anyone told Nathaniel who, exactly, Michael is. Was. Shit.

"Oh dear," Vivian says. "I'm so sorry. He was only a bit younger than you, wasn't he?"

"Irish twins," Patrick says, something he's said dozens, hundreds of times to explain how he wound up with a younger brother in the same grade. "This is Nathaniel, the new clerk," he adds in a rush, an obvious bid to change the subject, but Vivian takes it.

Vivian leaves without buying anything. No surprise there—every few weeks she'll buy something, but usually she picks up a book, hums consideringly, then puts it back on the shelf, muttering *coals to Newcastle*.

"Someone in my building moved out and left behind their baby carriage," Vivian says before leaving. "I nearly trip over it every time I go downstairs. If you'd like it, I'll give you my address."

Patrick thanks her and writes down where she lives.

As soon as the door shuts behind her, Patrick glances at his watch. "I need to check on Susan. I'll be back in five minutes."

Susan's fast asleep, which is good, and breathing, which is about as much as anyone could hope for under the circumstances. He takes his time going back downstairs, and when he gets there he pointedly doesn't count the cash in the till until Nathaniel's in the bathroom.

Again, nothing's missing.

He keeps an eye on Nathaniel for another reason. Unless Nathaniel is a lot denser than he seems, he picked up on the subtext of Patrick's conversation with Vivian. If he has misgivings about sharing close quarters with a queer man, he'll bolt, and he'll do it soon.

But he doesn't. That night, after Susan wakes up long enough to eat a peanut butter sandwich and fall back asleep in the bed of apartment 3F, Nathaniel moves his toothbrush into Patrick's bathroom and proceeds to use up the last of Patrick's shampoo.

Patrick spends the night snatching sleep in five minute increments, except for when Nathaniel comes in at two in the morning, says, "For the love of *god*," and picks the baby up. Patrick passes out almost immediately.

The rest of the night, Eleanor's either in Patrick's arms or asleep in a dresser drawer, which Mrs. Valdez assured him is perfectly safe for the next week or two. Even asleep, she somehow looks furious. It's the only trace of Susan he can find on her face.

3

Mrs. Valdez corners Patrick.

"You're in charge here," she tells him, an index finger firm against the placket of his shirt, her nurse's uniform bright in the gloom of Susan's kitchen. "You treat that baby like she's your own baby and that poor girl like she's your sister, you hear?"

Patrick can only nod. He'd watched with a secondhand sense of shame as Mrs. Valdez took in the empty bottle of Ballantine's on Susan's bedside table, the pills in the bathroom, the pervasive smell of weed.

"They're both healthy," Mrs. Valdez assures him. "Physically, at least. New mothers need meat. Can you cook liver?"

Patrick doesn't even have a real stove in his apartment, and that's on purpose. Instead, he orders so much takeout that, after the first few days, he starts giving Hector and Iris five dollars every morning and asking them to pick up

Chinese food, sandwiches, pizza—I don't care, surprise us, keep the change—on the way home from school. Just when he's starting to worry he's about to go broke, Susan remembers that she's earned four gold records and has a bank account full of money.

"I shouldn't be doing this to you," Susan says. It's three o'clock in the morning. They're in Susan's bed, Eleanor asleep on the mattress between them. Patrick should put her in the cradle Mr. Valdez brought home from work—a prop from a show that just finished its run—but if she wakes up again he's going to need to scream into the pillow.

"You know I want you here," Patrick says, when what he wants to say is *just please don't die*. All week long he's been reminding himself that Susan's been in a band for years. Valium and whiskey aren't the worst she's done. They aren't even the worst she's done around Patrick. "Just be careful, okay?" And then, feeling shitty about it before the words even leave his mouth, "If you die, your parents will take Eleanor." The Larkins aren't bad people, but there's a reason Susan's here instead of their comfortable Long Island split level.

"Go to hell," she says. "I'm not trying to die. I just don't want to be awake and sober for this."

"People die without trying all the time." Patrick hears Susan's sharp intake of breath. Obviously people die without trying, Patrick, you fool, that's the reason they're in this mess.

"Okay," Susan says, a little wetly. He rolls to his side and attempts to stroke her hair, but he's terrible at this, just truly the world's least comforting human being. He keeps thinking she needs to wash her hair.

"You trust him," Susan asks a few minutes later,

waving a hand in the direction of the living room. Through the bedroom door, Patrick can see Nathaniel passed out on the couch, an arm flung over his eyes. "I'm not insane for letting a total stranger rock my kid to sleep?"

Patrick doesn't know a single thing about Nathaniel except that he takes his coffee black and has something against dust.

But you learn a lot about someone when you spend practically every waking minute with them for a full week. He's kind to Iris and Hector, patiently listening to their tales of ninth grade drama and correcting their algebra homework. A lot of people would judge Susan for—well, for everything about how she's handling things, frankly— but Nathaniel doesn't so much as look at her funny. He seems to save any malevolence for Patrick, and even that's just a gentle cattiness: some scathing commentary about a used tea bag he found in the military history section, some pointed words about grown men who don't understand that babies need to be burped. Nothing's gone missing, no sinister strangers have come around asking for him, and Patrick would swear he isn't using.

That much Patrick's sure about: Nathaniel's rarely more than a few feet away. Patrick would know if he had so much as a cigarette.

And then there's the fact that he's helping at all. It's not like anybody asked him to—it wouldn't have occurred to Patrick to ask his bookstore clerk to sterilize baby bottles, and it wouldn't have occurred to him to ask anybody in the world to spend their nights walking his niece back and forth in front of the window until she falls asleep.

"He's taking good care of that baby." Patrick doesn't

add: thank god *somebody* is. Patrick's trying his best but every time he picks her up he's sure he's doing something wrong, and from the way she carries on, she seems to agree. Susan's trying too, but she isn't in any shape to look after a newborn on her own right now.

"It's so sad," Susan says.

Patrick doesn't even need to turn his head to know that she's crying again. The past few sentences were probably the longest non-crying conversation they've managed since she got here. He reaches for her hand. "Why's it sad?"

"Because he must have had kids. Where are they now?"

Patrick could point out that men leave their families all the time, or that Nathaniel's experience with babies might come from younger siblings or nieces and nephews. But it all boils down to the same question: where are they now?

The next morning he shows Nathaniel where he keeps the stamps and envelopes. "If you want to send any letters," Patrick explains.

"Thank you," Nathaniel says, straightening out the roll of stamps before putting it back in the drawer.

"Just stick your letters in the tray with the other mail and I'll make sure the mailman picks them up," Patrick says.

"You can use the phone if you don't want to write," Patrick says a few days later when no letters from Nathaniel appear in the mail tray. "Long distance, too."

"No thank you," Nathaniel says, a little testily.

"Sometimes you need to," Patrick says, "even if it's just to stop yourself from feeling guilty."

Nathaniel looks up at him, something flinty in his expression. "Nobody's worried about me. God knows I'm guilty, but not of that."

In tenth grade, there was a kid who kept getting sent to the nurse's office for burning himself in chemistry lab. "Just wanted to see how long I could keep my hand there," he'd say after getting sent back to class, his hand bandaged in gauze. The next time the Bunsen burners came out, he'd do it all over again.

Reading the newspaper begins to feel like that, like an obvious danger that Patrick should have the common sense to avoid. Instead, he walks to the newsstand when it's still dark and the streets are almost quiet, Eleanor bundled in a blanket inside his coat, and reads the front page of the *Times* while standing on the sidewalk. At least the sanitation strike is over, and Patrick can carry out this masochistic ritual in reasonably fresh air.

He doesn't know what he expects to see. Every day the body count climbs higher, and Patrick reading about it in the early edition isn't going to make it stop. He can't tell if it's his imagination or if even the reporters seem sick of the war now. The other night, Walter Cronkite—not exactly a long-haired leftist agitator—went on air to more or less say we aren't going to win this war, and should negotiate a way out.

Today, on the front page, is the news that President Johnson—Patrick can't even think his name without something livid and dangerous curdling inside him—ended draft deferments for graduate students. Even if Michael had stayed in grad school, he could have been drafted anyway. It doesn't matter—Michael is dead, it's final, Johnson can't kill him twice—but Patrick wants to kick something. Who even fights a war with unwilling graduate students? It sounds like the setup to an unfunny

42

joke.

When Patrick gets home, fingers white with cold and Eleanor furious as usual, he checks on Susan, then goes to his own apartment and makes a pot of coffee and a bottle for Eleanor. Nathaniel comes out of the spare room, bleary-eyed and rumpled, a blanket still around his shoulders. Patrick hands him a mug and the paper. When Nathaniel's done with it, it'll get shoved into the bottom of the trash can, because they've entered into an unspoken conspiracy to hide the newspapers from Susan.

"Cold out," Nathaniel mumbles as he pours himself a second cup of coffee. It isn't quite a question. Nathaniel isn't capable of speaking with punctuation until he's fully awake, one and a half cups of coffee in his stomach. Patrick's added that to his meager stockpile of things he knows about Nathaniel.

It's gray, windy, and colder than yesterday, but it seems unfair to inflict that information on someone who's still mostly asleep. "It isn't raining," Patrick says.

Eleanor's fussy this morning—fussier than usual, which is really saying something—so Patrick types out a few letters one handed while trying to soothe her. At noon, Susan wanders into the shop, actually dressed and only slightly out of it. For a minute Patrick lets himself believe this is progress, but then she catches sight of Patrick holding Eleanor and abruptly goes back upstairs.

Patrick shuts his eyes. When he opens them, there's a fresh cup of coffee on his desk.

"Thank you," he says, but Nathaniel's already gone. The smell of Windex drifts down from upstairs.

Patrick keeps thinking that Michael's going to be horrified when he learns what a state Susan is in. Every few hours, the thought pops into his head and stays there for a precious few seconds until Patrick remembers that Michael isn't going to be anything, not ever again.

It's like the most important fact of his existence keeps slipping his mind, like where he put the phone bill or how many copies of *Billy Budd* they have in stock. How can you just forget that a person's dead? When Patrick's parents died, he hadn't forgotten.

He wants to ask someone whether this is normal. Mrs. Kaplan would know, but she believes long distance phone calls should last under sixty seconds. This does not feel like an under sixty seconds kind of conversation.

"I keep forgetting he's dead," Patrick tells Nathaniel. "I keep thinking, Christ, what would Michael do in this situation?"

Nathaniel pauses, one hand still holding the wadded-up sheet of newsprint he's using to clean the glass case. "Well, what *would* Michael do?"

It's a stupid question, because "what would Michael do about Michael being dead" is pure nonsense. Patrick knows the answer anyway.

Michael, with his boundless faith in experts, his belief that everything would work out just fine so long as you followed the rules, his conviction that the rules were on his side, would call the doctor. The doctor would do what doctors do, and it would end with Susan in Bellevue—or, more likely, a nicer, private psychiatric hospital upstate.

Maybe that's the right answer, but Patrick knows a couple people who've wound up in that kind of place and come out worse. Last spring, Mrs. Kaplan took in a girl who'd just gotten out of an institution. She'd been even paler and warier than Nathaniel, but when she warmed up enough to talk, she told him stories that gave him goosebumps. As far as he cares, the hospital is a last resort.

"Huh," he says.

"This is what happens when you don't have a funeral," Nathaniel says, his back to Patrick as he wipes a smudge off the glass. "Funerals make it feel real."

Susan decided to leave the entire business of Michael's burial to the Army and Patrick can't blame her. Michael would have loved to do their aunt and uncle out of a chance to play the part of dutiful guardians by showing up at a funeral.

But now he knows something else about Nathaniel: he's lost someone too.

At the beginning of March, when the baby's one month old and the telegram is three weeks old, it starts to snow. It's nothing special, just the kind of dusting that'll melt as soon as it hits a subway grate.

Patrick's trying to type a letter to a collector in Minneapolis who wants to buy an inscribed Melville that Patrick picked up at an estate sale last fall, but he keeps getting distracted, his attention divided between Eleanor asleep in the carriage from Vivian's stairwell and the snowflakes settling on the car parked across the street.

Susan comes into the shop from the street door, wearing jeans and an old cardigan of Patrick's. It turns out her suitcase had nothing in it but diapers and formula and tiny little cotton gowns that Eleanor's nearly outgrown. Well, and a few bottles of Valium and more grass than Patrick's ever seen in one place. She's been wearing Patrick's clothes, hems and sleeves rolled up an improbable number of times. So has Nathaniel, but with less cuffing and rolling. Laundry day is starting to feel like a weekly emergency.

"It's my disguise," Susan says when Patrick asks whether he's ever getting his clothing back. "Anyone who might recognize me won't expect me to be dressed like an elderly librarian." The familiarity of Susan mocking his clothes makes something in Patrick's chest loosen, like maybe the real Susan is in there, and that one day this will all be over and she'll come back.

"I do just fine," Patrick says.

"Not lately," she says, frowning, and she's right—he hasn't gone anywhere more exciting than the bank in weeks. "Sorry about that." She picks up the dust rag that Nathaniel pointedly left on Patrick's desk and starts wiping down a shelf.

"Don't you dare apologize," Patrick says. "I can screw and get screwed after Eleanor starts sleeping through the night." He's trying to make her smile—she's always been susceptible to anything even slightly risqué—but it doesn't work.

"Yeah, but—"

A crash comes from the back room.

"You can leave it, you know," Patrick calls out, for probably the hundredth time. Nathaniel's been working on that room for days. Patrick can't imagine why. It's filled with junk. Upstairs, piled against the walls and wedged between the bookcases, is more junk. It's the natural state of Dooryard Books. You can clear a surface, shut your eyes, and when you open them, a coffee mug, a Hawthorne early edition, and a badly rolled joint will have materialized out of thin air.

From the back of the shop comes the scrape and thud of boxes being dragged around and restacked. Then there's a dangerous silence, the painstaking hush of a muffled sob coming from Susan's direction, followed by something he's never heard in the shop.

"Is that a violin?" Susan asks, the dust rag going still.

"Good god, it's out of tune," Nathaniel calls out. He plays a few notes. "It needs new strings." A disapproving noise. "And the bow needs to be rehaired." There's a pause as, presumably, he does whatever needs to be done to make violins play in tune. Then he plays a scale, or maybe an arpeggio, or whatever it's called. "Strike that," he says. "The bow needs to be replaced entirely."

Susan wipes her eyes on the back of her hand, leaves the dust rag wedged between *Meditations in an Emergency* and *Lunch Poems*, then heads toward the back of the shop. "Is my guitar back here?"

Before this month, Patrick hadn't known Susan could go twenty-four hours without picking up her guitar. It's a desperately bad sign, maybe even worse than the pills and the booze and the fact that she came here in the first place. She hasn't even put on a record, and so neither has Patrick.

He holds his breath. It's just a few strings being plucked, two instruments being tuned. He should type his letter, ignore it in case paying attention makes them stop, but he's spent half his life listening to Susan play the guitar and he's spent the past three weeks worried out of his mind. He wants to take this shred of normality and put it somewhere safe. He gets up and goes to the back of the shop, wheeling Eleanor's carriage along with him.

Susan's in one of the metal folding chairs by the table, the guitar on her lap. Nathaniel's leaning against the wall, the violin tucked under his chin. They're both pale and thin with dark hair, a matched set. When customers see Patrick holding Eleanor, with her tuft of straw-colored hair and cloudy blue eyes, they assume she's Patrick's. It makes his stomach drop every time.

"What do you play?" Susan asks.

"Absolutely nothing," Nathaniel says. "Not since college."

Patrick thinks he recognizes the violin as a relic from the old shop, one of the many non-book secondhand items that used to find their way into bookshops back in the old Book Row days. Mrs. Kaplan would tell customers that the violin was part of a lot that came from the estate of a man Walt Whitman corresponded with, the implication being that the violin might once have been in the same room as Whitman. At the new location, Patrick put his foot down: there's just no room for musical instruments, hat stands, or cigarette cases of dubious provenance. But sometimes he misses the feeling of working inside a cabinet of curiosities.

Nathaniel starts playing something Patrick dimly recognizes as Christmas music, maybe.

"Is that 'Greensleeves'?" Susan strums along, picking up the harmony.

Patrick wonders if Nathaniel chose this song on purpose as something Susan might like; he can't have spent three weeks in the shop without figuring out that Susan is Suzie Larkin, and Suzie Larkin in synonymous with a certain kind of folk music. A kind of folk music, she keeps saying, that got worn out by 1965.

After a moment, Susan starts singing. Every now and then one of them makes a change Patrick can just barely perceive, and the other shifts whatever they're doing. After a few minutes, they're playing something completely different than what they started with.

"What next?" Susan asks.

"I don't know anything new," Nathaniel says, "but I'm

not bad at picking things up by ear. Or, well, I used to be able to."

Susan raises her eyebrows. "Can you really? How about—what's something everybody knows? Patrick, help me out."

The obvious choice would be the Beatles, one of those songs whose chords every teenager with a guitar knows by heart. But if the memory of Michael sitting cross-legged on the floor of Susan's old MacDougal Street apartment, playing *Revolver* from beginning to end, again and again until Susan and Patrick were both ready to shake him—if that memory makes Patrick want to lock himself in the bathroom and punch the wall, then he doesn't even want to think about what it would do to Susan.

"'Love Is All Around,'" Patrick says. "There's a violin part in that." Well, he thinks there is. It might be a cello.

"I don't know that song," Nathaniel says.

"They played it everywhere for a few months last year. You couldn't get away from it," Susan says. "You know, it's this one." She plays a few bars and sings a few lines, enough that Patrick is going to have it stuck in his head for the rest of the day, but Nathaniel shakes his head.

"Susan," Nathaniel says, amused, "I'm nearly forty years old."

"What, did your ears stop working? How about 'Light My Fire'?" Susan strums a few bars.

"I think my line is that all music recorded after 1955 sounds like noise."

Susan narrows her eyes. "I don't buy it."

Nathaniel makes an aggrieved sound and starts to play something classical.

"Oh wow, Patrick, he's playing Bach. We have a serious musician on the premises." Susan's voice drips with sarcasm.

The sight of Nathaniel playing classical violin sets off an alarm bell for Patrick. It isn't even the first one that Patrick's had since Nathaniel arrived. He doesn't fit the pattern of the other strays. No track marks, no dog tags, no unsavory friends calling in at the shop. Patrick would swear on a bible that the man hasn't touched any kind of drug since moving into this building. He hasn't even helped himself to the beer in Patrick's refrigerator.

It's only a matter of time before he dusts himself off and goes back to whatever life he left behind. It's a good reminder that Nathaniel is as temporary as anyone else. So is Susan, for that matter—she'll get back on her feet and buy a ticket to San Francisco, taking Eleanor with her.

Nathaniel segues from Bach to "Love Is All Around," the same exact notes Susan played a few minutes earlier, and Susan laughs. It's a sound he hasn't heard since she came here. She joins in.

Something warps and twists in the music. Susan says, "Okay, okay, I see where you're going" and the sugary pop ballad transforms into something moody and strange, like it's been filtered through Bob Dylan by way of a haunted house.

Through the back window, the snow dusts the branches of the dead tree in the yard, before settling on the ground in wet clumps. The song twists and shifts again until it's something almost cheerful. The radiator clangs in a messy counterpoint. The baby stirs, and when her eyes open, she gazes at Patrick.

4

Patrick's about to close the shop when someone walks in.

"Gracious," the new arrival says, dramatically stepping backwards and clutching his chest when he sees Patrick holding Eleanor. "Tell me you didn't make that."

"Okay, first of all, fuck you," Patrick says, leaning in to kiss Jerome's cheek. "Second, there's nothing wrong with babies."

"Of *course* not, darling. But when an old queen—"

"I'm twenty-seven!"

"Like I said. Nobody's seen you in weeks, and now I know why. *Procreating.*"

"She isn't mine."

"Exactly how sure are you about that?" Jerome asks, one plucked eyebrow carefully arched. He has on a fur coat but no wig or makeup. It makes Patrick panicky when Jerome goes out in drag—it's only a matter of time before he gets arrested—but when he told this to Jerome, he got an earful about how wearing false eyelashes in broad daylight isn't any more of a crime than Patrick going home with every queer rare book collector on the East Coast. The worst part is that he was right. "I always thought all white babies looked the same, but they can't *all* look just like you."

"She's my niece," Patrick says.

The expression of camp scandalization drops from Jerome's face. "Your brother?"

It hits Patrick that he's going to have to go through this every time he tells someone about Eleanor. "Not coming home."

"Well, shit," Jerome says. "I'm sorry, baby."

Patrick shakes his head. "What do you have for me today?"

Dooryard Books has some regular book scouts who come by every couple of weeks or months with a few well-selected books they think Patrick might want to buy, but they're the minority. More common are those who arrive with an A&P bag containing two decent books and a lot of nonsense, and Patrick buys the entire lot so that way they don't go elsewhere the next time they find something precious. There's a man who drives his 1949 Buick up to the store, double parks, and insists that Patrick look at whatever he has in the trunk. There's a retired schoolteacher who Patrick meets in a parking lot in Hoboken, like they're selling heroin or machine guns rather than copies of *Little Women*. There's a man with what Patrick swears must be a false mustache who arrives twice a year with a milk crate full of books so good that Patrick can only hope they aren't stolen.

Jerome is in a class of his own. A few years ago, he walked into the shop, asked for a copy of *Go Tell It on the*

Mountain, then had a lot to say about race relations when it turned out Patrick didn't have any James Baldwin in stock. When he came back a week later with a stack of James Baldwin and Richard Wright and one inscribed copy of *Invisible Man*, Patrick bought them all.

Today he has a Bloomingdale's bag full of nice enough leather-bound books, probably part of a set that got split up, a flawless first edition of *Manhattan Transfer*, one paperback with a lady in a nightgown fleeing an old house, and a book Patrick's never heard of called *Ladies of the Rachmaninoff Eyes*. "Very funny, very gay. Elderly lesbians," Jerome says, like this is a crucial selling point, and maybe it is. "Make sure you read it before you sell it."

"Okay," Patrick agrees.

It's nearly closing time, and Patrick was alone in the shop, but he's been waiting for an opportunity to show Nathaniel the process for purchasing and pricing books. He picks up the phone and dials Susan's apartment. When Nathaniel isn't in the shop, he's usually with Susan, whispering, their heads bent together, their instruments in hand, increasingly eerie music drifting out of Susan's apartment and into the stairwell. Otherwise, Nathaniel is across the hall. If Mrs. Valdez is home in the afternoon, she and Nathaniel watch soap operas on the Valdezes' color television while Mrs. Valdez irons her uniform.

"He's with the Valdezes," Susan says. "They're watching *Laugh In*. Want me to send him down?"

"Ask him to run down during the next commercial break, if he doesn't mind. Tell him it'll take less than three minutes." He hangs up. "Be nice to him," he warns Jerome.

"I can be terribly nice," Jerome says, in what he probably thinks is a sultry voice.

Nathaniel comes in from the street door and doesn't flinch when Jerome makes a spectacle of himself, kissing Nathaniel's hand.

"Anyway," Patrick tells Nathaniel, "we write the seller, title, description, and purchase price in this book. Then we give the seller a receipt." He turns to Jerome. "I'll take everything but the paperback. We don't sell paperbacks."

"It wasn't for sale. I finished it on the subway and dropped it in the bag."

"Maria reads these," Nathaniel says, frowning at the paperback. "I don't think she has this one."

It takes Patrick a moment to realize that Maria is Mrs. Valdez. Nathaniel's been here for less than a month and apparently they're on a first name basis.

"For you, it's for sale," Jerome tells Nathaniel.

The cover price is fifty cents. "I'll give you a quarter," Patrick says.

"Thirty cents," Jerome counters. "It's a good one. I do love a sexy evil man in a frock coat."

That's a good candidate for the gayest sentence ever uttered, and Patrick figures Jerome earned the extra five cents just for the effort. He digs a quarter and a nickel out of his pocket and drops them on the counter. Then he pulls ten dollars out of the cash register for the rest of the books and watches as Nathaniel records the sale and writes a receipt.

"How do you know what to pay?" Nathaniel asks.

"Baby, he makes it up," Jerome says.

Patrick sighs. "Jerome gets a forty percent cut of what I think I can sell the book for. Good copies sell for fifty percent of the cover price, but anything rare or special I have to figure out using—"

"Tea leaves," Jerome says. "A crystal ball. Your

womanly intuition."

"Using my decade of experience. Speaking of which." He rifles through the papers on his desk until he comes up with the latest issue of *Antiquarian Bookman,* the trade magazine where booksellers list books for sale and books they want. Patrick scans it every week for books he has in stock, then sends a postcard with a quote to the bookseller who wanted it. When he finishes with an issue, he lends it to Jerome or one of his other favorite scouts, so they'll know what to look out for.

"Pleasure doing business," Jerome says, giving a demure wave of his fingers before leaving the shop.

"Is he your friend?" Nathaniel asks while Patrick is lightly penciling in the price on each book's flyleaf. Patrick can't figure out if the subtext is *why would you be friends with someone like that* or *are you lovers* or if Nathaniel's just curious.

"Yeah," Patrick says. "But if you're asking whether we're—uh." He suddenly just does not have what it takes to say "lovers" or "fucking" in front of a man over ten years his senior. Nathaniel has to know that Patrick's queer, but the world is full of people who spend their whole lives pretending not to notice anything they don't like. "Not lately," Patrick finishes, hedging.

"I see," Nathaniel says, apparently satisfied, which makes Patrick suspect he answered the question Nathaniel meant to ask.

This is where most straight men hurry to explain that they don't know anything about any of that business because of how normal they are. Nathaniel doesn't do that. Instead he leans over and puts a cap on the ballpoint pen that's sitting on Patrick's desk.

Still, Patrick expects Nathaniel to seize any reason to

leave. Maybe he'll say he wants to finish watching *Laugh In* or he needs to bring that book to Mrs. Valdez, anything to get him away from a conversation about Patrick's gay sex life. Patrick almost doesn't blame him; he'd climb out a window if he had to hear about a straight person's sex life.

"I can close up on my own," Patrick says, feeling merciful, "if you want to finish whatever you were watching with the Valdezes."

But Nathaniel stays, never more than a few feet away as Patrick runs the cash register tape and locks up.

"Where do you get a violin restrung?" Patrick asks one morning when Nathaniel emerges from his bedroom. He's wearing one of Patrick's t-shirts. Patrick tries not to notice the way the threadbare shirt shifts on Nathaniel's shoulders as he reaches for a cup of coffee—he's not as skinny as Patrick first thought.

"It's just that you mentioned your violin needs work," Patrick says when Nathaniel's starting in on his second cup of coffee. He doesn't add: Susan asked me to flush the pills down the toilet and then she cried; the only time I've seen her smile in the last month is when she's making music with you.

"It isn't my violin," Nathaniel says, finally looking up from his coffee mug. "It was in your shop."

"Pal, that violin cluttered up the shop for years. I lowered the price to two dollars and still nobody bought it. It's your violin now, good riddance to it, no take-backs."

"Two dollars," Nathaniel repeats, and now he's all the way awake. "Two *American* dollars?"

"No, two Klingon dollars."

"What in *hell* is a Klingon dollar?"

Patrick decides then and there that he's closing the

shop early on Thursday so Nathaniel can get some culture. "So, where do you get violins restrung?"

"Around here? I wouldn't know," Nathaniel says. "In general, a luthier. Anyway, I ought to save my money."

"Shit." Patrick scrubs a hand across his beard. On his desk is a letter from Mrs. Kaplan, explaining that her sister is back in the hospital with an infection, so Mrs. Kaplan will be in Florida for at least another few weeks. Patrick should have looked at the calendar and realized it was his responsibility to figure out what to do with Nathaniel. "I owe you a month's wages. Jesus. I'm so sorry."

"You paid me two weeks ago."

Two weeks ago, Susan gave Patrick an apparently random amount of cash for February and March rent. Before taking the money to the bank, Patrick gave Nathaniel a handful of ten-dollar bills, said "Wages?" and then forgot about the entire transaction until this moment.

"Okay, New York minimum wage is a buck sixty or seventy, I can't remember. Let's call it two dollars. You're easily working eight hours a day, so that's forty hours a week."

"Not really. Some of that time I'm looking after the baby."

"This is shitty bookkeeping, but I'm just going to consider baby work and shop work as the same thing, two bucks an hour, eight hours a day, five days a week. That's eighty dollars a week." Patrick will chip in half that amount for the babysitting. Eighty bucks a week is probably fifteen more than anybody's ever made as either a babysitter or a bookstore clerk, but Patrick isn't nickel-and-diming the only person on this planet who Eleanor can stand. "So, I owe you one eighty for the last two weeks."

He unlocks his desk and reaches for the checkbook.

"No," Nathaniel says.

Patrick still with his hand in the desk drawer. "I can't really pay much more—"

"I won't take money for taking care of Eleanor."

This might be some kind of macho refusal to get paid for women's work, but Patrick feels like that kind of man would refuse to do the work in the first place. "It's work. There are people who take care of babies for a living."

"Obviously," Nathaniel says, peeved. "That isn't the point."

"What, exactly, is the point? I'm not letting you work for free."

"How do you plan on stopping me? You can't force a person to take money."

Jesus Christ. Patrick doesn't have the patience for this. "Fine, be my guest." He begins to fill out the check. "A hundred ten, then." Nathaniel, who apparently does algebra with the Valdez twins for fun, can divide one eighty by two and discover it isn't a hundred and ten, but he only makes an exasperated noise.

"Cash would be better," Nathaniel says.

"Don't worry, I made it out to cash." Patrick manages not to roll his eyes. Does this guy really think that Patrick was going to make out a check to "Nathaniel Smith"? It takes Nathaniel three or four tries to remember to answer to "Mr. Smith" when Hector and Iris are trying to get his attention. They've started to call him Nathaniel, which means Patrick might finally win his campaign to get them to stop calling him Mr. Fitzgerald.

"When will you want me to leave?" Nathaniel asks, folding up the check and putting it in his pocket. "Mrs. Kaplan said you'd put me up for a month."

Patrick feels like the rug's been pulled out from under him. More fool him. Usually, if one of the strays has done any work whatsoever, Patrick finds them work at another bookstore. There isn't enough work at Dooryard Books for another employee. They just don't do that much business. It's the rare book sales that pay the bills, and Patrick handles those. When he needs time off, or he has to be at an auction or book sale, either he closes the shop or Mrs. Kaplan pitches in for a few hours.

Now, though, even with Nathaniel sometimes manning the cash register, Patrick's behind on everything else. There's a lot of work he can do while holding a drooling baby, but he draws the line at repairing century-old rare editions.

And then there's Eleanor: they need the extra help. Susan likes Nathaniel, the baby likes Nathaniel, and that's a majority vote, so Patrick doesn't need to consider whether his decision has anything to do with the fact that *he* likes Nathaniel.

"Who said anything about leaving?" Patrick tries to sound impartial. "If you want to stay, there's work for you here. If you want to go, I can find you work at another store. Either way, you can stay in the spare room if you want."

Something frustrated and tired crosses Nathaniel's face. "Of course I'll stay."

Patrick tries to look like someone who isn't giddy with relief. "Same deal? Five days a week, time off as needed?"

"I've been working every day."

"So now you have two days off. Slow days are Monday and Tuesday," Patrick says. "Go have fun."

Nathaniel's lips are pressed into a tight line.

"Or you can stay here," Patrick says. "You live here.

Nobody's kicking you out. Read. Watch television. Get stoned with Susan. Watch *As the World Turns* with Mrs. Valdez."

"That was one time. What about rent?"

Nobody should pay rent on an eight-by-ten room with no furniture other than a single bed, but Nathaniel doesn't look open to that argument.

"I pay a hundred dollars a month, and it's only that cheap because Mrs. Kaplan hasn't noticed it isn't 1935 anymore." And because Patrick's apartment is only a couple of storage rooms that happen to have access to a bathroom and a fire escape. And also because he's basically the building's superintendent, but Nathaniel doesn't need to know any of that. "The going rate for a furnished room in this neighborhood is something like twenty-five a week, but a room at a bare bones hotel over on West Street would be something like fifteen." Patrick's well aware that his spare room—hell, his own room—is closer to the latter. "But I can't charge you fifteen a week, because then you'd be paying most of my rent for me. So, seven a week, and I pay for groceries and utilities?"

Nathaniel sticks out his hand, and Patrick instinctively grabs it. "Thank you," Nathaniel says without letting go. And then, surprisingly earnest, "I don't want to be a charity case."

"I've been a charity case, you know," Patrick says. "Mrs. Kaplan's charity case, as a matter of fact. Nothing wrong with that, not when you need the charity."

"Oh. I didn't mean—"

"No harm done." He hasn't let go of Nathaniel's hand, and Nathaniel hasn't let go of his. At this proximity Patrick can't help but notice that he's—well, it isn't any of Patrick's business what Nathaniel looks like. He's Patrick's employee, his tenant, and, in a way, his responsibility. He drops Nathaniel's hand and takes a step backwards. "Now, let's see where to get a violin restrung."

Susan tells them that if the man who runs the guitar shop on MacDougal doesn't stock the right kind of violin strings, he'll at least know where to send them.

"You two go. Eleanor and I will stay at the cash register and grumble at anyone who comes in," she offers. "That's the job, right?"

Patrick rolls his eyes, but it's a good sign if Susan's teasing him. He puts on his coat, notices that Nathaniel's only wearing a sweater, then takes off his coat and gives it to Nathaniel. He puts on a leather jacket that someone left at the shop ages ago.

Nathaniel hesitates at the door, still holding Patrick's coat. In the month he's been here, Patrick's not sure Nathaniel's left the shop for longer than it takes to put out the trash. He spends plenty of time looking out the window—the shop window, and the window in Susan's living room that looks out over Jones Street. There isn't anything to look at: wintry trees and dirty sidewalks, parked cars that shift back and forth according to alternate side of the street parking rules. Nathaniel looks outside in the same way that he looks at pizza, at a fresh pot of coffee.

"Have you always had a thing about going outside?" Patrick asks. "Susan's like that about heights."

"No. No, I just…" Nathaniel makes a noise like he's thoroughly disgusted with himself.

"You can stay here, and I'll go to the guitar shop," Patrick offers, quietly enough that only Nathaniel will hear. "Or we can take a cab."

"Why are you doing this?" Nathaniel asks, an edge to

his voice. "You let me eat your food and wear your clothes and watch your television, and now this?" He's holding Patrick's coat up like it's Exhibit A and he's Perry Mason.

This is mighty rich, coming from a man who not five minutes earlier refused to take money for babysitting. But it's not like Patrick's never asked himself the same question, especially after one of the strays stole his typewriter a couple years ago. His only answer is that he doesn't like to think about where he'd be if Mrs. Kaplan hadn't helped him in 1958. He can't walk past someone if there's a chance he can do half as much for them as Mrs. Kaplan did for him.

It isn't even like he's doing that much, really. Usually, all he does for the people Mrs. Kaplan brings him is train them to work in a bookshop and give them lunch a few days a week. Maybe take them to the doctor or help them apply for jobs. It's more than most people would do, but most people don't have an old lady presenting them with good deeds that are ninety percent complete, a paint by numbers project.

Mrs. Kaplan calls it a mitzvah. Patrick, who hasn't set foot in a church since his parents' funeral, sometimes thinks it might be a sacrament, but then gets embarrassed by the thought.

"Look, the day Mrs. Kaplan met me, she put three stitches in my forehead because I wouldn't go to the hospital. See that scar?" Patrick pushes aside his hair and points to his eyebrow. "Any normal person would have told me to get lost, but she fixed me up, bought me a sandwich, offered me a job, and gave me a place to sleep."

Patrick hates telling this story. He doesn't want to remember that kid: that kid had lost all his illusions and he'd lost them too fast. Patrick wants to avert his eyes.

Maybe that's why he makes himself tell the story—to all the strays, and to a lot of other people besides. It's a kind of offering. It keeps him honest.

A man once told him that at AA meetings, you introduce yourself as an alcoholic because it's a reminder of the problem you all have in common. Patrick figures anyone who winds up needing his help might want to know that he's been there, that he's part of the fellowship of people who could not possibly have gotten their shit together without some help. Sometimes, knowing about Patrick's crummy past gives a person permission to accept half a sandwich or a five dollar bill or a bus ticket home.

"And so that's why you gave me your coat," Nathaniel says, the edge still in his voice. "And why you're taking me to get violin strings? Because Mrs. Kaplan helped you?"

That was the answer at first, sure. That was why Patrick bought Nathaniel's groceries and lent him some clothes and a spare bed. But now, for some reason, he says, "I gave you my coat because I have a lot more meat on my bones than you do." He's only been to the gym a handful of times since Susan moved in, but for the ten years before that, lifting weights was his only actual hobby. Pick the right gym at the right hour, and there's even odds you'll go home with someone.

Nathaniel's gaze drops to Patrick's shoulders, his chest, and it doesn't mean anything because when you're dumb enough to talk about the meat on your bones— Jesus Christ, Patrick, of all the things to say—people look at your body. It's inevitable. But Patrick, because he's truly on a roll, notices how long Nathaniel's eyelashes are, how his eyes are more amber than brown. How long it takes for his gaze to get back to Patrick's face.

"I've been brushing my teeth next to you for a month

and—" It shouldn't be embarrassing to say that he thinks they're friends, or something like that. "We're friends," Patrick says firmly, pretending his face isn't hot. His beard hides the worst of the damage. It's fine.

Nathaniel looks—the fucker looks *smug*, like he was baiting Patrick into admitting it. "Quite," Nathaniel agrees, before Patrick can get mad about it. "How'd you get hurt?" Nathaniel asks, looking at the scar on Patrick's forehead.

"Cops. All right, let's head out."

Over at the cash register, Susan is trying to look like she isn't listening. She's heard all this before, but to her it isn't the story of Patrick getting taken in by a lady who used her sewing kit to fix his face; it's the story of Patrick running away without telling her or Michael. Just because now she knows the whole story doesn't change what it must have felt like to them back then.

"All right," Nathaniel says, squaring his shoulders and holding on tight to the battered violin case. "Let's go."

It's a five minute walk to MacDougal. Patrick takes the quieter way, turning onto a stretch of West Fourth that's only a few blocks long and which hardly gets any traffic. It's almost pretty, with the first March leaves appearing on some of the spindly trees that line the street, but Patrick can sense Nathaniel's attention drawn to every piece of gum ground into the sidewalk, every nasty smell that wafts out of the gutter.

When they turn onto Sixth Avenue at a messy intersection of three streets, Nathaniel tenses beside him. He stops walking, so Patrick stops too. Sometimes Nathaniel seems to disappear to someplace else— someplace not particularly pleasant, by the looks of it. He goes perfectly still and rigid, like he's relying on the same prey animal instinct that makes deer freeze in the face of oncoming headlights.

Right now, they're blocking the sidewalk. Patrick takes Nathaniel by the arm and steers him off to the side, so they're standing against the plate glass window of a shoe repair place.

"You're all right," Patrick says.

"Lies," Nathaniel says, with a valiant but failed attempt at bitchiness.

"Want to turn around?"

"Of course I want to turn around," Nathaniel snaps. "But I won't."

"There's no shame in going easy on yourself."

Nathaniel looks like he wants to argue, but instead he rolls his eyes, like Patrick's being very silly about all this. "I need to try."

"All right."

"Just —don't leave me."

"I wasn't planning to," Patrick says.

Nathaniel's face reddens. "I mean, stay next to me."

"Sure," Patrick says, more surprised that Nathaniel made himself ask than by the actual request. He wouldn't be the first person to treat Patrick like a cross between a bodyguard and a Saint Bernard. The girl Mrs. Kaplan took in last year had practically glued herself to him.

"We'll cross at the corner," he says when they start walking again. "Nothing to worry about. Okay, let's go, the sign changed to Walk." Nathaniel keeps so close that their arms touch.

Patrick can practically feel the nervousness rolling off Nathaniel, but Nathaniel doesn't say anything, so neither does Patrick. By the time they get to the guitar shop,

Nathaniel is out of breath and noticeably pale.

The guy behind the counter has blond hair down past his shoulders, a Santana t-shirt, and a joint that he hastily hides under the counter when the shop door opens. He fusses over Nathaniel's violin like it's a newborn baby.

Nathaniel winds up buying a set of strings, a new bow, some resin, a new case, and some odds and ends that Patrick can't identify.

"Susan Larkin told me to say hello," Nathaniel says over his shoulder on the way out.

"Susan—*Suzie Larkin*? Jeez, man, you could have told me up front. Is she back in town? Wait." The man's eyes narrow. "I read that the band broke up. Are you playing with her now?"

"No," Patrick cuts in before this guy tells all his customers and his dope dealer, and Susan winds up reading about her alleged new act in the *Village Voice*. That's the last thing she needs.

"Okay, man," the guy behind the counter says, taking a step back, his hands up in surrender.

"Do you want to go straight home or stop for lunch?" Patrick asks when they're out on the sidewalk.

Nathaniel sticks his hands in his pockets and looks up at the sky. "I'm still coherent, so let's press our luck a bit."

They stop at the kind of place that has a jukebox and a liquor license, cigarette butts on the floor and waitresses who act like they're doing you a favor. Patrick orders a burger and beer. After a perfunctory glance at the menu, Nathaniel says he'll have the same.

While they're waiting for their food, Susan's single from last August plays on the jukebox. It's full of hand claps and tambourines. It's catchy. Patrick likes it. "This is Susan," Patrick says. "She hates it. The record company overdubbed drums and extra vocals. Last summer, radio stations would not stop playing it."

Nathaniel listens to the rest of the song in silence, his face gradually arranging itself into something tight-lipped and pensive. "Joan Baez but you can dance to it," he says eventually.

Patrick laughs, pleased by the bitchiness and surprised that Nathaniel apparently knows who Joan Baez is. Patrick's secret opinion is that it sounds like the Lovin' Spoonful, only prettier, but Susan would have to torture that information out of him.

"That's what Iris and Hector say," Nathaniel explains. "I don't think it's a compliment."

"No, it wouldn't be." Patrick digs in his pocket for change. "Hold on, okay?" He goes to the jukebox, drops his dime in the slot, makes his selection.

"This is one of Susan's first songs," Patrick says when his song comes on. It's "A Sailor's Life," a traditional ballad that Susan adapted pretty freely. He remembers her listening to a grainy recording on the three-album folk music anthology she bought with the money she got for her fifteenth birthday. He sat on the floor of her bedroom, doing his geometry homework while she was in her own world, strumming a few bars, scribbling something in her notebook, putting the needle back down at the beginning of the track, and then doing it all over again. Sometimes people act like Susan simply finds an old song and sings it, easy as that, but she labors over those songs just as much as the songs she writes from scratch.

"Oh," Nathaniel says after a minute. "It's lovely."

When Patrick pressed that button on the jukebox, he hadn't remembered that "A Sailor's Life" is about a woman whose husband dies at sea. He'd only been thinking of fifteen-year-old Susan, her hair in her face, her guitar in her lap.

Now he's thinking of Susan nearly thirteen years later. He's thinking about Michael. He's held it together for a month and he isn't going to get shaken up by a song on a jukebox, a song he's heard a thousand times. He takes a deep breath and finishes his beer. He's aware of Nathaniel—not watching him, but carefully *not* watching him, giving him space to be a basket case in private.

"What kind of beer is this?" Nathaniel asks when Patrick has a hold of himself. It's the most neutral question in the world and Patrick could hug him.

"It's just Schlitz," Patrick says, and Nathaniel takes a thoughtful sip like he's never had a Schlitz in his life.

They eat their lunch to the accompaniment of the random assortment of music that other patrons have selected on the jukebox—some old standards, some Motown, a lot of Top Forty. With each song, Patrick tells Nathaniel about the band or artist, and whether— according to Susan—they're drug fiends, philanderers, or sex pests. Nathaniel listens, amused by Patrick's gossip, but also intrigued by the music, not at all like a man who thinks everything recorded after 1955 sounds like noise.

When they get back to the shop, Patrick hauls the record player down from his bedroom and plugs it in at the back of the shop. Then he fills a milk crate with records and carries that down too.

"Have at it," he tells Nathaniel.

Susan raises her eyebrows, but she comes to sit next to Nathaniel on the floor, the baby on her belly next to them, gnawing on the edge of a Rolling Stones album.

5

In the middle of March, Patrick comes home from an estate sale to discover that Nathaniel finally got the back room cleared out. Susan's in the back of the shop, curled up in an armchair she dragged in from the street, Eleanor in her lap. They all take a moment to stare at what Nathaniel's uncovered.

"That's a kitchen," Susan says, pointing out the obvious. "Or at least it was forty years ago."

Sure enough, there's a sink, an enormous white and green oven, and an ancient icebox made of dark wood with blackened iron hinges.

"It doesn't plug in," Susan says, peering behind the icebox.

Nathaniel starts laughing. It's not the first time Patrick's heard him laugh, but it's rare enough that Patrick has to stop what he's doing and just...take it in. "You put ice inside," Nathaniel says, "and it keeps your food cold."

"Ask Mrs. Kaplan when she comes back," Patrick says when Susan's still peering skeptically at it.

"Are you sure?" Susan asks. "But where did the ice come from?"

"The iceman," Patrick says—because, seriously, they had icemen when he and Susan were kids.

"The iceman," Nathaniel agrees.

Susan looks back and forth between them like she thinks they're both pulling her leg.

"This room is bigger than I thought it would be," Patrick says before they can get into a fight about ice, even though a quarrelsome Susan is a normal Susan, and therefore a relief.

"Imagine," Susan says. "A room seems bigger when you take out four hundred boxes of books."

"Don't worry," Nathaniel says. "I put the book boxes upstairs, where all the other book boxes will keep them company." There's a bit of acid in his tone and a glint in his eye.

"It wasn't only books," Patrick grumbles, playing along.

"True. There were invoices from 1928, a file folder of recipes cut out of magazines, and a pipe. A chest of drawers that's now in my bedroom, a highchair—"

"I want that."

"It's already in your apartment," Nathaniel says.

"You gave him a key?" Patrick whispers when Nathaniel is up front, talking to a customer.

"You live with him. So does Eleanor, half the time. Are you telling me *now* that you don't trust him?"

"That isn't it." Patrick doesn't know how to explain that it's one thing for him to give someone a key to his home, the shirt off his back, the money from his wallet, but he doesn't expect anyone else to act that way. "I'm glad you like him."

"I do like him. He's mean."

"Must be nice to have something in common."

"Where are you from?" Susan asks Nathaniel that night. They're all in Susan's apartment, finishing up Chinese food. Nathaniel ate his with chopsticks in one hand and Eleanor asleep against his shoulder.

"Boston," Nathaniel says.

Patrick looks up from his lo mein. Most people would say "I grew up in Boston," or "I came here from Santa Fe."

Patrick's bullshit detection has always been reliable. He'd been twelve when his parents died, and the sheer volume of lies people told him in the ensuing weeks, ranging from "they didn't feel a thing" to "everything happens for a reason" to "we'd be happy to have you boys come live with us" must have been enough for his internal bullshit detector to calibrate itself pretty accurately. Wherever Nathaniel's from, it probably isn't Boston.

"What do you do?" Susan asks.

Nathaniel gives her an arch look. "Well, Susan, I'm so glad you asked. I work in this bookshop you may have heard of—"

"Before," she says. Patrick sighs. Michael always said Susan would have been a terrific FBI investigator; Michael, of course, meant it as a compliment.

"If I start in on my sad stories, we'll all get indigestion," Nathaniel says.

Patrick gives Susan a look that says *drop it*. Susan gives him a look that says she's never done anything wrong in her life. "Let him be mysterious," he tells Susan, because so what if Nathaniel is keeping secrets. You don't wind up at rock bottom without some things you want to keep to yourself. Patrick would be a hypocrite if he argued otherwise.

"It's unfair, because you know my sad story," Susan tells Nathaniel.

"What's unfair is that your hellion daughter has decided to attach herself to me like a barnacle."

"I can take her," Patrick offers.

"That's quite all right," Nathaniel says, waspish, and shifts the baby higher on his shoulder.

Patrick leans back in his chair, reaching for the record player to put the volume up, hoping to distract Susan from her interrogation. Yesterday, a dozen boxes arrived from San Francisco. Three of them were labeled RECORDS in a stranger's handwriting—presumably Susan's manager or former landlord. Nathaniel carried those three boxes up to Susan's apartment, Patrick stacked everything else on the second floor. Nathaniel spent the rest of the day calling the second floor a shocking disgrace, a veritable pigsty, and a stain on his personal honor.

Before dinner, Patrick put on the new Byrds record, which came out too recently for it to have sad associations for anyone at the table. He can't tell if he dislikes the album or if he just isn't in a mood to enjoy new things.

"Put on Jefferson Airplane," Susan says, even though Patrick knows for a fact that Michael loved that band.

"Why don't you ask him what his deal is?" she asks Patrick later, when the two of them are alone in Susan's apartment and Nathaniel is across the hall watching *Batman* with the Valdezes. Eleanor's asleep in her crib and Grace Slick is on the record player.

"What do you mean, his deal?" He's sprawled in Susan's armchair. Susan's lying on the sofa, a joint dangling from her fingertips.

"You know perfectly well what I mean. What's he been doing for the past twenty years? He doesn't look like he's had a hard life."

"You can't always tell."

"His teeth are perfect."

"What a fucked-up thing to notice." Patrick noticed the exact same thing.

"He's obviously been through something awful. Why don't you just *ask* him? He talks like a banker, plays the violin like a professional, can't go outside without having a fit, and refuses to say a single thing about his past. I don't know why you *don't* care. Everybody loves a mystery."

"He's a person, not a mystery," Patrick says.

She groans and holds out the joint. "Obviously. Don't be sanctimonious, Patrick, you're better than that."

Patrick takes the world's tiniest drag and Susan lets out a breath of a laugh. He grins back at her, because they both know what a lightweight he is. This is the first time in over a month he's been anything other than sober. He's going in at the shallow end.

"I think he'd tell you whatever you want to know," Susan says, reaching to take the joint back.

"What's that supposed to mean?"

"He's your little shadow."

That's true, but only because Nathaniel's badly shaken up and Patrick is big and safe. It isn't personal.

"I've met a few of the men you've gone around with," Susan adds, handing him back the joint.

Patrick is kind of touched by *gone around with*. Ten years ago, that's how he would have described the boys who took Susan to the movies and brought her home from school on the handlebars of their bicycles. The distance between this apartment and Susan's pink-painted bedroom is in danger of collapsing, and any minute now Michael will walk in and demand that someone explain quadratic equations. He takes another drag and holds the joint out for Susan. "And?"

"And Nathaniel fits the profile. Older, smart, waspish."

Patrick considers explaining that his tastes aren't even close to that narrow, and that the men she's met are the men he's allowed her to meet. And those are the men he thinks will amuse her. That profile has more to do with the type of person Susan likes than the type of person Patrick likes. Still, though, she's right—those are the men Patrick likes best, too.

"There's no reason to think he's into men," Patrick says.

"You're complicating this," she says. "Just ask Nathaniel for his life story, and when you do it make sure you're doing pushups or something."

Susan's been here for six weeks, and this is the first conversation they've managed that doesn't revolve around the baby. Instead, it's about whether Patrick can seduce secrets from his employee.

"I love that you think I'm some kind of gay mata hari," he says.

"Nobody thinks that about you, Patrick." Susan starts laughing, and it's such a good sound. He's missed it so much, even if he can hear the sadness threaded through the laughter like a strange new instrument added to an old song.

It turns out that the only thing more annoying than a crying baby waking you up every hour is a crying baby not waking you up. Eleanor's too big to sleep in the drawer, so now she spends every night upstairs with Susan in a real crib. Patrick apparently forgot how to sleep for more than two hours at a go.

He gives up and goes out to the living room, thinking he'll put the television on and let the static hypnotize him into something resembling sleep. But he finds the tiny sofa already occupied by Nathaniel, a book in his lap and a flashlight in one hand.

"You can turn on the lamp, you know," Patrick says.

"I didn't want to wake you." Nathaniel swings his feet off the couch to make room.

Patrick sits. "Can't sleep? Or is the book just that good?"

"It's not the book." Nathaniel points the flashlight at the book's cover for Patrick to read. *Bleak House*. It's Patrick's own copy, a dog-eared and faded paperback he'd bought from one of those used book tables near Washington Square Park, nowhere near good enough to sell in the shop.

"Not my favorite," Patrick admits.

"I used to love Dickens," Nathaniel says, and Patrick thinks he learned more about Nathaniel with that one sentence than he has in the previous six weeks. "I loved this book," Nathaniel goes on, "but reading it now, I can't figure out why."

"I hate that feeling," Patrick says, "when something you used to love feels…broken." He'd been crazy about *Lord of the Rings* in high school, but when he tried to reread it last summer, he gave up as soon as he realized he was rooting for the hobbits to stay home. *No draft cards on Middle Earth*, Susan said when he complained to her about it. *No domino theory in Mordor*, Patrick agreed.

In the moonlight that makes its way through the dingy window, Patrick sees Nathaniel tip his head against the back of the sofa, a silhouette that's become familiar without Patrick noticing: straight nose, sharp chin. Pretty, his brain unhelpfully supplies. It's not the first time he's noticed, but it is the first time alone, in the dark, only inches apart. Patrick turns to look at the blank screen of the television.

"Who even likes Dickens?" Nathaniel asks. "What does that say about a person?"

"Probably that they'd love *As the World Turns*," Patrick says.

"One time!" Nathaniel protests, but even in the dark Patrick can tell he's trying not to smile.

"Sometimes when I'm reading a book, I'm secretly tracking down evidence of queer characters, and that's really hard to do with Dickens."

"Well, I imagine you're flat out of luck with the classics."

Patrick grins. "You'd be surprised."

Nathaniel's quiet for a moment. "Surprise me, then."

"Off the top of my head—*Moby Dick*? *The Great Gatsby*? Those are gay on the page. No fancy interpretation required. You don't even need to work hard. And if you include poetry, there's Whitman, of course."

"I have noticed you have a fair amount of Whitman," Nathaniel says, in the world's most egregious understatement.

When it comes to rare editions of a handful of nineteenth-century American writers, Patrick is one of the city's experts, at least if you employ a flexible definition of both *rare* and *expert*. But when it comes to rare editions of Whitman, Dooryard Books gets named by anyone who knows what they're talking about.

Patrick first read Walt Whitman in eleventh grade English class. The assigned text had been "When Lilacs Last in the Dooryard Bloomed," but Patrick, at that stage, wasn't stopping at the assigned texts. He knew he couldn't ask his aunt and uncle for college tuition, so he was going to need a scholarship. Not that it mattered, in the end, since he dropped out before graduating. After that, college was never going to happen.

In any event, he'd gone to the school library to find more Whitman. When he pulled *Leaves of Grass* off the shelf, it opened on its own to "I Sing the Body Electric." The significance of that wouldn't occur to him yet: the book's spine broken at that exact spot, proof that he wasn't the first boy hiding in the stacks, reading the words "you linger to see his back, and the back of his neck and shoulder-side," wondering if it could possibly mean what he thought it meant.

He put the book back, face red and heart pounding, like he was about to get caught shoplifting, and shoved the entirety of Whitman into the mental file labeled Things Never to Think About, a file that was already too full to manage.

He'd gone back two days later, taken the book off the shelf, read it again. This time: "a youth who loves me and whom I love, silently approaching and seating himself near, that he may hold me by the hand." There was only one way to interpret that, right? Or was Patrick taking something normal and innocent and infecting it with his own perversions?

But someone had taken a sharp pencil and used it to underline five words in that poem: love, hold, content, happy, together. If Patrick was seeing things, he wasn't the first one. He wouldn't be the last one, either. Even if he were laboring under the influence of a dangerous perversion, it seemed increasingly likely that Walt Whitman had written all these poems under that same influence. And Whitman was someone they read in school, so he couldn't be *bad*. He made wanting men sound like something noble. *And* he was from Long Island.

Two years later, Patrick had a job working for the city's preeminent expert on what collectors unironically refer to as Whitmania. An entire floor of the old Fourth Avenue location was devoted to Whitman. There were letters from Whitman, letters to Whitman, brittle yellowed newspaper clippings of stories and essays by Whitman, tintypes, telegrams, two draft manuscripts, postcards, a hat that Mrs. Kaplan was able to claim with a straight face Whitman had once worn, and—of course—multiple copies of several editions of *Leaves of Grass*.

It took less than a month of working at Dooryard Books for Patrick to realize that people *knew* about Whitman. They knew back then. They know now. There were lovers. There were *letters*. There was even a photograph. At no point in the past century has any of this been a terribly well kept secret. There's one review, circa 1870 or thereabouts, that basically said "so you're all going to take this pervert seriously?" and apparently the unanimous answer had been *yes*.

Granted, Patrick will never underestimate a person's ability to look away from an unsavory fact, but still. Whitman's probably the most regarded American poet of his century and people *know* about him.

"The Kaplans started collecting Whitman before I was born," Patrick tells Nathaniel now, "but, yeah, the fact that he was gay maybe makes me like my job more." When

Patrick took over as manager, he kept acquiring Whitman. He regularly checks in with collectors, in case they have a whim to sell. He goes to auctions. He lists Whitman and Whitman-adjacent titles in a catalog that a consortium of rare book dealers puts out every now and then.

"The *fact* that he was a…homosexual?" Nathaniel almost stutters over the word. Patrick gets the feeling he's never said it aloud.

"I don't know how a person can read *Leaves of Grass* and come to any other conclusion," Patrick says.

"Well," Nathaniel says, a little faint.

"Let's find you something else to read," Patrick says, figuring the middle of the night isn't the time to cite every egregiously gay line in *Leaves of Grass*. One in the morning is not the time for a conversation that requires footnotes. Nathaniel, like everyone who's ever worked in a bookshop, sometimes reads on the clock, but Patrick can't remember what books he's seen in Nathaniel's hands. He seems to flip through whatever's lying around. "What else do you like?"

There's a long moment before Nathaniel speaks. "I don't know anymore."

Patrick doesn't know what went wrong for Nathaniel, what brought him to Mrs. Kaplan, but he can see the shape of a life divided into before and after, and he knows how hard it is to figure out what you still have in common with the person you used to be. Maybe that's why Nathaniel fits in here. Maybe all three of them are dealing with the kind of grief that slices your life into clean pieces, the sharpest knife.

Patrick's had it before, that kind of existence-cleaving loss. First, his parents. Then, everything that happened when he left home. The different Patricks on either side of

Cat Sebastian

the cut are barely acquaintances. It's one thing for that to happen to him, but Susan? He's been thinking she'll get better, but even if she has *better* in her future, it won't be the same. She won't be the same. She'll have lost whoever she was. Patrick's eyes get hot and prickly.

He pinches the bridge of his nose, because he isn't doing this, not now. It must be obvious what's going on, because Nathaniel gets him a glass of water. Patrick needs to squeeze his eyes shut, because there's nothing worse than kindness. He drinks the water, thinks about how he needs to pay the gas bill, needs to hire an electrician to figure out why the Valdezes keep blowing fuses, and really should go to the grocery store to pick up some fresh fruit and vegetables. Susan's going to get scurvy.

When he trusts himself, he turns to Nathaniel, who's barely pretending to read the book that's open in his lap. The flashlight isn't even trained on the page.

"I'm sorry about whatever happened to you," Patrick says, sounding exactly like someone who's trying not to have a middle of the night breakdown.

Nathaniel shakes his head, fast, like he doesn't want Patrick's words any more than Patrick wanted that glass of water. "Whatever crosses I have to bear, I'm not sitting around in the dark, crying in my undershirt. And neither are you. Let's have some dignity, for heaven's sake."

Patrick snorts. "Let's find you something to read, then," he says, even though he already said it a minute ago. He slaps his thighs, brisk, like he has things to do, and those things don't include crying in the dark or making anybody else cry.

"Right, then," Nathaniel agrees, equally brisk.

"The thing with books is that there's always something. I mean, if you like reading, you'll find something else," Patrick says, like he's here from the Books Tourism Council, like his job is to sell Nathaniel on the benefits of better living through books. "Want to go downstairs and look?" Nathaniel spends hours a day in the shop. Why does Patrick think he wants to spend even more time there when he's off duty? Nobody has ever made him act this dumb, he swears it.

There's no reason to whisper when they go downstairs, no reason to turn only the one light on, no reason to stick together like they're worried about getting caught. He's hit with the memory of sneaking around with Susan their last year of high school—breaking into her dad's liquor cabinet, sneaking into the biology lab, Patrick always ten seconds away from a cardiac episode, his hand over Susan's mouth to keep her from giggling, Michael just as bad.

"Just give me some books that you enjoyed," Nathaniel says.

That Patrick can do. A Rex Stout. *Stranger in a Strange Land.* M.F.K. Fisher's memoir about Provence. *The Spy Who Came in from the Cold.* This is as weird a stack of books as any he's assembled for Mrs. Kaplan. He puts them all into Nathaniel's arms. "You can borrow books from the shop, you know. Take whatever you want and put it back when you're done."

Nathaniel frowns. "What if someone wants to buy it? How will you know whether it's in stock?"

"I don't exactly keep track of that."

Nathaniel makes a noise that's halfway between a tut and a sigh, pure disapproval, and Patrick doesn't know why that makes him smile, but it does.

Before they go back upstairs, Patrick swipes a commercial edition of *Leaves of Grass* off the shelf and puts it on top of Nathaniel's pile.

6

"This is very upsetting to me," Nathaniel says, sounding aggrieved enough that Patrick puts down the latest *Antiquarian Bookman* and turns his attention to what's going on at the back of the shop. Nathaniel is sitting at the table between Iris and Hector, correcting their math homework.

"It's the same material you were learning last month," Nathaniel says, tapping their textbook with the eraser end of a pencil. "Is your teacher obsessed with simplifying equations? Simplifying them stupidly, I might add."

Nathaniel's hair falls across his forehead as he scribbles something on a piece of paper. The radiators are having fits, so it's warm enough in the shop for Nathaniel's sleeves to be rolled up. On his left wrist is a watch: brown leather band, round face, gold details, in decent shape by the looks of it. Your watch is the first thing you pawn, so either that watch is an irreplaceable heirloom or Nathaniel never got to the point where he needed to pawn things.

"How do you remember this stuff?" Patrick asks. Years of calculating sales tax, mark ups, and the percentage he owes book scouts has left him able to do a lot of math in his head, but anything more advanced than solving for X got left behind in high school.

Nathaniel looks up. "It wasn't exactly irrelevant to my job," he says.

"What was your job?" Iris asks. "I mean, what kind of job do you need this for?" She sounds like a kid who just found out you can feed animals at the zoo for a living.

"Engineers use math a lot more advanced than this," Nathaniel says. "Economists. Statisticians, too." None of that answers what he did for a living. "Anyway." He taps the paper he just scribbled on. "That's what it should look like. There's a better book around here somewhere." He gets to his feet and scans the shelves. It takes him less time than Patrick might have guessed to find whatever he's looking for, but then again he's started inventorying the browsing stock on the first floor, insisting that Patrick's method of simply remembering what he has is deplorable, unseemly, and a crass embarrassment.

"Here," Nathaniel says, handing the book to Iris, open to a page with diagrams and equations.

"We carry math textbooks?" Patrick asks.

"Imagine, if only you had a list of books in stock," Nathaniel says, and Patrick supposes he walked right into that.

For the next hour, Nathaniel works with Hector and Iris. Patrick goes back to what he was doing at the front of the shop, but occasionally hears laughter. By the time the twins leave, Iris looks almost ecstatic.

"You're both too smart to be in that class," Nathaniel says. "We just covered a full unit in barely an hour."

The twins exchange a look. "Puerto Rican kids don't usually get put into the advanced classes," Hector explains. "At least, not at our school."

Nathaniel presses his lips together. "I see. Well, if they're going to teach you like you aren't capable of learning, you'll need to learn it on your own."

Patrick bristles, because the real solution would be for the twins to be in the correct math class, but Iris perks up like she's been offered an ice cream cone.

"It won't be so bad in college," Nathaniel says. "At least, I hope not."

"That was nice of you," Patrick says after the twins leave.

"It's an outrage," Nathaniel says. "Hector is smart enough to do whatever he wants with his life, but Iris is— well. It would be a bad thing for a mind like that to go to waste."

The door chimes ring, and Patrick turns to see who walked in. It's a man in a coat much too heavy for a relatively mild March day, and he's carrying a stack of books so high that Patrick can hardly see his face, just an unruly thicket of iron gray hair. He has an oilskin knapsack over his shoulder.

"Gary?" Patrick asks. "Put those down. Here, let me—"

"You can have them after you pay for them," Gary snaps, placing the teetering pile directly onto the floor.

"Sure, sure," Patrick says. Gary is one of the more peculiar book scouts. Seven or eight years ago, after a stint in the merchant marines, he hit hard times and Mrs. Kaplan took him in. From what Patrick can gather, he sleeps at YMCAs or in the back of the rusted out 1954 Hudson Jet he drives up and down the coast, scouring estate sales and church fairs, looking for books.

"Why's it so clean in here?" Gary asks, looking around him with an expression of disgust. "Ain't natural."

"Nathaniel here is relentless," Patrick says.

"Oh no," Gary says. "You need the dust. Makes people feel like they're getting a bargain." He turns to Patrick and takes a book out of what looks like an old pillowcase. "You'll want this. First edition, perfect copy, inscribed." It's Steinbeck's *Tortilla Flat*. And it really is perfect—there isn't a mark on it, no bumped corners, binding tight, not a single tear in the jacket. It looks like it's been on someone's shelf in an air conditioned room for the past thirty years.

"It's a beauty." He and Gary proceed to haggle, a well worn patter that they've been through a dozen times and could both probably predict the outcome down to the decimal point. As soon as Patrick writes the check, Gary moves the books onto Patrick's desk. "Nathaniel, take a look at this," Patrick says, holding out the Steinbeck.

"Where's Edna?" Gary demands. He's one of maybe three people Patrick's ever heard call Mrs. Kaplan by her first name.

"Florida. Her sister got her gallbladder out."

"Sylvia's all right, isn't she?"

As far as Patrick knows, Gary never met Mrs. Kaplan's family, but everyone who's spent time with her gets to know about the members of her family like they're characters in a soap opera. There's Sylvia in Florida, a pair of sisters-in-law in Brooklyn, a ne'er-do-well brother who ran away fifty years ago, and about twenty great nieces and nephews who Patrick could identify on sight thanks to all the photographs he's seen over the years. Even now, Patrick's hoping that Ezra makes first chair in the state orchestra and Sarah gets into Brandeis.

"She's on the mend," Patrick says. "How've you been?"

"Can't complain." Gary unbuttons his coat and shifts his weight. He looks like he could do with a place to sit and a hot meal, or at least something to drink, but they used up the last of the tea bags that morning and Gary doesn't drink coffee. "Spent the winter in Baltimore, then drove up through Pennsylvania and hit some book sales in New Jersey. Found that Steinbeck in a barn in Tom's River. Paid seventy-five cents for it."

"Where are you heading next?"

"Finger Lakes, then maybe Maine for the summer."

Patrick wishes him well, then watches as Gary leaves, his knapsack still slung over his shoulder, but fifty dollars richer.

"Does he have a place to stay?" Nathaniel asks.

"He doesn't stay in one place too long," Patrick says.

"A drifter, then."

"Nathaniel. *You're* a drifter."

"Hardly. I," Nathaniel says, "am a mental case."

Patrick snorts. "Point taken."

"I haven't drifted a day in my life."

Nathaniel gestures at himself with an ironic little flourish and Patrick arrests the motion, taking hold of his wrist. He taps Nathaniel's watch. "I'm no expert on watches, but I bet this is pretty nice. A gift?"

"I bought it for myself." Nathaniel doesn't make any move to take his hand back, and Patrick doesn't drop it, just shifts his grip so he's more or less holding Nathaniel's hand. Nathaniel still doesn't pull away.

"Bet you had a job with a pension. Bet you have a set of golf clubs somewhere."

"You're right about the pension," Nathaniel says. "Wrong about the golf clubs. But I do have a tennis racket."

Patrick notes the present tense, like that tennis racket is sitting somewhere right now, ready for Nathaniel to come get it. He probably has a whole life waiting for him, no matter what went wrong for him last winter.

Patrick squeezes Nathaniel's hand and lets it go.

"You can have your chair back after you've gone to the laundromat," Nathaniel says. He has his feet up on Patrick's desk, Eleanor asleep on his chest, *Leaves of Grass* open in one hand. "I had to wear my least favorite one of your shirts." He's wearing a pair of worn-out jeans and a plaid flannel shirt. "I don't look reputable at all," he complains.

"What a princess," Patrick mutters, and Nathaniel looks up at him, his expression torn between amusement and outrage. "Want to come with me? Susan will watch Eleanor and the shop if I do her laundry."

"Of course I don't want to," Nathaniel says. "But I should."

"That's not what I said."

"That doesn't stop it from being true. I want to find out where the limits are."

"The limits of what?"

Nathaniel sighs. "My sanity, I suppose."

Patrick gathers all the laundry in a couple of pillowcases and makes Nathaniel carry one of them around the corner to the laundromat. When everything is loaded into the washing machines, Nathaniel sits on a metal folding chair and resumes reading *Leaves of Grass*. They're the only two people in the laundromat, other than a bored-looking middle-aged woman behind the counter.

"What's the verdict?" Patrick asks, sitting in the chair next to Nathaniel's and gesturing at the book.

"I keep coming up with alternative explanations. He has a healthy appreciation for the male form, et cetera."

"Most people do that. For what it's worth, the letters are a lot harder to explain away."

"I'm not doubting your expert opinion." It's unclear whether the expertise he's referring to is Patrick as a bookseller or Patrick as a gay man.

"'When I Heard at the Close of the Day' is especially illuminating," Patrick says.

Nathaniel begins flipping through the book. Patrick takes it from his hands, finds the right page, and gives it back.

"You doing all right?" Patrick asks a few minutes later. "In terms of sanity?" He wouldn't have used that word if Nathaniel hadn't done so first, but it feels rude. He remembers Nathaniel stumbling over *homosexual*. There's no way to talk about being queer or having a fucked up brain without being rude about it, because you aren't supposed to talk about those things in the first place. You aren't supposed to be those things.

"Its limits have not yet been breached," Nathaniel says, eyes still on the book. He sighs and closes it, his finger marking the page. "I hate this, but it serves me right."

"No," Patrick says, a little too loud. Nathaniel startles, and Patrick lowers his voice. "You don't deserve to feel trapped."

"You don't know what you're talking about,"

Nathaniel says, and returns his attention to the book.

The door opens and a woman comes in, wrestling a wicker hamper. Patrick gets up to hold the door.

"Oh, Patrick," she says. "I hardly recognize you out of the shop. And Nathaniel!"

It's Vivian. It's always odd to run into a customer. Some of the regulars occupy that murky space between acquaintance and friend. After so many visits to the shop, Viv might be closer to the friend end of the spectrum.

Vivian's obviously never been to a laundromat in her life, because she has no change and only the vaguest sense of how to separate laundry. "Maryanne used to do it. I've been sending the laundry out, but it's ruinously expensive," she explains.

Maryanne, Patrick assumes, is the fedora-wearing woman who used to come in with Vivian. Patrick doesn't ask exactly how she left the picture. All that matters, really, is that Vivian doesn't sound pleased about it, and also that she needs help with laundry, so Patrick walks her through it.

"Is the baby sleeping through the night?" she asks when her clothes are loaded in the washer.

"When the planets are aligned," Patrick says.

"You need the book by that man—Spock. Dr. Spock."

"Excuse me, what?" Patrick is aware of one Spock, and he's on the bridge of the *Enterprise*.

"My sister had his book. I can't remember the title. You probably have one in stock."

"It's called *Baby and Child Care*," Nathaniel says, not looking up from his book.

"That's it!" Vivian agrees. "I see you've fallen prey to Patrick's influence. Whitman's completely out of my period but Patrick got me anyway."

"He's a dangerous man," Nathaniel agrees.

"Now all I can see is the longing. Not only for companionship," she says, in a way that makes it clear companionship is standing in for sex or romance, "but for community. He's looking for people like him." She pauses with a glance at the empty wicker hamper. "It's very touching, and very familiar, isn't it?"

Patrick realizes that Vivian thinks he and Nathaniel are involved. They're doing laundry together, which isn't something she'd expect Patrick to do with an employee. He can see the moment Nathaniel realizes the same thing—his eyes open a little wider, and it looks like he's about to say something, but when he opens his mouth, all he says is, "Quite," and then he and Vivian start talking about the Democratic primary. They both like Robert Kennedy, which isn't any kind of surprise when it comes to Vivian, but he'd been worried that Nathaniel might be a Republican.

"Call me Viv," Vivian tells Nathaniel. "Everybody does."

Nathaniel's been around for more than ten of Viv's visits to the shop—no, more than that, because she sometimes stops by on the weekend. Viv is only five or ten years older than Nathaniel. If, for Patrick, Viv is in the space between friend and acquaintance, for Nathaniel she may already be a friend.

"Call me if you decide to go see it," Viv says as Patrick and Nathaniel leave, talking about some or another movie they'd read about.

When they get home, Nathaniel corners Patrick in the back room. "Can I paint the kitchen?"

It takes Patrick a moment to realize that Nathaniel is referring to the back room. "Why?"

"The walls are stained. It's ugly. They sell paint at the hardware store, you know."

Patrick does, in fact, know, but it has never once occurred to him that he might want to put that knowledge to practical use. Still, Nathaniel needs some kind of job to do. The store is getting aggressively clean and Nathaniel has taken to wiping down surfaces while Patrick is still using them. His inventory of the downstairs books is well underway, and if Patrick doesn't play his cards right, it's only a matter of time before Nathaniel starts bugging him about unpacking the boxes upstairs.

"Sure," Patrick says. "Take the money out of petty cash."

Patrick offers to go to the hardware store himself, but Nathaniel insists that he can do it on his own. In the end, Susan goes with him, claiming that she needs to stretch her legs and that terrible things will happen to Eleanor's liver if she doesn't get sunlight.

An hour later, they come back with a gallon of paint in one of the uglier shades of green. It's the green of mouthwash and hospital linoleum, a green that doesn't and shouldn't exist in nature, or in bookstores, or anywhere else.

"It matches the stove," Nathaniel explains, visibly pleased with himself. Patrick doesn't have the heart to say that the stove is ugly too. He just opens all the windows so they don't asphyxiate.

When Hector and Iris come by after school, Hector crosses himself and Iris says "very bold" and then they change into old clothes and help paint the trim and cabinets white.

That night, while the paint dries, Nathaniel takes Patrick's coffee maker from upstairs and places it on the butcher block next to the sink. Next to it, he arranges Patrick's kettle and hotplate. Five coffee mugs that Patrick's never seen before hang from hooks under the upper cabinet.

"This way we don't have to run upstairs every time we want a drink," Nathaniel says. "And any customers who want some coffee or tea can help themselves."

"Any customers who want a drink can leave and go somewhere that serves drinks," Patrick says.

Something shutters in Nathaniel's expression and Patrick feels like an asshole, but seriously, this is a bookstore. The idea of people coming in and drinking his coffee and leaving mugs around his books makes him feel faintly ill.

"You *like* your customers," Nathaniel says. "You pretend not to, but I see the way you light up when one of your favorites comes in. I'm not saying you have to give refreshments to anyone who wanders in off the street, but this store is effectively your living room. When Jerome comes in, it wouldn't kill you to give him a drink and a place to sit. Viv would love an excuse to stay. The other day, Gary looked like he was about to collapse. You do less for strangers."

Patrick wonders how much this has to do with the fact that *Nathaniel* likes the regulars. He can barely stand to leave the shop, so customers and scouts are the only new people he can talk to. He'd seen the look on Nathaniel's face when Viv suggested they see a movie: he'd wanted to go, but was afraid he couldn't. He's effectively trapped in this store unless Patrick or Susan go with him.

But Nathaniel seems to believe what he's saying. He looks almost uncomfortably earnest; there isn't the faintest whiff of bullshit in anything he said.

"Most of the business is rare books," Patrick says. "We don't really depend on foot traffic. I've gotten into the habit of thinking of customers as a distraction. But," he says, with the feeling of edging out onto thinner ice, "of the two of us, you're the one who really likes the customers." And it's true. Nathaniel chatters with customers so well and so naturally that Patrick leaves the cash register entirely to him when he's working. "And I think you're lonely here. Most people would be," he hurries to add when Nathaniel looks insulted.

Nathaniel goes to the sink to fill the kettle with water. When he speaks it's with his back to Patrick. "I always worked in a busy office. The same people, year after year."

"You miss it," Patrick says. It sounds like Patrick's idea of hell.

Nathaniel looks like he's about to have one of his spells so Patrick grabs the kettle and plugs it in. It occurs to Patrick that Nathaniel waited until the shop was closed and they were alone to instigate this conversation, presumably to spare Patrick's feelings, only to have the tables turned on him. Patrick squeezes Nathaniel's arm.

"I do miss it," Nathaniel says. "God, what is wrong with me?" He draws in a breath. "In any event, it isn't safe to have the coffee maker balanced on a stack of books and plugged into the same extension cord as the refrigerator and hotplate, so the coffee maker needs to be moved down here anyway."

"It's a good idea. I might as well bring down my refrigerator too, or we won't have any milk for our coffee." It's only a little refrigerator, the kind that comes up to his knee, and it's no trouble for Patrick to carry it down the stairs himself.

"Thank you," Nathaniel says when Patrick's finished

plugging in the refrigerator and Nathaniel has poured them both cups of this revolting chamomile tea that Susan likes.

"Any time," Patrick says, and he means it.

"You *are* still here," says a voice that's all too familiar.

Patrick turns from where he's shelving some books. "Hi, Luke."

"You never write, you never call."

"How's California?" Patrick asks.

"It's great! I'm here for a week. You look good."

Patrick's pretty sure he looks like someone who gets up at six o'clock every morning to take a bright-eyed baby off Susan's hands. "So do you." Luke always looks good, in a neatly combed hair and collared shirt kind of way. He used to be one of the book and manuscript experts at an auction house in the city, but then he took a job with an auction house in Los Angeles.

Susan and Nathaniel come in from the street, Nathaniel holding the door open for Susan and the baby carriage. They'd walked over to the Salvation Army on Second Avenue, which might mean Patrick gets his clothes back sometime soon. Nathaniel has that shell-shocked look he gets after he's been outside.

Patrick watches Luke do a double take as he realizes he's seeing Suzie Larkin in the flesh.

Luke glances pointedly at Patrick, clearly wanting an introduction. It would be shitty not to go along with it, so Patrick introduces Luke to both Nathaniel and Susan. "We were together until Luke moved to Los Angeles," Patrick explains. He feels a little squeamish about that *together*, partly because he knows he made a mess of *together*, and partly because it's a slight exaggeration. But anything else would look like concealing the relationship.

"Such a fan," Luke tells Susan, managing to make it sound offhand and sincere at the same time. "Don't tell me this sweetheart is yours," he says, cooing at Eleanor. "And are you..." he gestures between Susan, Eleanor, and Nathaniel.

"I work here," Nathaniel says, but as he says it he takes a step toward Patrick. Luke's eyebrows shoot up.

"Let's go try out that new song," Susan tells Nathaniel, a hand on his elbow.

"Well," Luke says as soon as they're alone.

"It's not like that."

"We weren't *like that* either, not for months, if memory serves."

"I'm his boss, and I don't even know if he's—"

"He's wearing one of your sweaters."

"Are you serious? Did you memorize my entire wardrobe?"

"Wardrobe? Darling, you have four sweaters. Let's not get excited." Luke snorts. "Wardrobe. So, an older man."

"Luke." Nathaniel can't be more than two or three years older than Luke, but Patrick doesn't point this out.

"Fine!" Luke holds his hands up in surrender. "You seeing anyone?"

Patrick hesitates, because an immediate *no* might give Luke ideas.

"I'm not hitting on you. My god, Patrick, I'll find a way to resist."

"I'm not seeing anyone."

"I do have a nice hotel room, though," Luke says, and they both start laughing. They did get along well, while it lasted, and it isn't Luke's fault that Patrick is the way he is.

"Are *you* seeing anyone?" Patrick asks.

Luke makes a so-so gesture with one hand. "Want to have dinner? I really am only asking about dinner."

"Sure, why the hell not."

"Is that crepe place on Greenwich still open?"

"Oh Christ, that fucking place." They put things like seafood curry on pancakes.

"Come on," Luke wheedles.

"Fine, all right, whatever." He checks his watch—seven thirty, which is late enough that he isn't going to feel guilty about closing early. He flips the sign and locks up the shop.

They wind up splitting a bottle of wine and making it most of the way through a second bottle, so by the time they're done eating, Patrick's not even pretending to be sober. Luke tells him stories about the people he works with, none of whom Patrick has ever met or ever will meet. He doesn't pay attention, just listens to the familiar cadences of Luke's voice. There's a thread of bullshit working its way through Luke's monologue, like maybe he's trying to impress Patrick with stories about his new car and his new house and his new life. Patrick *is* impressed—he was impressed with Luke before they ever got together—so this is all pointless.

Michael used to tell him to get over it. People aren't honest, and it's a fool's errand to expect them to be. But it isn't the dishonesty that bothers Patrick. It's more that when he has the feeling that someone's lying, he knows there's something they're lying *about*. You only tell a lie when you have something to hide.

He feels like he's spying on Luke's new life through a peephole. He feels seedy, but also like he's being manipulated.

"You do look good," Luke says. "It's the hair."

Patrick self-consciously touches his head. He hasn't gotten his hair cut since Susan and Eleanor moved in, and he only trimmed his beard when Iris told him he looked like a hippie.

"It's so long," Patrick complains.

"All blonds should let their hair grow. More of a good thing," Luke says decisively. Patrick isn't even blond, not really. He has the color hair you get when you were blond as a kid: dirty blond, if he gets some sun in the summer.

"I should go," Luke says after they've split the check. Neither of them make any move to get up. It's dark, they're in the back of the restaurant, and none of the waiters are paying them any attention. Patrick knows of four gay bars in a two block radius and there are probably others he hasn't heard of. So when Luke leans in to kiss him, it's not an insane thing to do, even though they're in public. It's just this side of a peck, something between *goodbye* and *nice to see you again* and *remember?*

"I'm in town for a week," Luke says as Patrick watches him get into a cab. "I'm staying at the Americana."

Patrick won't call him, but it's embarrassingly reassuring to feel wanted, however idly. He walks the two blocks home, mildly annoyed with himself for having passed up what would have been a decent couple of hours, but mostly glad to be heading home.

When he reaches the shop, he's surprised to see a light still on. He lets himself in, locks everything back up, and feels an odd thrum of anticipation as he heads to the rear of the shop. He finds Nathaniel in the kitchen, sitting at the table, reading the John le Carré novel that Patrick lent him. It looks like he's still on the first few pages. On the table in front of him is a mug of tea.

"Want me to put on some water on for you?"

Nathaniel asks, looking up from his book.

Patrick shakes his head. Instead, he fills a glass of water at the sink and uses it to swallow a couple aspirin.

"That man," Nathaniel says. "Are you and he…"

"Not anymore." Patrick leans against the counter. Now that the paint has dried, the green doesn't seem quite so violent. Maybe it's grown on him. Maybe it's the wine.

"Why not?"

"He moved back to California."

Nathaniel has an expression that Patrick can't decipher. Some people are fine with a person being discreetly queer, but change their tune as soon as that person stops hiding. Even some queer people think everybody belongs in the closet.

And it hasn't entirely escaped Patrick's attention that Nathaniel might not be straight. When Patrick starts talking about this stuff, Nathaniel seems curious in a way that straight people seldom do. He doesn't seem comfortable—very much the opposite—but that combination of discomfort and curiosity is practically a mandatory stop on the trip to figuring out you're queer.

Or—maybe Nathaniel already knows. It's not like he goes around talking about who he used to fuck—or where he worked, where he went to school, or anything at all. The only thing Patrick knows about Nathaniel's past is that he used to work in an office and he stopped playing the violin in college. That level of cageyness ought to feel dishonest. If Luke's harmless storytelling rankles, then why doesn't Nathaniel's secrecy? They're both trying to cover things up. The difference, maybe, is that Nathaniel is practically announcing that there are things he doesn't want Patrick and Susan to know.

Patrick watches Nathaniel frown at a stain on the table

and tries to summon up some annoyance, but all he can think is that Nathaniel waited up for him.

So, yeah, Nathaniel might be queer, and he might think Patrick's being rude and déclassé by not hiding it, but those topics are too delicate to navigate half drunk and weirdly sappy. Patrick ought to go to bed and walk away from this conversation before it can get dicey, but the wine's loosened his tongue.

"Is this going to be a problem? Me being gay?"

Nathaniel's eyebrows shoot up. "No? Is this supposed to be brand new information? I've known since before I came here."

Patrick imagines that there's something so powerfully gay about his presence that you can see it from a cab several blocks away, even though it probably just means that Mrs. Kaplan screens her strays to make sure they aren't going to be a problem. *Extremely* bold of Mrs. Kaplan, but Patrick's given up questioning her methods.

Patrick's had enough wine to find all of this very amusing, or maybe he's relieved, so he laughs a little, and Nathaniel smiles up at him—the real deal, both sides of his mouth and everything. Patrick's just drunk enough to admit to himself that he'd do practically anything to guarantee a steady supply of those smiles. Appalling.

"And also," Nathaniel says, "I'm not an idiot. You've clearly fucked the entire male half of your clientèle."

"Not all of them," Patrick says, which sets them both off.

"Did you love one another?" Nathaniel asks when they've settled down. His tone is blunt, even unsentimental, like he's asking whether Patrick remembered to mail the gas bill.

"Me and Luke? No," Patrick says. "I liked him a lot. I

still like him a lot. And I guess he liked me a lot, but it beats me why."

"It might have something to do with the way you look," Nathaniel says, and Patrick watches in amazement as his cheeks turn pink. Patrick's own face is heating, but there's no way he's doing it as prettily as Nathaniel is. Nathaniel has more aplomb than Patrick's given him credit for, because he simply crosses one leg over the other and moves right along. "I mean, it probably isn't because of your personality."

Patrick bursts out laughing. Nathaniel looks terribly pleased with himself.

"You don't keep it a secret?" Nathaniel asks.

Patrick shrugs. "Depends. Susan knows, obviously. Mrs. Kaplan knows. Michael knew. The Valdezes have seen men coming and going at all hours, so they know. I'm more cavalier about it than most people." The fact is, once he told Michael, there wasn't anyone left whose opinion mattered.

Nathaniel makes a tsking sound. "Risky."

"If they can pretend we aren't here, they can pretend there isn't anything wrong," Patrick says. "It's time to stop hiding." It isn't anything he hasn't said before. It isn't anything he hasn't heard and read dozens of times. It feels odd saying it now, though, because if Nathaniel *is* queer, then it sounds like a criticism.

Nathaniel is quiet for long enough that his tea is probably cold. "I suppose things are different now," he finally says.

"I mean, you can still get arrested. The cops still raid bars." Patrick's been in two raids. The second time he managed to sneak out through the basement with a few other patrons. "This is a good neighborhood to be gay,

101

though."

Nathaniel, who started frowning when Patrick mentioned people getting arrested, now looks like it's taking him a real effort not to laugh. "I have noticed that. There's a gay bar on our street, Patrick. There's a gay *bookstore* a few blocks away."

"Well, shit. I didn't realize I was dealing with a regular expert." He sort of expects another blush, but Nathaniel just gives him a level look, and Patrick's face heats again.

"Maybe I will have some tea," Patrick says, mainly for an excuse to stay. "Want another cup?"

Patrick fixes Nathaniel's tea the way he likes it. He takes his coffee black: medicinal and bitter, a means to an end. But his tea is a different story: he adds enough milk to turn it the color of melted vanilla ice cream and so much sugar it never fully dissolves. There's always a layer of sugary silt at the bottom of his cup. He always looks a little guilty as he adds that fourth spoonful. Tonight, Patrick makes sure each spoon is as full as it could possibly be.

Part 2
FAINT INDIRECTIONS

Nathaniel

7

Nathaniel's only two sips into his first cup of coffee when Patrick, newspaper in his hand, says, "Shit."

Nathaniel doesn't pay much attention, because every day the newspaper provides a multitude of opportunities for any reasonable person to swear. But then Patrick clears his throat and says, "Martin Luther King's been killed."

"Who did it?" Nathaniel asks.

Patrick raises his eyebrows. "Some asshole? I mean, who do you think?"

Well, specifically, Nathaniel is taking a professional interest in whether Dr. King's murderer was some asshole employed by the U.S. government or some asshole operating on his own. After Kennedy, he'd thought that was the first question everybody knew to ask.

The newspaper coverage is useless, except for making it clear that the man's death was indeed an assassination. Nobody tried to make it look like suicide or an accident, which is interesting in itself. Nathaniel and some of his more realistic colleagues feared Dr. King would meet an untimely end due to faulty brakes or a gas leak, something mundane and unheroic. From what Nathaniel can tell, the assassin likely wasn't a government operative—either American or otherwise—which isn't precisely comforting, but at least it isn't compounding Nathaniel's paranoia.

Obviously, he tells none of this to Patrick. Instead he says, "My parents would have been secretly delighted," after he's thrown on some clothes and joined Patrick downstairs in the kitchen.

Patrick scoops some ground coffee into the filter. "Your parents sound like jerks."

"Quite." It's a bit of a thrill to be able to talk like this. During his time with the agency, he'd gotten used to being a cog in the machine, interchangeable with the other expensively educated men in adequately tailored suits, all with the same side part and country club background. If there was something about you that wasn't perfectly interchangeable, then you took pains to hide it away. If Nathaniel were to assemble an intelligence service designed to actually gather information—which is perhaps the task he'll be assigned in hell, if he's judged appropriately—he might not use "he went to Groton and can handle himself at a cocktail party" as the screening criteria.

"You never talk about your family." Patrick says this with no weight to it. It isn't a question. Patrick doesn't really ask questions, and Nathaniel can't tell if this is because he can sense just how much Nathaniel can't say, or if he's like this with everyone.

Still, at Patrick's words, Nathaniel's thoughts make a break for the abyss until he realizes Patrick's only talking about Nathaniel's parents. "Talking about them would involve thinking about them," Nathaniel says. "And I'd rather not." He pours himself another cup of coffee and downs half of it while it's too hot, letting the heat cauterize whatever the hell is going on in his mind. "They're dead now, anyway."

Patrick holds up his coffee mug. "Good riddance to shitty relatives."

Nathaniel clinks his mug into Patrick's.

"There might be riots," Patrick says a minute later. "Just so you know."

Nathaniel bites back a hysterical laugh. "Yes, quite."

"Last summer there were riots—protests, I guess—all over the country. Here, they started when a cop shot a Puerto Rican kid."

Patrick sometimes explains things to Nathaniel like perhaps he suffered a head injury or recently immigrated here from another planet. Which, come to think, isn't inaccurate, except the head injury is more of a psychological one, and the other planet is the Central Intelligence Agency. At first, Nathaniel thought Patrick was talking down to him, but soon realized Patrick is simply delivering background information that he thinks Nathaniel might need, and doing so as succinctly and neutrally as possible. One imagines the vagabonds and mental cases he and Mrs. Kaplan take in—Nathaniel very much included in that description—might from time to time need a refresher course in reality.

"Iris told me about that," Nathaniel says, very casual, as if he didn't once have a report cross his desk positing that the Soviets must be the ones fomenting last summer's race riots, because what other reason could there be for people to be so upset? "She said it wasn't even one shooting. She said it happens all the time."

Patrick pours out a cup of coffee and hands it to Nathaniel. "It's common enough that it isn't always first page news."

Nathaniel grimaces. "If this were a country with leaders we don't care for—someplace in Eastern Europe or Latin America or Southeast Asia—we'd call it an uprising instead of a riot." How very liberating to say something like that aloud. This is how the radicals lure you in. The marijuana and comfortable clothes are merely the thin end of the wedge; the next thing you know, you've condensed the last twenty years of American foreign policy and the entirety of your career into a few damning syllables.

Before he can drop some acid and burn the flag, Nathaniel heads into the shop and dusts the shelves angrily, alphabetizes angrily, and sweeps angrily, all the while refusing to pinpoint precisely what he's angry about. The loss of a good man? The setback this means to the movement? The worry that he might be complicit, in a literal sense, rather than a demographic one?

It's a chilly April morning, but when Patrick flips the sign to Open, Nathaniel props the door with volumes S and T of an outdated *Encyclopedia Britannica*. Then he drags the table to the front of the store, followed by the coffee maker and some mugs and a half empty box of Chips Ahoy.

Patrick watches all this silently, but instead of shutting the door and asking Nathaniel if he's gone nuts—which, yes, thanks, several months ago, no sign of it letting up any time soon—Patrick puts on a sweater and gives his spare cardigan to Nathaniel.

All things considered, Nathaniel might have found somewhere better to lie low than a building inhabited largely by political subversives. He thought a sleepy little side street bookshop owned by an old lady and attracting practically no foot traffic would be a perfect place to get his act together. For a man who spent over fifteen years in the business of amassing intelligence, it turns out he's an utter dud. Well, that's the CIA for you.

Patrick is a flagrant homosexual paying an employee under the table and running a business that likely receives as many stolen goods as any pawn shop. The sheer number of sexual deviants entering this store would be enough to merit a police raid. Men who say *darling* and wear scarves for decorative purposes. Women whose clothing was never bought in any ladies' shop.

Even the Valdezes are on the radical fringe. Mr. Valdez mentions his union alarmingly often. Iris will have an FBI file before she's twenty. Hector has mentioned Che Guevara in favorable terms more than once, even if one of those times was to point out that he was handsome; whether Hector is correct is beside the point. Maria seems normal but she can't possibly be, not if she's responsible for two children turning out like that.

And Susan—Susan is the worst of the lot. Before coming here, Susan Larkin had been a name typed on a file label, alphabetically between a Beat poet and a civil rights leader. There had been hundreds of names, telephone records, travel itineraries, photographs, lists of known associates. Nathaniel had been meant to look at each of those pieces of information as a data point and find a pattern of subversion. Instead the only pattern he could make himself see was that the CIA was illegally spying on Americans, which meant Nathaniel was effectively employed by the secret police.

He quietly photocopied as many of the files as he could fit into the inside pocket of his suit coat, quit his job, left town, and wrecked his life. Four months later, his shock seems painfully naive. Had he really thought the underhandedness was confined to foreign soil? There should be a stronger word than naiveté.

Those photocopied files are now at the back of Patrick's safe, stashed in an ordinary manila envelope and shoved behind some first editions that Patrick is saving for a rainy day. If Nathaniel's learned anything about Patrick over the past two months, it's that he's effectively blind when it comes to anything that might be paperwork.

Far and away the worst part is that Nathaniel likes all these radicals. The Valdez twins are brilliant. Susan has the kind of charisma that penetrates the cloud of misery engulfing her; he's slightly terrified to discover what she'll be like when that cloud dissipates a little. And Patrick is—

Patrick is a twenty-seven-year-old man who reads books approximately eight hours a day yet has the muscles of a stevedore. He has a deranged penchant for feeding the hungry and has, by all appearances, had sexual relations with the entire homosexual male population of the neighborhood, or at least those literate enough to set foot in a bookstore. He's utterly unbothered by the fact that Nathaniel can't leave the building without an emotional crisis.

At that, Nathaniel's psyche goes into free fall, as per usual. For the love of god, it's been months. He has got to snap out of it. That trip to the guitar store had felt like the Charge of the Light Brigade, and he can't even take the garbage out without his hands getting clammy and his heart thundering in his chest.

He's very much afraid this is insanity. Which would, of course, be one more reason for the powers that be at Langley to lock him up. You can't have disaffected analysts in possession of state secrets running mad in the streets. And Nathaniel knows a lot more secrets than what's inside the manila envelope.

"Your whole body just went rigid," Susan says. They're in her apartment, the baby asleep for once in her life, as he and Susan attempt to turn a perfectly decent folk song into the kind of music that's one step removed from inciting a riot. He's considered telling her that the government—he can blame the FBI—is fixated on celebrities, but that would probably only encourage her. In those files that he destroyed his life over were pictures of her at enough protests that it's a wonder she found time to do anything else. She apparently spent the entirety of 1967 at anti-war protests and the previous eight years at civil rights protests.

The fact that Nathaniel is going along with this is only more evidence of insanity.

She lights a joint and holds it out. He takes it, because it's one of the only things that keeps the panic at bay and the abyss at a comfortable distance. He's adopting a comprehensive approach to moral degeneracy, it seems.

He takes a hit and passes the joint back to her, not bothering to put the violin down. When he first came across it in the kitchen, he hadn't even hesitated before picking it up and tuning it. Fifteen years should have been enough to get him out of the habit, but here he is, like the intervening years never happened. Perhaps that's the appeal—the sense of turning back the clock to a time when his hands were clean, his future safe and certain. When he looks at Hector and Iris, he envies the blank slate in front of them.

"Oh brother," Susan says and hands him back the joint. "Whatever you're thinking about, either get it off your chest or think about something else. It isn't doing you any good stuck in your head."

"Take your own advice, madam," Nathaniel says, because the woman hasn't said a single word about her dead husband. It had taken Nathaniel weeks to figure out the man's name. Sometimes, Nathaniel can tell when a conversation is drifting too close to the subject by the way Susan and Patrick slam on the brakes.

But their grief is still there, right on the surface, nearly a palpable thing. Nathaniel remembers taking his own grief and tucking it away, far out of sight, never looking at it and certainly never letting anyone else see it. It's fossilized now, the hardened remnants of the place grief used to be.

"We'll play something cheerful," Susan says, and proceeds to sing a happy little song about overthrowing the government.

"We need ground rules," Susan says after they've spent a few weeks doing what she charmingly calls dicking around with music. Now, evidently, they're doing something more intentional—premeditated, even—and this requires rules. "No songs Dylan ever covered. No songs *I* ever covered. And none of those ballads about men on white steeds going off to war."

That's all perfectly unobjectionable but Nathaniel doesn't have the disposition to enter a negotiation without making his own demands. "No hand claps," he says.

"Nothing about falling in love."

"No tambourines." Nathaniel has nothing against tambourines in other people's music, but he needs to draw a line. He'll associate freely with long-haired radicals, but the tambourine is a line he won't cross.

"I'm so insulted that you think I own a tambourine," Susan says.

"Darling," Nathaniel says, "you have a harmonica. Get off your high horse." He's flat on his back and alarmingly high, high enough he can say things like *darling* and not worry about anything other than how he's ever going to get off this sofa. Somewhere else in the room, Patrick laughs, thrilled as ever by Nathaniel's bitchy turns. He's a terrible influence.

"What's even left for the two of you to play?" Patrick asks.

During Nathaniel's first year of undergrad, his roommate—currently an executive with an insurance firm in Hartford—had a collection of folk music records that Nathaniel was rather appalled to discover he enjoyed. He suspects Susan had many of the same records.

"Murder ballads," Nathaniel suggests.

"Murder ballads!" Susan agrees. "Oh my god, murder ballads."

"Do I even want to know what a murder ballad is?" Patrick asks. Nathaniel forces his head to turn to the side. Patrick is sitting cross legged on the floor, the baby chewing on his sleeve.

Susan's strums a few chords and begins singing about a murderer who lives in the moss and whose gruesome misdeeds are meticulously detailed in rhyming couplet. Nathaniel's never heard this one before.

"There's blood in the kitchen. There's blood in the hall," Susan sings. "There's blood in the parlor where my lady did fall."

Nathaniel listens as Susan sings through a few verses,

then picks up the harmony. It turns out he can play the violin while lying down. Every teacher he ever had would weep at the sight of him, but he isn't playing for the Philharmonic, and everybody who isn't in this room can rot.

Susan plays the song through, then makes an infinitesimal change that transforms the ballad into something deliciously creepy. Nathaniel gets goosebumps.

When he saw Susan's name on that file, he never wondered what her music might sound like. The only songs of hers that he's heard are what Patrick played for him on the jukebox. The music she's playing now is the chiaroscuro counterpart to those bright, sunlit songs. It takes all his meager skill just to keep up with her. Frankly, he's a little starstruck. At least once a day he wants to tell her that she might be a genius, but she plays like someone who already knows.

Over the next hour, Susan replaces half the original lyrics with her own grisly descriptions of what some elfin troublemaker called Lord Lankin will do to you if you chance upon him in the long grass or let him into your mead hall. Her voice—ethereally lovely, clear as a bell—contrasts eerily with the gruesome murders she's singing about. The ballad shifts from folk music to protest music.

"He'll burn up your bones and he'll cut off your head," Susan sings. "He'll scoop out your eyeballs and…" She strums along, obviously trying to come up with a rhyme.

"And leave you for dead?" Nathaniel suggests.

She sings it again with the completed verse while Nathaniel fiddles along, as softly as possible.

"And the thing is," Susan sings, reaching the chorus. "You don't get to complain."

"Well, no," Nathaniel adds, his bow still moving, "you're dead."

Susan laughs, then writes something down on the pad of paper she keeps on the end table. Nathaniel takes advantage of the pause to reach for the joint that's balanced on the edge of an ashtray on the coffee table.

Nathaniel's started writing things in his own notebook, one of those ten cent affairs you can get at any corner store, but which Patrick had to buy for him because Nathaniel can still barely leave the fucking building. The most recent page reads: Frosted Flakes, Eleanor's little shoes, Captain Kangaroo (in color), pizza. It's either a list of things Nathaniel likes enough that he won't deliberately fling himself into the abyss, or it's a list of pleasures Nathaniel in no way deserves. Sometimes he pores over list like he's cracking a code, trying to decide which it is, but the key is his own warped psyche.

"Let's do the song about the nightingale," Nathaniel says.

Patrick hauls himself to his feet, keeping Eleanor against his shoulder. Nathaniel misses a note, momentarily flustered by the sight of the tiny baby cradled in huge arms, one of Patrick's big hands on the back of her head. Since when does Nathaniel even care about men's hands? (Since 1945, if he's being his most truthful self, which, unfortunately, seems to be the case these days.)

He lets himself watch as Patrick fixes another bottle. When Patrick returns to the living room, Nathaniel bends his knees, making room on the sofa. Patrick takes the hint and sits. The cushions shift under Patrick's weight. Nathaniel can feel it, the next best thing to actual contact.

After a lifetime of extinguishing that kind of thought, he feels a nauseous little thrill letting it linger in his mind.

It's a lit match, but instead of dropping it to the ground and crushing it underfoot, he's holding it between two fingers, watching it burn. He keeps waiting for something terrible to happen.

All that happens is that Patrick looks at Nathaniel's sneaker and sighs. "Tie your fucking shoe," Patrick says. "You're high as a kite and you'll break your neck." When the baby is done with her bottle, Patrick lays her across his lap and ties Nathaniel's shoelace himself.

"You still shouldn't have thrown it back!" Iris yells at her brother. "We could've got *arrested*."

The Valdez twins walked out of school to protest the war. All spring, kids have been walking out of high schools and colleges across the country and around the world.

"This wouldn't have happened a year ago," Susan says. It's the third or fourth time she's said it, and she's probably right. It seems that, finally, the doomed nature of this war has become glaringly obvious, even to people who initially supported it. Patrick says that every time he walks past Washington Square Park, somebody's burning their draft card.

Just last month there was a big protest at NYU against Dow Chemical for manufacturing napalm. Last week, Columbia students held the dean hostage, although Nathaniel thinks that had more to do with racism than with Vietnam.

Every time Nathaniel looks at the newspaper, there's a protest in Detroit or Paris, Los Angeles or Mexico City. The entire world seems to have taken to the streets to protest a host of wrongs, and while Susan and even Patrick see this as a promise of change, Nathaniel's waiting for the other shoe to drop. Every protest reveals the opposition more clearly: people who *want* war and bigotry, who want teenagers to be shot in the street and Vietnam burned to cinders. None of this is a surprise to Nathaniel; he worked for that opposition, even when he didn't want to acknowledge it. It's the widening divide that worries him now. He's seen what happens in countries where there are irreconcilable factions.

Soldiers with machine guns were stationed on Capitol Hill during the protests after Martin Luther King, Jr. was killed. The National Guard drove tanks through downtown Memphis. It would have taken nothing at all for one of these soldiers to pull a trigger. It would have taken nothing at all for a cop at today's school walkout to have grabbed his billy club and put it to use.

Nathaniel likes these children; some tired and cowardly part of himself wants Iris and Hector to have stayed safe inside their classroom, even though he realizes this is impossible. The entire point is that they aren't safe.

"It really wouldn't have happened a year ago," Susan repeats.

"Wait. Who threw what?" Nathaniel asks, catching up. His gaze roams over the twins, looking for signs of damage.

"A counterprotester threw a rock into the crowd," Iris says. "Hector threw it back, but nobody saw. At least I don't think anybody saw."

"I didn't throw it back. I tossed it aside. Underhand."

"Who the fuck throws rocks at children?" Patrick asks.

Everyone stares at him. Patrick is not a man who swears in front of kids.

Iris recovers first. "The same people who want to bomb children and burn down their homes," she says, with an implied *obviously*. "And now Hector's going to get an FBI file and Mami will kill him."

"Nobody's getting an FBI file," Susan says. "You aren't getting arrested. There are probably five hundred other people they'd need to arrest first."

Nathaniel makes a choked sound, because he thinks Susan might be delusional. Patrick evidently agrees with him, because he catches Nathaniel's eye and winces.

Everyone falls silent, the only sound a Doors album playing in the back of the shop.

"Tommy DeAngelo enlisted," Hector tells his sister. "Remember him? He graduated last year. Glasses, stupid haircut?"

Iris is momentarily speechless. "Why?"

"Said he was going to get drafted anyway, and this way at least he could pick the navy. Navy's safer."

"But," Iris starts, and she's obviously going to start in on all the very good reasons nobody should enlist in this war or possibly any war, and how the government is lying and the war was ginned up by profiteers. She'll be right on all counts, but there's nobody in this room who needs to hear it.

Besides, Nathaniel has spent the last two months listening to people act like *not* dodging the draft is effectively a war crime. Maybe they're right—at this point, the one thing he's sure of is that he's the least qualified person in this building to make any kind of moral judgment. But he thinks it's missing the point to blame the men who either enlist or comply with selective service.

"Some people enlist," Nathaniel snaps. "Some people will always enlist," he repeats, a little less testily. "There will always be true believers. There will always be people who trust their government not to be embroiled in a gigantic, evil conspiracy or to be tragically incompetent. If the president says we need soldiers, the people who believe him are the optimists."

"They're wrong," Iris says.

"Of course," Nathaniel says, trying to remember that he's dealing with children, not jaded CIA analysts. "But I want to live in a world where the true believers are right."

8

One sunny morning in May, Nathaniel goes by himself to the A&P for a pint of milk. He manages to get almost all the way home before the abyss catches up with him. He unlocks the shop door with shaky hands, his heart thudding from the perils of the dairy aisle and a cloudless sky.

He heads directly to Patrick, because Patrick is...soothing, Nathaniel supposes. He'd be useless up against any actual threat—if someone tried to mug him, he'd buy the mugger a sandwich and give him the coat off his back—but against more existential threats, he's practically a magic amulet. He's *good* in a way that Nathaniel finds incomprehensible and which he's certain he doesn't deserve any part of.

But Patrick's in the shower and Nathaniel has just enough self-respect not to barge into the bathroom. He goes upstairs to Susan's on the pretense of getting

Eleanor.

"You look awful. Did you sleep at all?" Susan asks, instead of *good morning* or *thanks for taking my hellion daughter off my hands*.

"No, thanks for asking," Nathaniel says. Eleanor gurgles up at him. He lay awake half the night, enumerating his sins and dreaming up all the ways they might catch up with him. Hence, the early morning trip to get milk before he'd even had a cup of coffee. He doesn't even take milk in his coffee, for pity's sake. But Patrick does.

Susan's looking at him a little too carefully. Scrutinizing him, really, and he suspects she isn't only seeing the circles under his eyes. She shakes her head and pours him some coffee from her own pot. "It's my last cup, so you're welcome."

"Brew more, you harridan." He jostles Eleanor onto his shoulder and takes a sip. Susan's coffee isn't as good as Patrick's.

"Save your sweet talk for when Patrick's around to be impressed," she says, because she really is a harridan. But she does put on another pot of coffee. "Come here," she says, when the coffee machine is puttering away. She opens her arms.

Nathaniel squints at her and takes another gulp of coffee.

"Come on," she says, advancing on him.

"Truly unnecessary," he says, appalled, but she's already upon him, his coffee whisked away, her arms around his shoulders, her face smashed against his chest. She's tiny. Nathaniel is maybe slightly above average height for a man and on the skinny side, but having her up against him makes him feel like a lumbering giant. She smells like baby soap and marijuana and she will *not* let go. Eleanor, squashed between them, thinks this is all tremendous fun and celebrates by biting Nathaniel's neck with her toothless gums.

Susan removes the little beast and puts her in her crib, and Nathaniel thinks his trials have come to an end, but then she's back at it, her head tucked up under his chin.

It's that, maybe, the tickle of her hair against his neck, the sound of Eleanor making little noises in her crib, the old and unwanted familiarity of it all, that makes Nathaniel crack. He squeezes her back. He doesn't know how long they stand there, but his collar's damp from where she's been crying all over it.

"It'll get better," he says, because that much is true. She doesn't ask how he knows, and she doesn't point out that his voice is hoarse. "I went to the grocery store on my own. It was hellish."

"The fact that you did it at all is something," she says.

"Spare me," he says. She hauls him toward the couch, presumably as punishment, then pastes herself up against his side, halfway onto his lap. "If this is a seduction, I have terrible news," he says, shocking himself by coming so close to admitting the truth aloud, even though he suspects she already knows.

She looks up at him just long enough to roll her eyes, then puts her head back on his shoulder. Inspired by what he can only assume is a further descent into madness, he puts his arm around her and kisses the top of her head. It's…fine. It's nice. He's comforting a friend. He's letting himself be comforted. When was the last time he touched someone like this? Before coming here, he can't remember the last time anyone touched him at all, other than a handshake or a trip to the dentist.

The apartment door swings open. "There you are," Patrick says, sounding half frantic. "I couldn't find you." And then he takes stock of what he's walked in on. "Oh," he says, frozen in place on the threshold. "I should have knocked."

"Oh, be quiet," Susan says, not even bothering to extract her limbs from Nathaniel's person. "It's not like that."

"It looks like that," Patrick says.

"My husband died three months ago." Susan snipes at Patrick all the time, in the way people do when they've known one another so long that childhood patterns stay fixed. But this might be the first time Nathaniel's heard Susan sound genuinely angry at Patrick.

"Everybody grieves differently," Patrick says. Nathaniel bets he read that in the book on grief he keeps under his desk.

"Oh my god. Nathaniel's gay."

"Hey!" Nathaniel says, because Susan could have some discretion, even if, apparently, Nathaniel has none.

"Weird thing to say about your boyfriend," Patrick points out.

"We aren't sleeping together, you madman," Nathaniel says.

"I'm supportive!" Patrick says. "Oh, I get it. You haven't slept together *yet.*"

Nathaniel starts laughing. Beside him, the indignation is pouring off Susan, so he takes one of her hands in his and squeezes it. Patrick can do with that what he will.

"No offense, Nathaniel, but I don't want to have sex with you," Susan says firmly.

"Likewise," Nathaniel says, still laughing. "With all due respect," he adds, tipping an imaginary hat, which sets

Susan off laughing too.

"Okay! God! Sorry! You're cuddling platonically," Patrick says, more sarcastic than Nathaniel's used to hearing from him.

"Yes, Patrick," Susan says. "We're cuddling platonically."

"Should I start knocking when I come over?"

"Is it okay if I push him out the window?" Susan asks nobody in particular.

"I don't think that would help, exactly," Nathaniel says. He picks up Susan's wrist and glances at her watch; his own left hand is still wedged behind her back. "We need to open the shop. Perhaps some of us can find another time to be obtuse and dramatic."

Downstairs, Nathaniel flips the sign to Open while Patrick switches on the lights. "I apologize for making you worry," Nathaniel says, his attention on some books that a customer put back horizontally. "I went out to buy milk."

"You don't need permission to buy milk."

"Yes, well, I do know that. But we both know I don't go anywhere without a minder." Nathaniel means to sound matter of fact but it comes out pathetic. He pulls himself together. "I wanted to try. It was not a success."

"You got back here all right, milk and all. That's progress. Thanks for picking up the milk, by the way."

Nathaniel scoffs. Progress.

"Susan shouldn't have said that about you," Patrick says.

"Hmm?"

Patrick steps close, and when he speaks it's quiet enough that nobody else could possibly hear, even though there aren't any customers. "She shouldn't have said you were gay. Even if that's something you told her, she shouldn't have said anything."

"She isn't wrong," Nathaniel says, expecting an emotional free fall that doesn't come. Instead all he feels is embarrassed. To his surprise, most of that embarrassment has to do with how obvious he's been, and less to do with the shame he's been dragging around since he was a teenager. It's difficult to be too ashamed about that around Patrick. "What I mean to say is that she mostly isn't wrong," he adds, because he doesn't know how to make sense of this topic without papering over half a decade of his life.

"You don't have to explain."

Nathaniel almost wishes he did have to explain, about this and about everything else. Then Patrick would know exactly who he's been feeding and housing, exactly who's been rocking his niece to sleep. Nathaniel would have to leave, of course, but at least he wouldn't be enjoying all this under false pretenses.

"And she still shouldn't have said anything to me," Patrick goes on. "If you told her something in confidence…"

There's the faintest hint of a question in there and it takes Nathaniel a moment to figure out why. He's about to say that he hadn't actually told Susan, in case that's what Patrick's wondering about, but he effectively did tell her. *If this is a seduction, I have terrible news.* That *was* Nathaniel telling her. For weeks, she's been making it clear that she knows, easing him into the idea. *Save your sweet talk for Patrick.*

Nathaniel spent his career watching his painstakingly assembled facts get reshaped into something that wasn't the truth. Even as he wrote his reports, he knew which facts were so inconvenient they'd have to be ignored, and which were nearly desirable and therefore would get exaggerated. One of the things he likes most about Susan is that she'll have no part of that. Perhaps it isn't ideal to go around announcing other people's secrets, but the entire point is that it wasn't a secret, it was a fact they were all delicately sidestepping. "I'm glad she did," he says.

The shop door opens and they both pivot, like they've been caught in the middle of something more interesting than a conversation.

Mrs. Kaplan walks in. "I hardly recognize the place without all the dust," she says, gazing around in wonderment. "You can see through the windows. Who knew?" Her eyes linger for a moment on Patrick and Nathaniel, standing at a distance that Nathaniel now realizes is abnormally close.

"Welcome back," Patrick says, wry. "I don't need to tell you who cleaned."

Nathaniel raises a hand in greeting, feeling absurdly shy. The last time he saw Mrs. Kaplan, he'd been knee deep in a nervous breakdown, and he'd been a lot deeper than that when she'd taken him in. She's seen him at his worst and there's a cowardly part of him that hoped he'd never meet her again. He'd stumbled in here, half out of his wits, on an afternoon when she'd been working the cash register, Patrick apparently at a book auction. He barely remembers that day, only the matter of fact way she'd locked up the shop, hailed a cab, and brought him home.

"You look well," she tells him before wrapping him in a hug.

"Thank you." He hopes she knows he's thanking her for more than the compliment.

Mrs. Kaplan releases him only to immediately hug

Patrick.

"Have you been at the *beach*?" Patrick asks, holding her at arm's length and scrutinizing what does indeed appear to be a suntan. "Have you been playing shuffleboard and drinking whiskey sours for *three months* while the rest of us toil and strive?"

"Oh, take your mug and be quiet," she says, opening a purse the size of serviceable luggage and producing a mug that says MIAMI in bright pink letters alongside a flamingo on a surfboard. "Do I get to see this baby or are you all holding out on me?"

When Patrick goes upstairs to get Eleanor, Mrs. Kaplan turns to Nathaniel. "I wasn't sure I'd still find you here."

"I don't have anywhere else to go."

She gives him a once-over—tan cotton slacks, a white oxford, and scuffed penny loafers, his everyday uniform since that trip to the Salvation Army—and says, "I'm not sure about that."

Nathaniel could tell her that looking presentably employable—or like someone who was once employable—doesn't amount to much. But he suspects that what she's really getting at is that he walked away from something, and could theoretically walk right back to it. She probably thinks he worked at a bank or an insurance agency.

Patrick comes back down, carrying Eleanor, who is, thankfully, a distraction from Nathaniel's past. Mrs. Kaplan compliments Eleanor's fat little cheeks and wisps of sandy hair. "What color do you think her eyes will be?"

Eleanor's eyes started out a murky blue, but in the last few weeks they've gotten clearer. Susan's eyes are green, but that doesn't seem to be the direction Eleanor's are heading.

"Can't tell yet," Patrick says.

"Were Michael's eyes the same color as yours?" Mrs. Kaplan asks. "That bright blue? I can't remember."

"Yeah." Patrick swallows. "We both got our dad's eyes."

"You should see the back room," Nathaniel says, because Patrick looks like he needs a few deep breaths. "We painted it. There's tea back there, and coffee."

Mrs. Kaplan gives him a knowing glance, like she knows what he's doing, but she follows him to the kitchen and is duly impressed. "I don't know what you used to do with yourself," she says, "but I doubt you were a handyman or a housekeeper."

"I hate untidiness," Nathaniel says. "I can't think straight when things are a mess." His face heats, because he hasn't presented Mrs. Kaplan with much evidence that he's ever been able to think straight. "I've started inventorying the books."

"It looks like you're staying," she says.

"My plan is to stay until Patrick kicks me out," he says. It's the truth. It's not like he has any better ideas. He has a notebook full of reasons to stay, a notebook full of reasons why he shouldn't. "But I shouldn't overstay my welcome."

Something flickers across Mrs. Kaplan's face. "With Patrick, that isn't something you need to worry about."

Susan comes downstairs to hug Mrs. Kaplan and get congratulated on having produced such a lovely baby. Susan holds on to Mrs. Kaplan for a long time while Mrs. Kaplan speaks quietly into her ear, and Nathaniel remembers that Mrs. Kaplan lost a husband too.

They order Chinese food and Mrs. Kaplan stays for

dinner, all of them crammed around the table in the kitchen. She shows Patrick about a hundred photographs of her nieces and nephews and great-nieces and great-nephews. "Did Ezra make first chair?" Patrick asks. "Did Sarah decide whether she's going to Brandeis?"

Susan leans over and whispers in Nathaniel's ear. "He's never met any of these people."

Nathaniel is utterly charmed. He's so charmed he might black out.

"Fix your face, babe," Susan says. Under the table, he pinches her.

9

"It's stupid of me to get attached," Patrick mutters. They're at the A&P, trying to fill their cart with groceries that will form themselves into balanced meals without any intervention more drastic than a can opener. "It's not like Susan's going to spend the rest of her life upstairs. She'll take Eleanor back to California."

"She had her things shipped here," Nathaniel points out, stopping in front of the canned vegetables. The music piped in over the speakers seems designed to make you feel like you're in a movie about people buying groceries: nondescript and familiar, but somehow enough to convince you that canned beans are a bit of a thrill.

Patrick puts four cans of creamed corn into the cart. Nathaniel returns three of them to the shelf, let's not get carried away here. "I don't want Eleanor to leave."

It's possible—probable, even—that Susan will eventually move out. She and Michael moved to San

Francisco in 1966, right after they got married, with no plans of coming back east. "She's your niece," Nathaniel says. "She won't disappear from your life." He squeezes a jar of peanut butter until his fingers turn white against the glass.

"It makes me feel crazy," Patrick says. He puts a box of spaghetti into the cart. "Three months ago I didn't even know her, and now I'd lie down on train tracks for her, no questions asked. And she isn't even my kid. That's crazy, right?"

Nathaniel could explain that he's experienced this particular mystery, that he knows how the heart can generate devotion out of thin air and find a place inside you to keep it. He could also tell Patrick that he knows about what comes after, how the space remains, the devotion remains, even when its object is gone.

Instead he picks up a loaf of spongy bread that claims to contain vitamins. They need vitamins; he puts it in the cart.

"You take care of her every day," Nathaniel says. "Of course you love her. That's the entire point of babies. We would have gone extinct a million years ago if babies didn't operate that way."

"I didn't love her at first," Patrick says. "I kind of resented her. She was here, and Michael wasn't."

Nathaniel is a little touched that Patrick's telling him all this. And by touched, he means he's quite smug about it, actually. "And you did the right thing anyway."

Patrick makes a noise that somehow dismisses the idea that doing the right thing even bears mentioning. Nathaniel can't figure out whether Patrick is deluded enough to believe everyone is as good as he is or if he holds himself to a different standard.

"No, we can't get grapes," Nathaniel says in the produce aisle, putting the bunch of grapes back where they came from. "Susan says we're boycotting them."

"Why?"

"Farm workers are striking in California."

"Does that include wine?" Patrick asks.

"It can't," Nathaniel says, alarmed. He and Maria have been drinking a bottle of Burgundy that one of the doctors at work gave her. "French grapes are fine," he decides. "They have unions."

Patrick gives him an *if you say so* look that Nathaniel chooses to ignore. They get bananas.

Patrick is about to make another pass down the canned goods aisle. Nathaniel can't face the threat of green beans. "I'm requisitioning this cart," he announces, grabbing the handle and steering it toward the ice cream.

It turns out Nathaniel likes sexy evil men in frock coats as much as Jerome does. Last month, after Patrick bought that paperback from Jerome—paying for it with change from his own pocket, simply because Nathaniel mentioned their neighbor might want it—Nathaniel had meant to bring it right up to Maria Valdez, but he'd gotten distracted. During that night's bout of insomnia, he read the entire book. It was the least hideous sleepless night he's spent since 1961.

The next morning, he gave the book to Maria and asked her if she had any recommendations for something similar. It turns out there's an entire genre of fiction that's mostly about beautiful young women who start out in bad situations and wind up in worse ones before falling in love with a handsome doctor or the Duke of Lancaster. The rhythm of it all is a relief. The villains are worse than he is, straightforward bad guys who all but twirl their mustaches. The heroines tend to be optimistic naifs who are bad at noticing risk; he's decided not to evaluate whether that particular quality has any personal relevance. He and Maria began passing dogeared paperback romance novels back and forth.

Now, on the windowsill next to his bed, Nathaniel has a stack of Anya Seton and Daphne du Maurier paperbacks that Patrick bought him for ten cents apiece from a sidewalk vendor on MacDougal Street. In Nathaniel's notebook, he's written "Anya Seton," but in his mind he knows he means the books, talking about them with Maria, and the fact that Patrick bought them.

Also on the windowsill next to his bed are the books Patrick lent him last month. At the bottom of the stack is *The Spy Who Came in from the Cold*. It opens with bad intelligence getting people killed. He'd had a nasty moment when he wondered if Patrick was on to him, even though Nathaniel was an analyst, not the sort of operative most people imagine when they think of spies.

But of course Patrick doesn't know, because if he did, he'd have sent Nathaniel packing. Patrick had simply lent Nathaniel a book he enjoyed, and now that book judges Nathaniel every night, mere inches from his pillow.

In his little notebook he writes *Maria being funny about books*. Then he writes *As the World Turns*, even though Patrick must never know how sincerely Nathaniel enjoys it and how desperately invested he is in the fate of Penny Hughes. Next, he writes *pistachio ice cream*, which, inexplicably, he'd never tried until this month.

If he keeps going, his notebook will be full of all the loveliest things in the world, things that in any just world he wouldn't be allowed near.

"Did you ever play professionally?" Susan asks. The woman is relentless. Nathaniel's afraid she won't stop until she's assembled a full dossier on him.

They're in her apartment, listening to the Kinks. He'd like to think that Susan starting this interrogation in the middle of "A Well Respected Man" is a coincidence. However: guilty as charged, he supposes.

He tells her the truth. "I wasn't good enough."

At first he was afraid that if he said too much, Susan and Patrick would connect the dots, and someone would say something to the wrong person and it would end with Nathaniel in a secret prison in the Panama Canal Zone.

But he's been here for three months. He's talked to hundreds of customers. Faculty from various New York colleges visit Dooryard Books all the time, and there is no world as small as the world of people who went to a certain kind of school. Viv was finishing her graduate degree at Radcliffe while he was doing his undergrad at Harvard; they probably know people in common. One customer is the spitting image of a boy Nathaniel knew in prep school. A doctor Maria complains about shares an uncommon surname with Nathaniel's former secretary. It isn't like he's in deep hiding.

He wants this to mean that nobody's looking for him—surely they'd have found him already if they thought he posed a risk. But he's familiar enough with intelligence gathering to know that finding a single person is usually a matter of luck.

He has, however, had enough time to assess the nature of the threat. Even if they know he photocopied the files, they wouldn't kill him without finding out what he did with the copies. He can stop worrying about sniper rifles, at least. And if he really wants to be rational, he can find comfort in the fact that of all the underhanded things he's heard of the agency doing, he's never heard of anything suspicious happening to former analysts.

This should make it easier to go outside, but evidently his subconscious isn't interested in rational arguments. Or perhaps the danger that threatens to engulf him at his worst moments isn't the fear of a bullet to the head so much as it is the contents of his head.

"You weren't good enough for what?" Susan asks.

"Boston Symphony, New York Philharmonic, Chicago Symph—"

"Okay, so you weren't one of the fifty best violinists in the country," Susan says. "You realize there are professional musicians who aren't in world class symphony orchestras but also aren't playing on street corners while people throw spare change into their violin cases."

"I know," Nathaniel said. "But I was better at other things." One of his professors took him out to lunch and told him that the government was going to need mathematicians if they had any hope of fighting the Soviets. Nathaniel was flattered; his fate was sealed. He'd get a job doing something important, something special and valuable and useful. He could be that person, and not the person he was starting to fear he was. Working for the agency felt like putting on an unobjectionable suit, and what Nathaniel wanted more than anything was to be unobjectionable.

Susan sits up just enough to put on a different record. Still the Kinks, but this time it's "Sunny Afternoon," and now Nathaniel knows he's being roasted.

"It was 1950," he says. "I was terrified."

"About being gay?"

That wouldn't have been the word Nathaniel used back then, if he'd even let himself use a word. "About not being the right kind of person," he says. In 1968, that sounds weak and sad.

"Sometimes I still think I should be wearing little white gloves while I have lunch with the other ladies in the Junior League," Susan says. Nathaniel already guessed that she was raised like he was, more or less. In the refrigerator downstairs, there's a porcelain pitcher full of milk, because Susan insists that pouring milk directly from the carton into a coffee cup is disgusting for mysterious reasons she can't articulate. Nathaniel, for the same mysterious reasons, agrees. Patrick calls them both bourgeoisie collaborators.

Nathaniel opens his mouth to point out that ladies in the Junior League would simply never leave their gloves on during lunch, but Susan catches his eye with a look that's half amusement, half *don't you dare*. He knows that she knows exactly what he was going to say. There have been few times in his life he's felt as transparent as he does around Susan, and even fewer that he's wanted to.

"Are you still terrified?" Susan asks.

Nathaniel thinks about it. "Of being the wrong kind of person? I already know I'm the wrong kind of person." The last few months have etched that much into his bones. That, he supposes, is the first step. The first step toward what, he couldn't say.

10

"What're they doing?" Patrick asks. It's a Sunday morning, and Hector's sitting on the floor at the back of the shop, surrounded by the remnants of some old contraption the twins found in the basement. Iris is lying on her stomach, her chin in her hands, giving unsolicited advice.

"Whenever I ask what they're building, they get shifty," Nathaniel says.

"Is it for science class?" Patrick asks them.

"No," Iris says without elaboration.

"Very shifty," Nathaniel mutters.

"Nothing they do," Patrick says low, leaning close to Nathaniel's ear, "could be half as bad as what Susan, Michael, and I got up to, and we turned out—"

Patrick breaks off and Nathaniel winces. They really didn't turn out fine, did they. One dead, one still crying every day, and Patrick—Patrick is lonely for reasons that Nathaniel can't make sense of.

"What does 'turned out all right' even mean?" Nathaniel asks. "You had a family tragedy. It isn't a moral failing." He pushes an irritating strand of hair behind his ear—god, he needs a haircut—and when his arm drops, his knuckles brush against the back of Patrick's hand. It wasn't on purpose, but he keeps his hand there for a moment before sticking it in his pocket. On the radio, Simon and Garfunkel's "America" is playing.

"Nobody took your stupid wire," Iris says.

"It isn't a wire. I keep telling you, there aren't wires. It's a clamp."

"Nobody took your clamp either."

"I know! I didn't say they did."

"Well, find it, then."

Hector sighs, put upon, and hauls himself to his feet. He glances around the room, then crouches down and pulls something from behind the radiator. Hector has eyesight like a cat. "There it is. Somebody must have kicked it there. Oh—but this isn't what I need after all."

"There used to be radio supply stores," Patrick says. Both the twins jump, like they hadn't noticed him and Nathaniel standing there. "Downtown."

"That's what our dad said," Hector says. "Radio Row. They've all been knocked down to build that bank."

"It isn't a bank," Iris says. "It's the World Trade Center."

"Sounds like a bank to me."

"Also, we don't need radio supplies, because we aren't making a radio."

It doesn't look like a radio, that's for sure. It's made of dirty black metal, and the bulk of it is shaped like a barrel with a crank. Nathaniel's certain he's seen something like it, but he can't imagine when or where.

"Do you have a better idea?" Hector asks.

"Where did all those stores go, though?" Patrick asks.

Nathaniel gets the Yellow Pages and finds a radio supply store on Fourteenth Street, but when they call, nobody answers. There's another store on Laight Street, which nobody in the room has ever heard of. When they consult the road map that Patrick keeps by the cash register, it turns out to be near the Holland Tunnel. There's another store near the South Street Seaport.

"I'll be down there tomorrow," Patrick tells the twins. There's a huge old used bookstore near City Hall that Patrick periodically combs for anything he can resell at a profit. "I'll swing by Laight Street. If it's nice out, I could walk across town to the other store, too."

The twins look genuinely surprised, like Patrick's an ogre who's never done a single nice thing for them, rather than the man who's been buying them pizza and sharpening their pencils and proofreading their essays for the past two years.

"I'll come with you tomorrow," Nathaniel says when they're getting ready for bed. Whenever he steps outside, he feels like he's being plunged directly into the abyss, but each time it gets slightly easier. Or maybe he's just getting used to the contents of the abyss.

In the morning, they leave Susan in charge of the shop. After a cold and rainy April, May finally feels like spring, and they both wind up carrying their jackets.

"How far is it?" Nathaniel asks.

"Two subway stops."

Nathaniel has been on the subway, of course, when he visited New York years ago. But that was back when he was compos mentis. They're still on Jones Street and his hands are already sweaty. He resists the urge to hide in a doorway.

"Or we could walk," Patrick says. "It's only twenty minutes."

They walk down Hudson Street. It's not a particularly scenic part of the city, mostly filled with warehouses and former factories, with a few gritty-looking garages scattered around. Painted on the sides of brick buildings, faded advertisements promote stores that probably went out of business a decade ago. Every block seems to have a diner or lunch counter, and only half are still open.

"I wonder what this neighborhood is called," Patrick says when they cross Spring Street. "It's too far west to be SoHo. I'm not sure I've ever been over here."

"Really? Well, I'm glad I get to see it with you," Nathaniel says, dreadfully earnest. Good god. Patrick doesn't say anything, but he bumps their shoulders together.

Dooryard Books is in a part of the city that's busy and prosperous. It's filled with restaurants and little shops. But Nathaniel knows—from alarming personal experience— that a few blocks to the west, things get seedy.

This part of the city is seedy in a different way. It feels half abandoned, faintly apocalyptic. This is a place where things used to be.

"Artists will move in here, like they did in SoHo," Patrick says, like he's reading Nathaniel's mind. "If they haven't already started. Jerome lives in a loft with some artists on Chrystie Street and they have to take the subway just to get groceries. You can't buy so much as a loaf of bread anywhere nearby."

Nathaniel imagines these abandoned factories and warehouses filling up with drag queens and artists and is surprised to realize that the idea pleases him. He likes things neat and tidy, new and fresh and clean. His house in Virginia—he presses his arm briefly against Patrick's, keeping the abyss from getting too close—was always orderly. His desk at the agency was so pristine that it was a standing joke that he must never do any work. He spent his childhood obeying the logic of sheet music before realizing numbers could be made to follow the same rules.

Order and symmetry and rules have always made him feel peaceful; they were his allies, trustworthy and reliable. The fact that he can walk down this street—an old warehouse with broken windows on one side of the street, a boarded up bar on the other, a car with missing hubcaps slumped against the curb—and feel like he belongs here can only be a sign that something is wrong with him. But there is something wrong with him; he already knew that. Some fundamental part of himself got left behind in Langley, or in the cold winter streets, or maybe he lost it years ago at a graveside. Maybe that loss isn't gaping emptiness, but space; maybe there's room in him for something else. Maybe there's room for him to be something else.

The store, when they reach it, looks like someone took the contents of another, larger electronics store, tipped it on its side, and dumped it into this place.

"Bet you feel right at home," Nathaniel murmurs, and watches the corner of Patrick's mouth tick up.

Patrick starts combing through the store for the parts Hector wants, but Nathaniel goes up to the shopkeeper and hands him the sketch Hector made. The shopkeeper frowns, tilts his head, frowns some more, then disappears. He comes back ten minutes later with half a dozen mysterious objects. Nathaniel could not, if his life depended on it, identify a single one of them. He takes out his wallet.

"I've got it," Patrick says, reaching for his own wallet.

"No you don't." Nathaniel puts his hand on Patrick's wrist. Giddy sparks shoot up his arm. "You're always buying everything. Meals, drinks, snacks."

"That's our deal. You're paying for room and board. We shook on it."

"You get pizza for the kids, you picked up new violin strings for me when you were out last week, and I think you've been buying Susan's groceries since February. Let me get something for once. You're overpaying me—"

"I am not," Patrick says. He's a terrible liar.

"—and charging me next to nothing for rent. I can afford a couple antennas."

"Is that what they are," Patrick says, marveling at the weird coils of metal.

"Frankly, I have no idea."

"Three dollars and forty-eight cents," the shopkeeper says. Nathaniel lets go of Patrick's wrist and produces a five-dollar bill. Patrick puts his wallet away.

The shopkeeper wraps everything up in newsprint and puts it in a paper bag that Nathaniel insists on carrying.

"Susan chips in for groceries," Patrick says when they're on the sidewalk. "Neither of us are keeping track right now of who owes who, but I don't have less money than I did when she moved in. And I haven't been paying her when she covers the cash register at the store. Maybe I should."

"She'd laugh in your face," Nathaniel says.

From the electronics store, the bookstore should only have been a ten-minute walk, but they get completely turned around.

"Stop complaining," Nathaniel says after Patrick's

spent five minutes bitching about all the construction making it impossible to know where anything is. "It's a nice day. We're getting fresh air."

"Sure, except for the car exhaust. We'll both get miners' lung."

Nathaniel tugs Patrick's sleeve. "Come on."

When they reach the bookstore, Patrick finds what he declares are a decent Lowell and an excellent Dickinson, while Nathaniel amasses a stack of paperback Gothic romances.

"If I want serious literature, I can find it in the store I basically live inside," Nathaniel explains after Patrick's laughed at him. "But if I want Gothic mansions and the dastardly cads who own them, I have to look elsewhere."

"I can't believe they carry paperbacks here," Patrick grumbles. "There's nothing like used paperbacks selling for a dime apiece to make a store look unserious."

"You're unserious," Nathaniel says.

"Nobody made this store's manager put out free coffee," Patrick says a moment later, but he squeezes Nathaniel's arm while he says it. The quantity of unprompted touching happening this morning is making Nathaniel feel untethered.

They've walked a lot and probably ought to take a cab or the subway home, but Nathaniel doesn't want the day to be over. It's silly; they'll spend tomorrow together, and the day after that. They've spent three months of days together. The only difference is that they're out of the shop. They're running errands. There's nothing special about it.

He still doesn't want it to be over.

"Let's get lunch," Patrick says, his voice gruff, like maybe he's been thinking the same thing.

"Yeah, okay." Nathaniel lets the distance between them collapse to nearly nothing.

Before they find a place to eat, they walk past a man sitting with his back against a building, dressed in what looks like army surplus, a duffel bag at his feet.

"Can I get you something to eat?" Patrick asks him.

"Fuck off."

"Sure, but my brother just died in Vietnam and I can't buy him any lunch, so."

The man looks up at him, furious.

"Or, you know, money for a bus ticket or a night indoors," Patrick offers. "I can do either."

"I'm not going to your fucking church, man." He looks warily between Nathaniel and Patrick. "And I'm not coming home with you."

"Don't want you to." Slowly, telegraphing his movements, Patrick reaches for his wallet and takes out a few dollar bills and a business card, then bends and places them under the edge of the man's duffel bag. "Take care."

"Do you just *do* that?" Nathaniel asks when they've turned the corner. "Whenever you see someone who needs help? You and Mrs. Kaplan are going to get yourselves killed." He gets panicky when he thinks about Mrs. Kaplan sitting him at her kitchen table and giving him chicken soup a mere hour after meeting him.

"I can't walk past someone like that."

"He had a knife." It hadn't been a big knife, but it had been there, concealed inside the long sleeve of his coat.

"You'd have a knife too, if you were sleeping rough."

"That isn't the point. You don't owe that to anyone. Your safety isn't the price of Mrs. Kaplan helping you," Nathaniel says. "You don't owe a debt."

"Of course I owe a debt! I'm sorry I put you in harm's

way—"

Nathaniel grabs Patrick's sleeve and tugs him so they're facing one another. "I don't care about that! Tell me this isn't a death wish." Patrick has nobody to look after him. Mrs. Kaplan would, but she's in Queens. Susan would, but she has her hands full looking after herself.

"Susan thinks it's some kind of guilty Catholic martyr complex. It isn't. It's—" Patrick shuts his eyes. "I want—I *need*—other people to have the same chance I did."

Nathaniel searches Patrick's face. "All right." He isn't convinced that Patrick *isn't* doing this from guilt. He's either a saint or he's burdened by a tragic guilt complex. Or he's a saint burdened by a tragic guilt complex; that seems par for the course when it comes to saints. Not a famously well-adjusted bunch.

"When Mrs. Kaplan helped me I thought I'd lost everything. I didn't know how I was supposed to keep going. By the time I finished the sandwich she gave me, I knew I could hang on. And so I get this life. I get this." Patrick gestures around them at some uninspiring office buildings and sluggish midday traffic, but also the blue sky and some pigeons. "I get this," he says again, and now he's almost pointing in the direction of home. "Sometimes it doesn't take much to do that for someone. Sometimes it's just a reminder that you aren't alone."

Nathaniel sucks in a breath. "Patrick."

"I know four dollars isn't going to save anybody's life. But I want to try. It isn't a penance."

They're standing in front of the Western Union Building, and workers are spilling out onto the sidewalks for lunch. It isn't the right place for this conversation. There isn't a right place for this conversation.

Nathaniel thinks of the notebook in his pocket, thinks

of all the good things in it, and how they add up to a bulwark against the abyss. "It took a lot less than four dollars for Mrs. Kaplan to save my life, and for you to keep on saving it."

Nathaniel was planning to live out the rest of his days never admitting any of that aloud, or even in his thoughts, but he can't stand here silently while Patrick confesses more or less the same sad story.

"I wish we didn't have that in common," Patrick says. To Nathaniel's relief, he doesn't look surprised.

"Yes, well, we're both doing swimmingly now. You're a living saint and I went for an outing without nearly fainting." He touches Patrick's sleeve. "Patrick, I just wanted to make sure you weren't trying to hurt yourself."

Patrick looks like he wants to fight about that, like he can't take the idea of his safety being anybody else's problem. But he deflates and says, "Fine, okay, sure."

They walk a few blocks in silence, but when their shoulders bump, neither of them moves apart.

11

Nathaniel shuts the algebra textbook with an air of finality. "If you don't both get an A on your final exam, I'll burn down your school." From the front of the shop, he can hear Patrick snort.

"It's the Regents we have to worry about," Iris says.

"You don't have to worry about anything." Nathaniel taps the book. "You know all of this. This summer we can do trigonometry, if you like." His theory is that if he can teach Iris and Hector a year's worth of math over the summer, the school might let them go directly into calculus, and then they'll be on track to do advanced math in college.

"Could we really?" Iris asks.

"I'd rather die, no offense," Hector says.

"Fair. Can you get your hands on the textbook they use?" Nathaniel asks Iris. "Maybe get a calculus textbook too, just in case."

"We aren't supposed to take books home over the summer," Iris says, but she says it like the infraction is an enticement, not a deterrent.

"Then it's a plan."

Nathaniel gets to his feet and leaves the twins to study for another class. As he works on the inventory, he hears them gossip about their cousin, debate whether a boy named Raul has a crush on Iris, and complain that peace talks are meaningless if people are still dying.

Iris, in particular, reminds Nathaniel of people he used to work with. She's just starting to figure out that she's smarter than practically everybody she knows. The best he can hope for is that she finds a good use for that mind. She's planning to go to college, thank god.

He's embarrassed by how much he envies them— envies all the time they have, the chance to do things right. He'll be forty this summer; he's crossed the likely halfway point of his life. And what does he have to show for it? Practically nothing. Less than nothing.

"How many pages is that?" Patrick asks, glancing warily at the composition notebook containing the inventory.

"You don't want to know."

"Oh, don't I?" Patrick asks, standing a little too close. Nathaniel feels his pulse pick up at the proximity, and at the flirtatious edge to Patrick's words.

"Nuh-uh," Nathaniel says, shaking his head, not breaking eye contact.

There's something crackling and hot between them. Nathaniel's instincts all tell him to walk away, to put some space between them. Instead he leans in a little closer, egregiously close now. "Twenty-six pages," he says. "One for each letter of the alphabet."

It isn't that funny, but when Patrick laughs, Nathaniel can feel it, hot on his cheek.

"I'm starved," Jerome says. He's on his second cup of coffee, lounging on a diseased-looking armchair Susan rescued from the trash collectors and dragged to the back of the shop. It's Nathaniel's day off, but Susan banished him from her apartment so she can call her manager. He's spent the morning drinking coffee with Jerome. Patrick looks incredulously at both of them every time he walks past, which only encourages Nathaniel to stay put.

"We only have teething biscuits and creamed corn," Nathaniel says.

"Or we could go out to lunch."

An excuse is on the tip of Nathaniel's tongue, but what the hell. Jerome spent the last hour regaling him with stories of backstage drag show drama. He won't be shocked by anything Nathaniel says.

"Sometimes I get nuts when I go outside," Nathaniel says.

"What kind of nuts?" Jerome asks, leaning forward, intrigued.

"Frightened."

Jerome shrugs, clearly unimpressed, and gets to his feet. "What do you need when you go nuts?"

"Stick close to me."

"Not a hardship," Jerome says with a showy little leer. "Let's go."

On the way out, they run into one of the regular customers. Beverly is a reporter at the *Times*. She wears a trench coat, big orange-tinted sunglasses, and Coco Chanel. Nathaniel would have thought she covered fashion or style, looking like that, but he's seen her byline on national news. She must live in the neighborhood, because she often comes in with a net grocery bag over one arm.

"I need something for a flight," she says today. "Quick."

"*One Flew Over the Cuckoo's Nest*," Nathaniel suggests, because he just finished it and knows it's still next to the cash register where he left it.

"Already read it," Beverly says.

"*Ladies of the Rachmaninoff Eyes*," Patrick says. "Loved it, by the way," he tells Jerome.

"I told you," Jerome says. "But are we letting straight people read it?"

"Oh for f—pete's sake, go have lunch and stop cluttering up my shop."

Outside, the vertigo hits Nathaniel before they're at the end of the street, but it isn't bad enough that he needs to stop walking. The restaurant is only ten minutes away, on the corner of Greenwich and Charles, and Jerome chatters the entire time.

As soon as they're seated, Jerome leans forward. "Are you and Patrick—" He tips his head to the side and lets his silence finish the question.

"Ah, no."

"Why not?"

Nathaniel truly does not know how to answer that, so he just stares.

"I mean, you should, if you swing that way," Jerome says, then waves at someone across the room and blows them a kiss. "I'd be first in line if I were still in the market for moody white boys."

This is where a person should say that he isn't like that. Nathaniel says, "The chicken sandwich looks good.

149

Moody?"

"Get the ribs. He has a chip on his shoulder." Jerome touches his temple, the place where Patrick has a scar. "He tell you about that?"

"Yes," Nathaniel says. He knows that Mrs. Kaplan gave Patrick stitches after he had a run-in of some sort with the police.

"Plenty of folks who get arrested get fucked up about it and stay fucked up about it. They print your name in the paper when you get caught in a raid, you know. You take a kid like Patrick—nice, middle class, probably got straight As—and throw him in the Tombs? His aunt and uncle can suck my dick, pardon my French, oh *hello*, Richie!" He waggles his fingers at someone passing by.

"Right," Nathaniel says, trying to make sense of what Jerome is telling him and square it with what he already knows. He spent his career assembling facts into coherent explanations and this set of facts isn't particularly difficult. Patrick got arrested in a raid and beaten up, his aunt and uncle kicked him out, and then somehow he came to Mrs. Kaplan. Nathaniel doesn't know the details, doesn't know why Susan and Patrick maintain a silence around this topic as sharp and as deep as the silence around Michael. "And he was so young," Nathaniel says, a little guilty about fishing for information.

"Still in the twelfth grade. Anyway, he keeps everything locked up tight. He's always ready for people to sail right out of his life. To leave him on the curb like an old mattress. The only people he even halfway believes in are that old lady and his brother. And, well. I guess that only leaves the old lady. Anyway, can't blame him, but a girl likes to be trusted. Two orders of the ribs," Jerome tells the waitress. "Extra coleslaw. Amazing lay," he tells

Nathaniel. "In case I didn't make myself clear."

"Good to know."

"Isn't it *just*."

The ribs are, indeed, delicious, and so is the coleslaw. So is the company. It reminds Nathaniel, in a bizarre, fun-house-mirror kind of way, of long lunches with colleagues, the kind where you order a second drink and cheerfully complain about everyone else you've ever worked with. Except it's extremely unlikely that the person across from him at this chipped formica table will be even slightly responsible for toppling any Latin American democracies.

Jerome walks him home. Nathaniel tries to thank him but Jerome waves it away. "I'm not having you lose your marbles on my watch. Kiss kiss!"

Patrick's at the cash register exactly where Nathaniel left him. Does he keep it all locked up tight, as Jerome said? Is he untrusting? Maybe Nathaniel can't see it because he, himself, isn't particularly open or trusting. He remembers Patrick, at the grocery store, fretting about Susan leaving. Maybe it isn't that he doesn't trust people, but that he doesn't trust them to stay.

"Have a good time?" Patrick asks.

"We talked about you the whole time."

Patrick sighs. "Where did you go?"

"Some place called Mama's."

"Jesus Christ, that place is about as gay as a bathhouse."

"I did notice that."

Patrick laughs, warm and bright and louder than usual, and the sound fills the entire shop.

"Let's go out," Susan says, walking into the shop, the chimes ringing as the door swings shut behind her.

"It's only six," Patrick says.

"I'm talking to Nathaniel," Susan says. "His shift was over an hour ago. I hope he's paying you overtime," she says, directing her attention to where Nathaniel is sitting with his feet on Patrick's desk, reading a book about a governess falling in love with her Byronic, mysterious, widowed employer. You could stock a modestly sized bookstore with novels that are effectively Brontë retellings and Nathaniel would read every last one of them.

"What's the going rate for reading paperbacks and drinking coffee?" Patrick asks.

"You can't afford me, darling," Nathaniel says. "This is pro bono." He turns to Susan. "Where do you want to go?"

She's dragged him out a few times to listen to music. Once, they went to a coffeehouse a few blocks away where they listened to some friends of hers play some music with entirely too much banjo. Another time, they went to a jazz club uptown. They'd taken a cab there, but on the subway home Nathaniel was braced for disaster; instead he was charmed by a rat eating a donut, a busking saxophonist playing songs that were popular twenty years ago, and a few teenage girls jumping the turnstile.

"We'll sit near the door and hit the bricks if you need to," Susan says, which isn't an answer. "I won't ever be more than a few feet away."

Nathaniel will never get used to people talking about his weaknesses so openly. "All right, then."

"I'll take Eleanor all day tomorrow," Susan tells Patrick.

Patrick frowns. "You don't need to do that. I wasn't going out tonight anyway."

Nathaniel's been watching Patrick and Susan dance

around this issue for months. Susan thinks Patrick's doing her a favor and feels guilty about imposing on him. Patrick seems to grasp that he isn't babysitting so much as raising a child, but doesn't know how to point this out without overstepping. Nathaniel just hopes that Susan doesn't decide that the best way to stop imposing on Patrick will be to move away.

"What do I wear?" Nathaniel asks Susan.

After a few thrift store excursions with Susan, Nathaniel now owns three pairs of cotton trousers, three plain white collared shirts, a camel-colored sport coat, a decent belt, and penny loafers. He also has a pair of jeans that feel much too tight but which Susan says he needs so she can take him places without anyone thinking she's with a cop or a sugar daddy.

The first time he put on a shirt with a collar after months of wearing Patrick's t-shirts and too-big sweaters, he'd been delirious with relief. It probably says something terrible about him, his longing for conformity, his gut instinct to preserve the status quo. Or maybe he's just used to the way certain garments feel against his skin.

"Jeans," she says. Oh well.

The shop door opens before Nathaniel can go upstairs and get changed. It's Nathaniel's least favorite customer: square jawed, broad shouldered, clean cut, like somebody ordered him right out of the catalog. The shop always smells like his cologne for a full ten minutes after he leaves.

"Oh, hi, John," Patrick says.

John scuffs his toe along the carpet, all bashful innocence. Nathaniel wants to be sick. "I was looking for a Whitman biography," John says, words calculated to go straight to Patrick's heart. For Christ's sake, the man doesn't even need a Whitman biography; just get Patrick started and you'll know all you need to know before the night is through.

"Settle down," Susan says once she and Nathaniel are on the stairs.

"I don't like him," he says.

"No kidding."

"He's up to something."

"He's working up the courage to hit on Patrick."

"I know *that*," Nathaniel says. "He's laying it on too thick. The downcast eyes, the stupid little smile. I was looking for a Whitman biography," he mimics. "If he knew anyone in common with Patrick, he'd know that Patrick isn't exactly a challenge."

"Did you just call Patrick easy?"

"Am I wrong? Anyway, he clearly isn't part of whatever network of homosexual literati Patrick's been sleeping his way through, so how did he even find Patrick? How does he know about Whitman?"

"Okay, Miss Marple," Susan says. "Go take a shower."

They walk across town to get to Susan's mysterious destination. It's warm enough that neither of them need a jacket.

As they're walking along the south side of Washington Square Park, Susan touches his arm. "If I want to go to the opera, will you let me buy you a suit?"

He thinks about it. He has a closet full of suits at—he can't really call it home, now, can he? There was a time he'd have been offended and shocked by the idea of a woman—of anyone—buying him clothes. Now, the impropriety might be part of the appeal, like Iris and her stolen math textbook.

"I have a closet full of suits," Nathaniel admits.

"And where, exactly, is this closet?" Susan asks, just like Nathaniel knew she would.

"Virginia. Outside Washington, D.C."

Susan's quiet while they cross the street. "A tuxedo, too?"

"A tuxedo, too," Nathaniel concedes.

"I'd take a field trip with you, if you wanted to get your things. We could take the train or borrow a car."

Nathaniel's stomach swoops in terror, but he isn't sure at what. The idea of being caught? He doesn't think so, not anymore. There's nothing in that house he needs, anyway: some suits hanging in a half empty closet, some books on half empty shelves, and several months of dust.

"It's ill gotten gains, I'm afraid," Nathaniel says, and braces himself for Susan's next question.

But the question never comes, and when he glances at Susan, her jaw is set.

It's Friday evening and Washington Square Park is full of boisterous young people. There's a woman with a baby carriage and a few old men sitting on benches, but the crowd is mostly the right age to be college students. Some are singing along while someone else plays the guitar. They all look dirty and outlandish to Nathaniel's eye, but he means that in an affectionate sense. There was a time when he would have seen them as a threat; he still sees them as a threat, but he thinks he'd like to be just as much of a threat as they are.

"Susan, my love," he says. "I don't want to go back."

She loops her arm through his and they fall silent for a few paces. "There was this moment in 1960, '61, when it felt like this right here" —she gestures around them at the park and its neighborhood— "was the center of the world. Nearly everyone I knew lived in a ten block radius. If you walked through the park on a Sunday you'd run into someone you knew playing the guitar. We knew what we wanted our music to sound like. We had a vision, and it was—don't make fun of me—it was beautiful."

Nathaniel's been secretly listening to the music Susan recorded back then, playing the records as quietly as possible when she isn't around. "It was."

"Folk music doesn't really exist anymore. The definition stretched until it stopped meaning anything. People moved on. That's fine—it's *good*—but it's a crazy thing to feel like a has-been when you aren't even thirty. There's no going back, even if you are, actually, back. I couldn't make that music now if I tried."

He can't tell if that was an allegory about his not wanting to see his house again, or Susan being confronted with the sight of people ten years younger than her having their own turn at the center of the world. "Forgive me for sounding like an old man, but you have your entire life ahead of you."

"So do you."

"Hardly."

"You have, what, ten years on me? Eleven?"

"Something like that." It's twelve.

"Pocket change. You think I wouldn't move heaven and earth to be twenty again and to have the next few years in front of me? Or maybe I wouldn't. Maybe I've missed some big cosmic point, but really I just want Michael back, and there's something you want back, but neither of us are getting it."

Nathaniel would do practically anything for a few hours in the winter of 1961. But the rest of it—he'd like to seal it off wherever they put nuclear waste.

"You won't get that, but you'll get other things," he

tells Susan.

"Will I? And I guess you'll spend the next fifty years getting the sad, bad things you think you deserve. Good plan!"

It's some comfort that Susan wouldn't sound half so smug if she knew precisely what Nathaniel did deserve.

Tonight's outing turns out to be the polar opposite of opera. Even as they crossed Third Avenue, Nathaniel had been holding out hope that they'd be going to another jazz club, but Jimi Hendrix is not a jazz musician, and the Fillmore East is certainly not a jazz club. Susan pulls a joint out of her pocket, in plain view of however many hundreds or thousands of people are in this theater, and lights it. She takes a drag and passes it to Nathaniel. "Shut your eyes and listen, and if you need to go, we go." She holds out her hand and he takes it.

At first, all he can think of is how to leave. As Susan promised, their seats are off to the side, near an exit. After that, all he can think of is how loud the music is. Then, at about the time the high starts to set in and the opening act has left the stage, he listens to the music.

Iris and Hector have a Jimi Hendrix record they play when their parents aren't home. Nathaniel's heard it reverberating through the stairwell. It has nothing in common with the music Susan usually listens to. It has nothing in common with anything Nathaniel's ever chosen to listen to at any point in his life.

But he does what Susan says: he shuts his eyes and listens. He can feel the bass in his bones, and the drums somewhere even deeper than that. But the guitar— Nathaniel can't imagine what it's like to be able to take an instrument and do something like that. The feedback and other noises are discordant, even troubling, but it's like

157

exuberant graffiti or those kids in the park. It's breaking the pattern.

During a rare quiet moment, Susan leans in close. "If American music is a family tree, can you see how folk music gets you here? Not only folk, not even mainly folk, but can you hear it?"

Nathaniel can't, not even when Hendrix plays Dylan's "Can You Please Crawl Out Your Window?" so he squeezes her hand and thinks about how a year ago he would have hated this, how he would have been frightened by the possibility of enjoying it. Maybe he can leave the person he was in the past. Maybe he does have a future in front of him. He lets the music seep into him.

They take a cab home and find the light still on in the shop. Patrick's waiting up for them, Eleanor asleep against his shoulder.

Nathaniel's heart does something terrible. Maybe the music has made him susceptible, because he feels like he's seeing something impossibly lovely, instead of Patrick in an old t-shirt.

Eleanor wakes up, sees Nathaniel, and reaches for him. When he moves to take her, his hands brush Patrick's. Because of warm weather and Jimi Hendrix and the fact that he smoked most of that joint by himself, he puts a hand on Patrick's arm and leaves it there, his fingertips resting against the warm skin above Patrick's elbow, and lets himself believe in something different.

12

By now, Nathaniel recognizes most of Dooryard's regular customers. A Melville collector in New Haven takes the train down once a month to make a circuit of half a dozen bookstores. A married couple in the neighborhood stops in every few weeks to ask whether there's any new Longfellow.

And then there's George, a professor at Columbia, who comes by whenever he's in the Village to look at any Whittier rare editions that Patrick's managed to get his hands on. He's forty-something and wears wire-rimmed glasses and black turtlenecks. There isn't a doubt in Nathaniel's mind that George is one of Patrick's conquests, or possibly vice versa.

"Don't tell Patrick," George says when Nathaniel's ringing him up, leaning close to Nathaniel's ear. They didn't have any Whittier in stock, but George bought a copy of *The Valley of the Dolls*. "I need to think about my reputation."

Nathaniel leans in too, mirroring George's posture and echoing his tone. "Patrick read this book last month." That wasn't particularly funny or insightful, but George laughs anyway. Nathaniel feels impossibly bold.

"Forgive me if I'm making the wrong assumptions, but I'd love to buy you a drink," George says.

They've hardly interacted, which means that George's attraction to Nathaniel is purely physical. He's never considered being picked up for his looks. That happens to women.

He thinks he likes it.

"No hard feelings if you'd rather not," George says, winking, and writing his phone number on the back of his receipt before handing it to Nathaniel.

Nathaniel stares at it for a few seconds before putting it in his pocket.

"Susan says I should take you to a bar," Patrick says later that day. "Because apparently you're getting picked up by every eligible queer who walks through the door and she wants to make sure you know you have options."

Patrick sounds gratifyingly annoyed about all of this, maybe even jealous. "I realize you fuck strangers as a sort of extended handshake, but I'm not—" Nathaniel reaches for something appropriately cutting but what he winds up saying is, "I'm not there yet."

The *yet* makes him almost dizzy. He couldn't possibly explain to Patrick that not only has he never touched another man that way, but until the last few months he's hardly let himself think about it.

Patrick sticks his hands in his pockets and looks at the ceiling. "You can just go and see what it's like. Or not. It's a standing offer."

"Fine," Nathaniel says.

"Want to go to Julius?" Patrick asks as they're closing up. "It used to be a great bar for closet cases but there was a sort of protest a few years back and it got written up in the *Times*. Now the closet cases have to find someplace else, I guess. It hasn't been raided in a while, though, so it's about as safe as we can get."

Nathaniel has no idea if he's being called a closet case—accurate—or if Patrick's trying to tell him that this bar is relatively subdued. The idea of a raid—an arrest, the police, being *found*—makes him want to curl up under the desk and stay there. But what good has playing it safe ever done him?

"Do I look all right?" Nathaniel asks when they're getting ready to leave. He's wearing exactly what he had on all day: slacks and a white button-up, nothing special.

"When don't you?" Patrick grumbles, put-upon. He says it loud enough for Nathaniel to hear, but low enough that Nathaniel can pretend not to have heard.

Nathaniel doesn't pretend. He flicks a deliberate glance at Patrick's shoulders, the folded up cuffs of his shirt, the stretch of denim across his thighs.

It's a warm May night so they sling their jackets over their arms and take their time walking the ten minutes to the bar. "You ever done this?" Patrick asks.

"No," Nathaniel says, because that's the answer to any question Patrick could possibly be asking.

"Look, Julius isn't usually a handjobs in the bathroom sort of bar," Patrick says right before they go inside, "so if you go back to someone's apartment, call me when you leave. I'll pick you up in a cab."

Patrick is being kind, but Nathaniel thought he had made this clear. "You really have no idea, do you? I've only been with women, and I only did that because I was supposed to. I know that sounds tragically repressed—"

"No," Patrick says, and you really have to be one of the world's worst liars to give yourself away with a single syllable.

"Of course it's tragically repressed! But I'm not going to achieve complete sexual liberation on your timeline. Or, possibly, any timeline."

Patrick touches Nathaniel's elbow. "Hey. There isn't a timeline. If you don't want to—"

"Wanting to isn't the problem." He feels like they're speaking completely different languages. He's twelve or so years older than Patrick, but right now they're from different planets. The generation gap evidently fissured at some point between 1928 and 1940. But even that isn't accurate: the professor who tried to pick him up that morning is older than Nathaniel. Viv is older than Nathaniel. There are plenty of homosexuals older than Nathaniel. Patrick's generation didn't invent the concept.

But they may have invented the idea of not hating yourself for it. Nathaniel doesn't know. He deliberately doesn't know; he made sure never to look around or pay attention.

"We can go home," Patrick says. "I shouldn't have pushed you."

"Well, now I *need* a drink," Nathaniel says. He pulls open the door to the bar.

It's hot and stuffy, loud with conversation and music. It's a bar, nothing special about it; it's almost pointedly nondescript.

A few weeks ago, Jerome told him that during the day, Julius attracts middle-aged writers from established New York periodicals, and that at night it's filled with gainfully employed queer white men. Jerome meant it as a caution—don't go there, darling, you'll be bored out of your mind. Right away, Nathaniel can see what Jerome meant. The prevailing aesthetic is so neatly combed and tidy, so very middle class, that Nathaniel wouldn't have stood out here a year ago. Now, with his hair two inches longer, his clothing casual and a bit rumpled, he still fits in. There are a few men wearing suits that Nathaniel might once have owned. A few patrons are young enough to be college students, but he isn't by any means the oldest person here.

"Do you need me next to you?" Patrick asks.

Nathaniel would like to know exactly how Patrick thought any of this would work if Nathaniel still needed him in arm's reach at all times. "Go make friends," Nathaniel tells him. Patrick fades into the background.

Nathaniel finds an empty stool, orders a drink, and checks the clock over the bar. It takes two minutes before someone slides onto the seat next to his and offers to buy him another. Nathaniel glances over long enough to see that the man is about his own age, blond, and wearing a shirt with the first two buttons undone, tie loosened around his neck. "I'm waiting for someone," Nathaniel says. The man goes away.

Another five minutes pass, during which Nathaniel nurses his drink and watches the bartender mix and pour and stir. The man is in his early twenties, and handsome enough that Nathaniel has to wonder if it's a job requirement. He helps himself to a cigarette from a pack someone left on the bar. At some point during the time he'd been losing his mind, he accidentally quit the habit and now the smoke in his lungs is simultaneously foreign and a sudden relief.

Finally, Patrick slides onto the empty stool and waves the bartender over. "What are you drinking?" he asks Nathaniel.

"An old fashioned."

"Two old fashioneds," Patrick tells the bartender and slides three dollar bills across the bar.

Nathaniel thinks he understands why Patrick picked this place. He wanted Nathaniel to know that he could walk into a bar full of gay men and blend in, and that the crowd of people is the same as he'd expect at a nice restaurant or an art museum. These aren't Patrick's people or Jerome's people. He's letting Nathaniel know that he can have this, that he can be this.

He's also, apparently, letting Nathaniel know that all he has to do is sit on a stool and someone will effectively offer to have sex with him. Honestly, Nathaniel hadn't thought it would be that easy. It gives him that same feeling he'd had when George asked him for drinks, the sense that he's something of an object. It makes him hot with embarrassment, and then even more embarrassed that he likes it.

"I can't believe people bother with these when there isn't even any grass in them," Nathaniel says, stubbing out the cigarette and pushing the ashtray away. "You've made me into a radical dope fiend, Patrick, and I'm looking at all these nice, clean-cut young people like they're cops."

Patrick gives him an odd look, like he's waiting for the punch line.

"Take Me Home," Susan's song from last summer, comes on the jukebox. Nathaniel and Patrick exchange a glance that's half wince, half amusement, and Nathaniel feels like they're alone here, like everyone else in this bar, in this city, on this planet is far away.

"What are we drinking to?" Nathaniel asks when the bartender puts two old fashioneds in front of them.

"Courage," Patrick says.

Nathaniel lifts his glass. "Drink on, drinkers." After a few months at Dooryard Books, you start quoting Whitman, apparently.

Patrick grins, sudden and surprised. "That poem was about a gay bar. Kind of."

They leave once they finish their drinks, taking the long way home.

"I had a good time," Patrick says when he's unlocking the door. It's dark enough in the shop that Nathaniel would be afraid of tripping if he couldn't navigate this place blindfolded by now.

"You don't need to sound so surprised," Nathaniel says. "I know I'm not the most thrilling company, but we make do."

"Who's surprised? I always like being with you," Patrick says, simply enough that Nathaniel couldn't doubt it if he tried. "But I don't think you had a good time." He holds out his hand for Nathaniel's jacket, then hangs it up on a hook by the door next to Patrick's own jacket.

"I always like being with you," Nathaniel says, and it shouldn't feel like such an admission, not after Patrick said it first. The light switch is right beside the coat hooks but neither of them reach for it.

Instead Nathaniel heads toward the back of the shop and puts on the kettle. As Patrick reaches for the box of tea bags, his hand lands on Nathaniel's hip, just a careless motion to steady himself. But Nathaniel's spent weeks paying attention to the way Patrick touches him and he thinks all these little gestures are questions, all easily ignored if Nathaniel didn't want to be asked, didn't want to answer.

Nathaniel puts his hand over Patrick's, keeping it there on his hip. The abyss—the fucking abyss—of course he couldn't do this without feeling like he's plunging into shark infested waters. The fact that he wants it is, naturally, irrelevant.

He interlaces their fingers, probably gripping too tightly, erring on the side of seeming decisive. Patrick puts the box of tea on the counter and steps closer, close enough that Nathaniel can feel the heat of him along his back, solid and safe and familiar. To hell with shark infested waters. The only people in this kitchen are him and Patrick. No sharks here.

He lets go of Patrick's hand and turns, and now Patrick has a hand on both Nathaniel's hips. They're close enough that Nathaniel has to look up to meet Patrick's eye. He watches as Patrick's gaze drops to his mouth.

Nathaniel could lean in, close the gap. But he wants Patrick to do it. He wants to be the one who's kissed. There isn't much he's sure of, but he knows that much.

"I want you to kiss me," Nathaniel says. Shaping his mouth around the words feels like swimming upstream, like each sound costs something. "Just a kiss," he adds, more for his own benefit than Patrick's, a reminder that the line he's crossing isn't even a terribly significant one, or at least it doesn't have to be.

Patrick lets out a breath and nods his head—once, quick, message received. Slow, he lifts a hand and pushes a strand of hair off Nathaniel's face. Nathaniel had been thinking that a kiss was the smallest denomination of affection, that he could start with a kiss and build up his tolerance. But that touch already overwhelms him, those few fingertips lighting up his nerves and sending his thoughts careening.

"Okay?" Patrick murmurs. His hand is on Nathaniel's shoulder, heavy and warm through the thin layer of cotton.

"Okay," Nathaniel says. Patrick leans in. His lips are soft and his beard is scratchy. He tastes like whiskey and bitters. They're barely touching. It's the first kiss Nathaniel's ever wanted, and they both know it.

Patrick pulls away, but keeps his hand on Nathaniel's shoulder, his thumb moving back and forth, soothing.

"Thank you," Nathaniel says.

Patrick snorts, and whatever tension was snapping between them breaks. "Any time, happy to help."

They get ready for bed the same way they have for the past three months, as if the kiss hadn't happened, as if it didn't matter, except when Patrick says good night, he reaches for Nathaniel's hand and gives it a squeeze.

Part 3

A City Invincible

Patrick

13

Somebody gave Mrs. Kaplan two tickets to tonight's Mets game, and she—inexplicably a Yankees fan—foisted them off on Patrick. Patrick in turn tried to give them to the Valdezes, but it's a weeknight and Mrs. Valdez won't let the kids go out. Mr. Valdez is working. Patrick thought Susan and Nathaniel might want to go, but Susan says she's managed to live this long without seeing any professional sports and isn't quitting now.

"Do you want to go to a Mets game?" Patrick asks Nathaniel. Patrick doesn't particularly want to watch a baseball game, and he doubts Nathaniel does either—he doesn't read the sports section of the paper and when the sports reporter comes on the eleven o'clock news, Nathaniel picks up a book.

"With you?" Nathaniel asks, letting the hammer fall to his side. The other day, Nathaniel found some framed botanical prints in one of the more derelict corners of the second floor, and now he's hanging them downstairs on the few patches of wall that aren't covered by bookshelves. He's standing on a chair, and Patrick has to resist the urge to remind him to be safe.

"Yeah, with me." Patrick's not sure if this is a deterrent. It's been a few days since they kissed, and Nathaniel hasn't made anything resembling another move. Patrick isn't chasing after an employee, so that's that, then. Presumably, Nathaniel wanted to prove to himself that he could kiss a man, and now he's accomplished that: excellent work all around, Patrick's job here is done.

But even before the kiss, things between them had been—not strained, exactly, but careful. Especially after the trip to the radio supply store. Sometimes he catches Nathaniel watching him. Patrick feels exposed, like he typed up a list of his weaknesses, an illustrated guide to his worst moments, and stuck it on the bathroom mirror for Nathaniel to reference.

"They have hot dogs and beer," he adds, as if that's any kind of incentive.

But Nathaniel smiles, just this quirk of one side of his mouth that Patrick's coming to realize is Nathaniel's version of a full-blown grin. "I'd like that," he says.

"We should leave at six. God knows how long it takes to get to Shea Stadium."

"Where is it? Queens, right?" He steps down from the chair, using Patrick's shoulder to steady himself, then goes over to the subway map.

Before Nathaniel agrees to go anywhere, he needs to find it on the map, needs to see his route laid out in front of him. At first, Patrick thought this had something to do with Nathaniel's nervousness about going outdoors, but now he wonders if Nathaniel's just the kind of person who likes knowing exactly where he is in the world.

Patrick puts his finger on the Willets Point subway stop. "You've been to Queens. Mrs. Kaplan's house isn't even that far from the stadium."

Nathaniel makes a doubtful noise.

Plenty of New Yorkers treat visiting the outer boroughs like going on safari. Patrick used to think it was because they thought they were too good for it, but now he realizes it's because they don't understand the bus system outside Manhattan. Which is fair, because neither does Patrick. But he doubts that's Nathaniel's rationale—he doesn't understand public transit within Manhattan either. This will be the farthest Nathaniel has been from the shop since he got here.

A month ago, Patrick would have been patient and gentle and understanding, but now he knows what Nathaniel looks like when he wants a push. "Oh, for fuck's sake," Patrick says. "You can go to Queens, you snob."

They wind up on an especially wrecked Queens-bound subway car. This spring, graffiti artists are going all out. Either that, or the city doesn't have the money to paint over and scrub off the graffiti.

Patrick always expects Nathaniel to be put off by these signs of decay. After all, he keeps the shop in an unnatural state of cleanliness. He tends to stare at litter and graffiti, wads of gum ground into the pavement, cab drivers swearing at one another across traffic. But Patrick is all too familiar with Nathaniel's less impressed expressions, and right now he looks perfectly content.

Patrick points to a crude drawing. "People drew dicks on the walls of Pompeii."

"We're participating in a great human tradition,"

Nathaniel agrees. "An unbroken chain of penis graffiti dating back thousands of years."

Patrick's aunt and uncle used to bring him and Michael into the city twice a year: once to visit his uncle's office, once to see the Rockefeller Center Christmas tree, boxes ticked off on some imaginary How To Do The Bare Minimum By Your Orphaned Relations checklist. The New York City of the early fifties was bright and sparkling, steel and glass, everything gleaming with the polish of prosperity. Everyone wore hats and had their shoes shined, and Patrick sat on the subway with his hands folded in his lap like he was in church. The trash didn't dare linger on the streets, and cabbies didn't shout, and neither of those things can possibly be true but Patrick will swear by them anyway.

In 1958, when he realized he couldn't go home—or that the city was his home, now—the shine hadn't worn off quite yet. Only in the last few years has he really had the sense that he's in a place that's past its prime.

But the seedier this town gets, the more it feels like home. He doesn't have any business with bright and sparkling; he doesn't want to wear a hat or get his shoes shined, either literally or metaphorically. Fifteen years ago, there was barely room in this city for people like him, or at least that's how it felt. Maybe a place needs a layer of grime and an aura of rot before anyone's willing to cede territory to the undesirables.

Their seats are in the upper deck behind third base.

"I'll get some beer," Patrick says.

"Priorities," Nathaniel agrees.

When Patrick gets back, Nathaniel is regarding the field with an odd expression. When the game starts, Nathaniel leans forward in his seat, his hands clutching his knees, Patrick still holding both beers. The first three innings pass like this, Nathaniel studying the game with a strange intensity, and Patrick wishing he had binoculars to get a good look at that shortstop.

"The Mets," Nathaniel finally says, taking the beer that Patrick presses into his hand. "The Mets didn't exist the last time I watched a baseball game."

"What team did you root for?" Patrick asks, taking advantage of Nathaniel being in the mood to talk about his life.

"Growing up, the Red Sox."

"Oh, so you really are from Boston?"

"I grew up in Vermont," he says easily, having evidently forgotten that he once said he was from Boston. "I had a boss who always had Senators games on in his office. He'd make people stand behind the television and read their reports."

"That doesn't seem like a great way to watch baseball or do a job."

"Patrick, you have no idea."

It's a weeknight game, early in the season, so the stands aren't full. Around them, empty seats give the illusion of privacy.

Nathaniel leans back and puts his feet up on the back of an empty seat in front of them. "Once or twice a year," he says, something taut in his voice that's belied by the looseness of his posture, "we'd drive up to see the Orioles play the Yankees. My ex-wife was a Yankees fan." He takes a sip of beer, his gaze fixed straight ahead.

Patrick isn't sure whether he's more surprised Nathaniel was married or that he's mentioning it. "Is that what went wrong?" he asks, because he doesn't know how else to ask if the divorce is what made Nathaniel lose his mind a little.

"We got divorced in '62," Nathaniel says. Patrick assumes that's a *no*.

Patrick flags down the beer man and buys two more overpriced Rheingolds. Then he gets some ice cream from the next vendor who passes by. Beer and ice cream might not be a decent dinner, but he's glad to see Nathaniel eating something.

"How long were you married?" Patrick asks.

"Three years."

The next question, the obvious question, is *do you have any kids*. If Nathaniel got divorced in '62 and he was married for three years, his kids wouldn't be older than eight or nine. The world is filled with men who walk away from their families, but Patrick can't imagine that Nathaniel wouldn't even send a postcard. He remembers how firmly Nathaniel insisted he had nobody to write to, nobody who was worried about him.

But he remembers, also, Susan asking how Nathaniel learned to take care of newborns. Patrick hopes he's added all of that up and come to the wrong conclusions, but the way Nathaniel's hand is clenched on his thigh tells its own story.

When Nathaniel gets like this, he likes the reminder that he isn't alone. At least that's how Patrick's explained it to himself, the way Nathaniel shadows him after a bad day. Right now, slouched in their seats, their upper arms are already touching. Patrick hopes that everyone in the stands behind them is too busy watching the runner on third base to pay much attention to Patrick's hand. He reaches over and pries Nathaniel's fingers off his thigh and leaves his own hand covering Nathaniel's for a second before pulling away.

"I used to root for the Red Sox too," Patrick says.

"I thought you were from Long Island."

"Only after my parents died."

"Ah, when you fell into the clutches of the evil aunt and uncle."

"They weren't so bad to Michael." They were neglectful, mean, stingy, and hateful, and they let Patrick sit in jail instead of coming to bail him out. But they tolerated Michael, at least.

"Well, as long as they were fine to Michael, it doesn't matter that they kicked you out," Nathaniel says. He's apparently been talking to Susan.

"They didn't kick me out. I ran away." Patrick could have gone home after getting out of jail. He could have gone home, could have let Michael and Susan know he was alive, could have finished high school—but he didn't know how to do any of those things.

"Susan thinks they smacked you around."

"Only a normal amount," Patrick says.

"It's very distressing when I'm the sane one here. What would be the normal amount for someone to smack Eleanor around?"

Patrick thinks he might be sick. "Stop being reasonable."

"My parents were the same way." He raises a hand to flag down the beer man. "And look at me now, not a trouble in the world."

Patrick starts laughing, which is just totally inappropriate, what the hell. But Nathaniel has that little twist of a smile he gets when he's pleased with himself. Nathaniel takes out his wallet and buys a pair of beers, something deft and second nature about it, and Patrick catches himself wondering if Nathaniel bought drinks for his wife at Orioles games.

They're well on the road to tipsy at the top of the seventh inning, and all the way there by the time the crowd starts filing out as soon as it's clear that the Mets aren't going to win this one.

"This has been lovely," Nathaniel says. "Really lovely."

Patrick doubts anybody's ever called the Mets lovely, but he can't disagree. The infield grass is unnaturally green under the stadium lights, and the smell of Cracker Jacks and spilled beer is the kind of familiar that passes for comfortable. The sky is dark except for planes taking off from LaGuardia, and Nathaniel's arm is still pressed against his own.

On the subway home, Nathaniel takes out his little notebook and writes something in it.

"What's in there?" Patrick asks, feeling bold.

"It's a list of my sins," Nathaniel says, and sticks the notebook back in his pocket.

14

One morning early in June, Patrick's slow to get ready and Nathaniel announces that he'll go out to get the paper by himself. It's been over a month since the last time he tried leaving the building alone, although last week he picked up a pizza with only Hector for company.

Patrick absently takes out a dime for the paper.

"You have to be kidding me," Nathaniel says, and sweeps out of the apartment.

When fifteen minutes pass, Patrick isn't worried, even though the trip to the newsstand and back shouldn't take more than half that time. After half an hour, Patrick grabs his keys and goes out. He finds Nathaniel on the corner, reading the paper.

"What's the matter?" Patrick asks, because he could have guessed that much even without seeing the worried look on Nathaniel's face.

"Robert Kennedy's been shot. In the head." Nathaniel

doesn't lift his gaze from the paper. He's been out here for half an hour; he must have already read the article several times. "But they aren't saying who did it. 'A youth.' That means nothing."

That had been Nathaniel's question after Martin Luther King, Jr. was killed this spring. "Let's go back," Patrick says. "We have to tell Susan before she hears it on the news."

She'd taken Martin Luther King badly, but at that point she'd still been pretty fragile in general. Now, two months later, Patrick wouldn't say that she's okay, because she isn't, not even close, but he isn't worried about her. If she had a nine-to-five job, she could go to the office and type letters and say hello to the elevator operator. She's taking good care of Eleanor. She's eating. Patrick's stopped covertly sweeping the apartment for pills. She's probably doing as well as she possibly could be.

"It's not only that he promised to end the war," Patrick explains when Nathaniel looks at him blankly. "His wife's pregnant." Dr. King's baby had been even younger than Eleanor. Susan just isn't dealing well with fathers of infants being killed, which is a statement that wouldn't have made a grain of sense a year ago. He's furious that it makes sense now.

He nearly has to wrestle the paper out of Nathaniel's hands to bring it up to Susan.

"What does it mean that I'm not surprised?" Susan asks after Patrick's told her.

Patrick's afraid it means that they both see the good in the world dissolving like sugar in tea. Once, Susan told him that an earthquake felt like her whole building was shaking itself apart. That's how this year feels, like the world itself is shaking in its foundations, and it's anybody's guess what will be left when the shaking stops.

He isn't going to say any of that, so he goes around the apartment, picking up stray coffee mugs and hair brushes and guitar picks and putting them where they belong.

"Now who's going to be the Democratic candidate for president?" Susan asks when Patrick finishes puttering and sits on the sofa.

Patrick hadn't even thought that far, but now that Susan mentions it, this can't end well. It feels tawdry to measure the loss of a person in practical terms, but Kennedy's campaign was promising in a way that not much is this year. It had been nice to be hopeful. Robert Kennedy felt like the only way this war would ever end. Every day there are more dead bodies. And every day more people change their minds. Peace talks are happening. But Patrick can't make himself believe that anybody in Washington cares enough to make it stop. They have their own agenda, and it doesn't involve peace.

Nathaniel comes in then, shouldering open the door while somehow holding three cups of coffee. He glances between Susan and Patrick and cracks a tiny little one-sided smile before distributing the mugs. Then he scoops Eleanor out of her crib.

"You're in my place," he tells Patrick, because he truly believes there are assigned seats in Susan's living room. He proceeds to wedge himself between Patrick and the armrest. There's nothing for Patrick to do but put his arm around Nathaniel's shoulders, and to keep it there.

In the middle of June, right before the school year ends, the Valdez kids come in carrying a package of filth that turns out to be a dog.

"We found him on the way home from school. He

was in that vacant lot on Seventh Avenue," Iris says. "Where the diner used to be."

"Absolutely not," says Mrs. Valdez, looking at her kids' faces and guessing their agenda. "Not a chance."

"Not it," says Susan.

"What are you going to name him, Patrick?" Nathaniel asks.

Patrick sighs and goes out to get a leash and some dog food.

Nathaniel and Hector give the dog a bath in Patrick's own bathtub, with Patrick's own shampoo, after which it's easy enough to identify it as the type of breed that's basically fifty pounds of hair and ears in a roughly canine configuration.

"Standard American Shaggy Dog," Susan says.

"Bookstores have cats," Patrick says to nobody in particular after putting down a bowl of kibble. "Not dogs."

The consensus is to name the dog Walt, because they're all fucking comedians.

"People will think I've named him after Disney," Patrick grumbles.

"You're named after the poet Patrick has a crush on," Nathaniel whispers to the dog.

There's a part of Patrick that's annoyed by all this. You can't just foist a dog on someone. It's the same part of him that's annoyed when he opens a dresser drawer to reveal zero clean shirts because Susan and Nathaniel have stolen them all, or when he goes to make lunch only to find that Susan's eaten the last of the leftover dumplings. Sometimes, the sound of Nathaniel and Susan going on and on and *on* about some new and fascinating way to tune a guitar makes him want to tell both of them to can it. He lived by himself for ten years. He's used to being alone. He's used to keeping the perimeters of his life clear and well-guarded.

But there's something superseding the annoyance, something fond and dumb and a little embarrassing. Susan grew up with dogs. Iris and Hector have spent years trying to badger their parents into getting a dog. Patrick likes that he made them happy in the same way that he likes finding Susan's coffee cups in his apartment and his own books on Susan's counter—the same way he likes seeing Susan and Nathaniel on his furniture, in his clothes.

He knows, too, that if he'd put his foot down and said absolutely not, he did not want a dog, Susan would have taken Walt herself. He hadn't, and so she didn't.

That night, Walt jumps onto Patrick's bed and falls asleep. His fur is matted in places, but he doesn't seem to have any fleas, so Patrick supposes he can stay there. When Patrick pets his back, his ribs feel too close to the surface.

Nathaniel appears in the doorway, backlit by the hall light so he's nothing more than a familiar silhouette.

"I don't even like dogs," Patrick complains half-heartedly as he combs his fingers through the dog's fur.

"Neither do I," Nathaniel says. "But everybody else does." Walt shifts in his sleep, resting his chin on Patrick's ankle. "I was about to put on the news, if you think you can extract yourself."

On the sofa, Patrick can't focus on the Channel 2 news. Nathaniel is a few inches away, wearing a t-shirt that used to be Patrick's. The building still echoes with the sound of everyone shrieking and laughing about the dog. But the television is a reminder of everything that exists outside the walls of this building. Some people were convicted of encouraging draft resistance, and Patrick feels like he's in a pot that's coming to a boil.

"Isn't that the man who wrote the baby book Viv wanted us to read?" Patrick asks. How many Spocks can there be, after all. "And he's going to jail?"

"Hey," Nathaniel says. He puts his hand on Patrick's thigh. "For what it's worth, they're pleased with themselves." The men on the television are, in fact, smiling. "They did the right thing, and if they're being made an example of, then maybe that'll bring things to a head." Nathaniel sucks in a breath. "They did the right thing," he repeats, like he's just heard himself.

Patrick puts his hand on top of Nathaniel's and leaves it there. "You sound like Susan. You sound like *Iris*. Next thing you'll be telling me about American imperialism."

"And I'll be right," Nathaniel says. "God help us all, but they're right." He pulls his hand away from Patrick's and tips his head against the back of the couch with a discontented sound.

"We should get ready for bed," Patrick says, because sitting this close is going to make him want things. No—he already wants things, but sitting like this is making it hard to pretend he doesn't. Nathaniel's a few inches away, the stretched out collar of his—*Patrick's*—t-shirt revealing a bit of collarbone and a glimpse of chest hair. His lips are slightly parted, his hair rumpled, and Patrick should turn his head and watch the television, but he can't look away.

Nathaniel rests his cheek against the back of the couch, looking Patrick dead in the eye. His face is lit up by the flickering light from the television.

Patrick feels like there isn't much ambiguity here, but when he reaches out to touch Nathaniel's thigh, Nathaniel practically flinches.

Patrick pulls his hand away. "Sorry," he says, mortified to have gotten that wrong.

"Don't be." Nathaniel makes an impatient sound. "I don't know how to do this."

"You don't have to."

"I know that," Nathaniel snaps. It reminds Patrick of all the times Nathaniel got frustrated with himself for not being able to go outside. "I mean, I don't know *how*."

"It can't be that different."

"The difference is that I want to."

Patrick feels his face heat, his own want coming into perfect focus, like the television antenna is finally pointing in the right direction. Nathaniel hasn't let himself want this, but now he is, and what he wants is Patrick. Patrick hasn't ever been particularly attracted to inexperience. He understands the appeal, in an academic kind of way, because he remembers when men saw that quality in him. But he's afraid that he'd be drawn to whatever attitude Nathaniel had, that he'd be hungry to give Nathaniel whatever he wanted.

"I'm nearly forty," Nathaniel says, dropping his forearm over his eyes. "This is absurd. I'm not some blushing ingénue."

Patrick snorts. He pulls Nathaniel's arm away from his face and doesn't let go. "You're a blushing *something* all right."

"It's dark. You can't prove anything."

Patrick rubs a thumb over the bones of Nathaniel's wrist. "You did okay last time."

"Damned with faint praise. Besides, you did all the work."

"I can do all the work again."

"I don't want to impose."

Patrick feels faintly hysterical. "Jesus Christ, impose all you like."

"Fine," Nathaniel sighs.

Patrick can't take it anymore. He's either going to start laughing or he's going to kiss Nathaniel and he thinks the latter option will be more enjoyable and less embarrassing for both of them. He gets a hand on the back of the couch and leans in, halfway to a laugh when their lips meet.

Last time, Nathaniel hadn't kissed back. It hadn't really been that kind of kiss. This time, he still isn't really kissing back—but his hand is on Patrick's shoulder and his lips are soft and he's very much letting himself be kissed. He makes a soft noise when Patrick deepens the kiss.

"You want this?" Patrick asks, his lips moving against the corner of Nathaniel's mouth. He wants to hear it. He wants *Nathaniel* to hear it.

In answer, Nathaniel bites Patrick's lower lip. Patrick hears himself make a noise, low and shocked, and he presses close. Nathaniel starts to lean back. If Patrick goes with him they'll be lying on the couch. That's fine, more than fine, but maybe not tonight.

Patrick pulls back, then, for good measure, gets to his feet. Nathaniel opens his eyes and gives Patrick one of his more withering glances. "So much for impose all you like," Nathaniel says.

"If you imposed any more we were going to ruin my couch."

"It's a horrible couch."

"I want you to keep wanting it," Patrick says, and it feels like a confession, feels like they both know he meant *I want you to keep wanting me.*

"There's some awful commotion on the roof," Susan says

one morning when Patrick comes to get Eleanor. "Last night it sounded like someone was jumping around up there."

Patrick frowns, because from Susan's apartment she shouldn't be able to hear anything on the roof. "It's probably squirrels in the attic."

"There's an attic?" Nathaniel asks.

"You can see it from the street," Patrick says. "What did you think those dormers were?"

"I thought they were decorative," Susan says. "How do you get to the attic?"

"The stairs? Honestly, where did you think the stairs went?"

"The roof?"

Now Susan and Nathaniel want to see the attic. Whatever wild animals are up there aren't any kind of deterrent. They leave Eleanor asleep in her crib with Mrs. Valdez and Patrick unlocks the door to the attic stairs. The lock is rusty enough that the key barely fits, but the door swings open easily enough.

The attic is a single low-ceilinged room with a pair of dormered windows at each end. There's no electricity up here, and the sunlight that filters through the dirty windows doesn't do much good. Patrick switches on his flashlight. It's hot and stuffy, but when he tries to open a window, he finds that it's been painted shut.

"I've only been up here a couple times," Patrick says. He wasn't storing anything under a roof that might leak, in an attic that might be full of mice and other creatures that like to destroy books.

It's too dark to see much more than shapes, even with the flashlight. He doesn't hear any animals scurrying away, so that's promising, at least.

"Ooh," Susan says when the beam from Patrick's flashlight lands on a piano. It's just a little upright—a spinet, he thinks it's called—wedged against the sloping roof.

"Careful," Patrick says as Susan crosses the room, picking her way around some junk.

She sits at the piano bench, dislodging a cloud of dust that briefly turns the flashlight beam into a solid thing, and plays a scale. "It's flat," she says. "But only a little." She starts to play "Heart and Soul," then slides over. "Come on," she says, obviously expecting Nathaniel to play the other half of the duet. But Nathaniel doesn't move, so Patrick sits. The bass part of "Heart and Soul" is the sum total of what he can play on the piano.

It's like being dragged back in time to 1955, both of them sitting at the piano in the Larkins' living room, Patrick dutifully turning the pages of whatever sheet music Susan bought with that week's allowance. "Unchained Melody." "Mr. Sandman." Like she's reading his mind, she starts to play "Only You." If Patrick shuts his eyes, he can believe that Michael is on the sofa behind them, calling out requests. He can imagine that Mrs. Larkin is in the next room, making sure the Fitzgerald boys don't get any ideas, but also making sure that they don't go home without a serving of pot roast or meatloaf or whatever else she's cooking.

Susan's playing it all from memory, even though she can't have played these songs in years. What must it be like to have all that stored up in her bones and tendons, the music and everything else that's tangled up with it? Patrick doesn't envy her.

Susan begins to play "Que Sera, Sera," and all Patrick can think of is the way Michael used to pester her to play it. And *Patrick's* the one who turned out to be gay. Susan isn't singing along, but Patrick hears the lyrics anyway, and it doesn't matter that they're sentimental. Most of the time he accepts what happened—not just Michael dying, but everything that came before it. He can look at Eleanor and look at Susan and even look at his own life, and he can feel almost good about it all, practically hopeful.

But when he thinks of them as kids, it all shatters. He can't stand the thought of anything bad happening to those kids.

When Susan finishes playing, Patrick scrubs his sleeve across his eyes, hoping it looks like the dust has gotten to him. When he stands, he promptly hits his head on a rafter. He knew there was a reason he never comes up here. He hears what might be Susan sniffling or might not be anything at all, but if he stops to check they'll both wind up crying. That won't do anyone any good.

"I'll get Eleanor and open the shop," he says. He doesn't wait to see if Susan and Nathaniel follow him.

When he enters the shop fifteen minutes later, a cup of tea is on his desk, and so is Nathaniel, sitting on the edge like he's lying in wait.

"I realize this is wildly hypocritical of me," Nathaniel says. "But even though I'm very much against emotions when they happen to me, I think it's possible that refusing to feel anything at all fucks you up fairly comprehensively in the long run."

"Susan doesn't need me weeping all over her."

"What makes you so sure?"

"Give me a break."

Nathaniel's lips press together in plain disapproval. "I have a lot more experience than you do with all this. I wish I didn't."

Patrick doesn't ask what *all this* means. He isn't sure he has to, at this point. "And you don't even talk about it."

"Like I said, I'm a hypocrite. Also, not to be a terrible show-off, but I'm fantastic at repressing things, as you may have noticed." He sighs. "I'm trying to do less of that. Drink your tea before it gets cold." He stands, but before he leaves he puts a hand on Patrick's shoulder.

15

"Well, that's almost a set," Susan says. "Ten songs."

Nathaniel looks up from where he's tuning his violin. "A set?"

"We could play somewhere. A coffeehouse, or that place we went to the other night."

When Susan takes Nathaniel out to listen to music, she wears what she calls librarian drag—one of Patrick's cardigans and her hair in a bun, as if she seriously thinks people won't notice Suzie Larkin in the audience of a venue where she herself played only a few years earlier. Patrick usually stays home with Eleanor, waiting up for them on the new sofa that's in the back of the shop next to the ratty armchair. Susan says she found the sofa on Christopher Street, but he thinks that might only be true in the sense that she found it in a store located on Christopher Street. It doesn't smell like furniture you find on the street.

Sometimes, though, they pay Hector and Iris to babysit and Patrick lets himself get coaxed into coming along. He doesn't really care about the music, but there's something quaint about Nathaniel holding the door for Susan, and Susan letting Nathaniel order her drinks. That's the real drag they're doing, this playacting at courtship. There's a healthy coating of irony, even camp, over the whole performance. Susan tolerated none of this from any of the men she dated, including Michael, but with Nathaniel they both know it's make-believe.

"Do I want to play music in a coffeehouse," Nathaniel repeats now, sounding baffled. Patrick had wondered if there was a goal to Susan's songwriting this spring, or if she was whiling away the time.

"It wouldn't have to be a big production," Susan says. "I could call the owner and ask if they'd let us play a few songs. No big deal, but you can say no."

"Let me think about it."

"It might not be safe," Patrick says. "You don't have papers," he tells Nathaniel. "Doesn't he need a cabaret card?" he asks Susan. He remembers this being a giant pain in the ass for Susan and a lot of other musicians; the city fingerprints performers and might not issue a card to anyone with a record. There's also a slate of unevenly enforced rules about whether dancing is allowed at places with liquor licenses. The point, according to Susan, is to make it difficult for jazz musicians—specifically Black jazz musicians—to make a living.

"The law changed last year," she says. "Nathaniel won't need a card. Venues still need a permit, but performers don't."

Later, Patrick finds Susan while Nathaniel is at the grocery store getting a box of macaroni and cheese for dinner.

"Are we sure it's safe for Nathaniel to do a show with you?"

"Why wouldn't it be?"

"Because he's hiding, right? He still asks me to make his checks out to cash."

"Not everybody has a bank account."

"Do you really think Nathaniel doesn't have a bank account?" Patrick asks. "He wears penny loafers and told me to pick up a bottle of chianti the next time I pass a wine shop." Patrick can come up with ways someone like that might fall on hard times, but not for them to stay there.

"What would he be hiding from?"

The problem is, Patrick doesn't know.

When school gets out for the summer, Patrick starts paying Iris to work the cash register from six to closing three nights a week. Patrick swears he used to run the place single-handed, but now he's barely getting by.

Somehow, word got out that Suzie Larkin is sometimes behind the cash register or playing the guitar in the back of the shop. It was only a matter of time: she's been on *Ed Sullivan* and her face is on the covers of record albums owned by a hell of a lot of people. But the people who stop by to gawk at her don't usually buy anything, so that doesn't explain why the shop is bringing in twenty percent more this year than it did last summer. Maybe it's the free coffee. Maybe it's the dog. Maybe it's just that Nathaniel's better at talking to customers than Patrick ever was.

"She's robbing you blind," Mrs. Valdez says one night after Iris helps close the shop. "Tell me you aren't paying that child two dollars an hour."

"After taxes, she's only collecting something like minimum wage." He's kind of proud of himself for having figured out payroll tax.

Mrs. Valdez frowns at him for a long moment. "I think you really do believe that's how minimum wage works," she finally says. "All right, let my daughter shake you down. It's no skin off my back."

Patrick isn't letting a high school student—however responsible—run the shop alone, not in a city where businesses get held up at gunpoint practically every day of the week. But if Susan's in the shop, and one of Iris's parents is upstairs, Patrick thinks it's all right to step out for an hour or two.

"Want to go for a walk?" he asks Nathaniel.

"Only if we can stop at the barbershop." He runs a hand through his hair. "I can't take it anymore." Nathaniel's hair is long enough now to be nearly at his chin, and he fidgets with it constantly.

Patrick takes him to his own barber, who wastes no time telling Patrick he's the one who needs a haircut. "Not today, Bill," he says.

"You looks respectable," Patrick says fifteen minutes later, when half of Nathaniel's hair is all over the barbershop floor.

"That doesn't sound like a compliment." Nathaniel's gaze is fixed on his reflection, as he turns his head this way and that. He has a neat side part, honey-brown hair sweeping over his forehead and just barely reaching his collar. Sometimes Patrick looks at Nathaniel and sees the ghost of whoever he used to be.

"I think the usual word is distinguished," Patrick says.

"For pity's sake, you can call me distinguished when I

turn forty, which isn't for another two months, thank you very much." Nathaniel gets to his feet, pays the barber, dusts some hair off his trousers, and heads out to the street.

"The other word is pretty," Patrick says, once the barber shop door is shut behind them. He nearly said handsome, which would have been accurate, but less precise, and a lot less loaded.

"I think that expired ten years ago," Nathaniel says.

"No, I don't think it did."

Nathaniel runs a hand through his hair. "It's still longer than I used to keep it."

"We just need to get you some beads and a scarf to tie around your head and you'll be a regular hippie."

Patrick didn't have any particular destination in mind, but now he's thinking of strands of beads and scarves with psychedelic prints. "Let's go to St. Marks Place." The other day, Susan and Nathaniel went to the Museum of Modern Art. This, Patrick figures, will be a nice counterbalance, culturally speaking.

To get there, they walk past Washington Square Park, which is somewhat depopulated now that the college kids are home for the summer. There are still grass smoking hippies and folk singers, but an equal number of old men playing chess, children balancing on the edge of the fountain, and middle-aged couples walking their dogs.

"The old store was a few blocks up from here," Patrick says once they've reached Astor Place.

"Show me."

There used to be dozens of secondhand bookstores up and down Fourth Avenue between Union Square and Astor Place. Squinting, Patrick can only make out a few that have held on.

Now an art gallery is on the ground floor of the old building, and in an upstairs window is a sign for an employment agency. Next door, the windows are soaped up.

"I swear it never got above sixty degrees all winter, and Mrs. Kaplan used to keep the upstairs lights off unless a customer wanted to go up there. The new place is a stately pleasure dome."

There's nothing to look at, but Patrick doesn't move. This old shop is the first place Patrick felt safe. They'd moved everything that mattered to Jones Street, but when he looks inside the shop window, he can imagine that he's seeing the three-legged stool where he sat while Mrs. Kaplan stitched him up like there was nothing unusual about it. He'd been nearly delirious with hunger and beside himself with shame. The future that had once been laid out neatly in front of him was nothing but a gaping pit, and Mrs. Kaplan chattered about the best deli for corned beef and asked him what he liked to read. All he could think was that this must be what it was like to have a grandmother.

They head back toward St. Marks, and it's like they've stepped into another dimension. Gathered on stoops and in clusters on the sidewalk are some of the same people you see in Washington Square Park: men with long hair, women in long skirts, a feeling that maybe everyone could do with a shower and a trip to the laundromat. But there's a harder edge here, a sense that the squalor is intentional and cultivated, that it's something more pointed than an aesthetic designed to trouble people over thirty-five. Washington Square is filled with hippies. These people are radicals.

Patrick glances over at Nathaniel, who isn't looking

around but is taking it in anyway; he isn't a man who needs to stare in order to get the lay of the land.

"Want an egg cream?" Patrick asks. His first apartment was an illegal loft conversion nearby on Astor Place. There was a dive bar on St. Marks that wasn't exactly a gay bar but was still gay enough that cruising was a sure thing. One night, he and the man who'd picked him up went to get an egg cream at Gem Spa. Patrick had the sense that everyone in the place had either just committed some kind of misdemeanor or was on the way to do one. But when he'd come back during the day, school kids and old ladies sat at the soda fountain, innocently drinking milkshakes out of straws.

"I have no idea what that is," Nathaniel says, probably because they don't have egg creams anywhere other than soda fountains in New York.

"It's like a milkshake but without milk or ice cream, and its carbonated."

"You can't be serious."

"Deadly."

Near the cash register, there's a rack of mimeographed pamphlets for sale. While they're waiting for their egg creams, Nathaniel begins picking up the pamphlets and examining them. Over his shoulder, Patrick sees that they aren't pamphlets, but underground newspapers and zines that range from anti-war manifestos to collections of poetry. Susan once mailed him a zine put out by San Francisco hustlers and transsexuals. Patrick was sure they'd both get arrested for breaking federal obscenity laws, but he'd read that thing from cover to cover and then over again before passing it on to Jerome.

Nathaniel slides a few coins across the counter and chooses a few zines apparently at random, then tucks them under his arm while he bemusedly sips his egg cream.

It isn't a date—Patrick doesn't know how it could be, when they do this kind of thing all the time. It had been like this during the baseball game, too, like there's something bubbling between them. He feels like that all the time, but maybe bringing that sensation outside and into the light of day reveals it as something worth noticing, something that adds up to more than a few kisses.

They take their time walking home. It's midsummer, and the sun's still out. Their hands brush with every stride.

Before this year, Patrick would wake up early nearly every Saturday morning to scour estate sales. He checked the classifieds in the *Times* and some of the downstate newspapers, then borrowed Mrs. Kaplan's station wagon in case he found more books than he could carry home. If he played his cards right, he could return her car and be back in the city to open the shop by noon.

Now that they're settling into something like a rhythm, Patrick's started going to sales again. This morning he drove up to an estate sale in Dutchess County and took his time driving home, stopping at junk shops and church sales. It's nearly three in the afternoon when he parks the car on Jones Street.

As soon as he gets out of the car, he can hear the music. They must have left the door open to take advantage of the weather. He opens the trunk and lifts out the milk crate of books he bought that morning, trying to place the song that's coming from the shop.

Nathaniel's sitting at the cash register playing Susan's old guitar, and Susan's playing a new guitar on a beanbag chair that absolutely wasn't there a few days ago. Eleanor's asleep in the carriage.

When Patrick realizes what they're playing, he nearly laughs. It's an appallingly folksy rendition of Stevie Wonder's "I Was Made to Love Her."

"This is terrible," Mrs. Valdez says, walking into the shop a few minutes later. She still has on her nurse's uniform and it looks like she's coming home from a long shift.

"I'm passing around a petition to make them stop," Patrick says, heading to the back of the shop to pour her a cup of coffee.

"I'll sign it," Mrs. Valdez says.

"So mean," Nathaniel says, but he and Susan have a wordless conversation and start playing one of the prettier murder ballads. The dog nudges Patrick's leg until Patrick scratches his head.

He knows it isn't forever; he knows they'll leave. But today he isn't letting that fact stop him from feeling almost unfairly lucky.

16

Walt can usually be relied on to sleep until somebody jangles his leash at him, so Patrick isn't expecting to wake up to a wet nose in his face and the sound of whimpering. When Patrick opens his eyes, Walt is staring tragically at him. It's barely light out.

"All right, all right." Patrick scrambles to put on some pants and shoes, then snaps the leash on Walt's collar and opens the apartment door as quietly as possible so they don't wake Nathaniel. Walt tugs at the leash. Usually Walt has to be practically dragged around the block in the morning, then passes back out a few minutes after they come home. Whatever labor union he belongs to regards forty-five minutes as the longest shift anyone can work without a nap.

But today Walt is bounding down the stairs faster than Patrick would like, when Patrick stops dead, the leash going taut in his hand. Books are all over the floor. It looks like the shop's been ransacked.

And the sound—he can hear the traffic coming from Bleecker. The front window is smashed, and there's glass all over the floor.

Patrick drops the leash and runs back upstairs to check the safe. It's closed. The glass case, however, is empty, one of its sides shattered.

He should call the police. That's what you do when there's a break-in, right? You call the cops, and they take down your name and contact information and don't do anything about it other than notice if you have a record. Practically everybody he knows has had a burglary in their building at some point, and all the police have done is confirm that, yes, there sure are a lot of burglaries in the city these days, have you thought about putting in an extra lock?

Walt starts poking his nose into Patrick's leg, which puts Patrick in mind of the only thing that's clear: dogs need to get walked no matter what. He picks Walt up so he doesn't get glass in his paws and only puts him down on the sidewalk when he's sure there aren't any shards of glass.

When he gets back, he finds Nathaniel standing in front of the cash register, ashen.

"There you are," Nathaniel says. "I thought you'd been—I don't even know what I thought. Don't you ever, ever do that again."

Nathaniel gets peeved and cross every day of his life but this is something else. "Don't disappear after the shop's been robbed?" Patrick asks, aiming for levity. He carries Walt into the kitchen and puts him down, then gives him a bowl of dog food. Nathaniel follows them, cornering Patrick against the counter.

"Yes! These are things nobody should need to tell you. I was worried sick." His fists are clenched and he looks furious.

"I spaced out," he says. "I wasn't thinking."

"That much is clear!" Nathaniel's hands are on Patrick's chest, now, his fingers digging into the fabric of his shirt and into Patrick's skin like he needs the proof that Patrick is really there. "Think of how you'd feel if you woke up and the shop was in mayhem and I was gone."

Patrick shudders. He takes Nathaniel's hands in his own. "I would have had a heart attack." He thinks he nearly did, just imagining it. Maybe if he were a little less frightened, a little less addled by the break-in, he'd be warier about how they're standing here, admitting— something. That they care about one another? That's hardly an admission. What, after all, have they been doing for the past few months, if not caring for each other? That isn't a secret.

But Patrick learned long ago not to let his happiness depend on anyone caring for him. Or so he thought— clearly the lesson hadn't stuck. Nathaniel bends his head and presses his lips to Patrick's knuckles and the sensation reverberates through Patrick's body, seismic.

"What did they take?" Nathaniel asks, disorientingly practical while Patrick's mind is still reeling from the shock of what Nathaniel just did, his thoughts ricocheting between imagining Nathaniel being hurt and the fact of him safe and close and having just touched Patrick in a way that doesn't allow any misinterpretation. Nathaniel drops Patrick's hands. "What did they take?" he repeats.

Patrick tries to get himself under control. "Everything in the glass case. Everything in the cash register, but that was only twenty dollars because I went to the bank yesterday. The typewriter. The safe is still locked."

"That's all?"

"Who knows? I can't exactly tell what's missing when half the books downstairs are in a heap on the floor."

"What about your files?"

"My *files?*" Patrick can't imagine what burglars would think they'd find in the file cabinet of a book dealer. Still, he turns toward the cabinet. It's on its side, its contents all over the floor.

Nathaniel takes a breath, lets it out. "Why would they take your typewriter?"

"Pawn shops are full of stolen typewriters. They're easy to grab, hard to identify as stolen." It isn't even the first time Patrick's had a typewriter stolen.

"Hmm," Nathaniel says, sounding skeptical.

Patrick doesn't know what there is to be skeptical about. It's a straightforward burglary, textbook in every way. The thieves grabbed whatever was portable and valuable, including some books—putting something in a glass case is a great way to let the world know that it's worth something.

Patrick calls Mrs. Kaplan, then calls the police, because they'll need a police report to collect on their insurance policy. She gives him the name of a glazier to fix the front window and the glass case.

"What happened here?" Susan asks when she comes down.

"We had a break-in," Patrick says. "Just the shop, not the apartment."

When he tells the Valdezes there was a break-in, they seem wildly unconcerned. They've lived in New York a lot longer than he has. Mr. Valdez shows him the police lock he has on the door, a metal pole that fits into the floor.

Patrick always thought this was paranoid, but then again he's always had doors too flimsy for that kind of system to make sense. The door to Susan's apartment is solid wood. He calls a locksmith right away.

Mrs. Kaplan gets there at the same time as the police. The cops take some pictures, act suspicious, complain about junkies, and leave before it's even noon.

"Thank you," Patrick tells Mrs. Kaplan. She didn't have to drive out here during rush hour to talk to the cops, when that's rightfully Patrick's responsibility.

"Nonsense. This isn't the first time I've had to deal with the police. There was a rock through the window in 1922, some teenage hooligans in 1938, and a hold-up in—it must have been '56 or '57, because Abe was gone and you weren't around yet."

Patrick has already heard all those stories, but he'd bet that Mrs. Kaplan really came because she knows Patrick doesn't like cops. Nobody with a record wants to talk to cops. It doesn't matter that Patrick's rap sheet consists of one count of disorderly conduct—that's what they charge everyone with who gets caught in a raid—and not anything to do with theft.

"Now," Mrs. Kaplan says, "somebody ought to tell Nathaniel that the coast is clear." Nathaniel made himself scarce as soon as the cops arrived. That's definitely something that Patrick ought to be worried about, but he has enough to worry about right now—that first edition of *Manhattan Transfer* he bought from Gary was in the glass case, and the loss makes Patrick's skin crawl.

He'd been waiting for a chance to get Mrs. Kaplan alone to ask her where she found Nathaniel, but right now he doesn't care. Nathaniel can keep his damn secrets; they aren't hurting anybody. And maybe Patrick doesn't want to know.

"I'll get him," Susan says. "He's in my apartment."

"I'll drive you back home," Patrick offers Mrs. Kaplan.

"I'll drive myself later on. You look like you'd break the steering wheel in two, and you have enough to do," she says, gesturing at the mess in the store. "Don't you have anything to drink around here?"

"It's barely noon."

"Put it in your coffee," Mrs. Kaplan says.

"I'll bring down the Ballantine's!" Susan shouts from the stairs.

It's going to take the rest of the day to get the books back on the right shelves. There isn't any point in opening, but Nathaniel goes to the Italian bakery anyway and comes back with three big white cardboard boxes filled with pastries; he also comes back looking only the slightest bit shaken, even though he went by himself. Patrick watches him take some dishes out of the kitchen and arrange them on the table by the door, alongside the coffeepot and the cups and that stupid porcelain milk pitcher.

"I wanted something nice," Nathaniel says by way of explanation. That apparently means spending too much money on snacks for customers who won't even buy anything, because the merchandise is mostly all over the floor.

Susan puts on some Motown. Nathaniel takes out the broom and borrows an extra dustpan from the dry cleaners across the street. Patrick puts the open bottle of Ballantine's next to the coffee and pastries, figuring that anyone who makes it that far into the store deserves it. The weather's warm enough that the breeze through the broken window is kind of nice.

It's the summer, so there's more foot traffic than

usual, even on a weekday. Some people look in, see chaos, and beat a hasty retreat. But a lot of regulars stay longer. After they help themselves to coffee and a pastry and gasp and cluck about the break-in, most of them shelve some books. Jerome comes by in street clothes but with the makeup only partly scraped off his face, clearly on his way home from wherever he spent the night. "Poor darling," he says, apparently to the store itself, and shelves all the nineteenth-century French novels.

Beverly, a *Times* reporter a few years older than Patrick and Susan, comes in wearing a three-piece suit that has to be sweltering on such a warm day, but she stays long enough to weed out some of the more damaged books and stack them off to the side.

Viv is on the verge of tears to see the shop in such a state. "I came in to ask if you had a bulletin board, but you have your hands full."

"We do have a bulletin board," Nathaniel tells her, and points to the wall behind the cash register. Right now, the bulletin board has a single piece of yellowed paper tacked to it, reading "NO RETURNS" in Patrick's handwriting; it's been there for so long that the edges are starting to curl. The bulletin board isn't a community message board. Except, apparently it is, because Nathaniel tacks up a note saying a 45-year-old woman is looking for a roommate, written in a slanting blue copperplate that must be Viv's handwriting.

John, a distractingly handsome square-jawed twentysomething who really isn't Patrick's type, but probably could be for an hour or two, comes in that afternoon. "Oh no," he says. "What happened?"

"We had a break-in," Patrick says. He thought that much was obvious. They didn't have a localized earthquake.

John puts a few books away. Nathaniel reshelves every one of them.

"I'm trying to figure out who's less subtle, Nathaniel or Captain America over there." Susan asks.

Patrick snorts. "Nathaniel's just being territorial."

"Is he, now?" Eleanor, in a shawl tied around Susan's back, tries to grab every book that comes within reach of her chubby fingers. "Is Captain America waiting for you to make a move?" Susan asks.

"I can't get a read on what he's doing. And he'd be a lot of trouble, anyway."

"How so?"

"Look at him. That is a man who's voting for Nixon. He's probably deep in the closet, probably hates himself a little. And I'm sorry, but I can't fuck someone who doesn't think we deserve to fuck legally and without feeling bad about it."

"How can you tell?" Susan asks. "His hair? His clothes?"

"You get to know the type."

"Is Nathaniel that type?"

Patrick hesitates. "Used to be."

They both glance over to where Nathaniel has stopped tailing John and is instead lightly flirting with a pair of elderly women in a way that Patrick can somehow identify as distinctly gay.

Patrick lowers his voice even more, nearly to a whisper. "He was married."

"I thought so. The two of you…"

Patrick hasn't mentioned anything to Susan about him and Nathaniel. For one thing, it's only been two kisses. But mostly he feels like he'd need to run it by Nathaniel first; Susan's his friend too. And he can't figure out how to ask whether he's allowed to tell his friend about two kisses without it sounding extremely junior high.

But he also isn't going to lie to Susan. "How bad is it that he works for me?"

"He can get work as a session musician whenever he wants, earning more than you pay him, and he knows it. He also knows he can have my spare room if he ever needs it."

"You've talked about this with him?"

"I've talked about this *at* him."

They're friends; of course Susan is looking out for him. But a few months ago she could barely take care of herself, and a few months ago Nathaniel didn't have anybody in the world. And now they all have one other, a thought that ordinarily would be too sentimental for Patrick to entertain, but it's been a long and dramatic day, so he kisses Susan's forehead and Eleanor's cheek.

Patrick isn't surprised to find Nathaniel awake late that night. He's lying on the sofa, his head on the armrest, a book face down on his chest and the flashlight dangling from his hand. When he sees Patrick, he tucks his legs up. Patrick sits and hauls Nathaniel's legs onto his lap. He's being a little touchier than he'd usually be, but he feels like they crossed some kind of Rubicon that morning.

"Want to watch television?" Patrick asks.

"It's nearly one. There won't be anything on."

"Want to talk about it?"

"Not at all," Nathaniel says. Patrick squeezes his ankle. The book Nathaniel isn't reading is *Alpha Centauri or Die!*, Patrick's own paperback copy from the shelf a few inches from Nathaniel's head. From the looks of it, he hasn't gotten further than the title page.

"I'm starving," Nathaniel says a few minutes later.

"There's still some fried rice downstairs," Patrick says, not feeling particularly thrilled about cold rice and even less thrilled about heating it up.

"I don't want fried rice. I want pancakes."

"Pancakes," Patrick repeats, his mouth watering at the thought. "We might have ingredients." He tries to remember if he's ever bought flour. Probably not.

"Having to make them ourselves would ruin it."

Nobody has ever been more correct about anything. "We could go out. The Waverly is open."

"Let's go someplace new."

"There's a twenty-four-hour diner on Twenty-second Street, if you're up for a walk."

They put on shoes and jackets and head toward Eighth Avenue. This neighborhood doesn't really quiet down until last call at four o'clock, and then it wakes up again two hours later, so right now there are about the same number of people on the sidewalks as you'd see in a smaller city in the middle of the afternoon.

When they get to Twenty-second Street, there's no sign of a diner, twenty-four-hour or otherwise. Either he got the location wrong or the diner shut down.

"There'll be something at Times Square, if you don't mind walking twenty minutes more. And if you don't mind a little sordidness."

"I love sordidness almost as much as I love pancakes."

Patrick snorts.

"I'm serious. I like the reminder that there's another way."

"Another way from what?"

"The right way," Nathaniel says, the word *right* soaked

through with scorn. "I wasted so much time making myself into the precise sort of person I thought I was supposed to be, and it didn't do me any good. It didn't do anyone any good."

It occurs to Patrick that whatever Nathaniel's doing right now, it's a choice. Whatever life he used to have, he could go back, or he could get steady work as a session musician. Instead he's sleeping in Patrick's miserable spare room and debating the finer points of guitar tuning with Susan. It might have started as a last resort but at some point Nathaniel decided to stay, or maybe just decided not to leave—or at least decided to stick around for a while.

"People don't always choose the other way, you know," Patrick says. "The hustlers and junkies might love the chance to have a pension and a mortgage."

"True." They're silent for a minute, the only sounds their shoes on the sidewalk and the sporadic hum of sparse nighttime traffic. "Did you make a choice?" Nathaniel asks.

"I dropped out of high school."

"Was that a choice?"

"I could have gone back to my aunt and uncle's house and finished school," Patrick says. "They didn't kick me out." He could have finished school; he could have done anything other than leave Michael alone with his aunt and uncle.

"You know," Nathaniel says, "you don't usually try to bullshit me."

"I could have gone back to school," Patrick repeats. "And I didn't." He used to think he should go to night school and maybe eventually get a college degree, but he had a job he liked; a degree seemed pointless. Sometimes he still thinks he should have tried anyway, should have taken the path that would lead toward a job at an insurance firm or someplace else boring and safe.

"Why not?"

That job at the insurance firm would have come with scrutiny and would have meant having a double life. Right now, Patrick doesn't have to hide, he doesn't have to worry about getting fired, he doesn't even have to worry about awkward interactions with his colleagues. "I think I would have been miserable if I'd tried to have that kind of life," Patrick says, very gently.

As they get further uptown, the sidewalks empty out. He wouldn't think twice if he was by himself. He's never been mugged, maybe because of his size or because he doesn't look like someone who has money, or maybe he's just gotten lucky. "Do you want to turn around and go to the Waverly?"

"Let's keep going," Nathaniel says.

"It's seedy," Patrick says when they get closer. "Just warning you. There are hustlers and prostitutes. Peep shows. Dirty movies."

Nathaniel makes a dismissive sound, but when they reach Times Square he goes still, looking up at the flashing signs, the billboards, the lights. There's an enormous advertisement for Gordon's, in which a bottle about the size of a city bus pours gin into a rocks glass. Right next to it is a billboard for another liquor. There are also at least four shoe stores, for some reason.

Patrick turns away from the signs and looks at Nathaniel, his face illuminated by the yellow lights.

"There's the diner," Nathaniel says.

It has exactly the sort of clientèle you'd expect at this hour: prostitutes, alone or in pairs; a few solitary middle-aged men; a group of giggling kids who look like they stopped here on the way home from a nightclub; some men in coveralls having lunch during the night shift. It's not a cheerful crowd, but most places get a little moody during that no man's land between late night and early morning. The air is thick with cigarette smoke and burned coffee. Frank Sinatra plays tinnily on the radio.

"Has it always been like this?" Nathaniel asks after they order their pancakes. Patrick doesn't need him to clarify exactly what he means.

"For the past ten years, maybe fifteen years, at least," Patrick says. "When I was in high school, there was an article in the paper about how this area was filled with undesirables, and I knew what that meant"—he points both thumbs at himself—"so I got on the train as soon as school let out."

"Didn't waste any time."

"It said something about how 'experts' agree that homosexuality has increased in the area, and I wasn't going to argue with experts."

"You're a reasonable man," Nathaniel agrees.

"The article went on and on about men in tight pants and makeup and I swear to god no travel agency has ever done a better job of selling a place. They practically gave the exact address—which entrance to which subway stop—where you could find the highest concentration of undesirables. It was like a treasure map."

Nathaniel laughs, bright and easy. After this morning it feels like a miracle. "What happened?"

"There must have been ten other men who read the same article. It was like the gay Bat Signal. We were all looking at one another and trying to find some degeneracy and I wound up getting picked up by one of the other tourists." It's a wonder nobody got arrested. The whole neighborhood must have been swarming with cops.

The man who picked him up told him about a bar on Charles Street. A few weeks later, Patrick got back on the train after finishing his homework on a Friday afternoon. He went to that bar, got arrested in a raid, was handcuffed and booked, and when he called his aunt and uncle to bail him out, they said he'd made his bed and could sleep in it. He'd just turned eighteen. He's about to tell some version of that story to Nathaniel, but Nathaniel speaks first.

"It's like what Viv was saying about Whitman," Nathaniel says. "He was searching for other queer men. It's all over his poems. What's the line—I wonder if other men have these feelings?"

Patrick stares at him. The line is something like *I am ashamed—but it is useless—I am what I am.* And then *Hours of my torment—I wonder if other men ever have the like, out of the like feelings.* It's a poem about heartbreak, but specifically and recognizably queer heartbreak.

"He thought Shakespeare was queer," Nathaniel goes on. "And he wanted people to look back and remember that he loved men. It's all the same thing. He was always looking, just like you were looking."

Nobody falls in love in a diner, accompanied by the smell of fake maple syrup and the chatter of tired prostitutes. And maybe Patrick hasn't, either. Maybe it happened weeks ago, and he's only noticing now. There's nothing new in his heart, but now it has a name.

"What," Nathaniel says, when a minute passes and Patrick hasn't said anything, "I do pay attention when you talk. And I read the things you leave around the shop."

"I know," Patrick says. "I just wasn't expecting you to draw a straight line from Shakespeare to me getting blown in the pizzeria across the street."

Nathaniel looks over his shoulder, like he needs to catch a glimpse of this pizzeria, this landmark of queer existence. Patrick starts to laugh. He muffles it in his paper napkin.

"It isn't there anymore," Patrick manages.

"They should put up a plaque," Nathaniel says, and that sets them both off.

"Come on," Patrick says after they've gotten themselves together and Nathaniel tosses a five-dollar bill on the table. "There's something else I want to show you."

Around the corner is a sort of five-and-dime, only it sells dirty magazines and has condoms that aren't even behind the counter. There are also racks and racks of pulp paperbacks.

"In the back," Patrick says, leading the way. "Ha. I knew it." There's a spinner rack of gay pulp fiction. One's called *Gay Cruise*, the cover featuring an uncharacteristic number of fully clothed men. *Gay Whore* has significantly less clothing on the cover. There are several others, all obviously gay and obviously pornographic.

"I can't believe these exist," Nathaniel breathes, almost starry-eyed at the sight of so much lurid gay smut. It's two of his favorite things: paperback novels and—Patrick's starting to realize—a touch of seediness. More than a touch, in this instance.

"You can get them at a couple drugstores in our neighborhood," Patrick says, preening a little that he got this right, that Nathaniel likes this as much as Patrick thought he would. "But here—"

"You can't beat the ambiance," Nathaniel agrees.

"Exactly. They're not my cup of tea—some are violent, and you can't tell from the cover what you're going to get—but I'm going to buy some for Luke. He loves them." Realizing that it might sound strange to send pornography across the country to his ex-boyfriend, he adds, "I don't know if he can get the same books in California."

They both yawn all the way home, and yawn some more as Patrick lets them into the building.

"What if I don't brush my teeth?" Patrick asks, stumbling toward his bedroom.

Nathaniel redirects him toward the bathroom. "Don't get cavities."

"Hey, Patrick," Nathaniel says when he's done brushing his own teeth, "Thanks. That was fun."

"And educational?"

"Of course." His gaze drops to Patrick's mouth, and Patrick catches his breath, suddenly wide awake. He's been waiting for the next time, letting the anticipation simmer every time Nathaniel brushes his shoulder or holds eye contact. But, not wanting to push, he's been waiting for Nathaniel take the lead.

They're standing awfully close, close enough that you start to notice all the places your hands aren't. You spend the vast majority of your life with no doubts as to where your hands belong, but put someone less than a foot away from you and the fact that at least one of your hands isn't on that person's body becomes a glaring omission. At least that's how it feels for Patrick.

And for Nathaniel, too, apparently, because he puts a hand on Patrick's hip. It's feather light, not reeling him in, not doing much of anything except resting there. That's as much of a green light as Patrick needs.

Their lips meet in the cautious way that Patrick's been expecting, but before now Nathaniel has kept his hands to the same places he might touch Patrick even if they weren't kissing: his arms, his shoulders, maybe his back. Now, his fingertips are on Patrick's jaw, his cheek; he's feeling Patrick's beard. Patrick lets his own hands land on Nathaniel's waist. His fingers brush the bare skin between the hem of his t-shirt and the waist of his pajama pants. When Nathaniel draws in a breath, Patrick feels it on his own lips.

This time, Nathaniel kisses back. He kisses the way he does everything else: thorough and precise. It feels like he's inventing the concept of kissing from scratch.

Patrick tries remind himself that Nathaniel is figuring things out. Patrick happens to be the person who's around to figure things out with. But then he remembers the way Nathaniel had held on to him that morning after the break-in, the way he'd kissed Patrick's knuckles.

The kiss is soft and slow, worryingly tender, a kiss under a yellow porch light at the end of a date. It's a kiss by the luggage carousel, after someone's finally come back. It's the sort of kiss Patrick has always known is for other people.

Mrs. Kaplan comes back a few days later to inspect the work the glazier did on the front window and the glass case.

"Good as new," she says as she surveys the shop: books back where they belong, window repaired, new typewriter on Patrick's desk. "Oh, isn't this nice." She picks up the new Rolodex. The old one was cracked beyond repair when the cash register landed on it. Susan bought a new one, made of sturdy metal, and transferred all Patrick's addresses, rewriting the cards that were torn or crumpled. That morning he'd looked up the address of a Thomas Wolfe collector to send them a quote on a fine first of *Look Homeward, Angel*, only to find their address written out in Susan's handwriting.

It'll be strange, months from now, years from now, to come across her loopy scrawl, unchanged since the seventh grade. Everyone who's worked in the shop has left their trace. On the flyleaf of some of the older stock, the price is written in an unfamiliar hand that must have belonged to Mr. Kaplan. It was Gary, the book scout, who decided fiction had to be organized by period, and now Patrick wouldn't be able to find anything if they adopted a more sensible strategy. Laura, a girl who stayed with Mrs. Kaplan for a few weeks in 1965, used random pieces of paper to level all the bookcases so they'd stop wobbling on the uneven floors; sometimes he'll come across some playing cards or a folded envelope and think of her as he shoves it back into place. People come; people go. Patrick knows this. He doesn't like to think of a time when Susan's handwriting will be her only presence in the shop. When Nathaniel goes, there won't be a single corner of the shop that Patrick can stand to look at.

Mrs. Kaplan stays long enough to have Chinese takeout with them for dinner. It's the third time that week they've had Chinese food. Patrick is starting to worry that someone in this household will have to learn to cook.

It's dark, so Patrick drives Mrs. Kaplan back home. "You haven't sent me anyone in a while." He doesn't mean to sound so petulant.

"I think you have your hands full," Mrs. Kaplan says. "Nathaniel's settling in well?" She asked him the same question months ago.

"He's great." It's the same answer he gave the last time she asked.

She's quiet for a moment, the only sound the echoey

thrum of traffic in the Queens Midtown Tunnel. He knows it's a tactic but he falls for it every time.

"I don't know what we'd have done without him. He's good with Eleanor," Patrick goes on. "And Susan."

"And you?" she asks.

He can't tell whether she means anything by it. She's always known about him. It was Mrs. Kaplan who bailed him out of jail. Another man who'd been caught in the raid had been talking to Patrick in the cell, trying to calm him down. He'd used his phone call to get in touch with Mrs. Kaplan and asked her to bail Patrick out too. Last Patrick heard, he was working in a secondhand bookstore in Tucson.

As soon as Patrick started working for Mrs. Kaplan, she started dropping pointed references to "people like that" who she'd known over the years, as if she were giving him her credentials: gay book collectors, lesbian vaudeville stars, her nephew Roger in Wilmington and that nice man he lives with. Patrick had been—well, mostly he'd been mortified, but he'd appreciated the sentiment.

At a traffic light he slants her a look that he hopes is sufficiently severe, and she beams innocently back at him.

"Where'd you find him?" Patrick asks. At this point, he's all too aware that no answer she gives will change anything.

"Rude," she says, with no heat in it. "Like he's a penny I picked up off the sidewalk." She turns on the radio and pretends to be fascinated by the Mets game.

"Do you even know his last name?"

"Why, it's Smith," she says, not particularly bothering to make it sound like anything other than bullshit. "Does it matter?"

"I don't even know him. I don't know anything about

him. But I—" He swallows and decides *to hell with it*. "I'm in pretty deep, I think."

"I knew Abe for two months before we got married. My parents liked him, he had steady work, and he made me laugh. Did I know him? Maybe not. Did I love him? Who knows. I loved him for the next forty years, though, I can tell you that much." She shrugs. "Knowing someone isn't the same as knowing facts."

Patrick can't imagine what it's like to meet someone and decide you're going to trust them for the rest of your life.

"He isn't being honest," Patrick says. Dishonesty's always made his skin crawl, and Mrs. Kaplan knows it.

"You don't seem to care."

He groans, because she's right. That's the worst part. He's always relied on that distaste for bullshit to keep him safe from all the frauds; it's his own personal burglar alarm and for some reason Nathaniel isn't tripping the wire.

Patrick sees Mrs. Kaplan inside, waves away her offer of money for cab fare home but takes a jar of chicken soup. He leaves her with three books: a du Maurier that Nathaniel recommended, Patrick's own copy of Richard Brautigan's *Trout Fishing in America*, and a paperback mystery about a literature professor who solves murders.

"Nathaniel came into the shop after getting mugged," Mrs. Kaplan says as Patrick's getting ready to head out the door. "I think you were at an estate sale. End of January."

When he gets home, it's late enough that he expects Nathaniel to be asleep, but the apartment's empty. At Susan's door, he can hear the muffled sounds of a television. He isn't sure whether to knock or let himself in, so he knocks lightly before turning his key in the lock.

They're on the couch, Nathaniel's head on Susan's

shoulder, his eyes shut and his mouth half open. Eleanor's on Susan's lap, also asleep.

"Turn the TV off," Susan whispers. "I'm trapped."

Patrick puts the jar of soup into Susan's refrigerator, then turns the dial until the television clicks off.

"Come here," she says, patting the sofa cushion. "Closer. Jeez, Patrick, I took a shower and everything, get over here."

He does as he's told, until Susan's arm is around him, pulling him into a one-armed hug, Eleanor between them. "This is platonic cuddling," she whispers, then tightens her arm when he tries to pull away. "We used to do this."

They'd stopped, maybe because she'd gotten serious with Michael and it was just too weird, maybe because Patrick got out of the habit of touching anybody except the men he brought home.

Loving Susan is easy and obvious, plain in a way that isn't covered by *friend* or *family* and made *sister-in-law* feel like an inside joke. Maybe she got grandfathered in before he forgot how to care about people—not just care *for* them with bus tickets and sandwiches, but care *about* them in a way that feels like putting cash on a card table.

"So loud," Nathaniel mutters from Susan's other side. "Harridan." Patrick feels like he's waiting for the roulette wheel to stop spinning, his heart in his throat, his wallet empty; it isn't even a new feeling, where Nathaniel is concerned.

"Stop thinking," Susan says. "You aren't any good at it." He kisses the top of her head. She smells like baby formula and incense. So does he, probably. When he slides his arms around her, her chin digs into his shoulder and her hair gets in his mouth, just like it always did.

17

A hell of a lot of people manage to spend years of their lives collecting books without noticing that most books aren't particularly valuable, and virtually anything you do to them is only going to make them worth even less. Patrick's lost count of the number of people who've told him about the whole room they have—on the Upper West Side, in Ossining, at their summer house on the Cape—that's filled with books. Patrick could tell them that he, too, has rooms full of books and it's not like people are beating down the door to pay a fortune for most of them.

Still, he humors collectors, at least those within a subway ride, because book people don't usually consider parting with their collections unless they're hard up for either money or space. Patrick will comb through what they've got and offer a fair price for anything he thinks he can sell, as long as he doesn't already have multiple copies of it in stock.

Answering that last question was always a bit of a mystery. Did he still have those three leather-bound copies of *The Golden Bowl*, or had he sold them? Or was it *The Bostonians*? But Nathaniel finished his inventory, and Patrick now has an alphabetized list of nearly all his books. It's eighty pages long, typed. Nathaniel punched holes along the side and bound it with brass brads.

"But what if I buy more books," Patrick had asked.

"You'll pencil them in and cross off whatever you sell. Then you'll retype an updated list next summer. Or I will." The prospect of retyping eighty pages brings Patrick no joy, but the idea that Nathaniel might be around this time next year is good enough that he doesn't care.

So when Patrick enters Viv's apartment, he can tell almost right away that he'll need to come back with a hand truck.

"The problem," he tells her, "is that you and I have identical taste." Clearly, she had the right idea with all that muttering about coals to Newcastle. "I'm going to go broke today."

He spends the entire morning going through her shelves. She has first editions of Virginia Woolf, Djuna Barnes, Gertrude Stein, Carson McCullers, and Anaïs Nin. None of them are perfect. They were clearly bought to read, and some have underlinings and dogeared pages. Some have "Maryanne Verdano" written on the flyleaf in faded blue ink. Patrick doesn't have the heart to tell Viv that all these signs of use detract from a book's value. Instead he offers her what he thinks is a fair amount for a total of fifty books and the standard half the cover price for another hundred.

She sighs. "I don't know what I'll do with the rest. I can't take all these books with me, and I can't afford this place on my own."

"Nathaniel will be sorry to see you go."

"I'm only moving to Barrow Street. You'll see more of me than ever."

He declines her offer of a drink, writes her a check, suggests that she call that bookstore on Worth Street to unload the rest, and is about to leave when he sees another shelf in the doorway to the kitchen. This is the sort of apartment where bookshelves have been shoved against every wall, wedged between every piece of furniture. It's a mode of living that Patrick's only too accustomed to.

He can see why she didn't draw his attention to these books in the first place. They're paperbacks, and not even nice-looking paperbacks. There isn't an unbroken spine among them.

"Are these Gothic romances? I don't mean *The Monk*. I mean the sort of books with women in nightgowns running away from creepy houses on the covers?" A closer inspection reveals that they are.

Viv sighs. "They were Maryanne's. I wasn't sure what to do with them, other than take them with me. I can't throw them out."

Patrick had assumed Viv and Maryanne broke up, but that isn't how you talk about someone who's still alive. He clears his throat. "Do they have sentimental value or are you willing to part with them?"

"Everything in this apartment has sentimental value, but I can't keep it all. I don't even want to keep it all."

"I'll take them all for…thirty percent of the cover price? Nathaniel's crazy about them. He'll be over the moon."

"Anything for Nathaniel." She has a little twinkle in her eye that lets Patrick know she assumes he and

Nathaniel are together. He's not going to correct her, because this isn't about the particular nuance of his and Nathaniel's friendship, and at this point he doesn't even know if she's wrong. It's about this woman giving her late partner's books to someone who will know exactly what they're getting.

Patrick takes another look at the shelf itself. It's shallow, the perfect depth for paperbacks. It has the rough look of something made by an eighth grader in woodshop. "I'll make you an offer on the shelf, too, if it's for sale."

He loads as many paperbacks as he can carry into a milk crate, promising to come back later in the week for the shelf and the rest of the books. "I'm not going to write you a check for the paperbacks," he says, taking out his wallet and counting out some bills. "Because this isn't a business expense."

No matter how many times Patrick attempts to lug home a milk crate filled with books, it's always heavier than he expects it to be. By the time he's shouldering open the door to the shop, he's sweaty and a little out of breath. Nathaniel's at Patrick's desk, mending a torn page with glue and wax paper the way Patrick taught him. Nathaniel isn't particularly interested in book repair, but this technique is a bit of a magic trick and doesn't require that much skill. He's showed Iris too.

"Walt tried to eat a bee," Nathaniel says. "Susan dosed him with hay fever medicine and he's sleeping it off upstairs." He puts down the paint brush he's using to apply the glue and looks up, taking a gratifying moment to let his gaze sweep over Patrick.

"These," Patrick says, putting the crate on the counter, "are for you. There's more where these came from."

Nathaniel's gaze darts between the books and Patrick's

rolled-up sleeves and then to his face. He lifts some of the books from the top of the crate and examines the next layer. It isn't the first time Patrick's bought him books. It is, however, a hell of a lot of books. It's extravagant, possibly even showy. This is the kind of gesture that's one level up from a dozen roses or a box of chocolates: it's a nice bracelet, or a bottle of perfume, if he's learned anything from Doris Day movies. He hadn't been thinking in those terms when he bought the books. He was only thinking that Nathaniel would love them. Patrick can't decide if that makes it better or worse.

"Thank you," Nathaniel says, getting to his feet.

"There's also a shelf."

Nathaniel comes out from behind the desk and flips the sign on the door to Closed, then slides the deadbolt and draws the blinds.

There's no preamble this time, just Nathaniel gripping Patrick's collar and pulling him in. The kiss is fast and hard, Nathaniel's mouth soft and wet and open for Patrick. Patrick gets a foot between Nathaniel's, nothing more than a thought, an invitation, and Nathaniel presses into Patrick's thigh. Nathaniel takes a step backward and Patrick follows, until Nathaniel is sitting on the edge of Patrick's desk, Patrick standing between his legs. Like this, Patrick looms over him. He has to tip Nathaniel's head back to kiss him. Nathaniel gets his hands on Patrick's belt loops and tugs. If Patrick had known that all it would take to get this kind of reaction was a crate full of tawdry paperbacks, he'd have cleared out the Worth Street bookstore of every damn book with a spooky house on the cover.

"Do you want—" Patrick starts, but Nathaniel pulls him close again, looking for friction. When he finds it they both groan.

Patrick's never had sex at work and he wasn't planning on starting today, but at this point he'll do whatever Nathaniel wants, however and wherever Nathaniel wants. Nathaniel wants to fuck in the shop? They'll fuck in the shop. He gets his hands under Nathaniel's ass and lifts him so they're pressing together at a better angle.

"We can, if you want," Patrick says into Nathaniel's ear. "Your call."

Nathaniel pulls back and looks at him. His mouth is red and wet, his hair rumpled. "I'm not using you."

"You could," Patrick says, maybe a little too quickly. He shifts his grip so Nathaniel is sitting on the desk again, and slides a hand up Nathaniel's back. "If you want."

Nathaniel makes a sound.

"Yeah?" Patrick asks. "You like that?"

"Maybe," Nathaniel says, breathless. "Yes. No. I don't know. I keep thinking about it."

"What do you think about?"

Nathaniel is quiet for a minute, his gaze darting helplessly between Patrick's eyes and mouth. "I know you'd make me feel good."

Patrick doesn't know if that was calculated to basically incapacitate him but that's what it does anyway. He kisses Nathaniel, breathless and desperate, fitting their bodies together as best he can. "That's what I want too. Can I make you feel good now?"

There's only the tiniest hesitation before Nathaniel says, "Please."

"Is the door upstairs locked?" Since the break-in, they've been careful about that. Nathaniel nods.

Patrick kisses Nathaniel again, hard, then undoes both their belts. He gets a hand under Nathaniel's shirt, seeking out the hidden skin at the small of his back, just getting Nathaniel used to the idea of Patrick's hands on him. They're just breathing into one another's mouths, hardly kissing at all. Patrick isn't sure what the right move is here. When he pulls Nathaniel out of his pants, he half expects Nathaniel to tell him to stop, but he just says Patrick's name, again and again.

It's nothing fancy—Patrick licks his palm and does what he's done more times than he can count—but his gaze keeps flicking between what he's doing with his hand and Nathaniel's face. When he slows down, Nathaniel makes an aggrieved sound, low and gratifying. When he tightens his grip, Nathaniel pants into his mouth.

"Patrick," Nathaniel says, warning.

"I've got you."

Nathaniel's perfectly quiet when he comes, nearly still, his eyes shut and his mouth half open, until he reaches into his shirt pocket and hands Patrick a handkerchief.

Patrick waits until Nathaniel's eyes are open, then showily licks his hand clean before returning Nathaniel's handkerchief to his pocket. Nathaniel looks like he might not be breathing.

"You," Nathaniel says, reaching for Patrick, less articulate than Patrick's ever seen him. "Let me. Show me."

And so Patrick shows him.

"Well, well, well," Susan says when Patrick and Nathaniel come over with a box of pizza for dinner. "What do we have here?" She sounds like the villain in a Saturday morning cartoon.

"What are you talking about?" Patrick asks, mainly to be difficult. It's not like they were going to try to keep this from her, but how the hell did she know as soon as she opened the door?

"You don't need to be a detective to figure this out, boys. Nathaniel, you look like somebody scrubbed your neck with steel wool. Patrick, you need to use hair conditioner in your beard."

"Oh my god," Patrick says, his hand going automatically to his beard.

"I'll lend you a bottle," Susan says cheerfully.

"I think we should play your song," Nathaniel says after they've eaten. They're in what's become their standard positions: Patrick with Eleanor on the floor, Nathaniel sprawled across the sofa, and Susan cross-legged in the armchair. Walt is prowling around the edges of the apartment like he's on security detail.

"What song?" Susan asks.

"'Take Me Home.'" That's the song you couldn't walk down the street without hearing last summer. The one Susan hates down to her toes.

Patrick looks up from where he's been trying to detach Eleanor's jaw from his collar. She's teething, and the only joy she has in life is gnawing on people's clothes.

"It's trash," Susan says.

"You wrote it. I checked the liner notes. Forget the horn section and the—"

"The xylophone," Susan says dolefully.

"Forget all that and look at the song you actually wrote." Nathaniel sits up and reaches for Susan's hand. "It isn't going away. You might as well make it yours again." He hasn't said that he likes the song, or even that it's any good. But he's right that the song isn't going anywhere— it's been a year since it came out, and radio stations aren't playing it as often as they used to, but they play it enough that you're never surprised to hear it.

Susan looks at him like she's been betrayed, and Patrick thinks she has a point. "We don't play love songs." Her fingers are wrapped tight around Nathaniel's.

The next afternoon, Patrick's sulkily unpacking and inventorying one of the mountain of boxes on the second floor, because Nathaniel's been bribing him with donuts every Sunday if he's unpacked a box that week. He's deciding what to do with copies of *Life* magazine from the thirties when the opening chords of that song drift in from the stairwell.

Glad for an excuse to abandon the books, Patrick quietly climbs the stairs. When he cracks open the door, he sees Nathaniel sitting on the sofa, Susan's guitar in his lap, playing the song. He's slowed it down, about as slow as you can get and still call it music. Patrick's no expert but he thinks it's in a different key, mellower but also a little unsettling. Patrick slips inside.

"A little faster, maybe," Susan says. And then, a few minutes later, "You're making it sound like something you'd play. I mean, it feels like the murder ballads and those pieces we've been tinkering with." By tinkering, she means actual songwriting. Patrick isn't counting, but there are probably six original songs they wrote together.

"You wrote it," Nathaniel says.

Susan lets out a shaky breath.

"Look," Nathaniel says. "I'll drop it if you want. But I've seen how you get when that song comes on and I want to help fix it before—"

"Before?" Susan asks. "You have somewhere to be?"

"There's nowhere I'd rather be," Nathaniel says, which is about ten times as earnest as he usually is. It's also not an answer to Susan's question.

The next morning, when Patrick stops by Susan's to take Eleanor, he finds Susan already awake and Eleanor still asleep in her crib, slack-jawed and fat-cheeked. Susan's eyes are bloodshot and puffy. Used tissues litter the bed.

"Stupid fucking song," she says.

"If you ask him to back off, he will. Or I can ask. He doesn't want you to be miserable."

"Michael loved that song, you know. I mean, it's sugary and has a catchy chorus, of course he loved it." Susan's never said outright that she wrote the song for Michael, but it was practically designed in a lab to appeal to him.

"He did love a chorus," Patrick agrees.

"Never met a chorus he didn't love." She's crying again, so he sits on the bed and puts an arm around her and lets her cry all over his shirt.

Patrick wants to know why, of the two and a half decades of memories he has of Michael, it's the dumb, mundane, slightly embarrassing ones that hurt the most. The other night he'd dreamed that he and Michael were sitting around, Michael whining about an overcooked burger while he stole all Patrick's fries. "Pat. *Pat*. Are you listening to me? Patpatpat. It's *charcoal*." He'd woken up, remembered, and the whole next day felt like he was unfolding that telegram for the first time. How is a man supposed to sleep when he has that waiting for him?

He has an inkling that his grief might stay fresh if he keeps brushing aside every awful thought that occurs to him. Maybe, if he made himself think about how much he misses his brother, and how he'd started missing his brother long before he went to Vietnam, then he'd be less torn up when that kind of thought shows up out of the blue. But when he tries to think about it, everything in his mind slams shut.

Still. He can do something.

"Right before the two of you started dating," he says, his voice steadier than he expects it to be, "he couldn't shut up about you." At that point, Patrick knew what was going to happen, but had no idea if Susan and Michael knew. They'd all been living in New York, Patrick on Astor Place, Susan on MacDougal Street, Michael finishing up at Columbia. "Once, he said, 'You know what I really like about Susan's music? It's just so *catchy*.'"

Susan gasps and pulls away to stare at him. "He didn't."

"Hand on a bible," Patrick says.

"You never told me!"

"I wanted you to keep liking him!"

"He had such a tin ear."

"I think he wanted to say something nice about you, and catchy was legitimately the best compliment he could pay music."

"Oh my god," she says, incredulous. "What a dope."

They both seem to realize, at the same time, that they won't be able to mock Michael to his face. Susan opens another box of tissues. It's too much for Patrick to expect some kind of catharsis after telling one anecdote. Nearly five months of stomping on practically every thought about Michael might have broken some part of him.

But now he can think about that one conversation, how open and hopeful and lovestruck Michael had been, how it had taken all Patrick's self-control not to laugh in his face. He can hold that memory in his mind, and that has to be worth something.

18

Patrick's not sure he can take the sight of people lighting fireworks and being festively patriotic, and he doubts Susan will be in the mood for that either, so his big plan for the Fourth of July is to draw the blinds, close the shop, and spend the day watching whatever they can get on Channel 13.

Nathaniel has a better idea. "Let's go to the beach."

"It's supposed to rain tomorrow," Susan says, checking the paper.

"Well, it'll be that much less crowded, then," Patrick says. Nathaniel catches his eye and gives him a minuscule nod, and Patrick catches on: Nathaniel wants to get Susan out of the city, someplace new and different where she won't be tempted to turn on the television and see footage of either parades or flag-draped coffins.

Patrick hasn't been to the beach since 1962. Susan was still living in New York. Michael had just graduated college and was working a summer job at the Metropolitan Museum of Art and sleeping on the couch in Patrick's first apartment, an illegal loft conversion. This was right before Michael and Susan got together, and he remembers it as the summer he had to watch two intelligent people exchange longing glances and come up with dumb pretexts for seeing one another.

What he mostly remembers from that summer was that they'd both asked for his permission. "I'm not secretly in love with you," Susan said. "I'm not working through my feelings for you by falling in love with your much better-looking younger brother. Don't flatter yourself." Patrick had said that he loved the idea of his two favorite people being together, and he'd meant it.

Michael bluntly said that he was in love with Susan but wouldn't do anything about it if it bothered Patrick. Patrick repeated exactly what he told Susan, then added that it definitely wouldn't be a problem for him, as he wasn't interested in women anyway. And then everything went to hell. Maybe Patrick just hasn't met the right girl yet. Doesn't Patrick want to have a family? What if he changes his mind? Isn't he worried about getting arrested?

At that last question, Patrick had spat that it was too late to worry about that, and told him about the raid, about his aunt and uncle refusing to post bail, about how he didn't know how to go home after that. Patrick expected—he didn't know what he expected, but he'd been keeping that secret for years, never sure which would be worse: letting Michael think he'd abandoned him for no reason, or Michael knowing the truth.

But Michael had simply said that he hoped Patrick didn't go to that kind of place anymore—it didn't sound very safe. Patrick has never come so close to hitting another person as he did to hitting his brother that day.

But first they'd gone to the beach, Susan borrowing a friend's car and driving them out of the city. Jones Beach was hot and crowded. They all got sunburned and then spent two hours in wet, sandy bathing suits in traffic back to the city.

Patrick, somehow, remembers it as a good day, one of the best days. He doesn't know if that's because it was one of the last good days, and he's exaggerated it in hindsight, or if it was good in the uncomplicated way that things only can be when you don't quite believe it will ever end. Even Patrick was capable of that kind of hope at the age of twenty-two. Maybe everybody was in 1962.

None of them have bathing suits, so they all go to Macy's, because it's the easiest department store to reach on the subway.

"I can't remember the last time I was in a department store," Patrick says.

Susan glances sadly at his clothes. "Are we supposed to be surprised? I'll meet you back here in half an hour."

It takes Patrick and Nathaniel all of five minutes to find swim trunks, leaving them with plenty of time to visit the children's department, where they discover that they make swimsuits for babies.

"I need to get it," Nathaniel says, holding the hanger tight in his hand. "It has a matching sun hat. I'm getting it."

"Not if I get there first," Patrick says, and that's how Eleanor winds up with a swimsuit that will make her look like a strawberry, a matching red sun bonnet, and a hooded terrycloth bathrobe.

"She can't even walk," Susan says when they show her. "She can't even crawl. She could've sat in a tide pool in her diaper like all the other babies."

Before leaving the store, Patrick remembers to buy film for his camera and for Susan's Super 8.

In the morning, it's just as gloomy as the weatherman predicted, but they put on their swimsuits and various combinations of t-shirts and shorts, fill one of Mrs. Valdez's enormous beach bags with snacks and towels, and get on the subway to Coney Island.

It takes an hour, which brings even Nathaniel to the limits of his enthusiasm for subway graffiti, although he spends the entire trip holding the baby while Susan falls asleep, her head on his shoulder. Somebody left a newspaper on the seat, so Patrick reads aloud the interesting parts of any articles that he thinks Nathaniel will like.

Patrick's been to Coney Island—not the beach, but the boardwalk. It's the kind of place that answers the question What Should We Do Today when the weather's decent and you don't want to go to the movies. People say it's gone to seed, but there's something inherently seedy about eating hot dogs while playing rigged games to win painted dolls. Is there a non-seedy place to pay a psychic a quarter to guess your name, weight, and occupation? Patrick isn't sure he'd want there to be.

But it's seedier than he remembers. The colors are faded and the paint is peeling. Maybe it's the cloudy weather, but the crowds are thin. A bunch of stalls are shut down. It looks like the Parachute Jump closed since the last time Patrick was here, but it's still standing, looming and quiet. Some property developer demolished the rest of Steeplechase Park a couple years ago. That same dickhead bought up a bunch of buildings and evicted everyone in order to put up some ugly high-rises. If there's one thing that Patrick's learned from ten years in this city, it's that around every corner is a dickhead trying to stop you from having fun in public, especially if you aren't middle class, white, and visibly straight.

The plan is to buy three ice cream cones, rent an umbrella, lay out their towels, and—Patrick isn't sure about the rest. The water will be cold. Eleanor's barely old enough to sit up, and probably won't have much fun besides her usual amusements of being tickled and held.

Before they can do any of that, Nathaniel sees the roller coasters.

"It's been twenty years since I've been on one of those," he says, eying the Cyclone like he's sizing up an opponent.

The Cyclone is an enormous wooden deathtrap that looks like it might fall over if you lean on it too hard. Patrick hasn't been on a roller coaster of any kind since junior high. He isn't even too crazy about it when taxi cabs take sharp turns.

But Nathaniel watches the cars fly along the tracks as if it doesn't look like an obviously bad idea.

"You got nervous on the escalator at Macy's," Patrick says. "How can you think that looks like fun?" He gives Susan a pleading look but she shakes her head. She's always hated roller coasters. She won't even go on the Ferris wheel.

Nathaniel glances between them. "I want to see if I can," he says, and Patrick isn't going to argue with that. "Do we have time?"

"We don't have a schedule," Patrick says. "The ocean isn't going anywhere."

"I could go for a ride and meet you back here for ice cream. There isn't a line."

"I'll go with you, if you want company," Patrick says. Nathaniel still doesn't like going anywhere farther than the grocery store by himself, but the truth is that Patrick will go wherever Nathaniel goes, unless he isn't wanted. That's just the state of affairs and he probably ought to get used to it.

"Really?" Nathaniel asks, one corner of this mouth twisting up. "Susan, will you take our picture?"

Susan does better than that. She takes the Super 8 out from under Eleanor's carriage and makes a movie of them waiting in line, waving at the camera, paying for their tickets, getting into the back row of the horrible little train car.

The seats are plain wooden benches with a metal rail that lowers over their laps. At the front of the car are parents with two kids and a high school-aged couple. They all look like sensible people without any kind of death wish, but looks can be deceiving.

Patrick forgot how loud roller coasters are. At no point are you allowed to shut your eyes and forget exactly how rickety the entire contraption is. That doesn't mean he won't try.

"You can open your eyes," Nathaniel says. "The ride hasn't even started."

Patrick doesn't want to be a spoilsport, so he opens his eyes.

"You can keep them shut, it's fine," Nathaniel says. "You're being very brave."

Patrick attempts to sink in his seat, but the ride operator comes around and lowers the safety bar.

You'd think they'd start out slow, but the first drop is a dramatic plummet. Everyone on the ride screams, but Nathaniel gasps and starts laughing. Patrick clutches the lap bar. There's nothing to stop them from sliding against one another when the ride makes one of its sharp turns. Nathaniel being next to him isn't a novelty; Nathaniel touching him isn't even a novelty at this point. It's distracting, though, enough to take the edge off the certainty of disaster. Nathaniel's hand closes over Patrick's on the bar. "You're doing so well."

"Don't patronize me," Patrick complains, which only starts Nathaniel laughing again. The ride makes another drop. Nathaniel doesn't let go of Patrick's hand until the ride stops. There's nobody who can see.

"So," Nathaniel says when the car finally stops. "It turns out I hate roller coasters. Let's go find somewhere nice to be sick."

Susan reveals her true monstrous nature by filming them as they get off the ride, their hair windblown, their faces probably green. Patrick gives the camera a rude gesture. Nathaniel grabs Patrick's hand and pulls it out of view. "Eleanor will watch that someday."

Patrick doesn't know how it's never occurred to him that one day all of this will be told to Eleanor as a story, that one day she'll hear something along the lines of "when you were a baby, we went to live with Uncle Patrick." Or maybe it'll be Patrick telling the story: You came to live with me. We had a dog named Walt who stole your teething biscuits and let you pet his ears.

These will be the stories that all children hear, the stories about a time before they can remember, but in which You is still the protagonist.

There's no way to tell any of those stories without including Nathaniel. He'll be in every story for the first few months of Eleanor's life, and longer, Patrick hopes. But how much longer? Why does this have to enter his thoughts now, when his hand still feels hot from where Nathaniel gripped it? He finds his sunglasses in the beach bag and puts them on. The breeze from the ocean is cool, and there isn't enough sun.

"You don't look great," Nathaniel says, eyeing him carefully. "Let's never go on a roller coaster again."

"It's a deal. Let's get ice cream and walk to the beach," Patrick suggests.

The water is freezing but Nathaniel says, "Oh, to hell with it," and goes right in. Patrick strips off his shirt and follows.

"What the hell," Patrick says as soon as he's knee deep in the water. It's freezing. He didn't know water could be this cold in July.

"You'll feel better if you come in past your shoulders," Nathaniel calls. He's already several yards out. This is a man who showers in boiling water. Patrick doesn't know how he can stand it. "Come *on*."

Patrick sighs and goes in further. He does feel a little better once he's in up to his neck, but he isn't happy about it, so he splashes Nathaniel. Nathaniel retaliates immediately, then ducks underwater.

"It's the only way to deal with cold water," Nathaniel says. "You just have to throw yourself in."

Or you could stay on the warm dry sand, but Patrick doesn't say that. Instead, with his back to the beach and nothing in front of him but Nathaniel and the Atlantic Ocean, he lets his gaze drop to Nathaniel's wet shoulders, to the hair on his chest, which he can just make out underwater. He's seen it all before, but not in broad daylight.

Later, Susan wades in with Nathaniel—sensibly only going in up to her knees—while Patrick watches Eleanor attempt to crawl on the beach blanket but mostly attempt to eat the beach blanket. When Nathaniel and Susan come back, Patrick gets some hot dogs from a vendor and Susan produces a thermos of whiskey sours. They don't have cups, so they pass the thermos around.

The beach is relatively empty. About twenty feet away, a couple is kissing. A few yards in the other direction two older women sunbathe on faded pink towels, the straps of their swimsuits pushed under their arms so they won't get tan lines. Latin music is playing on somebody's radio. Patrick is pretty sure he could close his eyes and fall asleep.

He does lie down, and he does shut his eyes. When he opens them, Nathaniel's looking at him out of the corner of his eye, doing the same thing Patrick had done in the ocean, only more discreetly. Patrick watches Nathaniel look at him, a closed loop, something sparking through the circuit.

When they get home, they're all tired and sandy and mildly sunburned despite all the clouds—except Eleanor, who had her strawberry sun hat. Susan walks the dog while Patrick rinses Eleanor off in the bathtub and Nathaniel unpacks. By the time they've all finished with their showers and Eleanor's had a jar of mashed peas and fallen asleep in her crib, it isn't even dark out, but they're all ready for bed.

"Well, good night, boys," Susan says, stretching. "You don't have to go home but you can't stay here."

The Valdezes are at a cousin's block party uptown, so the building is quiet as Patrick and Nathaniel go downstairs.

"Come here," Patrick says as soon as the apartment door shuts behind them. It's only when the small of Patrick's back hits the wall that he realizes Nathaniel's pushed him there. Well, steered him there. Guided him there. Patrick doesn't know if the whiskey sours have loosened Nathaniel up or if he's just gotten bolder. It doesn't matter. Patrick isn't complaining.

"Wanted this all day," he says, his lips moving against Nathaniel's, one of his hands in Nathaniel's hair and the other pushing up the back of his shirt.

Nathaniel slows things down—Patrick has no illusions about who's doing the speeding up and slowing down around here—and everything is careful and gentle again but it's the carefulness and gentleness of two people who have already established that they're going to push one another into things.

"Will you take this off already?" Nathaniel mutters, tugging at the hem of Patrick's t-shirt. "Walking around shirtless for half the day and now—for God's sake, Patrick, let go of me so I can get this thing off of you."

Patrick pulls his own shirt off and is rewarded by both Nathaniel's hands on his skin, forceful enough that Patrick can let himself feel pinned against the wall. He brings a hand to Nathaniel's hip, cupping his palm around the curve of bone under cotton. When he skims his fingertips inside Nathaniel's waistband, he feels Nathaniel suck in a breath, his mouth against the skin of Patrick's throat.

"Can you—" Nathaniel starts.

"Anything you want," Patrick says, too fast, not knowing what Nathaniel is going to ask for, but knowing it doesn't matter. The answer is still yes.

"Can you make it different?"

"Sure." Patrick's about to ask what, exactly, Nathaniel wants him to do differently, when Nathaniel speaks again.

"I've never liked it before. Christ, that sounds awful. Ungrateful. Hell. What I mean is, I don't want to think about all the times I made myself do that. I want it to feel different."

Jesus. That asks more questions than it answers. Patrick doesn't know what kind of tragic obligatory straight sex Nathaniel's been enduring. Patrick doesn't know much about straight sex to begin with, except what gets hinted at in movies, but he can put together a rough sketch: the man's on top, the man's in charge. He's the subject; she's the object. If that's similar to Nathaniel's experience, and he wants something different, Patrick can maybe flip that around.

"Yeah," Patrick says, his voice rough. "Yeah, I can do that." He turns them, pinning Nathaniel against the wall, caging him in. "Is this different?" he asks, speaking the words into Nathaniel's ear. Nathaniel nods. "Was what we did the other day in the shop different?" Nathaniel nods again. Patrick toys with the hem of Nathaniel's t-shirt. "Will you let me?" He can feel Nathaniel swallow.

He pushes up Nathaniel's shirt and skims a thumb over his nipple, going slow and taking his time, kissing him all the while, feeling Nathaniel's skin warm under his touch. With his other hand, he uses his thumb to stroke the fly of Nathaniel's jeans. Nathaniel makes a noise that shoots through Patrick like some drug that hasn't been invented yet.

"We can do this in bed," Patrick suggests when he's on the edge of getting desperate and thinks Nathaniel might be getting there too. "With as much of my clothes off as you want. Yours too, ideally."

In bed, Patrick kisses the sunburned curve of Nathaniel's shoulder, the sharp edge of his collarbone. Nathaniel's hands are on him now, exploring and insistent.

As Patrick gets the rest of their clothes off, he takes an

inventory of all the places Nathaniel likes being kissed, the places where his breath hitches when Patrick's fingers make contact: the hinge of his jaw, the small of his back, the curve of his ass in the palm of Patrick's hand. He makes a noise that sounds pleased and surprised when Patrick kisses the spot under his ear, like maybe he didn't know he liked that until now, and that thought makes the heat in the room go from summer-warm to something incandescent.

Patrick braces himself over Nathaniel on one arm, then thinks better of it and lets Nathaniel feel his weight—it isn't lost on him that Nathaniel's spent the last half hour paying attention to his shoulders and his arms, the breadth of his chest. If he likes Patrick's size, then he can have it.

He doesn't know if it's possible to have sex so good it eradicates the memory of sex that felt wrong or made you feel wrong. He doubts it's as simple as making sure Nathaniel remembers he's with a man—if that was what Nathaniel needed, that's probably what he'd have asked for. If Patrick had to guess, he'd say that Nathaniel doesn't exactly know what he needs.

He bends his head and brings his mouth to Nathaniel's nipple, kissing it almost reverently, then sucking it into his mouth. Nathaniel makes a shocked sound, then one of his hands lands on the back of Patrick's head, keeping him there.

Patrick gets a thigh between Nathaniel's legs. "Just like this. Okay?" Nathaniel presses up, looking for friction, and Patrick gives it to him. He shifts them around a little, putting his hand where his mouth was, and kisses Nathaniel's neck, his jaw, his mouth. The slide of their bodies makes Patrick groan. At the sound, Nathaniel moves one of his legs aside, making room.

Patrick's been where Nathaniel is, and if you put your mind to it, you can imagine that you're getting fucked. He doesn't know if that's what Nathaniel's thinking, but the possibility that he might be is enough to make Patrick's mind go blank.

When Nathaniel comes, he muffles the sound of it in Patrick's shoulder, then lies back, panting and glassy-eyed, the angles of his face stark and lovely in the half light from the hall. Patrick finishes himself off, aware of Nathaniel watching, then collapses messily onto him. Silently, he starts counting.

Before he gets to thirty, Nathaniel pushes at him. "We need showers."

Patrick smiles into the skin of Nathaniel's neck, delighted to be right, delighted to know this man well enough to guess. He rolls away and starts the shower.

"Stay," Patrick says after they've cleaned up. "In my bed."

Nathaniel is still in Patrick's bed the next morning, cranky and incoherent, the way he is every morning. Patrick puts on the coffee and they get ready for the day, then Patrick opens the shop while Nathaniel gets Eleanor. It's like the pattern of the last five months has simply shifted around a few degrees, all the pieces precisely where they belong, solid enough that Patrick can nearly trick himself into believing it could stay this way.

Part 4

SOMETHING FIERCE AND TERRIBLE

Nathaniel

19

"It's a yes or no question," Susan says, and Nathaniel realizes he's been staring at the kitchen cabinets for long enough that Susan's finished washing the bottles. Nathaniel picks up a bottle and starts to dry it. "Do you want to play a few songs at the Gaslight next week or not?"

"Are you sure you need me?"

"I'd lose at least half the spookiness without the violin." She pulls the plug from the sink and the suds swirl down the drain. "Also, you wrote some of those songs."

"It's more like I was in the room while you wrote them." Nathaniel has a realistic view of their relative contributions. He's helped, but mainly he does what Susan tells him.

Susan snorts. "I've written plenty of songs in the same room as useless people and that wasn't what we were doing. What if I made a record? What if *we* made a record?

Would you want to do that?"

"Yes," Nathaniel says, surprised by how easily that answer came. Being a folk musician—or whatever it is Susan and he are doing—isn't exactly his life's ambition. But it's not like his ambitions have done him any good. Doing this, he's useful to Susan and he's having fun.

She puts away the bottles that Nathaniel dried. "Then play a few songs with me at the Gaslight as a dry run. You can lurk in the shadows if you're feeling shy."

"I'm not *shy*," Nathaniel says, and flicks her with the wet dish towel.

"Prove it."

When Nathaniel got off the train in the wretched new Penn Station last December, he'd meant to get a hotel room, take some flowers to the graveyard, and then— there's where things got hazy. Maybe he'd jump out the hotel window. Maybe he'd swallow some pills. Maybe there was some other way to take his leave from the mess he made of his life without causing too much inconvenience for the hotel maids.

He hadn't even gotten as far as booking the hotel room. He couldn't leave the train station without the sudden, visceral conviction that he was going to be snatched off the street and sent to a secret prison in Panama. Addled, he walked in the wrong direction and in short order got mugged by a couple of teenagers by the piers. In his confused state, he'd thought they were agents sent to take him away. When they left with only his luggage, wallet, and overcoat, he was only more befuddled. They hadn't even taken the file, rolled up and tucked inside his suit jacket.

Cold and frightened, he headed away from the water. When it started to rain, he stepped into a shop that seemed safely empty. It was a bookshop, and behind the counter was an elderly lady. When she asked him if he needed help, Nathaniel said that of course he didn't need help, and somehow within fifteen minutes was being bundled into Mrs. Kaplan's station wagon and whisked off to a warm house in Queens. His suit was ruined, but the files barely got wet.

Now he's trying to figure out whether agreeing to perform on stage with Susan Larkin, using his own first name, is the bloodless form of suicide he was looking for all those months ago. Is he daring the agency to come and get him?

But even in his more paranoid moments, Nathaniel has to admit this makes no sense. The CIA can't assassinate, imprison, or otherwise neutralize every disgruntled former employee—and Nathaniel can't be the only disgruntled former employee. By the time he left, nearly all the analysts he knew thought the U.S. had to get out of Vietnam—or at least would point to the intelligence and say that the war was unwinnable, which amounts to the same thing.

He knows this, just like he knows the break-in was nothing but garden variety robbery, not spies trying to get his files. Even the least competent CIA operative would have picked the lock of Patrick's safe, but Nathaniel's files are still there, safely tucked away behind the deed to the building.

His mind has been playing the same trick on him since December, taking his looming sense of peril and ascribing it to the likeliest villain: if Nathaniel feels hunted, and he has a file proving exactly how unscrupulous the CIA can be, then it's only Occam's razor to connect those two dots.

But there's another explanation, one that's been creeping up on him all spring and summer. Maybe what happened to him this winter was the culmination of too many secrets, an ever widening gap between the truth and his actions, between the feelings that lurked beneath the surface and what he allowed himself to feel, between what he knew and what he wanted to believe. Maybe reality started to feel less real because he'd lost touch with it years ago.

"So?" Susan asks. "What's the answer?"

Nathaniel dries the last of the bottles. Maybe there's only one way for him to sort out what, exactly, he has to be afraid of. He's always needed evidence.

"All right," he says. "Let's do it."

Patrick takes him to bed—and that's the correct phrasing, as they're both perfectly aware who's doing the taking and why he's doing it—every night for a solid week. After a trip to the laundromat, Nathaniel folds the sheets for his own bed and puts them in the bottom drawer of the dresser in his apparently former bedroom.

"That way they don't get dusty," Nathaniel explains, feeling like god's greatest idiot. Patrick likes having Nathaniel in his bed: he paws at Nathaniel for half the night, then wakes up and smiles like a dope. Even the CIA could make sense of this fact pattern.

"Sensible," Patrick agrees, looking far too amused, damn him. Then he backs Nathaniel into a wall and drops to his knees. The practiced efficiency with which he accomplishes this and the extent to which he obviously loves it are tangled up with Nathaniel's pleasure, as much a part of it as the feel of Patrick's mouth, the sight of him.

Nathaniel spent half his life fighting his body on this

one basic matter and the experience of *not* fighting it is a dizzying rush—it's releasing the brakes at the top of a hill, letting gravity and momentum and the inexorable forces of nature do their job. It's *easy.*

This is why he never used to let himself think about it, why he never let himself imagine the scratch of a man's beard on the inside of his thigh, the heat of a man throbbing in his hand: he knew he was susceptible. He was right. He could have measured the path of the last six months in the ever-collapsing distance between plain imagination and sweaty desperation.

"Sleeping in your bed," Nathaniel says, managing, with some effort, to sound passably sane, "would make it easier for you to fuck me."

Patrick sits back on his heels and Nathaniel wants to beg him not to stop, but he has an agenda here.

"You'd want that?" Patrick asks, sounding more suspicious than intrigued. And then, after studying Nathaniel's face and whatever he sees there, "You want that."

"Jerome seems to think you're good at it."

Patrick gets to his feet but he keeps his hand in Nathaniel's jeans. "Jerome wouldn't know."

Nathaniel swallows. "He had all kinds of flattering things to say."

"I mean, sure, but he likes to be on top, so."

The image that flashes in front of Nathaniel's eyes makes him feel like he might black out. What if Jerome was wearing false eyelashes? Lipstick? A dress? Nathaniel might not survive. "I see," he says.

Patrick looks like he's on the verge of laughing but he doesn't stop stroking Nathaniel. "We can do it either way. Or neither way."

Nathaniel doesn't have any answer to that, but Patrick must not expect one, because he pushes Nathaniel onto the bare mattress—he should never have put the sheets away, more fool him—and pulls his clothes off.

They don't do anything they haven't done before, not really, but Patrick's hands linger in new places, and he says things like "Can I" and "Will you let me," hushed and wondering, like he's waiting for an answer.

The night before the gig, Nathaniel wakes up at three in the morning, the building silent around him except for the muted ticking of Patrick's alarm clock. He can't remember the last time he slept through the night, but he must have been a child, because the pattern of repeatedly waking, ruminating, and either falling back asleep or staring into the darkness is the only way he knows to pass a night.

He sleeps just as terribly in Patrick's bed, but now when he wakes he has a momentary thrum of contentment to know that Patrick is there, inches away, warm and real. And then, guilt: at this point, not telling Patrick is the same as deceiving him, but Nathaniel can't bring himself to do it.

He slips out of bed and goes down to the shop. Out of habit, he starts tidying up the receipts and stray bits of paper near the cash register. It's mostly a collection of notes from Iris to Patrick and back again: we're out of stamps, Jerome is coming tomorrow at three, I found the gas bill.

Iris doodles on the edges of her notes, distinctive floral swirls that Nathaniel also finds strewn across her math homework, a stroke of whimsy that some bitter and rotten part of Nathaniel wants to tell her to crush underfoot. *You aren't a man and you aren't white*, he imagines telling her. *You need to make sure you fit the mold in every other way.* But he doesn't need to tell her that. Not because it isn't true—it's sickeningly true, even in 1968—but because Iris already knows. She can make her own choices. He puts the notes in a neat stack on Patrick's desk.

Upstairs in the safe, the photocopied files are still hidden in the back. If something happens to him, Patrick will eventually find them, but that could be years from now, and he wouldn't even necessarily connect those pages with Nathaniel. Why would he? He wouldn't know what to do with them.

But Nathaniel doesn't know what to do with them either. When he was making those copies—half past five, telling his secretary she might as well go home, he could manage the Xerox machine on his own, thanks—he was only thinking that he needed proof. But he hadn't thought about who, exactly, he'd be proving it to, or even what he'd be proving.

He loads a clean sheet of letter paper into the typewriter and types out everything he knows about the CIA's surveillance program and everything else he suspected. The typewriter is loud in the nighttime hush, and part of him wishes that Patrick would wake up and ask him what he was doing. But Patrick, who's as miserable a sleeper as Nathaniel, chooses tonight to sleep like the dead.

Written out, it's as much an indictment of Nathaniel as it is of the CIA: three pages of facts that Nathaniel could have inferred years earlier if he'd paid attention, if he'd been willing to see the organization for what it was. It was his job to analyze facts, and if he'd treated what he knew about his employer as carefully as he treated intelligence about foreign enemies, he'd have known which way the wind blew as early as the Bay of Pigs.

Back upstairs, he spins the lock on the safe in the combination Patrick never bothered trying to conceal from him. He slides the typed pages into the manila envelope and puts it back into its hiding place.

Then, feeling like a burglar, he lets himself into the apartment and climbs into bed. Patrick reaches out, the way he often does in the middle of the night when Nathaniel is lying there, restless. His fingers slide under the hem of Nathaniel's shirt, hot against his skin.

"I'm awake," Nathaniel whispers. Patrick takes this as the invitation it unfortunately is.

"Settle down," Susan tells Patrick on the day of the gig, when Patrick can't stop pacing the shop. "I've done this hundreds of times. It's a coffeehouse. Not Shea Stadium. Not even the Fillmore East. We're just dropping by to play a few songs. Stop being sweaty."

"I can stay home with Eleanor," Patrick offers.

"Iris is babysitting," Susan says, after she finishes rolling her eyes. "She's thrilled to have my telephone to herself for a few hours."

Susan wears jeans and a white oxford straight out of Nathaniel's closet. Nathaniel, at her direction, wears jeans and a t-shirt. "It's a small venue," she says. "Bigger venue, bigger outfit."

The Gaslight is a filthy, smoky basement with no ventilation and no liquor license. The walls are rough brick and the ceilings are so low Patrick nearly walks into a light. Every seat in the place is occupied, and there are people standing around the edges of the cramped room.

As soon as Susan sits on the stool at the front of the room—there's no actual stage—you could hear a pin drop.

They open with the murder ballad that they turned into a protest song. It's catchy, and it's angry, and the crowd eats it up.

Between songs, Susan leans toward the microphone and chats with the audience as she tunes her guitar. "This winter," she says, "my husband died in Nha Trang. He really liked this song." The crowd is quieter than Nathaniel would have thought possible. They launch into "Take Me Home."

After, they're both a little giddy. Susan goes off to talk to a couple of men who Nathaniel is sure he ought to recognize. Nathaniel makes a beeline for Patrick.

"There's a bar upstairs, isn't there?" Nathaniel asks.

"There sure is."

Maybe spending the past half hour playing music that's a giant middle finger to everything Nathaniel used to stand for has made him brave. He straightens Patrick's collar, letting his knuckles brush against Patrick's neck. He leaves his hands there, resting on Patrick's shoulders for a moment. "How about you buy me a drink."

20

At the sound of his name, Nathaniel pries open his eyes, expecting to find Patrick on the other side of the bed. But when he reaches out, Patrick's side of the bed is empty, the sheets cold.

"Sorry to wake you up," Patrick says from the doorway, "but Maud Dempsey died. I need to go to uptown."

"I'm sorry to hear that," Nathaniel says, trying to remember if he's supposed to know who Maud Dempsey is. He sits up, and Patrick hands him a cup of coffee.

"I never met her. She was a Whitman collector. She's been collecting since Whitman was alive. Her lawyer just called. I want to see if it's worth making an offer for the lot. I could use a second set of hands, if you're interested."

Nathaniel could not be less interested in Whitman collections, but Patrick looks like he's about to vibrate out of his skin. "Of course."

"Wear professional drag."

Nathaniel finally notices what Patrick's wearing: a shirt, a tie, and pants that aren't jeans. He does a double take. Patrick doesn't even wear a tie to book auctions.

"Where are we going?" Nathaniel asks.

"Sutton Place. 56th Street, maybe 60th—something like that—all the way on the East Side."

Nathaniel sighs. Manhattan has such a nice, sensible grid system with predictable numbering, but at the edges it all unravels and you never know where you are. The entire Village is an exercise in frustration. Jones Street is a single block long, which should be illegal.

"I can open the store at ten," Susan says when they run into her on the stairs. Patrick thanks her, then goes back up a few steps to kiss Eleanor. Nathaniel catches Susan's eye and doesn't even care that she can tell how smitten he is.

"Look," Patrick says when they're on the subway. "I wasn't looking forward to her death or anything, but I've definitely been looking forward to getting a look at her books, and so have a whole lot of other booksellers and collectors." And the lawyer thought to call him first, is what Patrick isn't saying. He wipes his hands on his trousers, clearly nervous.

In the lobby of the apartment building, Nathaniel sticks close to Patrick in a way he hasn't done in a while, like maybe proximity will soothe Patrick's nerves as well as it soothes Nathaniel's.

"Ten full stories of millionaires," Patrick mutters. It's the sort of building where the lobby has a golden chandelier and marble floors, and things seem to sparkle without any clear light source. The elevator operator has gold braid epaulets.

When Patrick introduces himself to the woman who answers the door—presumably someone from the lawyer's office—she flicks a skeptical glance over both of them, finishing up with the most infinitesimal of raised eyebrows at Patrick. She's about forty, wearing a black dress, three strands of pearls, and a little hat. Nathaniel, in his thrift store clothes, feels like a peasant. He's met hundreds of women of this mold and even more of her male counterpart. A year ago he *was* her male counterpart.

"She thinks I'm your kept man," Nathaniel whispers when they're alone in the library, a high-ceilinged room with a rolling ladder.

Patrick coughs to cover up his laugh. "I think it's the other way around. The real substance of the insult was something along the lines of 'you both seem pretty homosexual to me.'"

"How does she know?" Nathaniel, at this point, knows that he can seem gay when he lets it happen. But that's an affect he can put on and off as he pleases, like Jerome swipes on his lipstick and wipes it off.

"I, well." Patrick adopts his most innocent expression.

"Oh for heaven's sake, who did you fuck this time?"

Patrick attempts again to cover a laugh with a cough. "I spent a weekend with Maud Dempsey's grandson on Fire Island in 1965 after he stopped by the store to buy a present for his grandmother."

"You fucked the next of kin," Nathaniel says. "Naturally." He's pleased to note that Patrick seems much less nervous now than he had in the elevator.

"Here, look at this," Patrick says a few minutes later, holding a leather-bound *Leaves of Grass*. Nathaniel is underwhelmed. At any given moment, there are never any fewer than a dozen copies of *Leaves of Grass* in stock. But sometimes a collector will write in, asking for a particular volume—a certain year, a specific binding—and Patrick will sell it to them for a sum so staggering that it keeps the shop in the black for a month or more, so Nathaniel is well aware that these volumes are precious to the right people, however unremarkable they seem to him.

"Is it a first edition?"

"First of all, it's enormously sweet that you think I'd be let within five city blocks of an actual 1855 first edition of *Leaves of Grass.*" By now, Nathaniel knows this was barely more than a pamphlet of twelve poems, typeset by Whitman himself. Whitman added to the collection throughout his life. Patrick points at the flyleaf. "It's a first edition of the 1881 edition." On the fragile ivory paper, there's a handwritten label with a man's name and the words *from the author.* "I can't make out the handwriting."

"Looks like C.F. Blaylock."

"Thanks. Obviously, someone could have pasted this label on at any time, but—"

"My grandmother said she bought it from a gentleman in New Jersey who used to dine with Whitman," says the woman who'd let them into the apartment—apparently *not* from the lawyer's office, then. "That's how she got the letters, too."

"I'd love to see these letters," Patrick says.

By the time they leave, Patrick's written a check for an indecent amount of money, but which he says he'll make back from the sale of that one book alone.

Patrick arranges to have most of the books and letters delivered, but he insists on taking home the inscribed edition himself.

"You're a little kid carrying her new doll home from the toy store," Nathaniel tells him in the cab, because apparently this book is too good for subways. He puts his hand on Patrick's knee, too low for the cabbie to see in the rearview mirror. "You're still smiling. It looks good on you." He pulls his hand back, but only after a moment.

Patrick opens the book gingerly. "Look, you can't tell me that he writes this and every literate gay man in the country *doesn't* seek him out," he says, as if they're continuing some earlier conversation. "At that point you effectively have a public homosexual for the first time in American history."

Nathaniel doesn't argue. He knows what's coming next, because he's heard it all before, but instead of being bored, he's charmed; it's an old song, and knowing the tune doesn't make it any less worth listening to.

"Besides," Patrick says, turning pages to find the engraving of Whitman that's in virtually every edition. "I mean, seriously."

In this engraving, Whitman has on a shirt that's open at the neck, with what might be a glimpse of chest hair if you really put your imagination to work. No necktie, no waistcoat, no jacket. One hand is on his hip and the other is jammed in his trouser pocket. He has a beard and a rakishly tilted hat and an expression that Nathaniel sometimes sees directed at Patrick when they're walking down Christopher Street.

"Let's say you're a queer man in 1855," Patrick whispers, so the cabbie can't hear him over the man on the radio who's shouting about draft dodgers. "And you see this man's picture in a book of fantastically gay poetry. You're writing him a letter, right? You're angling to meet him. You're—"

"You're horny for Walt Whitman."

Patrick sinks lower in the cab seat, like maybe that'll

hide that fact that he's blushing. "You shouldn't say things like that."

"What? You mean facts?"

"He wasn't perfect," Patrick says. "I mean, the things he said about—"

Nathaniel leans back against the vinyl seat and lets Patrick's lecture wash over him.

When they get back to the shop, they find Susan at the cash register and Eleanor in her lap. "Wow," she says, glancing between them. "Things went well, I'm guessing?"

"He found a book his boyfriend *touched*," Nathaniel says. They both start cackling, and Eleanor joins in. That's a new trick of hers.

Patrick spends the rest of the day restless, pacing the shop and apparently unable to spend more than two minutes at a time at his desk.

"I will do whatever you want," Nathaniel tells Susan, his voice low, "if you take over the shop and mind the baby for the next two hours."

"Sure. Two hours," Susan says. "Wow, ambitious."

"What—no, you creep, I was going to take him out for dinner." But now that he's thinking about it, they can get dinner later. Susan really is a genius. "Come on," he tells Patrick, pulling him toward the stairs. "It's not like you're getting any work done."

"Where are we—oh."

He steers Patrick toward the bedroom, pausing only to switch on the record player—he likes the privacy of an added layer of sound. There's a Rolling Stones album on the turntable—not what Nathaniel would have chosen, but now is not the time to be picky.

Once Patrick is on the bed, Nathaniel straddles his lap. Usually, Nathaniel wants the weight of Patrick on top of him, wants the newness of it. It hasn't escaped his attention, though, that Patrick likes when Nathaniel pushes him around a little. And why shouldn't he—Patrick likes it when Nathaniel pushes him around, figuratively, in every other context. Nathaniel can take turns; Nathaniel can be generous.

Patrick loosened his tie and undid the top button of his shirt as soon as they left Maud Dempsey's apartment. Nathaniel presses his mouth to the exposed V at his collar and breathes in the scent of him, then starts working off Patrick's clothes. When he takes his own clothes off, his skin prickles with the awareness of Patrick's gaze on him. He makes himself slow down.

Maybe there will always be a voice in his head telling him that it's wrong; maybe there will always be an answering voice that sounds a lot like Patrick saying "you want this." If those two voices coexist for the rest of his life, that'll be good enough. Maybe he doesn't need to get all the psychic shrapnel out of his mind, just find a way to live with it.

While they're kissing, Patrick reaches up to the headboard to steady them, and Nathaniel has to stop what he's doing. He's seen Patrick's arms dozens of times. He's had his hands on them; he's had his mouth on them. They're thick and they're muscled and they feature in most of Nathaniel's more pornographic imaginings. He knows every contour of them by heart. But something about Patrick reaching over his head and holding the rail of the headboard lights a fuse in Nathaniel's belly.

"Can you do that again?" Nathaniel asks.

Patrick raises his eyebrows, but he wraps his hand around the rail. It just does something to the muscles in his biceps, Nathaniel supposes. Then Patrick does it with his other arm, too. Nathaniel's face must show exactly what he's thinking, because Patrick grins and says, "Oh *really?*"

Nathaniel's mouth is dry. "You look good like this."

"You could tie me up," Patrick offers, easy as anything. He's probably done it before. He's probably done it in this bed. Nathaniel might pass out.

"I don't want that," he says. "I just want you to stay like that for a minute." He touches Patrick's chest, then trails his hand down Patrick's stomach, along hair and sweat and warm skin. When he wraps his hand around Patrick, he keeps an eye on Patrick's face and his arms and—Christ. He doesn't know why this image is working for him. He keeps his grip loose, probably annoyingly so. Patrick strains a little, his arms flexing, putting on a show: he knows exactly what he's doing.

Nathaniel knows by now what Patrick looks like when he's enjoying himself, and right now Patrick is taut with desire. He bends his head and takes him into his mouth, not something he's done before. Patrick makes a noise that he might have muffled in his forearm or the sheets if he could. The moment feels weighted with everything Nathaniel isn't supposed to want and isn't supposed to be. Somehow, in the syrupy logic that belongs to warm sheets and fading sunlight, that old wrongness doesn't quite become right, but it finds a home here in the same way that Nathaniel did.

"I had no idea you could cook," Nathaniel says. "You've been holding out on us."

"It's just a stir fry," Susan says. "It's tofu and broccoli with some Minute Rice. Calm down. I was going to riot if I had to eat another night of takeout."

Nathaniel has never had tofu, and had vaguely supposed it to be an ingredient you succumbed to only after prolonged exposure to drugs and radical politics, but what have the last six months of Nathaniel's life been if not prolonged exposure to drugs and radical politics? It tastes like meat from the future. He helps himself to seconds.

"The two of you have to start cooking," Susan says. "Eleanor can't grow up eating nothing but takeout except for when I cook. Think about it."

"We have to do it for feminism," Patrick concedes.

"I clean," Nathaniel says. "Patrick does the laundry."

"Put all of us together and we're one adequate housewife," Patrick says.

"We just need a dad to mow the lawn," Susan says.

Nathaniel nearly points out that the courtyard in the back is a true health hazard, but he's not volunteering to be dad.

The next day, Nathaniel pulls a cookbook off the shelf of books that Patrick always swears he can't remember buying. *Mastering the Art of French Cooking* looks like it's for people who've successfully managed something more involved than toast. *The Joy of Cooking* isn't much better. Finally, he pulls down a spiral bound, cheaply printed affair called *Simple Dinners for New Brides*. Each of the recipes calls for fewer than six ingredients and the instructions are written so a not particularly bright eight-year-old could follow them. Perfect.

He goes to the grocery store and buys a chicken, some potatoes, and a bunch of carrots, then has to go back out to a hellish store on Fourteenth Street when it turns out Susan doesn't have a big enough pan. He doesn't especially want to roast a chicken, but he also doesn't want to scour the bathroom and he does that when the alternative is Eleanor taking a bath in a filthy tub.

It doesn't taste bad. It doesn't taste good, either, but Nathaniel thinks he can improve on it with some effort. Patrick and Susan seem impressed, at least.

A few days later, Nathaniel opens the same cookbooks and uses index cards to mark a few promising recipes that he thinks even Patrick can't mangle. He finds Susan at the cash register reading a magazine.

"Where's Patrick?"

She turns a page and doesn't look up. "Oh, it's a warm day, so I guess he's out buying ice cream cones for hobos."

"You're a terrible person," Nathaniel says, but he's laughing.

"Come on, you know he's done it at least once." Her eyes are lit up with trouble. "Bet you five dollars."

"I don't think we're supposed to say hobo."

"Please. Anyway, Patrick took Eleanor to the doctor."

Nathaniel feels like something icy is dripping down his spine. "Is she all right?"

"What? Of course. She needs to get measured and weighed and all that."

"And you sent her with Patrick."

She crosses her arms over her chest. "Are you saying I should have taken her myself?"

"No, settle down. It's good, that's all."

"It's good," she repeats.

It's none of Nathaniel's business to ask whether she and Patrick have had any kind of conversation about what their future will look like. But he doesn't see anybody else around here who's about to broach the topic, so it's up to him. "Her first day of kindergarten, he'll need to be there, you understand that, right?" He thinks of all the milestones parents line up in their minds, stretching forwards: the moments they think will go in the photo album. "Her first date and her college graduation. He'll need to walk her down the aisle. I don't give a damn if there's a stepfather in the picture, Susan."

Her jaw is set and she looks mutinous. "I know that."

"Does Patrick know that you know that?"

"I can't very well go up to him and say, hey, Patrick, you know how you've taken care of us for the past six months? Well, you're emotionally on the hook for the next eighteen years and more, thanks in advance."

"Be serious. Patrick wants nothing more than to be on the hook."

The door opens and Patrick comes through, tugging the carriage behind him, Eleanor asleep against his shoulder. "Did I interrupt another fight about mandolins?"

"Yes," Susan and Nathaniel say together.

Patrick narrows his eyes. "Okay, fine, lie to me."

"Meatloaf, pork chops, or pot roast?" Nathaniel asks, holding up the cookbook.

Patrick raises his eyebrows at the cover. "Which of us is the new bride?"

"New bride is a euphemism for helpless idiot. I'm afraid we're both very much new brides."

The meatloaf is serviceable. Nathaniel figures if they each make dinner once a week, they can have leftovers or takeout the other nights and not worry about Eleanor growing up with either a nutritional deficiency or insufficient feminism.

Whenever he catches himself thinking like that, he tries to stop. He isn't going to be a permanent part of the cooking rotation or anything else. They'll want him gone when they find out who he is and what he's done. But it's hard to remember that he won't be a part of this forever. He *isn't* a part of this. He happened to be there when Susan and Patrick needed help, and so they folded him into their fractured little family. None of that is permanent. Susan and Patrick treat him like it is, but that's likely because they haven't thought that far ahead, and also because at this point it's too late to draw a line between family and not family. The time would have been in February, and none of them were thinking straight back then.

If he were braver, he'd tell them now, but he wants to keep every minute of this that he's allowed. He pages through the cookbook, trying to decide what he'll make the next time it's his turn to cook dinner. The pot roast looks manageable, so he dog-ears the page.

It's slow in the shop, a rainy July weekday, so Nathaniel doesn't have much to do during his shift. The store is clean, the inventory is updated, and he's about to find something to read when the shop bells chime.

He's hoping it's Iris, arriving early for their daily trigonometry session, but he has to suppress a groan when he sees who it is. "Patrick isn't here," he tells John.

"Oh," John says. "When will he be back?"

He'll be back any minute now, since he only went to the bank to make a deposit. "Who knows?" Nathaniel says.

John begins fiddling with a few books on a shelf near the cash register. That shelf has held the same three Whitman biographies since February, if not longer. Nathaniel stopped paying any attention to them. If John decides to buy one in order to impress Patrick, maybe Nathaniel can convince Patrick to put something other than another Whitman biography in its place.

"That's funny," John says. "When did you start carrying these?"

If John is confused about why Patrick stocks Whitman biographies, there's really nothing Nathaniel can do for him. But then he sees what John is looking at. They aren't biographies, or even any kind of book, but more of those pamphlets like the ones Nathaniel bought at the soda fountain earlier that summer. Zines, Patrick had called them.

At first he thinks he must have brought his own copies downstairs and Iris or someone tucked them away in a random place while tidying up. But, no, this is a different issue of one of the same publications, a cheaply printed black-and-white affair called *Louder* with a drawing of a dangerous-looking flower on the cover.

He'd enjoyed that one. It was funny. It was also, arguably, seditious, in that it plainly encouraged draft resistance, called for a national strike and refusing to pay income tax to protest the war, and listed the bridges, roads, and buildings that would be effective targets for demonstrators to occupy. People have been arrested for less. He'd been half impressed, half appalled, by the brazenness of the writers.

"We don't carry those," Nathaniel says. "A customer must have left them behind."

"Six of them?" John flips through a copy, his eyebrows inching higher and higher. "Does Patrick know about this?"

Nathaniel actually laughs at the implication that he's the one stocking the shop with radical underground newspapers and that Patrick would be shocked by their content. Has this man ever even talked to Patrick?

John narrows his eyes. "The old Jewish lady who owns the place, are these hers?"

Judging by the sheer quantity of old issues of *The Daily Worker* in boxes upstairs, Mrs. Kaplan wouldn't even blink at the contents of *Louder*. But John doesn't need to know that, even if he hadn't phrased that question as offensively as he had. "Like I said," Nathaniel says, out of patience and not bothering to hide it, "someone left them here."

John leaves the zines next to the cash register and leaves. Alone in the shop, Nathaniel picks one up and opens to the middle. "Every soldier is a POW" is printed in blocky capitals. He reads the issue from cover to cover—well, almost from cover to cover, because the back half is a Spanish translation that he can only partly make out. He flips back to "Every soldier is a POW," and is still looking at that page when Patrick comes back.

"Where did these come from?" Patrick asks, pointing to the zines.

Nathaniel isn't surprised that Patrick didn't notice them. Patrick is disorganized and the shop is too crowded for even Nathaniel to keep track of everything. "They were on the shelf with the Whitman biographies," Nathaniel says. "Your friend John noticed them, and he was very odd about it."

"He isn't my friend," Patrick says. "You aren't jealous of *John*, are you?"

Of course Nathaniel is jealous of John, handsome, twenty-five, and—by the looks of it—gainfully employed. "Don't be silly," he says.

"I don't want John. Do I need to spell this out for you?"

"I can't imagine what you're talking about."

"It was in this very room," Patrick says, pointing at his desk, "that you lectured me about emotional honesty."

It wasn't a lecture, and it wasn't about emotional honesty—Nathaniel's not sure he could even say emotional honesty with a straight face—but rather about how repressing grief can make you go crazy, but none of that is important right now. "You need to read that thing. It's one of the zines I bought at Gem Spa with you, but I don't know how six of them got into the shop."

Patrick sits at his desk and starts to read. Five minutes later he puts down the folded newsprint and says, "Well. Really decent writing, I'd say."

That was Nathaniel's first reaction too, but the quality of the prose isn't the crucial point here. "When I read it, I thought to myself, these people must want the FBI to start paying attention to them."

Patrick, who had been examining the art on the zine cover, looks up sharply. "Do you think John is some kind of cop? Creepy. I knew I didn't like him."

If that's how Patrick feels about a cop spending a few minutes in the store, Nathaniel doesn't want to imagine how he'll react to finding out who's been living under his roof.

"It's easy to imagine that man in a shoulder holster," Nathaniel says. "But, no, I don't think he's a cop, just a reactionary busybody. I'd like to know how these got here." He gets to his feet and puts the six zines back next to the Whitman biographies, assuming that whoever left them there might come back looking for them.

21

When Eleanor turns six months old, Susan buys a bottle of champagne and they drink it in front of the television while Eleanor chomps on a teething biscuit.

"This is where my expertise runs dry," Nathaniel says, trying and failing to pitch his voice to something casual. "It's all uncharted territory from here on out."

The temperature seems to drop ten degrees, and the way Patrick and Susan go perfectly still confirms Nathaniel's suspicion that they both figured it out already.

Sure enough, when Susan says, "Nathaniel," she doesn't sound surprised, only terribly gentle.

"I thought I should let you know," Nathaniel says, eyes on the ceiling so he won't see it when Patrick and Susan inevitably look at Eleanor and think about how unendurable it would be if something happened to her. Because it *would* be unendurable. But what does it mean to endure something? Life's worst miseries rarely kill you, but he isn't sure how much of himself survived past 1961.

This is more than he's said about Christopher than he has in seven years. A few people at work gave him stoical nods of condolence and his secretary brought him casseroles for a while, but nobody wanted him to talk about it, least of all Nathaniel.

He shouldn't have said anything tonight. At the very least he could have waited until they weren't drinking celebratory champagne. It'll only make them sad, and it won't make Nathaniel feel any different. A year from now, Nathaniel will be someplace else and having had these few moments of sympathy won't matter anymore.

Still, though, it has to count for something that Nathaniel can talk about it now—well, more like talk around it, allude to it, encode the entire sad story in an easily cracked cipher and then leave it in plain sight—with only the faintest call of the abyss.

The sofa cushion to his left sinks, and at first he thinks it's Susan—Patrick will have gathered that Nathaniel's just trying to hold it together, and affection would ruin everything—but he gets a wet nose to his face. "You're the worst," he tells Walt. "Nobody raised you and it shows." He threads his fingers into the long, scruffy fur at the base of the dog's neck.

"Here," Susan says, and passes him a joint that she hadn't been smoking two minutes ago. From Susan, this is the equivalent of a black-bordered sympathy card.

"You know," he says, "when I got here, I thought, well, these two kids have no idea what they're doing. At least I'm good for something. I thought, it's a good thing I'm not dead, which was a refreshing change, so thank you for that."

"You are so emotionally stunted," Susan says. "I love

you from the bottom of my heart, but how come nobody born before 1940 has feelings? Somebody should look into that."

"She means thank you," Patrick says.

"Oh, fuck you," Susan says, "he already knows I'd be in a padded cell without him."

"No, you'd be drying out someplace scenic," Nathaniel says, dizzy with the relief of having talked about it without having had to actually talk about it. "*I'd* be the one in a padded cell."

"Where are they buried?" Patrick asks that night when they're getting ready for bed. Nathaniel's brushing his teeth and Patrick's leaning in the door to the bathroom, so Nathaniel doesn't have to actually look at him or say anything for a moment.

"He," Nathaniel says. "Christopher." It was a mistake to say his name, such a mistake. He focuses on the tube of toothpaste, rolling it up from the bottom. Patrick squeezes it from the middle like some kind of hooligan. "Brooklyn," he says when he can trust himself to speak. "It happened when his mother was visiting her family for Easter." He squeezes out a perfect line of toothpaste onto Patrick's brush and rests it on the edge of the sink. "Flu."

"If you want to visit, I'd go with you."

Nathaniel hasn't been since the funeral. The idea of visiting his infant's grave with his gay lover feels instantly, egregiously inappropriate for the ten seconds it takes for his brain to stop living in 1961.

One of his goals in coming to New York had been to bring flowers to the grave. It seemed like the bare minimum: drop off some carnations, make sure the place isn't overrun with weeds.

He shouldn't let Patrick go with him. The memory of

Patrick will get tangled up with the graveside, so that later on Nathaniel won't even be able to think about Christopher without thinking of Patrick. He shouldn't be that cruel to himself.

"I'd like that," Nathaniel says.

The next morning Nathaniel finds the cemetery on the map and looks up what trains will get them there. They leave the shop in Susan's hands and take the subway to Brooklyn.

There's a flower shop across from the entrance; no bouquets of red roses for sale here, only tastefully subdued arrangements of lilies and gladiolus. The funeral parlor had been overrun with white flowers of every variety; he'd forgotten about that. There'd been a blanketlike arrangement on top of the little casket, purchased, presumably, by his former in-laws.

Nathaniel chooses a bouquet of yellow lilies, then immediately regrets it. He doesn't care one way or the other about lilies, and babies are too young to have a favorite flower, and even if he were alive he'd be seven years old and unlikely to give a fig about flowers. Christopher isn't even there anyway, so who are the flowers for? He finds that he's stuck, unable to cross the street.

Patrick takes the flowers from his hand and murmurs, "We can turn around," just like he did those first few months when Nathaniel couldn't go anywhere. They cross the street.

It takes them twenty minutes to find the grave, because Nathaniel forgot exactly how enormous this place is. He glances at the engraved name only long enough to confirm that he's found the right headstone.

It's a grave: gray stone on green grass. He didn't

expect to feel anything about it. Nobody's here and he wouldn't want it any other way. But placing the flowers at the foot of the stone feels anticlimactic. Insufficient. Irrelevant to the carefully buried knot of sadness that Nathaniel tries not to think about carrying around with him.

It's a Tuesday morning, and the graveyard is empty enough that the nearest people are a hundred yards away, but even if someone had been staring directly at them, Nathaniel wouldn't have shrugged off Patrick's arm when it wraps around his shoulders.

"Collins?" Patrick asks as they make their way back to the street. That, after all, is the name on the gravestone.

Nathaniel is struck by the sudden absurdity of the fact that the man he's been living with, the man he's been sharing a bed with, been falling in love with, hadn't known his last name. It makes the last six months feel even less substantial.

"Collins," Nathaniel admits.

"I never thought it was Smith."

Of course he hadn't. Of course Patrick took for granted that the man he was feeding and housing and taking care of was using an alias for perfectly good reasons. He remembers that man downtown, how Patrick hadn't cared in the least that he'd had a knife.

"I thought I was lying low when I came here."

"Is Nathaniel your real first name?" Patrick asks, instead of asking who Nathaniel thought he was hiding from.

"Yes."

"You did a shitty job of lying low," Patrick says.

They manage to get lost on the way back to the subway station. "We should have brought the map,"

Nathaniel says.

"We should have brought the map," Patrick agrees.

They pass an old stone church they definitely didn't see on the way to the cemetery. Churches are scattered all over the city, most of them wedged unceremoniously between other buildings, across the street from dry cleaners and barber shops, or attached to the side of a school. This one's all by itself, severe and monumental, two stories high with a white bell tower that doubles its height. In the back there's a cemetery with sunken, crooked gravestones.

Nathaniel isn't sure which one of them slowed down first, but now they're standing still on the cracked sidewalk, the church looming over them.

"Never really went in for that," Patrick says easily, like he's talking about California wine or bowling leagues, something morally neutral, something optional.

Nathaniel did go in for it, or at least he tried—or at least he knew he was supposed to. He can't untangle those threads anymore, can't pull free the thread of truth from the entire skein of pretense, denial, and wishful thinking. But when he looks at the church, it feels like it's looking back in disapproval, which has to mean some part of him thinks it's real. Or maybe that's just more mental shrapnel.

They finally find the subway station, but it isn't rush hour, and this is a local stop, so they have to wait a while for a train. They sit on an uncomfortable wooden bench, no closer than two men ordinarily would. The station is hot and muggy, the only breeze coming from the occasional express train barreling through the station.

"You said you got divorced in 1962," Patrick says, evidently having noticed the date on the gravestone.

"We split up in '61," Nathaniel says. "A few days after

the funeral, there was an emergency at work and I didn't come home for a while." It had been the lead-up to the Bay of Pigs. "Helen was justifiably unimpressed. The widower next door was very comforting and the rest is history. They're married now, with two children." This fact always makes him feel marginally less guilty about having married her in the first place. When she announced she was leaving him for another man, he'd been relieved. Marriage transformed Helen from a friend into a round-the-clock audience for his deception. He'd been suffocated. She'd been miserable.

"It was wrong of me to marry her." Nathaniel stares straight ahead across the tracks at the ads on the far wall. "I knew—I should have known—" He nearly laughs, because how many of his sins can be covered by *I should have known*? "I almost took this away from her." He gestures between himself and Patrick, but they're close enough that his hand lands on Patrick's arm. He doesn't even know exactly what *this* means. Wanting someone and being wanted back? Falling in love? "I was thirty. People were going to start to wonder." Laying his reasoning out like that makes it sound exactly as bad as it should.

"That happens to a lot of us."

"It didn't *happen* to me at all. It was a choice."

"Still."

What might be worse than Patrick learning about Nathaniel's career and kicking him out might be Patrick learning about Nathaniel's career and making excuses for him. Nathaniel didn't know any better, Nathaniel was doing the best he could, Nathaniel couldn't possibly have known what he was aiding and abetting due to an excess of patriotism and the fact that his father never loved him.

Nathaniel doesn't think he could stand to hear it.

The truth is, he'd do the exact same thing for Patrick, if Patrick had any skeletons in his closet, and he doesn't know if that's yet another character flaw or something even more dangerous.

22

"I always forget how quickly the town empties out in August," Patrick says when a sunny Friday comes and goes with only a handful of customers.

Nathaniel could tell him that something similar happens in every city, with people decamping for long weekends at their second homes or those of their richer friends. But New York in August is uniquely revolting. When the city permanently smells like garbage and the sidewalks never cool down, when the subways are unbearable and the lights flicker from too many air conditioners running at once, anyone who can find an excuse to get out of this city grabs it and flees.

The number of customers dwindles to a trickle. The Valdezes are in Puerto Rico, so the building is quiet, and will only get quieter when Susan takes Eleanor to visit her parents on Long Island.

Nathaniel goes upstairs to help Susan pack. She's

staring with grim determination at a suitcase that's open on her bed. It's the same one she arrived with in February, a tan leather Samsonite thoroughly defaced with travel stickers.

"You don't have to go," Nathaniel says, folding one of Eleanor's little dresses and laying it in the suitcase.

"She's their grandchild."

"You still don't have to." Nathaniel doesn't add that he doesn't want them to go, because that's selfish and also embarrassing, even though he's sure Patrick feels the same way.

"They aren't bad people and I'm not doing Eleanor out of a chance to have grandparents. There's nothing they can say to me that I'm not ready for."

"What does that mean?"

"Oh, you know. I'll find someone new someday, I'm still young, at least I have Eleanor, et cetera."

"Ah."

"She means well. If she needs to spend the next week trying to reassure me that I'll meet someone new, I can ignore her." She picks up some rolling papers, sighs, and puts them back into her nightstand drawer.

He and Patrick wave goodbye from the curb when Susan and Eleanor ride off in the back of a cab.

"I'm going to miss them too," Patrick says. He holds the door open and they both return to the too-empty shop.

"What if she forgets us?"

"Do babies forget people after two weeks? Parents travel all the time and you don't hear about it ruining their kids' psyches."

"I don't know," Nathaniel says.

Patrick puts his arm around Nathaniel. "Even if she

does forget us, she'll remember us soon enough."

The weight of Patrick's arm and the gentleness of his voice are a disaster. Nathaniel blinks a few times. "All right," he says, aiming for brisk and falling a mile short. "I'm going to take Walt on a walk now."

He expects the walk to go poorly, that he'll revert to the way things were in February, but his heart only gives a perfunctory flutter. He stops at the deli around the corner and brings home a pair of corned beef sandwiches for lunch. Patrick's by the door when he gets back, trying to look like he wasn't waiting for him.

For the rest of the day, it's just the two of them, with a mostly comatose Walt napping wherever they happen to be. The city is barreling toward a heat wave. In two windows, Patrick has air conditioners, which he says he purchased a few years back when he realized that sauna levels of heat and humidity can't be good for books, so the shop is bearable, at least.

That night, Nathaniel finds Patrick on the sofa, reading a pulpy-looking science fiction paperback. When he sees Nathaniel approach, he slides over a few millimeters—an invitation not just to sit, but to sit nearby.

"Let me get a book," Nathaniel says. He's read all the books Patrick lent him except the spy thriller, which he abandoned after the first few pages. But Nathaniel's never been able to leave a job half done, so he gets *The Spy Who Came in from the Cold* from his old bedroom. When he sits on the couch, he twists around so his legs are in Patrick's lap.

He's expecting this book to be something along the lines of James Bond: glamour and intrigue, good triumphing over evil. Instead, it's the story of an already disillusioned agent getting two hundred pages of brutal evidence that intelligence systems can only function when they stop caring about anything resembling good and evil or right and wrong, stop caring about people as anything other than pieces on a game board. It has more in common with Dashiell Hammett than it does with Ian Fleming.

It shouldn't feel like anything groundbreaking. "Spies are up to no good" is hardly a new thought. But he's never really considered that there must be people around the world who've been caught up in a rotten system, for good reasons and bad reasons and reasons that made sense at the time.

"You read fast," Patrick says.

"It's my only party trick," Nathaniel says. "Give me ten minutes so I can see how badly this poor man gets screwed."

"Why did you give me this book?" Nathaniel asks as he closes the cover and straightens the dust jacket. He doubts Patrick thought it had any special relevance to Nathaniel, but there must have been some reason.

Patrick shrugs. "I enjoyed it."

Of course. Patrick took a look at Nathaniel—miserable, panicked, barely functioning—and decided to let him have things to *enjoy*.

Nathaniel's hand strays to the notebook in his trouser pocket, but isn't there. He must have left it somewhere. He hasn't written Patrick's name in it—what if it fell into the wrong hands?—but his name is the secret code woven into all the other items. He's the precipitating factor. The dividend. He's the key the music is written in.

"Did you like it?" Patrick asks.

Absolutely not, Nathaniel wants to say. But there's a moment in the book where the jaded spy tells his girlfriend that spies aren't *good*; they're horrible people doing horrible things to keep ordinary civilians safe. And that's more or less what Nathaniel told himself for his entire career. It's for a good cause. It's keeping people safe. You can't be decent when your enemies are ruthless.

Maybe that's true. Nathaniel doesn't know anymore. But that's what police say when they're shooting teenagers. It's what the president says when he drafts more soldiers and bombs more civilians.

"I need to tell you something," Nathaniel says.

"Can it wait?"

"Why," Nathaniel asks, incredulous, "are you busy?" Nobody has ever looked less busy than Patrick does right now, his head tipped against the back of the sofa, his book open face down on his thigh.

"I mean, I could be," Patrick says with a glance at Nathaniel's mouth, a leer he might have been able to pull off if he didn't look so shifty. "But you seem unhappy, like maybe you don't want to talk about whatever this is."

Patrick knows that he isn't going to like whatever Nathaniel has to say. This might be the first time Nathaniel's ever seen Patrick do something selfish. "All right," Nathaniel says. "Tomorrow, then."

When Patrick's hand slides up Nathaniel's thigh in a blatant attempt to change the topic, Nathaniel goes along with it. More than goes along with it, because he, too, wants this more than he wants that terrible conversation. If he gets one more night of being able to pretend, then he'll take it.

At nine o'clock in the morning, Susan calls to wish Nathaniel a happy birthday.

"The phone is right next to Patrick's bed," she says.

"It sure didn't take long for him to hand it to you."

"My god," Nathaniel says, still mostly asleep, "you're a regular detective." It's a terrible connection, like she's calling from much further away than Long Island. "What's the matter with your phone?"

"It's on your end. I just got off the phone with my manager and the connection was fine." He can barely hear her, what with all the static and clicking.

"How's Eleanor?" Nathaniel asks.

"Spoiled rotten," Susan says, as if the three of them don't spoil that child at every opportunity.

It's just a bad connection. But there's a voice at the back of Nathaniel's head insisting that it's a wiretap. Nathaniel doesn't even know what a wiretap sounds like. He knows his thoughts are driven by paranoia, not evidence. It's the same as when he thought the burglary was suspicious.

Will it always be like this? Will he always be afraid that every bump in the night is his past catching up with him, his guilty secrets threatening to come out?

"Where do you want to go for dinner?" Patrick asks when Nathaniel reaches over him to put the receiver back in its cradle. "It's your birthday, you can pick."

The sheet slipped to their waists, but it's already warm enough that Nathaniel doesn't bother pulling it up. This conversation will contaminate the bed, but there isn't anyplace it won't contaminate, and Nathaniel doesn't think he can stand another minute.

He rolls over to face Patrick, not wanting to take the coward's way out by addressing his words to the ceiling. "I need to talk to you about what I used to do."

"If you want," Patrick says. He rolls onto his back.

"I worked for the CIA."

Nathaniel makes himself watch as Patrick flinches. "Were you a spy?" Patrick asks after a minute.

"Not in the sense you mean. I had a desk job." He wants to say that he had nothing to do with Vietnam, nothing to do with Southeast Asia in general, but he promised himself he wouldn't say anything that's even in the neighborhood of an excuse. "I worked in signals intelligence," he says, "specifically traffic analysis."

Patrick furrows his brow, because of course none of those words mean the same thing to him as they do to Nathaniel. "Traffic?"

"Looking for patterns in how and when communications are being made. You can learn something even if the communications are encrypted. Helen's a cryptanalyst," he adds, even though that fact can't possibly interest Patrick. "That's how we met."

"I thought you did math."

"I did, sometimes." Never as much as he thought he'd be doing. "Mostly I wrote reports about Eastern Europe."

"Why did you quit?"

"It turns out," Nathaniel says, "that the agency cares nearly as little for Americans as it does for Vietnamese and Hungarians and Cubans. Evidently I can excuse a lot of evil, but I draw the line close to home. Or, I used to."

"Some people are true believers," Patrick says.

Nathaniel winces at hearing his own words echoed back at him. "I was. But that's no excuse. Listen, Patrick, I'll leave if you want me to."

"I'm not kicking you out."

"You wouldn't be. I'm offering. I saved nearly all the money I made this year."

"And you have that pension," Patrick says. "Probably other money, too."

"I'm not touching any of that. Ill-gotten gains." He'd told Susan the same thing.

"What would you do?"

"Susan says I can get work as a session musician. She won't want to work with me anymore when she finds out, but I think I could find work without her help. I was looking at the ads in the *Village Voice* and I think I can afford a room."

"Do you *want* to move out?"

"No! God, no. I'd stay forever, if I could."

Finally, Patrick rolls to face Nathaniel. "Then why the fuck are you looking at the classified ads?"

"Because I'm not going to ask you to share your bed and your"—Nathaniel gestures around helplessly—"your whole *life* with someone who stood for the opposite of everything you love in the world."

"I know who you are now. I don't really care who you used to be."

"Well, you should."

"Maybe, but it's too late. I love you, and I can't just turn that off, you know?"

Of all the things he's done, letting Patrick love him might be the worst. "I'm sorry."

"I'm not."

"You should be."

"Stop telling me what to think. The dog needs a walk. Are you coming or not?"

Nathaniel throws on some clothes, even though he wants to give Patrick an alphabetized inventory of all the reasons he shouldn't want to be around Nathaniel.

When they reach the sidewalk, they both squint at the sun. Walt looks over his shoulder, judgmental, when they don't get a move on. Patrick's hair is everywhere and he has a bruise on his neck from where Nathaniel kissed him. It's like looking at something he stole in the dead of night.

"Cornelia or Barrow," Patrick asks, naming the two directions for Walt's quick morning walk.

"Cornelia," Nathaniel says, and they turn right onto West Fourth. When they turn onto Sixth Avenue, the sounds of a basketball game—even at nine o'clock on a weekday morning—rise above the traffic.

Patrick buys a paper at the newsstand, sticking it under his arm without reading it. "I knew you did something you weren't proud of. I already knew that. And it didn't stop me from…"

So, Patrick isn't going to say it again, isn't going to repeat that he loves Nathaniel. It's just as well.

"What were you hiding from when you came here?" Patrick asks as he's unlocking the shop door and holding it open for Nathaniel.

"I copied some files. I was worried that they were going to make sure I didn't show them to anyone."

"And you aren't worried about that anymore."

"There are dozens of people who know the same secrets I do." Nathaniel knows that what he's telling Patrick is the truth, even though he isn't sure it's ever going to feel like the truth. "They might want to make sure I don't sell my secrets to Moscow. Or to the *New York Times*." Nathaniel hadn't intended to suggest that the agency considers Moscow and the paper of record equivalent threats, but that might not be inaccurate. "At worst, they'll keep an eye on me."

"What's in these papers?"

Nathaniel swallows. "Proof that they're spying on Americans they've decided are subversive."

"And that was what made you quit?"

"That was the last straw."

Patrick nods, like that's in any way a satisfactory answer, and proceeds to oil his typewriter. As he's loading a piece of letter paper, he mentions that he's writing to a San Francisco collector who wants an 1880s *Leaves of Grass*, and who Patrick thinks might be willing to pay for that inscribed book he bought from Maud Dempsey's estate. Nathaniel picks up takeout from the soul food restaurant on Grove Street for a late lunch, and they eat enough chicken and waffles to feel a little sleepy. It's such a normal day, such a lovely and boring and typical day, and Nathaniel can feel his heart breaking. Patrick's words, "it's too late," echo in Nathaniel's ears.

That night, Patrick says, "If Michael came home, and he'd done terrible things, I'd have loved him, you know? Loving him wouldn't have meant that I supported whatever it was he did over there. I'd be upset that he was put in a position—"

"Nobody put me in any position," Nathaniel says. "I could have walked away. I wasn't drafted, I wasn't under orders."

"I know. I guess what I mean is that you signed up for what you thought were good reasons, and—"

"Patrick, it will break my heart if I have to listen to you compromising yourself to make me into someone good enough for you to respect."

"For fuck's sake, I don't care if you're *good*."

"You practically stopped talking to your brother because he didn't fight the draft!"

"I was furious with him because I didn't want him to *leave*. I couldn't stand the idea of him dying for no reason and just going along with it."

Nathaniel could kick himself, because Jerome

practically told him as much. What had he said? Patrick's always ready for people to leave him on the side of the road like an old mattress. And here Nathaniel is, offering to leave. No—it's worse than that. Nathaniel has backed them both into a corner where the only solution is for Nathaniel to leave. He hurts Patrick if he goes, and he hurts Patrick if he stays.

Patrick rubs a hand across his beard. "I don't care if you're good," he repeats. "I care that you're you."

Nathaniel doesn't know what he could possibly say to that, so he gets Walt's leash and walks him around the block. When he gets back, he heads directly into the shower, hoping that by the time he's done Patrick will be in bed with the door shut, and they can avoid the issue of where Nathaniel is or isn't sleeping.

But when he comes out Patrick is waiting for him, leaning against the wall opposite the bathroom, like he needs to intercept Nathaniel before he makes a break for it. He isn't wearing a shirt, which is just unfair.

"Come on," Patrick says. "Time for bed." He points toward his bedroom, so Nathaniel can't even pretend to misunderstand. Nathaniel climbs into the bed, and Walt follows so they have to go through the usual routine of reminding him that he's a dog and doesn't sleep on the bed. It's basically the same as every night for over a month. Two seconds after Patrick pulls the chain to put out his bedside lamp, they're kissing, Patrick's hand on Nathaniel's jaw, his body heavy and warm.

"You are good," Patrick says. "I should have said that before. You're good to me. You're good to the Valdez kids, to Susan and Eleanor—"

"Being good to the people I love isn't the same. It just isn't." In the dark quiet closeness of the bed, it sounds like a plea.

Patrick kisses him again, harder this time. Nathaniel slides a hand along the muscles of Patrick's back, then tugs him closer.

"Yeah?" Patrick asks.

Nathaniel wonders how many people have ever been fucked to prove a point about wartime ethics, or whatever is going through Patrick's mind. Nathaniel knows that isn't precisely the point Patrick is making.

Later, when he's sure Patrick is sleeping soundly, he slips out of the apartment. He spins the combination of the lock.

He's been thinking of what he told Patrick, that what the agency would be most worried about is Nathaniel giving this information to the Soviets or the press. Well, he has no intention of giving anything to the Soviets. But the *New York Times,* on the other hand. That might accomplish something. Seeing those files with his own eyes had ruptured the last shreds of trust Nathaniel had in this organization—maybe in the entire government. It might do the same thing for other people. Things could change, not just with how the agency operates. People might demand a government they can trust.

Or it might just explode Nathaniel's life, get him charged with treason or something equally ruinous, and bring everybody he loves into scrutiny they don't want.

He imagines telling that to Patrick and Susan, imagines telling them he can't do the right thing because he needs to protect them. Susan would hand deliver the envelope to the *Times* herself. Patrick would be more worried about Nathaniel's safety, but love has made Patrick an unreliable moral compass.

He has the number of a *Times* reporter and not a single

excuse not to use it. When Viv put up that flier looking for a room to rent, Beverly left Nathaniel with her phone number to pass on to Viv. And he did pass it on to her, but not before entering it onto a card and sliding it into Patrick's new Rolodex.

He can't change the last twenty years, but he can make sure the next thing he does is something he can live with.

In the morning, he offers to walk Walt and pick up the paper. At the pay phone on the corner, he pulls the Rolodex card from his pocket and makes a call.

Part 5
A WORD UNSAID

Patrick

23

"What do you mean, you didn't hear about it?" Susan asks. She arrived home with twice as much luggage as she left with. Eleanor now has a wardrobe that'll be the envy of all the other six-month-olds. "It's all over the news. You should have heard what my father had to say. I'm kicking myself for not being there."

"We didn't watch much television," Patrick says. "Or read the paper." Patrick spent most of the week taking Nathaniel to bed every chance he got, like maybe if he just fucked him well enough, all their troubles would disappear.

Susan looks between them. Patrick's dealing with the mail he didn't open for the past few days, and Nathaniel's holding Eleanor, who reached for him as soon as she saw him and now won't let him go. "Anyway, the Democratic Convention? To choose a presidential candidate? You've heard of this, yes?"

"Yes, oh my god, get on with it."

"Anti-war protesters had a rally. Tens of thousands of them, including the weirdo wing of the anti-war movement."

"You're the weirdo wing of the anti-war movement," Patrick points out. "I'm the weirdo wing of the anti-war movement."

"Your point? Anyway, the mayor of Chicago orders the police to enforce a curfew, and thousands of cops show up in riot gear, throwing tear gas into the crowd, chasing protesters with clubs as they run away. And it was all on TV. Television reporters got beaten up. Television reporters!"

"Who was nominated?" Patrick asks.

Susan wrinkles her nose. "Humphrey. Did you two seriously not even turn on the news?" She glances at the pile of newspapers on Patrick's desk, perfectly folded and blatantly untouched.

Patrick doesn't look at Nathaniel. Instead, he flips through the newspapers, only reading the headlines. It's all unsettling but familiar. Not just the police being violent— Patrick isn't ever going to be surprised by that. Last month some cops in Washington Square Park tried to arrest a boy who climbed a tree to get his pet squirrel. It was a Sunday and the park was crowded, but the police ran into the crowd with clubs, supposedly in order to disperse the people who gathered to defend the kid. What surprised Patrick was that this all happened over a squirrel, rather than race or the war. But it didn't really have anything to do with the squirrel, just like he isn't sure that what happened in Chicago was entirely because of the war. The war is the main thing, but the people on the other side aren't just *for* the war: they're against people protesting.

They're fighting for the status quo, or maybe an imaginary past where nobody complained and people kept to their places.

He can't imagine Nathaniel having been one of those people. Nathaniel probably wasn't, not exactly. It sounds like he tried to disappear into the rules, to use conformity as a kind of camouflage, and got too caught up in his disappearing act to mistrust what was happening around him. Patrick doubts he would have liked Nathaniel very much if they'd met a few years ago.

Patrick always scorned Michael for being such a rule follower. The rules were all made for people like Michael; of course he liked them. Maybe if Patrick's life had gone a little differently—a little softer, a little smoother—he might have been the same way. He crosses the street at crosswalks. He's scrupulous about sales tax. But he's spent ten years enthusiastically committing a felony whenever he touches a man. It's difficult to retain much respect for the rule of law when he can't live a fairly sedate life without committing a crime. This country has made him a criminal; it took his brother's life and would have taken his own life too. He has nothing to say to anyone who thinks he should wave the flag anyway.

And yet—Patrick still believes the United States is worth something, despite Hiroshima, despite the Ku Klux Klan, despite this war and despite practically every page of every newspaper on the desk in front of him. He believes it, not because it's true, but because he wants it to be true, because he wants to believe the people in the streets and the people in this building will come out on top. He wants to believe that enough people want to do the right thing.

He doesn't know if that's delusional. He doesn't know if that's what Nathaniel thought, too. But he does know you can assume the worst of someone and also help them be better; he's spent ten years looking after people who might steal his typewriter or pull a knife on him. That's basically how he'll feel going into the voting booth this fall. Christ. He scrubs a hand over his beard.

"Susan," he hears Nathaniel say. "I need to tell you something."

Patrick stays behind his desk, Eleanor in his lap, while Nathaniel tells Susan the truth, feeling like he's watching his house burn to the ground. It's not that he thought Susan would take it well, but as Nathaniel talks, Susan draws away: she straightens her back, takes a step toward the door.

When Nathaniel's done, Susan turns to Patrick, her face blank. "How long have you known?"

"Since Nathaniel's birthday."

"And you're fine with it," she says, not a question.

Patrick hesitates, shifting Eleanor in his lap. "I know I will be."

"Just to be clear," Susan says, turning her attention back to Nathaniel. "We're talking about the same CIA that buys foreign elections, organizes coups, and infiltrates American student groups, right?"

"Right."

"All that was in the news a year before you showed up here. So you didn't suddenly learn that you were working for the bad guys and hand in your two week notice."

Nathaniel swallows. "No."

"So, why did you quit?" she asks.

"I couldn't ignore it anymore. It wasn't just things happening in other parts of the agency, it was work they were asking me to do. And I couldn't."

"What were they asking you to do?"

"It's probably classified," Patrick says.

"Do I look like I care," Susan says, at the same time Nathaniel says, "I couldn't care less." Then they both look embarrassed.

"They're spying on Americans, on American soil," Nathaniel says. "That was the last straw."

"What was the first straw?"

Nathaniel looks surprised, like maybe he hasn't thought about it before. "The Bay of Pigs. No, that's not right. That's what it should have been. I don't know. I don't actually know." Now he looks troubled. "Listen," he says, "I came here because I was cold and confused. I wasn't planning on this." He lets out a strangled laugh. "How could I have been? I knew it would ruin everything when you found out, but I stayed anyway. I'm sorry for that."

"Are you?" Susan asks.

"No. But I know I should be. If you want me to leave, then I'll go."

"Oh, no," Susan says. "You aren't going to make me be the bad guy. And nobody's kicking you out. It isn't like that."

The door chimes ring, and a customer walks in, a woman and a mutinous-looking teenager. "Are you still open? Oh thank god. Somebody—not mentioning names—was supposed to read *The Red Badge of Courage* before the first day of school."

Susan takes Eleanor from Patrick. "I'll see you later," she says, maybe to Patrick, maybe to both of them, and leaves through the front door.

"I can mind the shop," Nathaniel says, then mouths, "Go with her," to Patrick.

Patrick hesitates, because he doesn't think Nathaniel should be alone right now. But neither should Susan. Nathaniel makes a shooing motion, and Patrick heads upstairs. He knocks on Susan's door, stupidly unsure of whether he's allowed to let himself in.

"I don't know how you're fine with this," Susan says when she opens the door.

"We knew he was keeping secrets. We knew that whatever he used to be, it wasn't anything he was proud of."

"I thought he worked for Dow Chemical or some other war profiteer." She sits in the armchair and Patrick sits on the couch. Nathaniel's absence feels almost glaring, a gap in a tightly packed bookshelf, the silence when the needle lifts off the record.

"And that would have been better?" Patrick asks. "War profiteering?"

"No. I guess not. I thought I knew him. I wish he'd told us months ago."

Patrick keeps thinking the same thing. There's a point at which secrecy becomes dishonesty, but Patrick doesn't know where to draw that line. "Would it have changed anything?"

"I wouldn't have gotten so attached. What were we thinking, letting a total stranger into our lives? We didn't know anything about him. Eleanor loves him. I love him. And now what?"

Patrick can see it all crumbling to pieces. He thought he was ready for this. He knew it wouldn't last, but knowing it doesn't make it easier. Now, either Susan will move out or Nathaniel will. Even if, somehow, Patrick gets to keep them both, he won't get to keep them together.

"You're in love with him?" Susan asks.

"Yeah."

"I am happy for you, you know." There's the tiniest fragment of a smile on her lips. "It's nice, isn't it?"

"It's nice," he agrees, charmed, despite everything, by the understatement. How many songs has she written, how many songs has she sung, that try to capture the experience of falling in love? And now she calls it nice. But nice is as good a word as any, when there aren't any better words.

"I keep imagining him sitting at a long table with a bunch of men in the same suit and they're all cooking up reasons to go to war," she says.

"Me too," Patrick admits. On Susan's coffee table is a cheap notebook that he recognizes as Nathaniel's. He must have forgotten it here before Susan left for her parents' house. Patrick opens it to the middle. Nathaniel's writing in here is so much messier than it is on the notes he leaves for Patrick, some letters more gestures than actual shapes, some words abbreviated in a way that must make sense to Nathaniel. There are single capital letters that appear on nearly every page—E, S, I, H, M—all easy enough to decipher as the people he talks to every day. There's no P, but Patrick doesn't need to wonder why: some things aren't safe even when you put them in code.

He squints and tries to decipher as much as he can, rarely making out more than a few words per page. Eleanor's first tooth. Subway graffiti. Tofu. The slide guitar. Night games.

"Should you be reading that?" Susan asks.

"I don't know. Susan, he called it a list of his sins, but look at it." He holds out the notebook. She hesitates, but takes it.

"How are Eleanor's little shoes one of his sins?" she asks a moment later, and Patrick can see as realization dawns.

He makes sure she has enough food in the kitchen for some kind of dinner, then goes downstairs. It's late enough that Nathaniel should have closed up the shop, but their apartment is empty. "Nathaniel?" he calls. But there's no answer. The shop, too, is empty. The lights are off and the door is locked.

There's no note on his desk, and when he goes back upstairs there's nothing waiting for him there, either. Nathaniel's things are still in his room—well, mostly in Patrick's room, at this point. His violin is on the dresser. He'd come back for his violin, wouldn't he?

Patrick checks his bedroom again, like maybe Nathaniel will be there this time, but all he sees is a Walt-shaped dent in the mattress. Where the hell is the dog, anyway? He whistles, but doesn't hear Walt's usual put-upon sigh, followed by the scratch of nails on the floor as Walt trudges off to see what Patrick wants now.

Back downstairs, Walt's leash isn't on the hook by the door, and only then does Patrick arrive at the conclusion he'd have come to immediately if he'd been thinking clearly: Nathaniel is walking the dog. He puts on the shop lights and unlocks the door. Then, for good measure, he props the door open. He's sitting at his desk, trying to decide whether a book is worth rebinding, when Nathaniel comes in.

"You're letting all the cool air out," Nathaniel says, using his foot to nudge the stack of encyclopedia volumes away from the door. "Go, be free," he tells Walt, unclipping the leash. The dog scrambles over to Patrick.

"I thought you'd left," Patrick says, scratching Walt's

head. "I thought you were gone."

"I would have told you first," Nathaniel says. Not, *I won't leave.*

24

The next morning, the phone rings as Patrick's opening the shop. "The car won't start," Mrs. Kaplan says. "And I don't have anything good to read."

He leaves the shop in Nathaniel's hands, gets on the subway, then walks from the station to Mrs. Kaplan's house. She's waiting for him at the door and won't let him even look at the car until he's had coffee and some babka. The kitchen hasn't changed at all in the last ten years, or probably in the twenty years before that. Same yellow paint, same black and white linoleum, same milky-green coffee mugs.

"All right," he says when he couldn't possibly eat another bite. "Let's look at that car."

The battery's dead, which is always why Mrs. Kaplan's car won't start. Why her useless neighbors don't come over and ring the doorbell when she leaves the headlights on overnight, he'll never know.

Mrs. Kaplan sits in the driver's seat and steers, the car in neutral, while Patrick pushes it into the middle of the road.

"Okay, put it in second gear," Patrick calls out, even though by now Mrs. Kaplan shouldn't need to be told how to push start a car—she's done it as many times as he has. "And keep your foot on the clutch. Let go of the brakes." Patrick pushes the car hard and runs with it. "Let go of the clutch!" he shouts when he can hear the engine running. "Now brake! Put it in park." He opens the driver's side door and Mrs. Kaplan slides across to the passenger side. Patrick drives the car around the block and parks it right where it started. "Let it run for a bit, and it should be fine," he says.

She turns in her seat to pat his cheek. "You did good."

"I got the car started. It was nothing." Nothing he hasn't done a dozen times before, he doesn't add.

"I mean with everything. What would I do without you?" she asks.

He wants to tell her that she has it backwards; he's the one who's grateful. "You know a million people. You'd do fine without me."

"But you're the one who always comes when I call."

Patrick touches the worn cream leather of the steering wheel. "You taught me how to drive." He never learned in high school, partly because Susan had been more than happy to drive him around in her father's baby-blue Cadillac, taking turns at eye-watering speed, but mostly because he didn't want to ask to borrow his aunt and uncle's car. Mrs. Kaplan took him out to a department store in Flushing, early in the morning before it opened, and let him drive around the empty parking lot.

The fact that she'd taught him to drive isn't really the

point. His memories of his parents are fragmented and hazy, and he doesn't want any memories of his aunt and uncle. He didn't meet Mrs. Kaplan until he was eighteen, but sometimes he thinks she might have raised him.

"Nathaniel called me last week," she says, and then doesn't say anything else. Her silence, as always, works on him like a truth serum.

"He told you?"

"He told me more than one thing." Her voice is heavy with implication.

Patrick runs a finger over the stitching on the steering wheel. "I think he wants me to be mad at him."

"Aren't you?"

"Not at Nathaniel. Are you?" he asks.

"Well," she says, "why would that matter? He knows what he did. Now he has to make it right. Don't you think he wants to be better?"

"Yes," he says. "You don't mind that he and I are—" He breaks off, feeling silly that he's looking for her approval.

"Mind? You're good for one another. When I met him he was like a wet cat. Pitiful and screaming mad about it."

Patrick laughs, at the image and the accuracy.

"Exactly the way you were," she adds. "It's good to see you happy."

"No telling how long it'll last," Patrick says.

"How long do you want it to last?"

Patrick shuts his eyes and tips his head back, the only sound the rumble of the engine. "I'm not sure what I want is on the table."

Mrs. Kaplan hums. "Sometimes you have to give people a chance to let you down."

"What's that supposed to mean?"

"Maybe he'll stay, maybe he won't. But if you act like he already has one foot out the door…" She shrugs. "I take in some kid and he steals my television? I don't like it, but ten other people don't steal my television. What's the use in treating them all like thieves? Did you tell him you want him to stay?"

"He knows."

She makes a disapproving noise. "Knowing it isn't the same as hearing it."

Back inside, he fixes a dripping faucet and a wobbly table leg. On the kitchen table, he leaves the books he grabbed before leaving the shop: *The Coney Island of the Mind*, *Bonjour Tristesse*, and *Slouching Towards Bethlehem*, books Susan took with her to her parents' house and left on Patrick's desk yesterday before everything went to hell.

Nathaniel's at the cash register when Patrick walks through the door. There are a handful of people browsing, and Patrick has never resented customers more than he does today. Nathaniel, despite the circles under his eyes, chats amiably with each of them as he rings them up.

"Don't be a hero and decide that you're going to leave to do me a favor or to spare me some conflict with Susan," Patrick says as soon as the last of the customers has left.

"I think we've established that I'm a lot of things but a hero isn't one of them. I'll stick around until you ask me to stop."

"I won't."

"You can't know that."

"I can and I do."

"Because," Nathaniel says, his hands in his pockets and his gaze on the ceiling, "it's too late for you to feel otherwise."

Patrick winces. "I'm sorry. I shouldn't have said that."

"It's the truth, though, isn't it?" Nathaniel looks exhausted. He isn't sleeping; Patrick sometimes wakes to hear him puttering around downstairs. His lips are pressed together in a miserable little line, and his sleeves are rolled up with merciless symmetry. On his shoulder is a tiny stain that he must not know about, a drip of Eleanor's mashed vegetables that didn't come out in the wash. It's embarrassing how much Patrick loves this man.

"I'm so glad it's true," Patrick says. Nathaniel looks confused, so Patrick is going to need to spell it out. "Look. When I think about what would have happened if I'd missed the chance to have this, I feel like I've swerved away from oncoming traffic. Do you understand?" Nathaniel doesn't look like he understands a single goddamn thing. "Nathaniel, for god's sake. I can't stand the idea of not loving you."

Some of that must have gotten through, because Nathaniel takes his hands out of his pockets and clutches the edge of the desk that's between him and Patrick. "Me too," he says, and it isn't a promise, but it's something.

Lunchtime comes and goes, and Susan doesn't visit the shop. Patrick hadn't seriously thought that a good night's sleep would make everything right in the world, but he hoped it might anyway.

But when he stops by her apartment in the afternoon, she takes him up on his offer to take Eleanor. She has to know Nathaniel will see the baby too. That feels promising.

While Nathaniel is minding the shop and the baby, Patrick climbs up to the attic. It had been hot in June, but now it's sweltering. The air feels solid with humidity.

When Susan complained about noises overhead, he'd blamed it on cats or squirrels, but there weren't any signs of animals in the attic. It only smelled of dust and mildew. The attic door opened suspiciously easily.

He shines his flashlight at the miscellaneous junk on the attic floor: a broken chair, a folding table, some old milk crates. And then, over by the dormer windows, is the contraption Iris and Hector were working on that spring. Iris said it wasn't a radio, and she wasn't lying, because Patrick thinks he's looking at some ancient version of a Ditto machine. God knows where they found it—could have been up here, for all he knows, or in the mess of things on the second story, or in a trash heap somewhere else. The floor around it is neat, but wedged under the machine is a piece of paper. He crouches down and extracts it. It's a misprint of the *Louder* zine, the text cut off on the right side of the paper. He folds it and puts it in his pocket, then goes downstairs and shows it to Nathaniel.

Nathaniel huffs out a laugh; it's the first time he's laughed in days. "I knew they were up to something."

"Are they going to get in trouble? With the law, I mean."

Nathaniel flips through the zine again. "I don't know. Do you think that would stop them?" He glances up at Patrick. "Do you think it *should* stop them?"

At the idea of Iris and Hector getting questioned, getting arrested, Patrick's heart races. "No."

"I gave the files to Beverly."

It takes Patrick a minute to make sense of this—what files, and who the hell is Beverly? He sits down. "Are you going to be all right?" Nathaniel said he wasn't worried anymore about the CIA coming to get him, but Patrick is ready to believe the CIA is capable of anything. Even more realistically, there's no way that sharing classified documents is legal. "Are you going to jail?" he asks, feeling like a kid asking to be told that everything is going to be fine.

Nathaniel sits on the edge of Patrick's desk. "The *Times* will keep my name out of it, but the agency will know it was me. Or at least they'll suspect it. I don't know what will happen."

"I want you to be safe," Patrick says. The way they're sitting, he has to look up at Nathaniel, and the only convenient place to touch is Nathaniel's knee, so that's where he puts his hand.

"The point is that we aren't safe. Turning dissidents into criminals is the thin end of the wedge. It always is. The next thing you know there's a secret police."

"When does the article come out?"

"Not for weeks, maybe months. They have to do whatever reporters do. More sources, corroboration, I don't know."

It seems unfair that Nathaniel spent the first few months here terrified of getting found by the CIA, and now he's done something that practically guarantees that he's going to get found by the CIA, and face the consequences.

Nathaniel spends the afternoon in the patch of dirt that's technically their backyard. The door is next to the kitchen, and Patrick can go months without remembering that it is, in fact, a door, because there's simply no reason to open it. The yard contains several ancient and mostly decomposed cardboard boxes, some soda bottles, the spindly remains of a dead tree, bicycle parts, bare dirt, and whatever weeds can survive almost total shade and decades of use as a dumping ground.

"What are you doing?" Patrick asks when he brings Nathaniel some cold water.

"Cleaning it up." Nathaniel drops something into a metal trash can he must have pulled off the street. It lands with a plink. "If Walt comes out here, I don't want him to step on a nail or broken glass." He picks up what looks like a tile and drops it in the bin. "Eleanor will be crawling soon."

Patrick leaves him to it. The next time he looks out the kitchen window, Nathaniel has turned up a shovel from god knows where and is trying to dig out the dead tree. By the time the sun sets over the roof of the building next door, the courtyard is clear. Nathaniel doesn't come in until Patrick's closing the shop.

Patrick's about to ask what Nathaniel wants to do about dinner when he sees that Nathaniel is clutching a blood-stained handkerchief in one hand.

"Let me look," Patrick says.

"It was just a piece of broken glass."

Patrick goes to the sink and turns on the tap. "Come on."

Nathaniel's hand is still curled into a fist. Some of the blood on the handkerchief is dried and dark, so he must have cut himself a while ago and kept working anyway. Patrick pries his fingers open and puts his hand under the stream of water. The gash is straight across his palm and there's dirt in it, the idiot, but it doesn't look deep enough to need stitches. Nathaniel hisses when Patrick cleans the gash with a bar of soap.

"Sorry, sorry. Nearly done," Patrick says. "Okay, I'll be right back with some bandages."

"Don't bother. I need a shower anyway."

While Nathaniel's in the shower, Patrick finds the little jar of iodine he bought when Hector came home with a skinned knee.

"You don't need to do this," Nathaniel says when he comes out, a towel wrapped around his waist and a bloody washcloth in his fist. "I can do it myself."

"I know you can," Patrick says, even though it's a pain in the ass doing anything to your dominant hand. "I like taking care of you."

"You like taking care of everybody."

He isn't wrong, but he's deliberately missing the point. Patrick pauses in dabbing on the iodine long enough to give Nathaniel an unimpressed look.

"Let's go out to dinner," Patrick says when he's wrapped a length of gauze around Nathaniel's palm a few times and covered it in tape.

"Stop acting normal."

"How do you want me to act?" He lifts Nathaniel's unbandaged hand to his mouth and kisses his knuckles.

"I really wish I knew."

Nathaniel pulls his hand away and kisses Patrick on the mouth. Patrick's shoulders hit the wall, the towel rack pressing into his lower back. In the past month, Nathaniel has figured out exactly how to turn Patrick on. Now he deploys his tricks all at once: a thumb on Patrick's nipple, a thigh between Patrick's legs, a kiss that's messy and insistent and sharp at the edges.

When Nathaniel drops to his knees, Patrick isn't ready for it. He wants to tell Nathaniel that the tile will be too hard on his knees, but Nathaniel glances up at him and says, "Please," and Patrick isn't going to argue about tile floors.

There's something about the whole setup that feels

like penance, or at least penitence: Nathaniel on his knees, minutes after basically telling Patrick he should be mad at him. But Patrick is no stranger to using sex to obliterate everything that isn't another person's body.

Patrick pushes the hair off Nathaniel's forehead, then traces the shell of his ear. "Anything you want," he says, and flicks open the top button of his jeans.

The next morning, before he's even had any coffee, Nathaniel announces that he has to run an errand and will be back before it's time to open the shop. Patrick makes coffee and putters around the empty apartment, then putters around the empty shop, Walt at his heels. It's too quiet and subtly wrong, like everything in the building got replaced with nearly identical copies. It's somebody else's home, in some other dimension.

He goes upstairs to Susan.

"I want you to stay," he says when she answers the door. "Even if you and Nathaniel are never okay again, I still want you to stay. I know I don't have any right to ask, not after—" He hadn't meant to say that last part, but now there's no taking it back.

"Not after what?"

"After I left you. After I left you and Michael."

Susan draws in a sharp breath. "You didn't leave us."

The version of the story that Susan tells herself is that what Patrick's aunt and uncle did was as good as kicking him out. And that's true, in a way: they made sure he wouldn't come back but they kept their hands clean. He isn't sure any of that matters. "You thought I was dead or in the hospital."

Susan opens her mouth like she's going to deny it, as if she hadn't told him so at the time. "We knew there was a good reason you didn't call us."

"I didn't call you for weeks." Patrick can't even remember that time without a hot wash of shame. The whole time he'd been at Mrs. Kaplan's, he'd known he should call, but he couldn't make himself do it, didn't know what lie he could possibly tell. What if they'd seen his name in the paper? What if they hadn't? "He was so mad. So were you."

"Not at you." She scrubs the sleeve of her bathrobe against her eyes.

"That's such a lie."

"Patrick, I don't know what you want me to say. I was mad at you. I haven't been mad at you about that in ten years. As soon as I knew you were okay, it was obvious that something terrible must have happened and I could make a few guesses about what it was."

"Michael didn't have any idea."

Susan looks at him for a minute, searching his face and finding something there that Patrick would prefer not to think about. "Michael forgave you. Or—no—he understood."

"He never said anything."

"The two of you never said anything to one another! Did you expect a heart to heart? God, it's so shitty that you can't be having this conversation with him."

Her arms are folded across her chest and her eyes are wet. He can't take it, so he pulls her into a hug. "The shittiest," he agrees.

"Do you really want me to stay?" she says into his shirt.

"Yeah. It's good," he says, so severe an understatement it's nearly a lie. "It makes me happy," he adds, feeling like he's standing over a pit. "I wish you were able to be in San Francisco with Michael, all of you together, but instead—"

"I hated living so far from you. So did Michael. He was sure we could lure you to San Francisco eventually."

Patrick remembers all the comments about the food, the culture, the climate. He remembers Michael's strangled attempts to explain that San Francisco is a great place for "You know. Men who…" accompanied by a vague gesture. Patrick thought these were pointed jabs, not sales pitches.

"What happens when you meet someone new?" Patrick asks, not sure it's a question he's even allowed to ask.

"There's room here, don't you think?" She pulls back and looks at him squarely. "Look. You'll be there for her first day of kindergarten and when she drops out of college and runs off with a painter. You can bail her out of jail and hold her hand while she gets a tattoo. If you want to be there, you're there. Okay?"

Patrick tries to say that he wants to be there, but all he can do is nod and look away.

Susan follows Patrick down to the shop. The door's still locked but the lights are on, and when Patrick opens the door, he can hear Jefferson Airplane playing from the back. A warm breeze blows through the shop.

"He'll be in the yard," Patrick says.

"What yard?" Susan asks, but she follows him.

Nathaniel is in a t-shirt and jeans, digging a hole in the center of the empty space he cleared yesterday.

"I bet you bled right through the bandage," Patrick says. "What are you doing, anyway?"

Nathaniel doesn't look up. "Planting a tree. It's depressing out here."

The tree, if you can call it that, is two feet high and sad looking. "Where do you even buy a tree in Manhattan?"

"The answers to this and many more questions can be found in the Yellow Pages," Nathaniel says, turning around. The little twist of a smile drops from his face when he sees Susan.

"I want to make a record," Susan says.

Nathaniel's expression is perfectly blank. "Do you."

"I negotiated a pretty decent contract. Your name's on it. All you have to do is sign."

Nathaniel shuts his eyes. "Susan."

Susan reaches into the pocket of her jeans and pulls out Nathaniel's notebook. "There's a song in here."

"There's a nervous breakdown in there," Nathaniel says.

"Same difference. Are you working this morning?"

"No. I just need to fix this." He holds up his hand, showing the bloody bandage.

"I have Band-Aids and mercurochrome upstairs," Susan says. Nathaniel drops the shovel and follows her upstairs, brushing Patrick's arm with his hand on the way out.

Patrick spends the morning typing up letters to prospective buyers. He keeps the shop door propped open so he can hear the music drifting down from Susan's open window.

25

"I still can't believe you brought them on the plane," Iris hisses at her brother.

"I wasn't going to leave them in San Juan," Hector says.

"You should have left them *here.*"

"Hey, you two," Patrick says when he sees them. "How was your trip?"

"It's good to be back," Mrs. Valdez says, entering the store behind her children. She looks harried. She looks like someone who's spent two weeks with bickering teenagers. She looks like a woman who will be thrilled to go back to work tomorrow.

"There's wine in the fridge," Patrick says, because Susan's mother sent her back with three bottles of sweet white wine. "No wine glasses, but if you can put up with coffee mugs, help yourself."

She heads back to the kitchen like she doesn't need to

be told twice.

Sometimes, when Patrick watches Hector and Iris, he wonders if he and Michael were ever like that. He doubts it. They'd been less than a year apart, but Patrick felt every day of those extra eleven and a half months. Protecting Micheal had been his job—not just protecting him from bullies or their family, but from the knowledge that they were all alone.

Maybe everyone feels a sense of guilty failure when they lose a younger sibling, or maybe this is something his brain cooked up special just for him. Maybe if they'd been on better terms, Michael would have figured out some way not to go to Vietnam. But it's been seven months since he died, and Patrick is pretty sure that what he's really tearing himself up over is that he didn't make it right between them. He doesn't know what it would have taken, or what words he should have said, just that he'll never get a chance to say them.

Mrs. Valdez puts a mug of wine on his desk. It has the logo for Shell gas on it. Her mug says something in faded black, with WAFFLES the only word still legible.

"You looked like you needed it," she says. "Also it's only four o'clock and I'm not drinking alone."

He holds up his mug in a silent toast.

"How was your vacation?" he asks.

"About a week too long."

"Your kids are a lucky to have you."

She gives him a look. "You aren't wrong, but what's this about?"

Patrick just wanted to say something nice to a person who's been more than kind to him for the nearly three years they've known one another. They're friends, right? They're sort of friends. She's forty-five and he's never

315

called her by her first name, but he thinks they're friends.

"I don't think I ever thanked you for taking care of Susan and the baby when they got here."

"You thanked me. You also paid me. Thanks for helping the kids with their homework and feeding them, if we're spending the afternoon thanking one another for things we'd have done anyway."

The zines are inches away, in the top drawer of Patrick's desk. Iris and Hector are only sixteen. It's probably his responsibility to tell their parents what they're up to. But all he can think about is that phone call he made from the police station ten years ago. The Valdezes are better parents than his aunt and uncle ever tried to be. They wouldn't hurt their kids. But he still can't bring himself to open that drawer.

The next morning, Iris comes into the shop to work a shift. "Hey," he says. "Welcome back." He opens the drawer. "Are these yours?"

She draws in a breath and looks ready to lie her head off.

"I liked them," Patrick says. "So did Nathaniel and Susan. Did you write it all yourself?"

She shakes her head. "Hector assembled the Gestetner. When we found it in the basement it was in pieces. My cousin did the Spanish translations and our friend Raul wrote one of the articles."

"Why did you put them in the shop?"

"We told some friends they could grab a copy if they wanted one. Sorry."

"Just be careful."

"Sure," she says, not even bothering to make it sound like a convincing lie.

"You know, people have gone to jail for encouraging

draft evasion."

"There are dozens of papers like ours. They can't go after all of us."

Patrick might think this is the optimism of youth, except for how Susan has said the same thing.

"They've slowed down the bombing," Iris says.

"Only because of the election," Patrick says. "Johnson is worried the Democrats won't have a chance otherwise."

"Which is because Johnson knows people hate the war, which he knows because tens of thousands of people have protested."

"The point is that they don't need to arrest the publisher of every radical newspaper. They only need to make an example out of a couple of kids."

That night at the Times Square diner, Patrick described that *New York Times* article on deviants as a gay Bat Signal. That had been a bunch of men seeing a chance for casual sex and seizing the opportunity; it's not the same thing as writing a radical newspaper. But change can only happen if individual people know how to find one another and become a collective, a movement.

Patrick feels a swell of—not hope, exactly, but something like a contact high with someone else's hope. Hector and Iris's entire conscious life has been a period of time that Patrick can only think of as a steady downhill slide, but they still believe they can change things. Hell, maybe the reason they think they can change things is that it *is* a mess: nothing's solid anymore, so they can shape it the way they want.

"I want you to be safe," he tells Iris.

"Who do you think gets to be safe? You think this war will be over when Hector turns eighteen?"

Whitman said that he liked agitation but disliked

317

agitators; Patrick likes agitation and he loves agitators but, at heart, wants everyone to be safe and warm and fed.

"Also," Iris says, "I'm not the only person here"—she gestures between herself and Patrick—"risking jail time and a criminal record in order to do something they know isn't wrong."

Mr. and Mrs. Valdez have to know that Patrick's gay, but somehow he hadn't thought the twins would pick up on it. You can usually count on teenagers to be oblivious about adults' personal lives.

When Nathaniel asked why Patrick doesn't keep it a secret, Patrick told him that hiding makes it too easy for people to pretend there's nothing wrong. That's what Iris is talking about: taking what they stand for and bringing it out into the streets.

"The problem with you is that you're too smart. Do your parents know about this?" He holds up the zine.

She puts a hand on her hip. "Are you kidding me?"

"What happens if they find out?"

"They won't like it."

"Would they stop you?"

Iris is quiet for a minute. "I don't think so."

"Would you get in trouble? I'm in a rough position here, kid. I don't want to get you or Hector in trouble, but I'm friends with your mother."

"We don't really get in trouble. We get lectured." Iris sighs, but trudges upstairs. Half an hour later she comes back down. "They don't like it, but they say it's better than going out and getting pregnant like my cousin did when she was my age."

That's almost exactly what Susan's parents said when she dropped out of college to play the guitar in coffeehouses.

Patrick looks at the cover, the spiky flower, the hand-lettered title, the modest little "25c" in the top right corner. "I'll pay you twenty cents each, wholesale," he says.

"Do you mean it?"

"It's good business," he says, thinking of the rack of zines at Gem Spa and at the other places he's glimpsed them.

But mostly, he remembers how annoyed Nathaniel said John was to see the zines. Other people will be annoyed, too. And other people won't be. There's some value in letting people know what kind of place this is.

By the end of September, Nathaniel is down to working ten hours a week in the shop, less than even Iris. He and Susan have played two more gigs and they spend half their time hammering out the details of the record.

They're acting in a way that feels, to Patrick, about eighty percent of the way to normal. If Patrick hadn't seen the way they were that spring and summer, he wouldn't have guessed that something was off. It doesn't even look like Susan is upset—Susan's never been able to hide that. She usually doesn't even bother. It's more like a mutual uneasiness.

Tonight, Nathaniel and Susan are fiddling with matchsticks, sliding them under the violin strings to change the sound. Eleanor is on the floor next to Patrick, trying to crawl. She's rocking herself back and forth on her hands and knees, occasionally looking angrily at the floor and then her hands, like they must be defective.

Before Eleanor, he never understood what people were going on about when they said that babies looked like a parent or some other relation. Babies mostly look like babies. But when Eleanor gets that expression, she looks just like Susan. The rest of the time, she's all Michael.

Looking at Eleanor and seeing Micheal isn't desperately sad anymore—or, it is sad, and it probably always will be, but it's also something else. She's all he has of Michael, and he might be all she'll ever have of her father, and at some point those two truths solidified into something good. They're family.

"Another couple of days," Nathaniel says from the sofa.

"She'll be all over the shop," Susan agrees. They all grin at one another, like they've personally accomplished something here.

Eleanor starts to cry, a sign that it's bedtime. Patrick changes her and gets her a bottle, then puts her in her crib, fast asleep. Six months ago, he couldn't have guessed it would ever be so simple to get this child to sleep.

Back in the living room, Nathaniel moves to the edge of the couch closest to Susan, and Patrick takes the invitation to sit. He takes the joint Susan passes him and lets their conversation wash over him.

"I think we should try drums on this track," Nathaniel says.

"I can't play the drums," Susan says.

"Neither can I. But we can get a session musician."

Susan's quiet for a while. "I prefer that it's only you and me."

"Okay," Nathaniel says, and starts to talk about something else. Fifths or eighths or some other fraction that matters in music, Patrick doesn't know.

"Go back to the drums," Susan says a few minutes later. "Tell me why you want them."

"Don't worry about it."

"If it wasn't important, you wouldn't have mentioned it. And now I'm curious."

"I think drums—or really any percussion—would lay down the rhythm in a way that makes it less…pretty. Right now it's beautiful. And that's good, obviously. Nobody's complaining about a beautiful song. But I think the anger is getting lost in the prettiness."

Susan's quiet again.

"You wrote the lyrics," Nathaniel goes on. "You know they're angry. I'd want people to hear that. If they walked away from that song thinking it was *nice* I'd be annoyed. Remember *Guernica*?" They'd been to the Museum of Modern Art that summer. At the time Patrick thought it was a pretty questionable choice for Susan to want to sit on a bench in front of a twenty-five-foot-wide painting full of dismembered bodies, even if it is a Picasso and the bodies are basically just distressing shapes. "*Guernica* has drums. Do you see what I mean?"

Patrick is just high enough for *Guernica has drums* to be the most profound thing he's heard in his life, even if he doesn't understand what it means. "*Guernica* has drums," he whispers, amazed.

"But it'll be a good song either way," Nathaniel says.

"Why are you folding like that?" Susan asks. "You obviously want the drums."

Nathaniel laughs. "Wait, are you serious? Because you matter to me more than any music we're ever going to make. Come on, Susan."

"That doesn't mean you have to give in whenever I'm pushy. We can talk things out. And, for the record, you matter to me more than the music, too, so implying that caring about one another is something only you can do is rude. No offense."

Patrick opens his eyes just enough to see that Susan doesn't look mad. Neither does Nathaniel.

"I hadn't thought of it that way," says Nathaniel. "Sorry."

"Also, you can't let me have my way because you're afraid I'm going to be mad at you about your reactionary phase."

"You can't call it that!"

"I can call it whatever I want. I, apparently, am the only one here being spied on by the actual CIA, so I feel like that gives me some rights. Anyway, I said we're going to be fine and so we're going to be fine."

"I don't think that's how this works."

"Okay, too bad, I think it is. We decide we want this"—she gestures at their instruments—"and we want this"—she gestures around the room. "We decide it's worth it."

Nathaniel fiddles with one of the pegs on his violin. "All right. Then, I really want those drums."

"I'll want to hear both versions. Drums and no drums. We can record both versions. Hell, we can release both versions. Just something to keep in mind. Also, if we're hiring session musicians, I want to talk about a mandolin."

"Your white whale," Patrick says, sounding very far away. Nathaniel pinches his leg.

"An autoharp wouldn't kill you," Nathaniel says.

"So much for 'this is your music, Susan, I'm just doing what you tell me to do.'"

"It *is* your music."

"You made something good, Nathaniel. Nobody's letting you wriggle out of responsibility for it."

"Harridan," Nathaniel says. "Here, listen to this." On

Susan's spare guitar, he picks out a tune they've played before, but he's done something to it, made it less mellow, a little jangly.

Maybe whatever new dynamic exists between Susan and Nathaniel, it isn't worse than what they had before. Maybe it's just in a different key.

Patrick shuts his eyes again, and he must fall asleep, because the next thing he knows, they're listening to the Beatles' new single. Susan has the record, of course, but so does Patrick—he bought it as soon as he heard it on the radio, like the kind of overenthusiastic teenager he never was. He's played it probably a hundred times now. It's a good song. It's catchy. Patrick isn't going to dwell on why he needs a seven-minute-long reassurance that things are going to get better. Maybe everybody needs that.

"That bridge," Susan says.

"Micheal would have loved it," Patrick mumbles.

"Never met a bridge he didn't like," Susan agrees, and starts singing along. Patrick's spent his whole life listening to Susan sing along—she can't help herself, really—but he didn't need to hear her sing "Hey Jude." That's for strangers on the record player to sing to him. He turns his face into the couch cushion so nobody can see what his eyes are doing.

26

The school year has technically started, but the teachers are on strike. The Valdez kids have been home more often than not, which means Iris and Nathaniel have taken up residence at the back of the shop with a calculus textbook. From what Patrick has overheard, only about fifty percent of what's going on back there is calculus. The rest is Iris arguing that the government needs to be overthrown and Nathaniel saying things like, "Yes, clearly, tell me more."

It's past nine o'clock, so Patrick locks the door and runs the cash register tape, then begins turning off the lights. From upstairs, there's another ominous thud. He heads toward the back of the shop.

"One of us needs to check on her," Nathaniel whispers as Patrick passes by.

"On my way."

Patrick finds Susan cross-legged on the floor next to the stack of the boxes that her landlord shipped from San

Francisco that spring. She has a box cutter in one hand and a look of clench-jawed resolve on her face.

"I need to find my address book. If Nathaniel wants a drummer, then I need to call Jim." Jim was the drummer in Susan's old band.

Patrick sits down next to her and starts rummaging through the boxes that she's already opened. The first box he looks at contains Michael's clothes. Right on top is this awful red cable knit sweater he used to wear every winter. Susan clutches his arm, and they stare at the sweater like it might disappear if they look away.

Susan gingerly removes it and puts it on her lap. The rest of the box is jeans, t-shirts, a few oxfords. "Salvation Army," she says, and Patrick shoves it all into a corner to deal with later.

It's brutal. A hair comb, a razor. Michael's alarm clock. Mundane objects, most bought at a Woolworth or drugstore, now precious for all the wrong reasons. An entire box of ratty Agatha Christie paperbacks, mismatched editions, all purchased secondhand, usually by Patrick, and given to Michael as a too casual afterthought when they saw one another. He puts that box aside.

The cups and plates choke Susan up: hundreds of meals shared together on dishes with green and blue flowers. They picked those dishes out together, the pattern a result of a compromise as carefully brokered as the Potsdam Agreement. Patrick had mostly been shocked that Susan and Michael had *wedding china*.

"They're nicer than your dishes," Susan says. This is a fact. "If you want them."

Patrick isn't sure he does, but Nathaniel will—he likes nice things, no matter how much he pretends he doesn't care.

He feels like there should be something in here for Eleanor, something she could look at and treasure and know it belonged to her dad, but none of it's like that. Michael took his watch—a college graduation present, purchased jointly by Susan and Patrick—to Vietnam, and apparently it got destroyed right along with the rest of him.

In the top drawer of Patrick's dresser is the telegram, the paper creased and the ink smudged from the days it spent in Patrick's pocket. Maybe Eleanor will want that someday, not because of the words on it but because of the smudges and creases, the evidence of having been folded and unfolded so many times: maybe she'll want to know her father was loved.

"I sent Iris home," Nathaniel says when he comes upstairs. "Need help?"

"Sure." Patrick glances around at the wreckage surrounding them. "We're looking for an address book." Nathaniel sits next to Patrick and opens a box.

"Patrick," Susan says. She's looking at a photo album. Patrick already knows what's inside, because he pasted the photos in there himself.

"We don't have to look at it," he says, but it's already open on Susan's lap.

The pictures start in seventh grade, Susan in braids and braces and an evil smile, Michael laughing for probably the first time since before their parents' funeral. It was Susan's camera, but Patrick took most of these photographs, so it isn't until the third page that he appears, his hair in a crew cut, Susan's old poodle in his lap. Sometimes there's someone else—Susan's mother, a classmate, a cousin who got invited to one of her birthday parties—but mostly it's the three of them, during the six years between the day they met and the day Patrick left.

Patrick can barely stand to look at Michael, always grinning so hard his face must hurt. Patrick can almost hear him talking too fast, laughing at his own jokes, unable to resist an awful pun. Patrick refuses to be someone who looks at a picture of someone who's died and comments on how full of life they seem, but that's all he can think. It's an outrage and a waste that he isn't around anymore, that someone took this kid and made it so he didn't get to see his daughter, didn't get to turn thirty, didn't get to listen to boring music and complain about hamburgers.

It's only when Susan sniffles that Patrick realizes he's already rubbing his eyes on the cuff of his shirt.

"You look like twins," Nathaniel says. "I figured you'd have to, to explain Eleanor, but still." He traces a finger along the edge of a photograph, very gingerly, only making contact with the album.

It's a picture from prom night, Susan in a dress her mother picked out and which must have used all the seafoam-green tulle on the entire North Shore, Patrick and Michael in rented suits, Michael's date a pretty redhead whose name Patrick hasn't thought of in a decade.

The next day, Michael stumbled into Susan's living room hungover, wearing sunglasses, with a giant hickey on his neck. It was overcast and drizzly. They'd eaten celery sticks that Susan's mom filled with peanut butter and dotted with raisins, just like they had a hundred other afternoons. It was the last time Patrick set foot in Susan's house; he was arrested less than a week later.

It's difficult to look at himself—clean shaved and painfully young—and think about what's about to happen. It's difficult to look at that kid and blame him for fucking things up with Michael. Patrick did the best he could, and he's still doing the best he can.

It's Nathaniel who goes through the rest of the boxes, lifting and sorting and occasionally holding up an item for a verdict. By the time he's done, there's a stack of boxes by the front door that they'll bring to the thrift store tomorrow, a box of Agatha Christie paperbacks that Patrick will hang onto, the wedding china, and Susan's address book. It's past midnight, and Patrick feels like they've had the funeral that they should have had in February.

"I need to sell my house," Nathaniel says, apparently apropos of nothing, but Susan looks at him, sharp.

"I'm coming," she says, and he nods once.

Without Susan and Nathaniel, the shop feels abandoned. Even Eleanor, who's going through a phase where she babbles whenever she's awake, doesn't make a dent in the quiet.

But everywhere Patrick looks, there are traces of them. The kitchen is still a lurid green, and the coffee pot is never full because the regulars know they can sneak back there and help themselves. The bulletin board is layered with notices—people looking for apartments and jobs, a litter of kittens that need homes, an invitation to a jazz venue that somebody's opening in their loft on Prince Street, information about a protest in a few days. Walt is there, taking shameless advantage of Nathaniel's absence to claim his half of the bed.

The Valdezes bring him a plate of mofongo, like they think Patrick might not be able to feed himself without company. They're mostly right—he's been eating cold pizza and lukewarm canned soup. He would have sworn that he hadn't been lonely or unhappy before Nathaniel and Susan came—and maybe he wasn't, but his life has stretched and grown and shaped itself so thoroughly around them that he can feel their absence like something solid is missing, like bricks have been pried out of the shop wall and now he can feel the draft coming in.

The fall semester's in full swing, and when Viv stops by on the way to her morning class, she takes time to have a cup of coffee. Patrick hears her say, "Oh dear," from the kitchen.

"What's the matter?" Patrick calls out.

"Somebody needs to water that lilac. It hasn't rained in a few weeks, and lilacs are fussy."

"Lilac?"

"The little shrub you planted in the courtyard. It looked quite healthy the last time I saw it. If you take care of it, it might bloom the year after next."

"Nathaniel usually waters it." It's difficult to imagine that thing blooming. It's difficult to imagine it surviving, honestly. Patrick fills a pot at the kitchen sink and takes it out back.

One afternoon, Jerome comes in five minutes before closing with a stack of books, and the ink isn't even dry on his check when he's dragging Patrick out the door—"bring the carriage, nobody *cares*"—and that's how Eleanor goes to her first rent party. Jerome's friends all act like a baby is a thrilling novelty, like a two-way radio or a lava lamp.

The next day, Mrs. Kaplan comes by. "Give this to Susan when she comes back," she says, handing Patrick a stack of official-looking papers. "That's her copy." When he reads the heading, he sees that it's a twelve-month lease for the apartment. "Now you can take me out to lunch to celebrate."

He nearly asks, half-jokingly, whether all the people in

his life have organized behind his back to form a rota to check on him while Susan and Nathaniel are away, but he decides he doesn't want to know the answer.

A bookstore near Union Square is closing, one of the last holdouts from the Book Row days. Patrick stops by, ostensibly to offer wholesale prices for any stock he can sell, but mostly to pay his respects. The books are picked over, but there are two decent shelves left, solid wood infused with fifty years of cigarette smoke and dust. He buys them for eight dollars each, not because he needs them in the shop—he couldn't fit two more shelves in there if his life depended on it—but because if Susan is staying, she'll need bookshelves. The books have started to invade her apartment, piled against the wall and stacked on the coffee table. On impulse, he offers five dollars for a steel wire paperback spinner rack.

A week after Susan and Nathaniel left, Susan pulls up to the curb in the enormous Cadillac she borrowed from her father. Patrick stops what he's doing, takes Eleanor out of her playpen, and goes out to the sidewalk. When Nathaniel gets out of the passenger side, he's wearing corduroy pants and an argyle sweater Patrick's never seen before. He looks like he's barely slept the whole week, circles under his eyes and everything strung too tight. It's alarmingly similar to the state he was in when he arrived at the shop in February.

"It's not that bad," Nathaniel says when Patrick gives him a grim once-over. "I'm mostly rattled by Susan's driving."

Susan takes Eleanor from Patrick, then grimaces at him behind Nathaniel's back.

Patrick unloads the trunk of the car. There are two suitcases in addition to the suitcases they left with. Patrick grabs one in each hand. Nathaniel reaches for the other two. "I can get them," Nathaniel says before Patrick can protest. "I'm not *ill*. Susan took care of everything. She spoke to the lawyer and the Black Panthers and the bank and got everything straightened out."

"The Black Panthers," Patrick repeats, not sure he heard right.

"They're getting half the proceeds from the sale of the house and everything in it. Susan said Michael listed the Black Panthers as the beneficiary of his army life insurance and it seemed like as good an idea as any."

"He did?" Patrick feels a laugh—half hysterical, half plain amused—bubble up inside him. "Oh my god." The image of Michael writing in the Black Panthers on official army paperwork is something he'll cherish always.

Nathaniel's mouth ticks up at the side. "Right? She insisted that I keep some of the money to pay for a lawyer, if I need one."

"Are the two of you going to stand out here forever?" Susan says from the shop door. Patrick shuts the trunk and follows Nathaniel inside.

"What's in these things?" Patrick asks. One of the suitcases is heavy enough that it might be filled with bricks.

"You should open it," Nathaniel says. He's sitting in Patrick's desk chair. Patrick puts the suitcase on the desk and opens the clasps. It's filled with neatly stacked books. The first one he sees is *East of Eden*. He picks it up carefully, opens it and sees that it's a first edition. The next book is *The Old Man and the Sea*, from the same year, also a first edition. Both are in fine condition.

"Are they all firsts?" Patrick asks.

"Yes, I checked. I didn't collect them, but I bought

them when they came out. I thought—you know how you hang on to a few first editions of *Howl* and *On the Road* because the value keeps increasing? I thought you might like these."

"You thought I might like them."

"A present."

This, from a man who apparently walked away from all his belongings with nothing but two suitcases and enough to pay a defense attorney—and one of the suitcases is for Patrick.

"If you'd rather not have any part of it, I'd understand."

"Thank you. Nathaniel, thank you. They're going in the safe. What's in the other suitcase?"

"A tuxedo," Susan says. "And a few sweaters."

"That way I don't have to keep borrowing yours," Nathaniel says.

"You can always borrow my sweaters," Patrick says. "Always."

Nathaniel's gaze lights on the paperback rack, still empty, and when he catches Patrick's eye, there's something almost like a smile there.

Patrick makes dinner—the tofu and broccoli that Susan sometimes cooks, the recipe written out in her handwriting and attached to the refrigerator with a magnet. While he cooks, Nathaniel leans against the counter, occasionally grabbing a piece of broccoli or tasting the sauce.

"What I wanted," Nathaniel says, "was to go back and feel like the person who lived in that house was a stranger."

Patrick remembers, back in March, sitting with Nathaniel on the couch in his apartment, thinking about the things that split your life in two, the things that make the person you used to be into a stranger—or maybe make whoever you are now into a stranger.

"That didn't happen?" Patrick asks.

"I didn't think I'd miss that person. I don't like him, I don't respect him—and it's pathological that I'm talking about myself like that."

"What did you miss?"

"I used to know what was what." He reaches past Patrick to open a cabinet and take out three wine glasses. "I was wrong, obviously, but I got up in the morning knowing that I was doing what I was supposed to be doing. I was so good at being good." He fills the glasses from one of the bottles of wine that's started to appear in Susan's kitchen.

Patrick remembers Nathaniel plunging into icy water uncomplainingly and wonders if that was what it was like for him to be good.

"And now you're winging it?"

Nathaniel sips the wine and makes a face. "You're going to tell me everybody's winging it."

Patrick was absolutely going to say that everybody's winging it, at least everybody he's ever known. Instead he jiggles the handle of the frying pan and turns the heat down.

"Nobody should be winging it when they're forty," Nathaniel says, and it sounds like he knows it's grade A bullshit.

"You don't even believe that." The kitchen is starting to get smoky, so Patrick puts the stir fry into a serving bowl—they're too fancy to eat out of frying pans, apparently—and shouts "Dinner!" loud enough that Susan will hear it where she's on the fire escape, talking on the phone, the cord stretching to its limit through the window. "You know what matters," Patrick says. "You can't be good if you don't know what matters." Because that's what they're talking about, isn't it? Being good? Figuring out what *good* is in the first place?

Nathaniel gives him a funny look, not quite a smile—so rarely a smile—but something sweet and surprised. "Well," he says, and looks away.

The rice might be a little burned, but Patrick sprinkles chopped cashews over the top and everyone says "ooh" like they've never seen a cashew before. Eleanor has a smashed-up piece of broccoli. Tim Buckley's on the record player with a song that should be too sad, too elegiac, *remember me* sung too many times for anyone not to do what they're told.

But it isn't sad. Or maybe it is, but they're still eating semi-burned food while Nathaniel details just how frightening a driver Susan is, and Patrick tells a story about how Susan once got onto a highway via the off ramp, and the lights flicker because everyone who has an air conditioner is running it tonight, during summer's last gasp.

Susan falls asleep on the sofa while they're watching *The Tonight Show*, slumped against Nathaniel's shoulder. They aren't in their usual seats. Patrick's in the armchair because it gets a breeze from the open window, and he's completely lost patience with the heat; he's ready for fall.

"The two of you made things right?" Patrick asks, his voice low enough not to wake Susan, or Eleanor, who's asleep in the next room. All day, things between Susan and Nathaniel had been—not the way they'd been earlier that summer, but easy in some other way.

Nathaniel's quiet for a moment. He has an arm around

her shoulder, his fingertips making dents in the gauzy cotton of her shirt. "Yeah, things are better."

"Good."

Nathaniel kicks his feet up onto the coffee table. "I asked her what would happen when she met someone new."

A few weeks ago, Patrick asked Susan the same thing, but he hadn't told Nathaniel—it still feels like a question he wasn't allowed to ask. No—it feels like a question that shouldn't matter. Why does Patrick need to know what happens when his friend—his sister-in-law, even—meets a new man? How is that his business? He hadn't known how to explain that to himself, let alone to Nathaniel. But if Nathaniel asked her too, that has to mean something.

"I told her that I was worried whoever she met wouldn't like us very much," Nathaniel goes on, and that brings Patrick up short. That isn't what he'd been worried about, not exactly. He'd been thinking about Susan moving away, starting a new family. What Nathaniel's getting at is something different—Nathaniel's assuming that there is a three of them, that there's something here that matters, something worth hanging on to.

"What did she say?" Patrick asks, his throat tight.

"That she wasn't going to fall in love with anyone stupid enough to interfere with a good thing. And that anyone she got involved with would have to fit into this." With Nathaniel's free hand, he makes a circular gesture encompassing all of them.

"Good." Patrick can't find any other words. "Good."

"Obviously," Susan mumbles into Nathaniel's shirt. "Maybe the two of you can shut up now so I can get some sleep."

"Time for bed," Nathaniel says, getting to his feet and

hauling Susan along with him. "If you spend the night on the sofa, you'll wake up with your bones crooked." Patrick watches, his heart in his throat, as Nathaniel walks Susan to bed. She makes some unhappy sounds, and he tells her to quit whining, and Patrick thinks he could go on like this forever.

They shut the door to Susan's apartment as quietly as possible and go downstairs. Nathaniel takes a shower long enough that steam starts to creep out from under the bathroom door.

"I missed your water pressure," he says when he comes out, one towel wrapped around his waist and using another to dry his hair.

"Our water pressure," Patrick says, immediately feeling stupid about it.

"Point taken." Nathaniel nudges the dog with his toe. Walt, who's been napping in the middle of the hallway since that afternoon, doesn't even twitch. "*Our* dog might be in a coma."

"I made some room in the closet for your tuxedo," Patrick says. "Definitely not our tuxedo."

Nathaniel turns away to hang up the towel he was using on his hair, but Patrick still catches the twitch at the corner of his mouth. "Susan wants to go to the opera!"

Patrick doesn't bother arguing, but he does corner Nathaniel against the wall. Patrick only means for it to be a kiss—upstairs, Nathaniel was yawning, and there are shadows under his eyes. But Nathaniel kisses back, then mouths his way down Patrick's neck, pulling aside the collar of his shirt. He makes a dissatisfied sound. Before leaving, he'd kissed a bruise into the place where Patrick's shoulder meets his neck, and it's gone now.

"You'll just have to give me another one," Patrick says,

and feels the shudder go through Nathaniel. "Yeah?" he asks, like he doesn't already know. Nathaniel's only answer is to bite Patrick's lower lip, not particularly gently.

Patrick gets a hand on the back of Nathaniel's neck, feeling the damp strands of hair and the tension of the muscles beneath. Nathaniel tips his head back against the wall and lets himself be kissed.

It feels like it's been longer than a week, and not just because they'd spent weeks before that taking one another to bed at every opportunity. Patrick is hungry for the familiarity, for the way his hands and his mouth know Nathaniel's body as surely as he knows how Nathaniel takes his tea. He hadn't known it was possible to miss someone in a way that feels like continuously reaching out toward empty space. He hadn't known that there could be a pleasure in missing someone, when you know they're coming back.

They make their way to bed, eventually, and Nathaniel pushes Patrick so he's on his back, Nathaniel's damp hair in his face, Nathaniel's thigh between his legs. He lets himself get pinned in place. This isn't the way Nathaniel usually likes it, and Patrick has the sense that he's being indulged. He lets Nathaniel indulge him.

Through the open window comes the sound of "Little Green Apples" playing on somebody's radio, along with a breeze that cools the sweat on their skin. Everything is lush and slow; they're spending time like it isn't something that ever runs out. And maybe it won't. Maybe it doesn't. Maybe they get to have this for as long as anyone gets to have anything.

Epilogue
JOURNEYWORK

Nathaniel

Beverly gives Nathaniel a twenty-four-hour heads up before the first article goes to print, and so of course he doesn't get a wink of sleep that night. But in the morning, the world is precisely as it was the day before, with the addition of one front page article. He reads it at the newsstand on a chilly December morning, the dog tugging impatiently at his leash, then goes home with the paper tucked under his arm and gives it to Patrick in exchange for a cup of coffee.

"There are other sources," Patrick says a few minutes later. "And the byline is Beverly but also some man I've never heard of."

Nathaniel had given Beverly the names of some of his former colleagues who seemed unhappy and frustrated. He wonders which of them talked. He wonders if his ex-wife was one of them.

He doesn't know if this will change anything. Even if the CIA stops its surveillance program, the FBI and the even spookier agencies will still be up to their usual tricks. Will the idea of being spied on make people trust the government less about things that matter even more, or will they assume that anyone being snooped on must deserve it? Or maybe people will decide that privacy isn't worth it, not in the face of whatever dangers are hiding out there. Nathaniel may have only made things worse.

He wants to believe that he's done something good. It

isn't that he thinks one good deed will balance his scales, but he wants his career to have been worth something. He wants this path he took—this flawed and fraught path—to have led to something worthwhile.

Nathaniel spent most of October in the recording studio with Susan. He hasn't heard the finished album, but he keeps repeating to himself what Susan told him: you've made something beautiful. That's something, isn't it? If he's going to take responsibility for the bad things, he has to take responsibility for the good things.

"There's more in here than you ever told me," Patrick says, still looking at the newspaper.

"There's more in there than I ever knew."

"So, this article might not point directly to you," Patrick says, looking hopeful.

"Maybe not." He lets himself smile, a tiny, hopeful thing. On good days, he thinks this will end with some legal threats, maybe some agency goons paying him a visit.

It's Sunday, which means Iris will be in later, and somebody has to get to the record player before she takes it over or it'll be Big Brother and the Holding Company all day. Patrick gets there first and puts on the White Album, dropping the needle directly onto "Blackbird." Nine o'clock in the morning is too early for sad songs, but when the album came out a few weeks ago, Susan played both records from beginning to end, called the whole thing a frivolous mess, announced that Michael would have loved it, and then played it over again. Patrick can listen to his sad songs at any time of day he pleases.

Around lunchtime, a woman comes in looking rough enough that Nathaniel imagines secondhand books are the least of her concerns, but who knows. He'd wandered into a bookstore in a similarly bedraggled state. She has on tight jeans, a striped t-shirt, and a jacket that's next to useless on a day this cold. When she approaches the cash register, he recognizes her from the last time he had lunch with Jerome. They'd run into her on the street, and Jerome kissed her on both cheeks and introduced her to Nathaniel as "my friend Luisa, she and I have done shows together," stepping on Nathaniel's foot on the word *she* in case Nathaniel was too dense to notice the pronoun.

"Luisa is Jerome's friend," Nathaniel tells Patrick now.

"Good to meet you. There's a plate of donuts in the back room," Patrick says, glancing up from the book he's repairing. "And some coffee. Help yourself." He manages to make this sound plain and factual, like this woman has walked into a place where food and drinks are dispensed as a matter of course, rather than a bookstore. That was Nathaniel's favorite thing about Patrick in those early days, the way he'd looked after Nathaniel with no fanfare, not even any explanations. Some people might want a warmer touch, but Nathaniel doesn't think he could have endured it.

"You need a place to stay?" Patrick asks a few minutes later.

Luisa shakes her head. "Jerome said you might be hiring."

"Oh, thank god," Nathaniel says. "Patrick, I'm giving notice." Patrick rolls his eyes, because Nathaniel gave notice when he got paid after signing the record contract and it hasn't stopped him from—in Patrick's words—cluttering up the shop every chance he gets.

"Well, I guess you're hired," Patrick says, and goes back to doing mysterious things to the binding of *An American Tragedy*.

Nathaniel suspects Luisa does need somewhere to

sleep, but she has no reason to trust a pair of strangers. They can cross that bridge later. After all, nobody's using their spare room.

That afternoon, Patrick shows Luisa how to put ads in the *Antiquarian Bookman*. Eleanor's a few feet away, trying to figure out how to make a break from her playpen. Walt is fast asleep. From the back of the shop come the sounds of Susan's mandolin being tuned. This might be the calm before the storm or it might be just another day, but either way they get to have it.

The title of *Leaves of Grass* comes from the line "a leaf of grass is no less than the journey-work of the stars." The first time Nathaniel read that line, back in April or so, he thought it was a lovely if slightly silly way to talk about photosynthesis. "Typical Whitman," Viv said when Nathaniel asked about it. "Ashes to ashes but in a good way," was Susan's interpretation. When he'd asked Iris, she'd gone to the dictionary, the enormous Merriam Webster that isn't for sale. "Journeywork is the kind of work a tradesman does," she'd said, shutting the dictionary with a dusty thud. "So that line means the stars made the grass—and the rest of us—the way an electrician puts in a new fuse box. It's like he's telling you there isn't any magic, but then he talks about it like it's magical anyway."

When he'd read that line to Patrick, Patrick had frowned. "And a mouse is a miracle," he said, paraphrasing the end of the stanza. "It has to do with that business about every atom belonging to me as good as belonging to you." Nathaniel is fairly sure Whitman didn't mean that the entire universe is entitled to half Patrick's sandwich, but he's equally sure that Patrick would disagree.

On Nathaniel's bedside table is a cheap paperback

copy of *Leaves of Grass*, the first page of that poem discreetly dog-eared. Maybe there isn't any difference between magic and starlight; maybe there's no difference between starlight and doing something good.

Outside these doors is chaos. Appalling men are elected president. Every day's headlines are worse than the last. All year, it's been like that, and it isn't getting better. But it will. Meanwhile, there are donuts and a pot of coffee and work to be done: maybe not enough to tip the scales, but there anyway. Dooryard Books is here anyway. So is Nathaniel. So are all of them.

Acknowledgments

After Hours at Dooryard Books would never have seen the light of day without the help of Miranda Dubner, who saw the distance between what this book was and what it wanted to be, and figured out how to bridge the gap. My agent, Deidre Knight, believed enough in an early version of this book that I kept working at it. Katie Welsh provided incredibly helpful feedback on at least three versions of this book and is still talking to me.

Kelsey Bowman created the most perfect cover for this book and is, as always, a delight to work with. This is the third or fourth book Kim Runciman has copyedited for me, and I'm grateful for her keen eye and light hand.

My family were good sports when it came to hearing horrifying CIA trivia and listening to folk and folk-adjacent music in the car for a year. The period of time I spent writing this book coincided with a period of fairly intense personal upheaval, and I truly could not have done it (or anything) without my family being amazing, funny, supportive, and kind. Let's never move again, you guys.

Historical Note

I did my best to be faithful to the true, tumultuous history of 1968—at least until the final chapter. I didn't invent Operation CHAOS—the CIA's program for conducting espionage on American citizens on American soil—but I did speed up its exposure. In reality, it was exposed by journalist Seymour Hersh in the *New York Times* in 1974. By then, public trust in the government had diminished considerably in the wake of Watergate, the continuation of the Vietnam War, and the publication of the Pentagon Papers. It's impossible to know whether the public would have been equally outraged in 1968, a year when Americans were spoiled for choice for things to be outraged about.

There's some odd misinformation circulating about how the draft worked in the United States prior to the implementation of the draft lottery in 1969. Basically, there was a system of peacetime (or, "peacetime") conscription beginning in the 1950s, which ramped up considerably in the 1960s. It was common to enroll in college and graduate school to defer military service. Some men volunteered in order to have some control over which branch they served in. Many eligible men were never drafted.

In 1968, Richard Nixon ran for president on a campaign of ending the draft and ending U.S. involvement in Vietnam. The draft very much continued and the United States did not pull out of Vietnam until 1973. No author's note could do justice to the ongoing harm done to Vietnam, Laos, and Cambodia through U.S. military involvement.

In 1968, New York City was home to the creation of several music genres, a legendary and history-shaping drag scene, and vibrant queer communities. Stonewall is right around the corner and the queer liberation movement is already gathering momentum. Writing this in the United States in 2025, it's difficult to be optimistic about the direction this country is headed. Reading personal accounts of 1968, there wasn't a lot of optimism going around then, either. And that, in a small way, makes me hopeful that whatever's on the other side of this at least points us in the right direction.

Finally, this book is not meant to be an instructional manual for childrearing: please don't smoke or do drugs around infants. While we're on the topic, don't participate in war crimes either.

Content Notes

This book contains:
- Death of a spouse
- Death of a sibling
- Death of a main character's child (past)
- Suicidality (past)
- Drug use
- Panic attacks
- Physical abuse of a child (past)
- Arrest (past)
- Discussion of the Vietnam War

About the Author

Cat Sebastian is an award-winning author of queer romance. Cat's books include *We Could Be So Good* and *You Should Be So Lucky*, and have received starred reviews from *Kirkus, Publishers Weekly, Library Journal,* and *Booklist. We Could Be So Good* won a Lambda Literary Award in 2024. In her spare time, she acquires too many houseplants and misplaces things.

The best way to keep up with Cat's projects is to subscribe to her newsletter at CatSebastian.com.

Also by Cat Sebastian

Coming in March 2026: *Star Shipped*

Midcentury New York City (the *Chronicle* books):
We Could Be So Good
You Should Be So Lucky

London Highwaymen:
The Queer Principles of Kit Webb
The Perfect Crimes of Marian Hayes

Page & Sommers:
Hither, Page
The Missing Page

The Cabots:
Tommy Cabot Was Here
Peter Cabot Gets Lost
Daniel Cabot Puts Down Roots
Luke and Billy Finally Get a Clue

Sedgwick Series:
It Takes Two to Tumble
A Gentleman Never Keeps Score
Two Rogues Make a Right

Turner Series:
The Soldier's Scoundrel
The Lawrence Browne Affair
The Ruin of a Rake
A Little Light Mischief

Regency Impostor Series:
Unmasked by the Marquess
A Duke in Disguise
A Delicate Deception

www.ingramcontent.com/pod-product-compliance
Lightning Source LLC
Chambersburg PA
CBHW071918130726
47909CB00014B/2061